Praise for *Our Short History*

"In *Our Short History*, Lauren Grodstein breaks your heart, then miraculously pieces it back together so it's bigger—and stronger—than before. This novel will leave you appreciating both the messiness of life and the immense depths of love."
—Celeste Ng, author of *Little Fires Everywhere*

"Riveting . . . Like *A Friend of the Family* and *The Explanation for Everything*, two earlier Grodstein novels, *Our Short History* honors the power of family ties . . . It carries an important lesson about letting go."
—*The Washington Post*

"One of the best books of 2017 . . . Grodstein has not just written another beautiful book, but one with deep purpose and meaning."
—*Roar*

"Grodstein's heartbreaking, character-driven story is told in the remarkable, believable voice of a courageous, sympathetic character."
—*Library Journal*, starred review

"A tender tale . . . Grodstein has a fine touch, alternately sarcastic, perceptive and wistful."   —*Minneapolis Star Tribune*

"Lauren Grodstein has subtly written a cathartic and unexpectedly profound book . . . It's also impossible to put down."
—*St. Louis Post-Dispatch*

"Karen is a character many will love—determined, flawed, loving, witty . . . A poignant and realistic portrait."

—*Kirkus Reviews*

"A meditation on love and grief . . . Lauded novelist Lauren Grodstein plunges into both beautiful and ugly emotions without hesitation."

—*BookPage*

"[A] deeply affecting novel . . . This is a tearjerker of a story, but not a mushy one—and it provides a charming, occasionally funny portrait of a mother trying to come to terms with both her death and her legacy."

—*The National Book Review*

"Grodstein's writing is detailed, accurate, and emotional . . . Be forewarned that once started this book will be impossible to put down."

—*Portland* (OR) *Book Review*

"A quick, sad and heartwarming read."

—*The Seattle Times*

"Funny as well as poignant, sad but not maudlin."

—*Shelf Awareness*

"This gave me all the feels. I didn't want it to end."

—Jaime Herndon, *Book Riot*

"Both tender and tumultuous . . . Deft storytelling."

—*BUST*

OUR SHORT HISTORY

also by LAUREN GRODSTEIN

Our Short History

A NOVEL

LAUREN GRODSTEIN

ALGONQUIN BOOKS OF CHAPEL HILL 2018

Published by
ALGONQUIN BOOKS OF CHAPEL HILL
Post Office Box 2225
Chapel Hill, North Carolina 27515-2225

a division of
WORKMAN PUBLISHING
225 Varick Street
New York, New York 10014

First paperback edition, Algonquin Books of Chapel Hill, March 2018.
First published in hardcover by Algonquin Books of Chapel Hill
in March 2017.
Printed in the United States of America.
Published simultaneously in Canada by Thomas Allen & Son Limited.
Design by Steve Godwin.

This is a work of fiction. While, as in all fiction, the literary
perceptions and insights are based on experience, all names,
characters, places, and incidents either are products of the
author's imagination or are used fictitiously.

LIBRARY OF CONGRESS CATALOGING-IN-PUBLICATION DATA
Names: Grodstein, Lauren, author.
Title: Our short history / a novel by Lauren Grodstein.
Description: First edition. | Chapel Hill, North Carolina :
Algonquin Books of Chapel Hill, 2017. | "Published simultaneously
in Canada by Thomas Allen & Son Limited."
Identifiers: LCCN 2016038075 | ISBN 9781616206222 (hardcover)
Subjects: LCSH: Mothers and sons—Fiction. | Absentee fathers—Fiction. |
Terminally ill parents—Fiction. | Self-actualization (Psychology)—Fiction.
Classification: LCC PS3607.R63 O95 2017 | DDC 813/.6—dc23
LC record available at https://lccn.loc.gov/2016038075

ISBN 978-1-61620-801-1 (paperback)

10 9 8 7 6 5 4 3 2 1
First Paperback Edition

For Jessie and Elliot,
with love

Gone, I say and walk from church,
refusing the stiff procession to the grave,
letting the dead ride alone in the hearse.
It is June. I am tired of being brave.

—ANNE SEXTON,
"The Truth the Dead Know"

OUR SHORT HISTORY

ONE

Mercer Island

.I.

When I was a kid, not much older than you, I was certain I'd grow up to be a writer. I had a portable typewriter—my dad bought it for me at a garage sale—and late at night, when everyone else was asleep, I'd sit in the kitchen and painstakingly type out little scenes and scraps of fiction. I liked mystery stories a lot, suspense, moments of horror, and surprising redemption. I hoped one day to write something about the Holocaust, but give it a happy ending. This was when I was a teenager and thought I could rewrite any script.

Now I'm grown and know that very few of us get to become the people we thought we'd be when we were kids. I never did write a novel, is what I'm saying, or even a decent short story, although I found other successes and pleasures in life and don't regret most of the things I haven't done. That said, I still have time, Jake, and I still like putting down words on paper. So I've decided to write a book for you, with chapters, a title, maybe even an appendix of photographs. It seems like the right way to tell you everything I want you to know. And this island, my sister's guesthouse, the cloudy Northwest: it's all very conducive to writing. I have a comfortable chair here and a shiny new laptop. And there's so much I want to tell you.

As of course you know, this island where my sister lives with her family—Mercer Island—is all pine trees and lacrosse fields and half-caff americanos. You can see the churning waters of Lake Washington from every direction, usually iron gray but sometimes unaccountably blue. Seattle lies a few miles to the west. I've always thought it was peaceful here, and good for us, although I do miss our home in Manhattan. (Remember how you used to ask if we could build a tunnel from West Seventy-Fourth Street to Mercer Island? And because I thought I had all the time in the world, I used to say, maybe later?)

This will be a wonderful place for you to do the bulk of your growing up, after you've moved here for good. You'll have your cousins to hang out with, and your aunt Allie to make sure you eat your vegetables. And your uncle Bruce is one of the most senior people at Starbucks, which means that living here you'll be very nicely provided for. You'll ski at Whistler and spend Christmas in Hawaii and pass long summer weekends at the family estate in Friday Harbor. You'll learn to drive and then you'll get a car.

That said, I've instructed Allison to send you to one of the public schools on the island instead of the private cloister where she sends her own kids. Public school matters to me; I want you to know how the real world lives, or what passes for the real world here on Mercer Island. I can't bear the idea of you growing up amid all this privilege without some awareness that there are people who grow up on free lunch. Remember, Jacob, I spent my own childhood in a Long Island duplex, my father's parents in the apartment upstairs. As I've told you a million times—as I hope you still remember—my mother was the fifth daughter of a Bronx postman. My father was the only child of Hungarian immigrants who barely survived World War II. Neither one of them grew up with anything like luxury, and neither did my sister or I.

Allison and I frequently discuss issues of privilege and economy. She says it doesn't mean we have to raise our kids broke just because that's how we grew up. She thinks that insecurity about money doesn't necessarily make a person more empathetic or kind: sometimes it just makes a person nervous her whole life. And she's right, I know she's right, but still it irks me to think you'll never understand that you are, in so many ways, so very lucky. Allison says, But in at least one way you aren't lucky at all. None of us are. And money is no compensation.

There is no compensation. I am your only parent; I am forty-three years old; I have stage IV ovarian cancer. I have perhaps two or three years left in my life, and once I am gone you will move here, to Mercer Island, to live with my sister, Allison, and her family. You can bring your hamster and all your toys. You can bring anything you want. You know this, Jake. You know that if it were up to me, I would live forever with you in my arms.

This will be a strange exercise, this book, I can tell. As I type, I feel like I'm writing about someone else. Like this couldn't be happening to me, or to us. And then—there—I feel the port above my ribs, and there it is again, the staggering truth.

I still haven't decided how often I want you to think of me in the future, Jake, or what kind of memory I want to be. I mean, of course I want you to remember me—I want you to remember that I existed, and that I loved you, and that generally speaking we were pretty happy. But I don't know if I want you to remember every single specific about our life together, so that your life on Mercer Island always feels like your "new" life, as though you're comparing it to something that came before that was somehow truer. I want this to be your true life, and I want Allison and Bruce to be like your mother and father, and your cousins to be like your siblings, and for you to consider yourself one of theirs. I want them to be your soft place to land. This is, I think, the best thing a family can be.

But I also want you to remember days like last Monday, when I took you to the Woodland Park Zoo and we paid five dollars to feed a leaf to that giraffe and instead of eating the leaf the giraffe licked your hand with its prehensile tongue and you were so surprised you froze and she did it again. This time you shrieked and I shrieked too and then we laughed until we got the hiccups. The zookeeper said, *I've never seen her do that before! You must be delicious.* You blushed a bit and said, *That's what my mom thinks. That I'm delicious.* And oh, how you are, Jacob. You, with your soft longish hair and your feathery eyelashes, you have no idea.

Sometimes I find myself daydreaming—sometimes in the middle of a conversation, even—and I realize I'm imagining what you'll look like in a few years. Will your hair still curl around the edges? Will you still wear Derek Jeter T-shirts every day?

Since you were a toddler you've been a New York Yankees fanatic, but then the other day I caught you in your cousin Dustin's old Mariners jersey—I hadn't done laundry in a while—and I thought, There it is, the beginning of a kid I'll never know. The thought made me more curious than melancholy; I was like an anthropologist studying the future you. Your cousin Dustin was chasing you around the lawn while Allie yelled at both of you to come in for dinner, and I was just sitting on the dock, witnessing. Your life without me. Dr. Susan says this sort of witnessing is normal. This sort of floating away. You had a scrape on your shin I'd never noticed before.

"What time is it in New York, anyway, Mom?" you asked me at breakfast. I told you it was eleven, and you said that's what you thought. You said, "In New York, it's already the future."

Jacob, I promise, if I do nothing else with the time I have left, I will write this book. I'm not sure of its title yet—do titles matter if you have only one reader?—but I know what I'm going to include: whatever wisdom I have, whatever lessons I'd pass on to you later, if I were going to be here later, when you were old enough to need them. My hope is that whenever you miss me or whenever you just want to know more about the person I was, you'll be able to open this book and read these pages and remember me. Learn more about me. And that way, even though you won't always be with me, I will always, at least a little, be with you.

I plan to be honest here. I plan to be excruciatingly, extraordinarily honest. I will not edit out the truth; I will not try to make myself look better than I really was. Than I really am. If I can't tell you the truth, why should I tell you anything at all?

SO I GUESS I'll start with this morning, which was a beautiful morning, the sunniest since we arrived a week and a half ago. June 18, 2013. A meteorological surprise.

You and I were living in my sister's guesthouse with the view of Lake Washington and all those boats tied to all those docks. Across a broad, sloped lawn stood my sister's five-thousand-square-foot pile, cedar-shingled, multichimneyed. From the desk where I wrote, I could see you playing on the lawn between the houses, hiding in plain sight from your cousin Dustin, who didn't mind that you were terrible at hide-and-seek.

Dustin isn't the sharpest of my sister's three children, but he is, by far, the sweetest. (Is that still true, Jake?) Then there is brassy Camilla, with her nose ring and dyed hair, and gorgeous Ross, who at that moment was off doing charity tourism in Guatemala. Dustin, the baby, was almost eleven then, chubby and scared of loud noises and therefore the perfect buddy for a precocious six-year-old such as yourself. "Dusty!" you screamed, then dashed away to a new hiding spot by the hemlock tree. Poor Dustin whirled around but you were gone.

I knew I should stop spying on you and get back to work; I was a campaign consultant with my own shop and this was the start of our busy season. In previous years, when you were in preschool, I was able to consult on four campaigns at once, had assistants and pollsters and speechwriters on the clock January through November. But that was before the persistent bloat, the achy back I thought was stress. So for this round I had only Jimmy "Ace" Reynolds, New York City Council majority leader, to whom I was grateful for sticking by me, even though I tried to never let him know it.

Do you remember Ace? I first met the guy four years ago, back when I was so busy with you and growing our business that a city council race seemed like small potatoes. But Ace had been in the middle of an appealing scandal: the tabloids had exposed an affair with a college-aged staffer ("Ace Boffs Pace Soph," "Ace Faces Pace Disgrace," and my favorite, "Ace in the Hole"). Within two days of my hiring, I had assembled the necessary pieces, repentant Ace, supportive wife, forgiving children, adoring constituents ("I don't care what he does in his personal life as long as he does right by my neighborhood.") We went on a local media blitz, using, as surrogates, the 9/11 widows in Ace's district and the kids whose asthma the local hospitals were treating for free. They all stood by Ace. And, after all, it was a local race in an off year: we had 31 percent voter participation. In the end, it wasn't even close.

Since then, Ace's marital troubles had been long forgotten, but he still had reasons to keep me around: by 2017, he aimed to be the first Bronx-born mayor of New York City since Ed Koch. My job was to lay the groundwork with a big city council win, for of course Ace could not be mayor if he couldn't even keep his council seat. This campaign was his launch, and at this particular moment it was a good assignment: challenging but not too challenging, geographically limited, plausible. I'd help him win. I'd make him think he couldn't do it without me.

(By the way, I'd met the wife—her name was Jill—on several occasions, and she'd always struck me as smart, self-assured, funny. She was attractive. I had no idea why she stuck with Ace all those years, all those betrayals, but those were not my questions to ask. Maybe she wanted, one day, to be the mayor's wife?

It was her devotion that kept Ace in office, and her money that paid my bills.)

"Mom!" I couldn't see you, but I could hear you; out here, I kept the windows open whenever the sun shined. "Mom! Where are you?"

I shut off my computer, bustled down the guesthouse stairs. You were standing with Dustin, rackets under each arm. "We're going to play tennis," you said. "We'll be back for dinner."

"Since when do you play tennis?"

Your hazel eyes narrowed. "I've been practicing since we got here."

"Jake's got a pretty strong serve," Dustin said with a flat tone of authority. "I mean, for such a little kid."

"You do?"

"You want to see?"

Of course I wanted to see. Ace could wait.

We marched out of the cul-de-sac and down the road to the park, where, sure enough, you displayed a pretty strong serve for such a little kid. Dustin lobbed the ball back at you, and you and he went back and forth five times before you finally missed a shot. I couldn't believe it—I had no idea you'd been playing tennis. I was shouting from the sidelines like Serena Williams's father. I was a nut. "Jakey!" I said, picking sweaty you up despite your weight and the lingering weakness in my arms. "How come I didn't know you could play tennis?"

You shrugged, but you were smiling, bashful. "I wanted to surprise you."

"I'm stunned," I said.

"Can we keep going now? You're squishing me."

I planted myself down and watched you and Dustin practice for an hour, and even though Dustin was going easy on you—I think he was going easy on you—you raced around the court with your lithe little body, the last trace of your toddler's potbelly gone like a dream, and I saw something athletic in you I'd never seen in myself. You looked like a child, an honest-to-God child—you were not a baby anymore in any way. You were a child and you were learning how to play tennis, and one day, I thought, you were going to be really good at it. And if I wanted to it would be easy to think about how I wouldn't be there to see you win your trophies, but I didn't indulge myself. Instead, I stretched out in the priceless Seattle sunshine—there is nothing as luxurious as a stretch of Seattle sunshine—on the side of the red clay court and watched you and Dustin smack that ball back and forth with a grit all the more dramatic for its pointlessness. I was witnessing you; I needed to do nothing but witness.

When it was time to go home, you were sweaty and your knees were scraped from a half-assed dive you took toward the end. We walked up the road, the distant hum of I-90 traffic like electricity in my ears. You swung the racket back and forth between your hands.

"That was awesome, Jakey," I said.

"I told you he was good," said Dustin.

Characteristically, you said nothing.

"Should we sign you up for tennis lessons, honey?" I asked.

Someone was walking a huge slobbery dog toward us, more bear than canine. We paused to pet it, have some friendly Mercer Island chitchat with its owner. After a smiley five minutes, we went our separate ways. Under an alley of willows, covered in dog slobber, you said, "I don't know if I can handle one more thing."

DURING THE SHORT time we'd been on the island, my days were mostly like this: a little work, a little writing, a little spending time with you. I could have done exactly that forever, but the days felt all the sweeter because I wouldn't. For dinner, in the main house, your aunt was heating up a pan of my baked ziti for dinner (which you loved, and which I was trying to teach Allie to make the right way, even though I also planned on freezing like ten thousand pans of it before I went so that whenever you missed me there it'd be, something I made for you with my own hands; baked ziti keeps forever). Meanwhile, I was running a bath and drafting a campaign mailer when I heard a knock on the door.

"Mom, it's me."

This was around the time you'd started knocking on doors, that we'd stopped being casually naked around each other. I pulled my bathrobe tight. "Come on in."

You were still wearing your shmutzed-up tennis outfit and you still had dirt on your shins. You sat down on the tight Berber carpet, looking mournful. "Jake?"

You wiped your nose on your wrist, then idly wiped your mouth. If I were my mother, I'd have given you the what-for. "You're taking a bath?" you asked.

"Just thought I'd relax."

"Skipping dinner?" You didn't like it when I skipped meals.

"No," I said. "I'll be in, in a little bit."

You nodded, looked out at the enormous picture window. In the darkening evening, your own small face looked back at you.

"Is everything okay?"

"I still want you to do it."

"You do?" It took me a second to figure out what you meant. "Oh," I said. "Are you sure?"

"I'm sure," you said. You tried not to meet my eyes.

I suppose it must have been naive of me, but I was certain that since you were so happy here, since you were settling in so nicely, you wouldn't have any interest in my finding him. What could you have possibly wanted with a stranger in New Jersey? You'd never even met the guy, didn't know anything about him, had always shown a laudable lack of interest in him. This was perhaps because a good third of your classmates didn't have fathers— their moms were lesbians or fifty-year-old single women who went the sperm-bank route. Or maybe it's because I'd been so dementedly determined to give you everything you'd ever wanted, you never had a chance to think about this one big thing you didn't have.

"Supersure?" I asked.

You shrugged again. You fiddled a bit with your shoelace, and I remembered that I really needed to teach you how to tie your shoes better. "Supersure," you said.

Well. I guess I'd always assumed that the topic just wouldn't come up. The story, as far as it went, was that your father disappeared when I was pregnant, which was fine with me because I was so happy to take care of you all by myself. That happened to be true. But then a few weeks before we left for Mercer Island, I was having a particularly bad night; you found me sobbing and nauseated in the bathroom. That night, you asked if I thought I could find your dad.

I told you I'd think about it and that you should think about it too. I told you it would take me a month to figure out how to look for him. Of course I was just buying time.

I looked at the date on my iPhone. It had been exactly a month.

"Can you find his number?" you asked.

"Probably."

"Okay," you said. You looked just like him. The same hazel eyes, the same soft brown hair, the same full lips. He was probably a very good tennis player. "When?"

"Soon," I said.

"When soon?"

"As soon as I can."

"Okay," you said again, and now you looked at me; you looked suspicious.

The boiled-down version of your father: he was a one-term Democratic congressman from New Jersey, swept in by a minor Bush rebellion in 2002, swept out again in 2004. A perpetual bachelor, he was fond of Bud Light, classic rock, and Rangers games. He kept a thousand dollars in cash in his freezer for emergencies. When you were born at Columbia-Presbyterian, I remember nursing you and gazing out across the river, knowing that whatever else he was doing, he wasn't gazing back.

I knew I could find him. I guessed he'd understand.

"You said you wouldn't be upset."

"I'm not upset," I said.

"You look upset."

I stood to turn off my bath. "Jake, honey, I told you I would be happy to do it and I am. He's a nice guy." I hated lying, but it just slipped out. "I'll call him this week."

"Okay," you said. You were old enough to fake empathy but too young to really know how to feel for someone else. "Thanks." You skipped out of the room, leaving dirt marks on the carpet and me to my bath. The cell phone buzzed. Allison. The ziti was ready. I ignored it, sank into the water, closed my eyes.

Truthfully, Jacob, I hadn't seen your father since I told him I was pregnant. For all I knew he was married, had a kid or two of his own. For all I knew he was dead. No, he wasn't dead. Even a one-term congressman would have scored an obit in the *New York Times.*

Throughout my pregnancy (a thoroughly decent one, I should say, not a moment of morning sickness), I thought about him all the time, tried to imagine what he was doing, whether he was thinking about me. I was managing the Griffith senatorial campaign—this was 2006, an open seat—and I was crisscrossing Maryland twice a day, from Frederick to Baltimore, Bethesda to Ocean City, pancake breakfasts and chicken dinners. Standing a step behind and just to the left of my candidate, editing stump speeches, talking to journalists, doing debate prep, renting buses, fighting for more resources from the DNC. A small state like Maryland plus my background in local elections, I ended up running the thing like it was a congressional district, working even harder than I had to. But I couldn't help it. Work was the only thing that kept me from calling him. And at night—the Hampton Inn in Annapolis, the Courtyard in Chevy Chase—I'd rub my belly and I'd talk to you, Jake, and I'd tell you about everything we'd done that day. I'd take the Amtrak to my OB. Griffith—a nicer guy than the media pretends—would always stop to compliment my ultrasounds. I never called your father, stayed true to my own dumb promise to myself.

The week before the election we were ahead in the polls by eight points and I knew what that would mean—it would mean a bonus. It would mean scads more work down the pike. It would mean I could hire a nanny and take you with me on the road in 2010. Which I would. Which I did.

It would mean I would never have to call him and threaten to sue for child support.

He knew how to find me, Jake, but he never did. You should know that about your father. He was a man who should have known he had a child on this earth and never tried to find him and never called the child's mother and never looked across the murky sluggish Hudson to see the newborn child nursing peacefully in his mother's arms or the tears coursing down the mother's face.

Oh shit, Jake (Sorry! Darn! Shoot!): things are getting way too sentimental here and, worse, self-pitying. I have nothing to feel sad about! I have been blessed with you and you have been blessed with me, and your family is enormous: here on Mercer Island, with Allie and Bruce and the kids, and at home with me and Julisa and your friends and teachers and Kelly the hamster whom I hope to God Julisa is managing to keep alive. And I know as you get older you will create an even bigger family for yourself: more friends; more loves; a partner, one day, of your own. Children.

It's late, I'm shivering, I missed dinner. I hope you can forgive me for missing dinner, angel. I feel so sorry for myself right that second I couldn't believe I was even able to type. I hate self-pity—it's the most putrid of all emotions, literally rots a person's dignity, a person's grace. But right now I miss you so much and I am still here in this house, this room. The same square acre as you. How could I have missed dinner with you? That's an hour we will never have again.

It's the nature of this project of mine to assess where I've been and where we're all going, and Dr. Susan would say not to beat myself up about the self-pity thing. She disagrees that self-pity is putrid; she says it's natural and that certain situations, such as this one, even call for it. And she says that I should just ride it like a wave.

Remember, she says, even at the bottom of the wave, there is so much in the world that makes me happy. You are so lucky, Karen, to have had so much that makes you happy. Say it out loud like a prayer.

My work.

My sister, Allison.

My niece and nephews.

The Seattle sunshine. We're supposed to have yet another day of it tomorrow.

The water slapping at the rocks below this island.

You you you you you.

I press a button on my phone so I can look at your face. Then I turn back to my book, to these pages, this thing I have to finish soon. I hope I have time to write it all for you, Jake.

You are my happy ending.

2

As you might remember, throughout my treatment I tried to work as much as possible, because even more than taking care of you, work felt like taking care of *me*. It gave me a purpose, a hope that the world might notice me and maybe even remember me after I was gone. Working on campaign politics, I was changing facts on the ground for millions of our fellow citizens. Get the right guy elected and the right changes will happen. I always believed that, Jake. I hope you do too.

Still, lately I'd been too sick to be a strong advocate for my clients, and I was embarrassed about how much I hadn't been able to do. I was kind of a terrier once upon a time. When I was working on the Wallace campaign, for instance, still in my twenties, I found out that our opponent's daughter, a teenager in a fancy private school, had had an abortion a week before her junior prom. Listen, far be it from me to saddle a sixteen-year-old with a newborn, but her dad was one of those abstinence-and-Christianity jihadists who wanted abortions to be illegal even in cases of rape and incest. A bridge too far, my friend. I leaked the abortion news to a sympathetic reporter at the *Wilmington News Journal* and Wallace won by fifteen points.

Of course, I'd become much more temperate at work, when I was able to work at all. Chuck, my partner (remember him?), had been good about picking up the slack, and we'd hired a bunch of twentysomethings to take care of a lot of the detail stuff. And it was an off year—mostly just New York City local elections—so it wasn't like I was missing that much action, but still. Three years ago I was something of a regular on MSNBC. You probably didn't notice, but I hadn't been on television since my diagnosis.

I called Ace this morning, 6 a.m. Seattle time—I wanted to talk about the campaign mailer, or anything else. "You feeling good?" he asked.

I was not feeling good. I'd had more of those mystery pains in my side, I had almost vomited the night before, and I knew I should go to Hutchinson, but the thought of being admitted in Seattle, I just couldn't face it. "I'm great, Ace."

"Still got cancer?"

"I'm in remission." Which sounded better than it was.

"So you can do the job?"

"I wouldn't take it if I couldn't," I said. The woman we expected to be his opponent, Beverly Hernandez, was the daughter of Dominican immigrants; she'd risen up the ranks at Roosevelt Medical Center, and would probably appeal to a different demographic than Ace did. Still, City Council reps were basically reelected as a matter of course. We'd both have to screw up in a big way for him to lose his job. The goal here was for him to blow his opponent out of the water.

"Hernandez had cancer too, you know. Like you. Breast. She's always wearing one of those pink ribbons."

"I have ovarian," I said. "It's different."

"Right, I know," he said. "Listen, I'll have Amani give you a call to talk about scheduling. I just hired someone in the office, Haley's her name, she's the new assistant, so if you can't get a hold of Amani you can probably find her. Jill has me going on an anniversary trip next week, but if it's an emergency you can find me. Otherwise, Amani or Haley." Haley—sounded young. "And while I'm gone, find out whatever you can on this Hernandez," Ace said. "She doesn't seem like much, but we've still gotta take her down."

"That's my job, Ace."

"Twenty points," he said.

"Let's make it thirty."

Ace chuckled. "Say hi to your kid." He clicked off before I could say anything else.

Truthfully, on the Karen M. Neulander Scale of Objectionable Politicians, Ace Reynolds barely nudged five. Believe me, some of these mouth breathers I've encountered—some of them I've even worked for!—at least Ace remembered I had cancer. At least he remembered I had you.

So I filled out some paperwork to send back and then, while I was at it, sent an email to Julisa to see how the hamster was doing. At around seven, you knocked on my door—here you went to sleep early and woke with the light—and we decided to go downtown for breakfast, because it was a Saturday in June and nobody else in this house was going to wake up for another two hours. And because it was sunny out. And because you were hungry and I could fake being hungry for you.

THE BELL CAFÉ on the water had a whole salad-bar type setup of whipped cream and maple syrup: we went there often and early, before the crowds of fleeced-up Seattle parents or hungover musicians could stop us.

"Did you call him yet?" you asked as we parked around the corner from the Bell.

"Are you kidding? I haven't even figured out how to find him."

You looked stricken, but still, reflexively, you held my hand as we cross the street. "I thought you knew."

"I told you I could find out," I said. "I never said I knew. But it won't be hard. I'll Google him. We can find him this afternoon." This was much sooner than I'd planned on.

"What if he wants to stay private?"

"That's impossible, even if he wanted to. There's no such thing as privacy anymore. Besides," I said, nodding at the hostess, who knew us by now, and where we liked to sit, "he's a lawyer, and lawyers don't like privacy. They all want the world to know how great they are."

You nodded like this was gospel. "Will he be mad to hear from you?"

"No," I said. "He might be surprised, but he won't be mad." I hoped this was true.

We picked up our menus and casually perused, even though I knew what we were each going to have. I loved going out to restaurants with you. We'd been doing it since you were born—I used to nurse you in restaurants, and it was surprising to me that I would do such a thing, considering, before I had you, watching other women nurse was mortifying. But oh! As they say, there was so much you couldn't know until you had a child. I loved nursing you and did it until you were almost a year old and pushed the breast away as though you were embarrassed, like you couldn't stand it anymore. And I tried to force you! I remember wondering how I would live without the hormonal rush of nursing, the calorie-burning life-affirming sigh of it. But you squirmed your little head, and then finally you chomped down and I got the idea.

I had been so anxious with you back then—when you were a baby you'd fall asleep in my arms, and even though I was beyond exhausted I wouldn't let myself sleep, for fear you'd fall from my grip (as if I'd ever let you fall). But then every time I'd try to put you in your crib you'd wake up shrieking. So I'd just sit in that rocking chair, forcing myself to stay awake, playing Scrabble on my iPhone over your heavy little body, doing everything in my power not to nod off. And then one day, when you were five weeks old, Allie was visiting and she took a sleeping you from my arms, and magically, like a spell had been cast, you stayed asleep. And then she put a pillow under my feet, and we slept in your nursery, both of us, soundly, for six hours straight. It was undoubtedly the best sleep I got that year.

"Look at that kid," you said, after a cheerful lip-pierced waitress brought us our order. I turned to see a small child by the maple-syrup bar decked out in full Batman gear, cape and mask and shiny shoes. He was balancing an enormous plate of waffles and whipped cream and I could see what was about to happen, but like Cassandra, I knew were I to shout no one would listen.

I said it anyway, under my breath: "Careful!"

Batman started to run, and then it happened: he tripped on the edge of his cape, his plate went flying, whipped cream sprayed us like bullet fire, the kid hurled himself on the floor and started to wail, the other patrons looked up, surprised, and the kid's father, who had already made it back to his table, turned around, and yelled, *"Oh, for Christ's sake!"*

The room went cracklingly quiet. For a moment, all was still. Then the father had at it again. *"What the hell is the matter with you!"*

"Harry!" Mom was red-faced. The kid keened like an Italian widow.

"Why can't he watch where he's going?"

But Batman could give as good as he got. He rolled about on the floor and shrieked, "I hate you! I hate you!" as both father and mother rushed to his side to try to stand and shut him up. Meanwhile, the waitress brigade wiped up stray whipped cream while the busboys collected his shattered plate, and then the mother started to ream out the father for letting Batman carry his waffles back to the table by himself and the father reamed her out right back. And you and I couldn't help it: we looked at each other and started to laugh.

You had whipped cream in your hair. I laughed harder.

"You think this is funny, do you?" said the father, turning to us. He was much more aggressive than your average Seattleite.

"I'm sorry," I said, taking a napkin to wipe my eye.

"For your information, my son has serious behavior issues that *are not funny at all*."

"I'm sorry," I said again.

Meanwhile, Batman was rolling around back and forth and kicking his shiny little booties on the floor and screaming, "Get me a jetpack! Get me a jetpack! *I hate you!*"

"I think we should order that kid a jetpack," you said, and this cracked us up all over again. Batman was screaming, "Get me a jetpack! *I'm gonna kill you!*" as his mother picked him up under her arm.

"I said this wasn't funny!" the father yelled at us, but oh, how it was. We were still cracking up when we left the restaurant twenty minutes later; we had to stand outside the restaurant to collect ourselves.

"Jeez," you said when we finally did, "that was kind of hilarious." *Hilarious* was one of your new words; you used it all the time. I zipped up your jacket. "That kid's dad was really mad," you said. "Screaming across the whole restaurant."

"I know," I said. "I hate guys like that. So tightly wound you think they're going to snap."

"What do you mean?"

"You know, easily angered," I said. "Stressed out." After a minute I added, "A lot of dads are like that."

"Hmmm," you said. Instead of walking to the car we turned, drawn like seagulls to the waterfront. "I'm not sure that's true," you said, thoughtfully. My chest hurt from laughing; you let out a hiccup. We passed the converted warehouses lining the street, in and out of dappling shade.

"Kyle's dad isn't," you said. Kyle—I assume you remember this—was your best friend at home. He lived two floors below us on West Seventy-Fourth Street.

"You're right—I guess he's not."

"And Uncle Bruce isn't."

"That's true," I admitted.

"In fact," you said, after a gulp of air, "I think most dads aren't."

"But some are," I said, then realized already I was on a campaign to malign dads. We reached the park by the water, still empty in the dewy morning; we took side-by-side seats on the damp swings.

"Was your dad tightly wound?" you asked. "Stressed out?"

"Grandpa? Sometimes." Actually, Jacob, I can tell you now that throughout my childhood my father was catatonic with stress, retreating at all hours into the basement so that he could smoke his pipe in peace while the washing machine gurgled. He worked as an adjunct history professor at two different colleges, and my mother never really gave up hectoring him (if only he'd finish that dissertation and find a real job!) and my sister never stopped longing, loudly, for things they never could afford. My mother worked as a bookkeeper in a law firm, and it was from her that we got the health benefits, the extra bit of money for Hebrew school, and the sense that if only my dad had been a man of more conviction, our family's lot in life would have been a prosperous one.

What I remember most about being a kid were the fights that would end with my mother in tears and my father in the basement, smoke filtering through the floorboards. When it got bad enough, my inscrutable Hungarian grandparents—the great-grandparents you never met—would come down from the upstairs apartment, looking half-starved, wearing bathrobes like crazy people. "Sha," they'd say, "the whole neighborhood can hear you," as though our neighborhood was people in houses as opposed to the butcher shop next door, the dry cleaner next to him.

When my mother stopped crying they'd go back upstairs, shuffling, to do whatever they did all day, play cards, watch the news. My father said that they were just so happy to have safety, stability, to watch their grandchildren grow up, they really didn't need anything else in life. "Is that why they never get dressed?" I'd asked, and got smacked on the side of the head for being rude.

People say that childhood is the happiest time in your life, but I've always thought that was ridiculous—children are basically at other people's mercy at all times, powerless, subject to the tidal waves of circumstances they can't control. Homework, chores, dinner table discussion where you have nothing to say. Most of the time I hated being a child, living according to the fluctuations of my parents' moods, depending on whether my mom got a bonus check, my dad got an extra class at Hunter. In contrast, I found being an adult exhilarating: I had my own money and my own bathroom. And you were so quiet, which meant that if I didn't yell at home, I never had to hear yelling in my home.

"Do I yell?" I asked you.

"Not too much," you said, kicking your swing into the air. "Only when you really mean it."

Out in the bay, enormous ships were idling, packed with brightly colored container boxes, headed to China, Russia, God knows where. I remember once, when I was in high school, I asked my grandfather if he'd like to show me Hungary one day. He was born in Budapest, and this was right around when the Iron Curtain was crumbling and Budapest was a place you once again could go. He looked at me like I was crazy. Said I'd rather take you to hell, then died a few weeks later.

Well, maybe I was too hard on all of them. They did the best they could with what they had. And the truth is, after my grandparents were gone and Allie and I were out of the house, my parents did seem to relax, became much happier around each other. By the time my mother died, they had spent many peaceful years together. Even as my father started fading, my mother got slower, they were still more happy than they'd been when we were young.

"I think we should call him today," you said.

I pretended not to hear you in the wind, the cawing of seagulls. Somewhere out there, I was sure, a trawler was blaring.

"Mom," you said. You ran your feet along the ground, stopping your swing. I wasn't ready to stop yet. I kept kicking and kicking my feet into the air, flying higher and higher, my butt lifting off the seat a little—what a hoot to be so light, so featherlight, so ephemeral that I imagined if I could just kick a little harder I'd jet off into the atmosphere altogether. I could see over the tops of the multicolored shipping containers toward the forested islands beyond.

"Mom."

Below me, I heard you. You sounded half-annoyed, half-scared.

"Mom!"

I sighed. This thing about being a mother, about keeping my trajectory close to the ground. "Yes," I said after I skidded myself to a stop.

Your eyes were narrow, and you crossed your arms over your narrow chest. "I think we should find him *now*," you said.

"*Okay.*" I wanted to swing again, but you were already turning to march across the park, back toward the car. "But first," I said, because I was the mother, and because it was my prerogative to make you do things you didn't want to do, "first we're going to visit your grandfather."

"Mom!" You collapsed back down on a swing, started kicking your feet again.

"Don't whine," I said. My stomach was cramping. I ate more for breakfast than I'd eaten in a while, plus all the laughing—but still. Stomach cramps could equal anything: fluid, blockages, build up of scar material. They could also equal a recurrence sooner than expected, but they probably didn't. They usually didn't. I kicked through the pain; I wanted to be in the air again. And I didn't want you to know anything was wrong. "We've got to see him while we still can."

You'd known my father only as a silent widower, ravaged by early onset Alzheimer's. He might even have seemed frightening to you, since he stared so long and so intently at things nobody else could see. But he was more than that once. (I was more than this once.) When you were a baby, my father was still in okay shape, even managing to teach one last class. And I remember, the night you were born—he and my mom came to the hospital and oh! How they marveled at you. "He's just so beautiful," my father said, cradling you in his thin arms. "He's the most beautiful thing I have ever, ever seen."

"You think?" I asked, eager to hear you praised.

"The most beautiful, beautiful, beautiful," he crooned. "Have you finally decided on a name?"

"Jacob," I said. I'd been keeping it secret till you were born. "After Janos, you know."

"Janos," whispered my father, holding you close to him. Janos was his father's name, the man who'd survived the Nazis by hiding in the Gemenc forest eating squirrels, the man who spent his final years in a bathrobe in Rockville Centre. "Oh, I've never seen anything like him, this Jacob, oh . . ." My father was crying, which at some other moment might have embarrassed me but didn't then since I was crying too.

"Gil, you'll get germs on him," said my mother, who was sitting on the bed next to me, holding my hand. My mother was bony and brittle, she was like that all her life—birdlike, said my father—but her hands . . . I'll never forget, how warm and encompassing they felt, holding mine. How safe. "Gil, don't hold him so close to your face."

"Jacob, Jacob—" My father had turned it into a song and was waltzing, carefully, about that dumb little chamber on 168th Street where you would spend your first night on earth. I'd sprung for a private room, and since I was a single mom the nurses were a little bit lax about visiting hours, and though lights were dim in the ward, our room was lit like a holiday.

"Beautiful boy," my father said, twirling slowly with you. My dad was good at backgammon and great at chess, spoke some Hungarian, passable French. By the time you knew him, he was sitting in a chair eighteen hours a day in a high-end nursing home in Bellevue, facing a sea he thought was the Baltic.

I wondered if you'd like some of his clothing—for when you were older. Maybe you'd want something of the grandfather you never really knew. Those Homburgs, they were quality, and expensive. Maybe hats would be back in fashion by the time you read this. I had, in my bedroom, a big box of things from your grandparents that I wanted you to keep, not just the hats but all your grandfather's history books, and their photographs, and whatever meaning was packed into their lives.

My stomach cramped again, maybe just because I was anxious. I still had so much stuff to go through. So much stuff in the world. In my line of sight, all those shipping containers.

"I don't want to go!" you said, starting to swing again, since you'd rather have done anything else besides visit the home, even if it meant swinging next to your mother all day in this crappy little park. "I hate that place."

"I know," I said. "I hate it too."

"You do? I thought you liked it there."

"I like Grandpa," I said, "not the home," which I hated for all the reasons a normal person hates a nursing home: the disinfectant smell, the residents gumming their food, the dying droolers parked in wheelchairs in the hall. But I also hated it for all the other reasons you'd expect: I couldn't believe that this was who my father had become. When my mother dropped dead of an aneurysm last year, right on the floor next to him, he didn't even hear her fall.

"So can we not go?"

"We have to," I said, and it felt responsible to say it, but it felt just as good to swing through the crisp dewy air, so I kept going. Across from me, the Puget Sound, glittery whitecaps, gulls, mountains, shipping containers, this earth that went on forever.

"How about we go to the bookstore instead?"

You were such a conniver. You knew how much I loved the bookstore in Capitol Hill. I didn't answer you, just kept swinging. You kept swinging too.

After a while, you looked at me, grinned cunningly. "Mom," you said, "we're flying."

"I know," I said. "Let's keep going."

"But what about—" And then you shut up. Good. I wouldn't make you go to see your grandfather if you didn't make me find your father. Just for today. Tomorrow I would feel stronger. Tomorrow we'd visit him. Tomorrow I could do whatever you needed me to do. I could face it.

Tomorrow, I swore, I'd call the doctors.

THAT NIGHT, IN the guesthouse, I couldn't sleep. Instead, I used my frantic energy to research Ace's opponent, Beverly "Bev" Hernandez: 57 years old, the VP in charge of planned giving at Roosevelt, and generally speaking, a likable figure. Put herself through college while raising three kids, went on for her master's, graduated with highest honors. Spent her Sunday mornings praying upstairs at St. Boniface and afternoons dishing out meals in the soup kitchen in the basement. Bev didn't have an official campaign website yet, but she'd filed papers, and I wondered if she had any idea what she was doing with this campaign. I mean, not even a website! Jake, can you imagine a time when that was even possible?

Still, the election was five months away and if there was any-thing most New Yorkers were too busy to care about in June, it was electoral politics. So unless Ace really screwed it up—which is to say, unless the *Post* found out about some Haley or another—this was pretty much in the bag.

I texted Amani, Ace's longtime assistant, to schedule a confer-ence call with a few donors as soon as he was back in town. Then I turned my attention back to Bev. There was the biographical information on the Roosevelt website, a few pictures of her at various social functions, and a wide-open Facebook profile, full of family pictures, chubby grandkids in christening gear, some-one's quinceañera, someone else's wedding.

Also sprinkled throughout the Facebook page were various pink ribbons and Race for the Cure banners and buttons and updates on Bev's health. I clicked on a recent photo of her and could see them clearly, the marks of remission: the slightly off skin tone, the crispy hair. She was smiling, though—she had a great smile—warm brown eyes, a nice full mouth, good makeup. And she was wearing a better-than-average hospital administra-tor outfit, a suit I thought I recognized from Banana Republic. I wondered, after she was diagnosed, if she went to the same websites I did, the ones that urged you to "pamper yourself," schedule "spa days," get "makeovers," and here were the places that would do it for free since you've got cancer. After my diag-nosis I was too busy with you for spa days or makeovers, but once I dropped twenty pounds I did go shopping—Allie was in town—and bought a tight green jacket at Prada that I just loved and that I'd bequeath to Camilla unless Allie wanted it.

Behind me, I heard you sigh heavily. You'd fallen asleep in

my bed. We were talking about the video chat with Julisa and whether or not you thought Kelly the hamster looked lonely (Do you remember this, Jake-of-the-future? How sometimes you would get chatty before bed, expansive almost, and start talking about school projects or video game levels you were trying to beat? Do you remember that you wore footie pajamas well after you turned six?) and then you fell asleep just like that, the way you always had, so sudden and heavy I used to be afraid you were dead. I watched you sleep for a while and then I turned to my computer, and when I turned around again to look, you had established yourself in the sleep position you'd had since you were a baby, on your back, both hands thrown up over your head in surrender.

I lay down next to you for a while, hoping your breathing would hypnotize me to a calmer place. It used to, before all this.

But tonight, too much on my mind—Ace; Bev; my dad, who was napping when we finally hauled our asses over there, Allie and Dustin in tow, so instead of spending time with him we went over to Cupcake Royale, where you and I did a fairly decent impersonation of Batman and his lunatic father. And I must have laughed too hard today or thought too hard because my stomach hurt, my brain hurt, I was too tired to sleep.

Bev, Bev. Facebook status updates: "Blood tests looking right!" "Back at work! Office never felt so good." "Hickman cath successfully removed! I feel so free!"

I scrolled down through political rallies and pictures of kittens to find a picture of her kissing her husband on a Hawaiian holiday: "So blessed and grateful on one-year anniversary of kicking cancer's butt in Wikiki!" And they looked so happy and radiant that I couldn't hate her for being healthy, for being happily married, for being Ace's opponent, for misspelling *Waikiki*. I clicked on the picture to enlarge it. Once upon a time I might have used Bev's dicey health history to raise a few doubts about her fitness for office, but that sort of nastiness didn't seem necessary this campaign. Nor did it seem sporting.

It was two in the morning, almost sunrise in Manhattan. I needed to sleep. I'd never sleep.

The computer had been going so long it felt hot.

If I tried to curl up next to you you'd kick me at some point, you couldn't help it, you were a sleep kicker. I could have gone next door to your bed, but I knew it would be pointless; I'd never fall asleep in a twin. So instead I turned back to the sizzling computer.

I promised myself I would never do this, but then you asked.

His name was Dave Kersey, and when I met him he was forty-two years old.

He was a partner at Wales, Heinrich, a firm with offices in Florida, Philadelphia, Englewood Cliffs. Not particularly white-shoe, that is to say. He attended law school in Maryland. He did personal injury and made a small fortune, but it wasn't like he advertised on billboards or anything; he really did try to take on legitimate clients with legitimate complaints. He really did try to do the right thing. That's what his line was, anyway.

I'd met him at a fund-raising dinner for Griffith back in 2006, just after Griffith declared. Your father was tall, balding, gentle, with the kind of greenish hazel eyes I've always melted for. We sat next to each other and I told him about how, earlier that day, I had called my dad and it took him way too long to recognize my voice. I made the story funny. He laughed along. At the end of the evening he asked if I'd like to have dinner some time. I told him I was going to be all over Maryland the next few weeks. He told me he'd wait.

Dave Kersey, Dave Kersey. His name used to be a lullaby to me. I would sing myself to sleep, pregnant, whalish and sweating at the tail end of my third trimester, singing to myself and to you your father's name, unable to help myself. David Michael Kersey. A nice Irish Catholic boy, originally from Baltimore. David Michael Kersey, who told me he loved me but lied.

Google said that he still lived in Hudson Towers, that sprawling monstrosity along the Palisades. His apartment up there was so stupidly bachelor pad, I couldn't get over it: black leather couches and a fifty-two-inch television and a glass coffee table and just about nothing else. A six-pack in the fridge, some moldy bread. I asked him if he felt like a cliché and he sighed and said sometimes. He'd been a bachelor all his life, minus a ten-month marriage in his twenties. He drove a BMW, which he was (naturally) fastidious about. He'd been five years older than me. He was I supposed.

There, said Google, that was him on a panel at a trial lawyer's conference. There he was speaking against tort reform at a law school in Alabama. There he was, on Facebook, his arm around a woman who was possibly his wife. He looked the same as always, maybe a little more bald. The woman was pretty and blonde and younger than me. I clicked to find out more, but unlike Bev Hernandez, your father had the good sense to keep his Facebook page private.

Should I tell you that the sight of Dave Kersey with his arm around this beautiful woman was enough to send me to the bathroom to weep like a teenager? That it made me retch into the toilet with the violent emotion of the lovelorn, the spurned? Part of me wanted to keen like Batman or scream like Batman's father, but I couldn't, I would never wake you, and anyway, I was a grown-up. And anyway, it had been seven years. And anyway, I probably shouldn't have told you this. This wasn't how I wanted you to remember me, even though it was also the truth.

I had sat next to him at that dinner party for Griffith, where I was supposed to be schmoozing big donors, and we had talked and laughed and kept talking. I felt like we'd never run out of things to talk about. The brief interregnum where Griffith thanked everyone for coming, spoke a little bit about his boyhood in Baltimore County, summers in Ocean City, American values, last six years of Bush-Cheney, time to bring real change—he was using all my lines, my best lines, and usually when he used my material I'd feel a bit gloaty, but sitting next to your dad I felt nothing but bubbles. I barely heard whatever was coming out of Griffith's mouth. I was just cartwheeling inside, I was so happy that fate had sat me next to this man.

I almost never drank but that night I had two glasses of champagne.

"Where are you staying?" he asked, and I told him, and I let him drive me to my hotel on some weird man-made pond in Bethesda. I was back in New York two weeks later and he was in Englewood Cliffs and the first time we went out it was Friday night and we didn't leave each other's sight till Monday morning.

Should I have told you this? But you're an adult now, right? And even though we're always kids when it comes to our parents' love lives—I suppose I should tell you that, regardless of what happened then—of what happens next—once upon a time your father really was a gentleman.

You breathed deeply, kicked the covers off. I was glad I wasn't next to you. One time you kicked me in my abdomen, right in the burning scar.

Before I could talk myself out of it, I clicked on Facebook messages and wrote, "Dear Dave, I know it's been a long time, but I would very much like to get in touch. I have an urgent matter to discuss with you. You can call me if you'd like, or send me your number. This is a bit personal, so I'd rather not discuss it on email. Thank you for your attention. Yours, Karen Neulander."

I attached my phone number to the message and then I pressed Send and then I went to the bathroom and sat on the floor and waited for the sun to rise, or for you to, or for my jetpack, whichever came first.

3

That Thursday, your cousin Ross returned from Guatemala. This was very exciting because Ross was the Brad Pitt of my sister's household: gorgeous, interested in many things, not enormously articulate. Do you remember how he arrived at Sea-Tac at 9 a.m., all floppy-haired and sweaty, with a robust growth of beard and something that looked very much like a tattoo peeking out from his shirtsleeve? He passed out on the couch as soon as he got home, and for the better part of the morning we tiptoed around him, marveling at the celebrity unconscious in our midst. Dustin, who idolized his brother, cooked him a large and nasty-looking pot of scrambled eggs, which lay congealing, hours later, under plastic wrap. You yourself were less impressed by Ross, and annoyed he was sleeping in the den because the den was where you liked to play with Dustin's Wii, and there wasn't much else to do in the day's gusty rain.

My stomach had taken a turn for the better, so I'd decided not to call the doctors for the moment. Your aunt Allison was still after me; she said I hadn't been eating much, and she was worried about my strength. I could have told her the truth, that the thought of Dave Kersey made me lose my appetite, but then I'd have to talk about him and I just didn't want to talk about him. Anyway, you seemed to have dropped the topic, which reminded me how fickle you could be about your interests, how fickle all kids could be.

On the other hand, the day before you had again practiced tennis.

"He's awake!" Dustin shrieked at one in the afternoon, taking his cold pan of eggs into the den. And sure enough, Ross had risen from his slumber, showered, and resumed his place on the couch, wearing nothing but jeans, his polka-dot boxers showing decoratively above his waistband, something grotesque and tribal decorating his arm.

"Holy shit, is that a *tattoo*?" Camilla asked before Allie could speak.

"It's henna," Ross said. "Impermanent."

"It's very nice, Ross," Allie said, and Camilla rolled her eyes.

We'd assembled on the thick carpet of my sister's enormous den to hear Ross tell of his journeys abroad. He had set up various small objects on the coffee table, stones and scraps of metal and burlap, like the contents of a hobo's pouch.

"What have you got there?" Allie asked idly, fingering a little wooden statue but looking admiringly at her son, who was so strong and so interested in engaging the third world. I knew that gleeful look on my sister's face because I'd caught it on myself in photographs—it was the look on my face when I looked at you.

"That's for you, Mom," he said. "I got it in Petén, when we were meeting with the local indigenous woodworkers. It's a model of Ixchel, the Mayan fertility goddess."

"You're kidding."

"Asha," he said, "she's the one who painted my tattoo—she said that it's good for sleeplessness and stress if you meditate on it."

"Who's Asha?" Cammy asked.

"She's from India," Ross said. "She works at the NGO that organized our trip. An NGO," he added, in case we didn't know, "is a nongovernmental organization."

"There aren't enough poor people to help in India?" my sister mused. "She has to go to Guatemala?"

"She has special skills, Mom," Ross said. "She's like a social worker."

"What's for me?" Dustin asked, and received, with delight, a tooled leather ball. For Camilla and me, there were copper bracelets, and for Bruce, to be held by Allie until his return, a bag of fresh Guatemalan coffee beans, so he could taste *real* coffee—which I assumed tasted just like the hand that feeds you.

"And this," he said, picking up a totem and handing it, with great flourish, to you, "is a ceremonial power gourd."

"A who?"

"Is that really a thing?" Camilla asked, but you picked up your shriveled gourd and assessed it calmly.

"What does it do?" you asked.

"It protects you from any evildoers or those who seek to do you harm. It makes you very strong. If you sleep with it under your pillow it will keep spirits from haunting your dreams." And I was thinking, Really, Ross? This was the best you could do? But you gazed at the gourd with a steady, practical eye.

"Thank you," you said. "I think this will come in useful."

"You know spirits aren't real, right?" I said, because, Jesus Christ, the last thing I needed was for you to start having nightmares again. "You know that's all pretend."

"I *know*," you said scornfully. "But just in case," you added, and held the gourd in both hands while Ross divvied up the rest of his plunder, then retreated to call Asha during daylight hours in Mumbai.

"I can't believe he went all the way to Guatemala and came home with a squash."

"Mom, it's not a squash, it's a *gourd*." The distinction had been an important one to you ever since we went to the Hudson Valley to go apple picking last year and came home with more apples, pumpkins, and gourds than we could fit in our tiny kitchen, and ended giving some of them to the homeless guy who lives on our corner to sell to tourists.

"Asha, huh," Allie said. "What do you think we should think about Asha?"

"It's a pretty name," I said.

"It's about time he found himself a girlfriend," Camilla said, rolling over onto her stomach. "I was starting to think he might be gay."

"Cammy, stop."

"What's gay?" you asked, which was funny because usually you let what you didn't understand fly right by, which was how

I'd managed to schedule so much medical treatment right in front of you.

"It's when boys date boys or girls date girls," Dustin said. "It's weird."

"No, it isn't," Camilla said. "I mean, it's different, but it's not weird. I know like seven gay people."

"You do?" you asked, eyes wide.

"Totally. At least seven. And then some of the girls in my grade are bi."

"Whoo now, I think that's enough," I said. "Is it time for lunch yet?"

"What does that mean, bi?"

"Cammy, honestly," Allie said. "I'll go make a salad."

"It means when you like to date both boys and girls," Cammy said. "Because human sexuality is on a spectrum."

"Oh," you said. I decided not to chime in. After all, this was what it would be like when you lived here with them, when Dustin and Cammy became your de facto big siblings. I guess it seemed okay. I never had big siblings, and my parents were not really the type to talk to me about homosexuality, or heterosexuality, or even sex.

(I was the last kid in elementary school to find out how babies were made, and when I did, I was so repelled I raced home to ask my mother if it were really true.

"Yes," she sighed.

"You and dad—*did that*?" I asked, agog. *"Twice?"*

I remember her back was to me, she was doing something at the stove. Her shoulders were jiggling a little bit and I remember thinking she must have been crying, she was so embarrassed to have been caught.

"Yes," she said, jiggling away. "Twice."

"Hmmph," I said, still disgusted but also delighted, a little, at their forbearance in the name of making a family.)

I had actually thought more than once about sitting you down and explaining it all, where babies came from, what sex was—you were only six, but some of the books had advised explaining this sooner than later so that kids could grow up with a healthy understanding of human sexuality. I was of a mind that a healthy understanding of human sexuality for a six-year-old was *no* understanding, that a kid who still believed in the tooth fairy shouldn't have to know about erections and fallopian tubes. On the other hand, if I didn't tell you that meant you'd get your information from your blunt and mischievous cousins and maybe that wasn't the best idea either.

And if I told you about sex and where babies come from, we could end up having one of two—or even two of two—difficult conversations. The first would be about your father, and about the truth that your father and I did these very particular and slightly uncomfortable things we're talking about, and that I wanted to do them with him, and so on and so forth, and God, how awful to have to think of your mother that way.

But worse, if we really got into it, the uterus and the vesicles and the vas deferens, then you'd know that this part of me that brought you into the world—the best, most magical part of me—was that which was killing me now. It all seemed like too much.

Regardless, I thought this little project was as good a place as any to give the sex advice that I might have had the courage to give you when you were a teenager, although you should feel free to skip ahead if you find this mortifying. But if not—well, as far as sex goes, assuming you end up hetero (and believe it or not, I have no investment in your sexuality—do what you will, just please be safe about it), remember that for women, sex is relatively complicated. Young women often don't even *enjoy* sex their first several go-rounds; frequently, it's uncomfortable or even hurts. They might fake having fun, they might grin and bear it, they might go through with it just because they like you. But it's quite possible it's a performance—for me, at least, the first several times I had sex (college, frat brother, don't remember his last name), it was entirely a performance. Sex is not like it is in the movies, at least for women. So my advice here is to be patient with her, be as nice as possible, and for God's sake, call the next day. That might be why she's doing it in the first place—for the call the next day. Don't be a jerk.

And as for the physical stuff, the birth control stuff—if it's okay, I'm just going to assume you learned all about that in health class.

THE NEXT MORNING, I reflexively checked Facebook before I checked my email. The little mailbox image was lit up, and I knew what it was, and because I was doing this for you I took a deep breath and clicked on it. The computer froze for a second like it sometimes did when I was on Facebook and I could have used that second to shut it down, close the whole thing down—I imagined lying to you, saying, "I'm so sorry, honey, he never wrote back," but I'd already typed the truth (there it was, the mailbox, the computer screen, you playing Uno with Dustin and Ross in the big house across the lawn), so I couldn't take it back. I took my breath, clicked my click.

"Dear Karen, Great to hear from you. I hope all's well and am happy to discuss whatever it is. Mornings in the office before 8 are best, or you can try me during lunch, but I'm sometimes out with clients."

He included his office number, and that was all.

It seemed to me preposterous that he didn't know why I was writing—what else would I have to write to him about? Why couldn't he acknowledge even at this late date that there might have been a child? He knew I was pregnant. Shouldn't he have therefore at least wondered if a child had been born?

Well, Allie said, he assumed I didn't have you—that I had an abortion. (I'm sorry, Jacob, to even suggest such a thing to you now, but at the time, remember—at the time you were as unimaginable as the moon. And I told your father that I would never have an abortion. I told him this as part of the planned speech I had for the last time I ever saw him. It was a speech I never managed to finish.)

When I got pregnant, your father and I had been dating for five months, and though the fact that he never wanted to have children had always been part of his shtick, I assumed that once he found the woman he loved, he'd change his mind. Actually, what I thought was that I'd say "I'm pregnant" and that his face would go soft with tenderness and he'd take me in his arms and say something along the lines of "Marry me," and that by the time you were born we'd have nested in a center hall colonial in North Jersey.

Instead, he looked at me sort of funny and asked me to repeat myself. I was half-naked in his bed, expecting tenderness.

"That can't be right," he said, once I'd said it two more times, first coyly, then loudly. "I had a vasectomy three years ago."

"You what?" I asked. "You did? You never told me?"

"I told you I never wanted kids," he said. "I told you that between global warming and nuclear proliferation, I don't believe it's fair to bring more people onto the earth. Anyway, I have never for one second in my life wanted to have a child. I just don't."

"You don't want to have kids because of *global warming?*"

"I don't want to have kids because I don't want to have kids," he said. I'm sorry, Jacob—I know you might not be pleased to hear this, but it's the truth. "I never have."

"But why?"

"Why? I just told you why—"

"It's just hard to believe—I mean, you'd be such a great dad."

"I can't be a great dad if I don't want kids, Karen."

"It just doesn't make any sense," I said. "Everyone wants kids. I mean, deep down. Everyone does." Didn't they? Deep down where it counted?

"Not me," Dave said.

"I can't believe you had a vasectomy and didn't tell me." I pulled up the sheets around my torso, wishing I had something to put on besides the night before's black dress.

"Karen, I told you everything you needed to know," he said, as close to angry as I'd ever heard him. "I told you I don't want children. I know I told you that. I *always* tell women that when we're dating. And then they don't believe me. They think they can change me. My first marriage fell apart because she didn't believe me when I told her no children."

That was why? I hadn't known. I looked around the room, at his collection of Star Wars paraphernalia. "But Dave," I said quietly. "You have so many toys."

He put his face in his hands for just a second. He didn't touch me. And then he put on a T-shirt and stood there, looking ridiculous, half-dressed and half-bald. "You sure it's mine?" he asked. "Because vasectomies are ninety-nine percent effective. The doctor said."

That's when I started to cry.

Now I looked at the clock, and even though it was about 1 p.m. in New York, fuck it, I'd been raising his child alone for the past six years, so sorry if I was calling at a less-than-convenient time.

"David Kersey," he said before the phone had finished ringing twice. I'd been expecting a secretary. I reflexively hung up and panted a little, put my hand on my chest to calm my heart. I stared at the phone for a few minutes, expecting it to ring. It didn't. I took a deep breath, thought about taking a Xanax, half a Xanax, told myself not to be a dummy, besides I had a no-Xanax-before-lunch rule. Then I picked up the phone again. I dialed slowly, tried to breathe.

"David Kersey."

Right, I knew this would happen. His voice sounded the same, exactly the same. The same voice he used to say "I love you" with, the same voice with which he said he'd wanted to "avoid situations like this."

"Dave, this is Karen Neulander."

"Karen," he said. "Hey, nice to hear from you."

What were we, lacrosse buddies? Nice to hear from me? Hey?

"Yes, well," I said. I should have written something down. "Hello."

There was a longer than normal pause.

"Everything okay with you?"

I breathed deep, closed my eyes. One hand was on the phone; the other was gripping the ragged edge of my T-shirt, wringing it fiercely.

"Dave, I have a son," I said. "I mean, we have a son. I don't know if you remember—I mean—" Jesus Christ. I wrung a rip in my shirt. "Almost seven years ago, I told you I was pregnant. We have a six-year-old son. His name is Jake."

Now the radio silence was on your father's end, although I thought I detected an intake of breath.

"And he would like to meet you," I said after another silent minute. "And I told him I would ask you if you wanted to meet him too, but it's perfectly fine if you'd rather not. I know how you feel about children."

More silence. I didn't know what to add.

Finally: "We have a son?" he said, sort of half-choked.

"Yes," I said.

"A son?" he repeated.

"I told you I was pregnant," I said. "You know that pregnancy often leads to children, right?"

"But I didn't—I never in a million years thought you'd keep the baby. You said—"

"I said what?"

"You said you were going to—"

"He was born at Columbia-Presbyterian," I said, eyes still squeezed shut. "January 20, 2007."

"Karen . . . I . . ."

"You what?" I opened my eyes; I was suddenly itching for a fight. C'mon, Dave Kersey, say anything to me. Say anything, I dare you.

"His name is Jake?" your father said.

"Yes," I said. Your father didn't know your name till you were six, Jakey. Your father was asking me to repeat your name. "Jake," I said. "Jacob."

"He wants to meet me?"

"Yes," I said.

"Jake?"

"Yes, that's his name."

"Jake?"

And this is when I thought that maybe Dave Kersey had actually turned into a moron because wasn't that what I'd just said? Okay, you find out you have a son and you might have some original questions, like what does he look like or where does he live, but this guy, your father, just kept repeating what I'd already told him with this tone in his voice like he'd never answered a question before in his life.

"Jacob," he said, trying it out again.

"He wants to meet you," I said, quickly, to keep myself from raging. "I told him I would find out if you were interested. But if you're not interested, that's really fine. It doesn't matter to me either way. But he's my son and I love him, so I told him I would try."

"When?"

"When?"

"When can I meet him?" And now your father sounded actually breathless, Jake. Like maybe he was even crying. Jesus Christ. The fucking moron.

"We're in Seattle now."

"Is that where you live?"

"We live in Manhattan, but we're visiting my sister. Do you remember my sister, Allie?" I knew he didn't remember. "We're here through the summer and then we'll be back in the city. You can meet him then if you want."

"I have to wait till then?"

"Excuse me?"

"I just . . . Till the end of the summer?"

He had to be kidding me. Seven years ago he never wanted children no matter what and now he could hardly wait two months to meet one? How was this possible? And anyway, *two minutes before he didn't even know you existed!* Two minutes before he probably barely remembered who *I* was!

"I'm sorry, Dave," I said. "We're here in Seattle most of the summer. But if you're interested, I'd be glad to set something up when we—"

"I could come to Seattle."

"What? No, are you crazy? No."

"I could," he said, more insistently. "I could come—I mean, whenever it's convenient for you, of course, but really I could come whenever. I mean, I could come over a weekend or cancel some meetings."

"Why?"

"Why?"

"Why do you suddenly want to meet him now? What's this rush?"

"I just—" He sounded confused. "You said he wanted to meet me. I'd like to meet him?"

"Right, but—" And honestly, Jake, one of the reasons I was so good at my job, one of the reasons my clients just loved me is that I always knew what to say. I always knew how to frame an argument. I was never at a loss. "Dave, we live twenty minutes from you. Why do you have to jump on a plane? Can't you just wait till we get back?"

"I didn't know—" your father stuttered. "I just. I didn't know. I didn't know I had a son. You never—"

"How did you not know?"

"You never told me!"

"I told you *I was pregnant.*"

"But then the last time we talked . . . you said you would never keep—"

"You told me that you hated children. That you never ever wanted a child. You had a preemptive *vasectomy*, Dave. So excuse me for thinking you wouldn't want to be a big part of this child's life."

We both turned quiet. I guess, as a trial lawyer, your father was rarely out of words either, and some small guileless part of me couldn't help but be touched that he seemed so . . . so eager. So moved. So full of despair.

"Karen, honestly, it had never once occurred to me that you would have the baby."

"I never said I would have an abortion." (Jacob, please know that—from the moment I took the test I knew you were mine, I would have you, I would see your beautiful face.)

"I just assumed—" your father said.

"Assumed? Who assumes something like that?"

"I just . . . you know. A single woman with a big career. I just . . . Everything you said—"

"What did I say?"

"That you would . . . I don't know, and you were always such a fanatic about abortion rights."

Oh my God. "You assumed because I was pro-choice I'd have an abortion?"

"You went to that rally in DC," he said, sounding more than slightly crumpled, and now I knew for sure that no matter what else he turned out to be in life your father was also, indubitably, a moron.

"And when I never heard from you again, it seemed obvious— I mean it just seemed clear to me that you didn't have the baby. Because if you'd had the baby you would have told me."

"Why would I have told you?"

"Because I'm the father!"

"What about global warming?"

"What are you talking about?" Dave said.

"You said you hated children! You suggested the baby wasn't yours!"

"I was panicking!" he said. "You never let me make it up to you. I called you—you never returned my calls!"

"You never called!"

"Of course I did!"

He was lying; your father was a liar.

"You told me you didn't want children!"

"Karen—"

"Global warming!" I said, almost shrieked. "Nuclear *proliferation*!"

He paused for a long moment. "Karen!" he finally said, his voice breaking, really breaking. "Why didn't you tell me you had the baby?"

"Dave," I said. "Why didn't you ask?"

There was no getting around this one—we were just going to be in it for a while together, each crying on one end of this great North American continent, and I knew for sure that I was right, that when he kicked me out of the house that day after I managed to give him only half my speech, I knew the right thing to do—the *only* thing to do—was to dust myself off so that you and I could have our life together. Yet this small, guileless part of me wondered if the past seven years of our lives had been lived under the shadow of a horrible mistake.

And then I remembered that the only good thing Dave Kersey ever did in his whole life was get me pregnant with you, that apart from that he was a terrible person and I could not think that I had made a mistake because if I did I would never recover. I would die right now, before my official time was officially up.

"I'd really like to come to Seattle," he said. "I mean, if that's okay."

"But you said you didn't want children," I whispered, so he couldn't hear me crying.

"I'm different now," he said.

He was different. He was different. If it weren't for you, Jakey, I'd have hung up the phone and thrown it into the lake. But instead I wiped my nose with my ripped T-shirt, gave myself a second for my heart to come together. Out my window, across the lawn, the lake was fulminating under the assault of the storm. I could see cars backed up on I-90, the bridge to Bellevue. I had thought, more than once, about getting in our little rental Hyundai and hitting the road, driving up to Canada, I-90 to I-5, away from this dumb place and cancer and even you, my love. Just escaping all of it everything and dying alone.

"Tell me about him?" Dave said.

I wiped my cheeks. "About Jake?"

"Yes," Dave said. "Tell me—tell me anything? What's he like?"

The skin on my face was hot and wet. "Jesus, Dave, I don't even know how to start. He's beautiful," I said. And then, because it was true: "He looks a lot like you."

I shouldn't have said that. Your father started blubbering again, quietly but I could hear the restrained snorting.

I tuned him out. "He's very smart, but he's shy. He's intuitive. He learned to read when he was four. He loves video games. He has a ton of friends at school. He goes to PS 199. It turns out he's good at tennis."

"Can I see—can you send me a picture?"

"Well, sure, but . . . here," I said, wiping my cheeks again, my nose. "I just friended you on Facebook. Click on my profile and you can see everything. His whole life, pretty much."

There was silence on the other end. I heard, or thought I heard, the faintest of clicks.

And so of course while he was clicking on me, I was clicking on him. Dave Kersey. Dave Kersey. How many times I dreamed of this, cyberstalking Dave Kersey. I never let myself. But now I could.

Dave had just bought a summer house, a nice one, on Long Island. He still drove a BMW. His wife—well, of course there was a wife—her name was Megan.

She was young and blonde and she sure was pretty.

He scrolled through my life while I scrolled through his and we both breathed together, shuddered, sometimes whimpered on the phone, hoping the other wasn't listening or forgave what was heard. "Oh my God," your father sighed more than once. "He looks just like—"

"Oh my God," I said when I saw their wedding photos. Three summers ago. The Bronx Botanical Gardens, where I had always wanted to be married, should I have ever gotten married. Megan carried plumeria in her bouquet. She hyphenated her last name.

"He's beautiful," Dave finally said. "You're right."

"I know," I said. "And that's not nearly the best thing about him."

"He really wants to meet me?"

"Yes," I said.

"Can I come?" he asked. "To Seattle?"

"Are you going to bring your wife?" This was not what I wanted to say, but it slipped out the way things sometimes do. His wife. The reason, I assumed, he was different now.

"Megan's traveling a lot for business," he said. "I'd probably come alone."

"Okay," I said.

"Okay I can come?"

"Can I think about it?"

"Of course," he said, and though there really wasn't much left to say, neither one of us hung up.

"Jesus, I can't believe you never told me about him, Karen," he said after a while.

"I'm sorry," I said. This was another thing I didn't want to say, but again, it slipped.

"I am too," he said. "I can't believe what a . . . what an idiot I was. I can't believe what I've missed."

"Well," I said. "You can get to know him now if you want."

"I'd like to."

"Okay," I said. "I'll let you know when it's a good time to come." And just like that, your father was coming to Seattle.

"Thank you, Karen," your father said. "Thank you. I know . . . I know—"

What did he know? What on earth could he have possibly known?

"Thanks for calling," he finally said.

"I did it for Jake," I said, then hung up quickly before another thing I didn't plan on saying slipped out.

I GOT THROUGH the rest of the day and then the night, tucked you in, read you your stories, didn't say anything about your father. You were very happy because Ross was going to take you and Dustin to Alki Beach the next day, to the place that sold Hawaiian shave ice, and if it was nice out, which it almost certainly wouldn't be, you'd be able to stick your toes in the water.

I lay with you for a while after you'd fallen asleep, stroking your light brown hair. You were blond as a toddler, and only recently had your hair started to grow darker, but it still had that softness of a baby's hair, like angel's wings under my fingers. I felt your little earlobes under my fingertips. If I didn't know it would wake you, I would have traced your lips.

Later that night, Allie met me in the guesthouse study so we could pore over your father's Facebook page together. It was midnight and we were drinking white wine, both a little surprised at how often your father updated his status and how little he had to reveal. Since his marriage to Megan, the only big life events seemed to be the house in Quogue and a two-week cruise to Alaska. He still frequented Mets games in the summer and Rangers games in the winter, still favored, as far as his pictures proved, golf shirts and neatly creased Dockers.

Megan seemed to be a little bit more interesting; she invested in Latin American markets for Citibank and clearly racked up the frequent flier miles, at least as far as Dave's doleful status updates reported: "Little lady's in Lima again. Drinking a mojito in her honor" or "My wife went to Chile and all I got was this lousy sinus infection."

His friends seemed to be the same friends, his family the same family, and his car, even, the same car, although probably a newer model. And I couldn't help but think that while I was bringing you to the pediatrician and getting your hair cut and going to school conferences and interviewing nannies and cleaning your hamster cage and watching you earn your white, yellow, orange belts, your father was just living his dippy New Jersey life, full of Rangers games and sad-sack jokes.

"No kids, huh," Allie said after we'd gone through each picture in his file, one by one.

"I guess no kids, no."

"How old is he now?"

"Close to fifty."

"And how old is Megan?" Allie asked. "Ask Google."

I clicked around, found Megan's bio on the Citibank page, which said she graduated from Yale. Yale! A few more clicks and it turned out she was the class of 1992. Just like me.

"She's my age."

"She looks great," Allie said, enlarging her image on the screen. "I mean, not that you don't, but—"

"She doesn't have chemo hair," I said. Instead, Megan had blonde hair in a chic cut along her jawline, blue-green eyes like a Disney doll's. She seemed to have made a uniform out of gray sheath dresses and black jackets. Her smile, despite what you might think about a woman in her profession, with her degrees and her lithe little figure—well, her smile was unnervingly warm.

"I wonder why no kids."

"He had a vasectomy," I said.

"Yeah, but they can reverse them. And we know they're not always one hundred percent effective, right?"

"But also she's forty-two or forty-three. If they got married three years ago, then—"

"She's too old," Allie said. "So many women wait too long."

"Not everyone meets the love of their life in high school, Allie." My sister was the only smart woman I know who married at twenty-two, had children right away. At the time, I thought she was insane, starting a family at twenty-three, the same age our poor mother did, our mother who spent her whole life bent with the burden of us. But Allie loved being pregnant and loved being a mother, and of course her husband, unlike my mother's, went on to a multimillion-dollar career, which I suppose made the whole maternal enterprise a little easier.

"What do you think she'll make of Jake?"

"Megan? What do I care?" I said. "She'll never meet him."

"Why not?" Allie asked, enlarging an image of Megan's shoes. "She's his father's wife."

"So?"

"So don't you think they'll end up getting to know each other?"

I was galled. "Allie, I'm not setting this up so that they can have a tight relationship or anything. He wants to meet Dave, Dave wants to meet him. That's fine. It's not going to go any further. They're not going to, you know, hang out at each other's houses."

Allie looked at me like I was crazy.

"Look, at the moment I'm just afraid he won't even know what to say to Jake. He'll be some stiff weirdo and break his heart." Allie stared into space. "You remember how he hated even the idea of children?" I said. "How he freaked out when I found out I was pregnant? Is this the kind of guy who's going to know how to behave around a six-year-old?"

"Well," Allie said, slowly, "I mean, he wants to meet him, right?"

"Yeah, but . . . I think he's just curious. I mean, I'd be curious. But curious isn't the same thing as, like, suddenly he wants to be dad."

"What if he's changed his mind?"

"I'd be shocked," I said. "Anyway, even if he has, as long as I'm around, I'm not going to go setting up father-son camping trips or any bullshit like that. And once I'm not here anymore, Jake will be living in Seattle. Which is three thousand miles from New Jersey. Which means there won't be any relationship."

Allie pushed at a cuticle. "But what if they want to have one?"

"They can email," I said. "Dave can go to his, I don't know, his high school graduation. If he wants to."

Allie, who didn't like to wind me up in my delicate condition, made a few benign clicks on Dave's Facebook profile, away from Megan, toward the Rangers. But I could tell what she was thinking.

"Allie, I know lots of divorced moms who do it that way. They don't want the father in their kids' life, for whatever reason, so they just push him to the margins. Which is usually where the fathers want to be, anyway. It's not like every dad is superdad, like every dad is Bruce."

"I know," she said. "It's just . . . What if Dave and Jake want to spend time with each other? Like, I don't know, like quality time?"

"Impossible. You won't let them."

"I won't?" Allie stopped clicking. "That's a hard thing to ask. To keep Jake away from his father."

"I'm not asking you to do anything except to avoid facilitating a relationship. Dave and Jake will meet, I'm sure they'll get along fine, or maybe they won't, I don't know, and then Dave can go back to his corner and we can have our lives again. Without him."

"But what if they want more than that?"

"Dave is not allowed to have more than that."

"But—"

"But?" Rain in Seattle usually came and went with a certain shiftlessness, but all that day it had been crazy, nonstop. We listened to it drive against the windows.

"But, Karen, he's his father."

"So?" I said. I was still wearing my ripped T-shirt, Jake; I started tearing at the hem. I needed her to understand the man your father was. For some reason she refused to understand. "Allie, excuse me for sounding a little hysterical, but how is Dave his father, exactly? I mean, how is he a father any more than any other sperm donor might be a father? *I'm* the one who's taken care of him for his entire life, I'm the one who's remembered vaccinations and met the teachers and put food on the table, and I'm the one who's been the *father and the mother*, so I'm sorry but I just—"

"Karen, don't—"

"Please, Allie. Please," I said. "Don't let him worm his way in to Jake's life. He doesn't deserve that."

"I wouldn't do it for him," she said. "I'd do it for Jake." She wasn't looking at me; she was looking out the window, toward the rain and the implacable lake.

"But Jakey isn't going to want to know him," I said. "He's a kid. He might have forgotten about it already. He hasn't . . . he hasn't mentioned him or anything about him all day."

"He remembers."

Jetpack, I needed my jetpack. "Allie, please," I said. "Honor my wish."

"Karen—"

"My dying wish."

"Karen—" she said. Tomorrow both of us would pretend this conversation never happened, that I never got as manipulative as this.

"I'm asking you one thing, Allie," I said. "And if you can't do that, I don't know if I can let Jake stay here."

"Karen!" she said. She sounded slapped.

We used to fight a lot, Allie and me, when we were kids. Our bedroom was so crowded with Allie's stuff, her clothing and her makeup and her field hockey sticks and her bullshit, that just creating a little space of my own in there was next to impossible. When I finally escaped to college I couldn't get over how free it felt to have that spartan bedroom, that empty closet. And now here I was, living in her house, depending on her to keep me alive.

I didn't say anything and she didn't say anything either, for a minute, but then one of us changed the subject, a little bit creaky but we managed it. Soon enough we were talking about maybe going to the house in Friday Harbor next weekend or maybe going shopping, and of course we should visit dad soon, and what did we think of Ross's tattoo? Secretly, I mean we'd never say anything, but didn't it look a little bit cool? And a girlfriend in India! We'd both always been a little curious about India, maybe one day we'd go. Even me, I could probably still get there if I tried.

But just because we changed the subject didn't mean that I trusted her entirely, until she said, "I miss Mom," which was exactly what I'd been thinking; I missed our mother. And because we were thinking the same exact thing and remembering the same exact person, I was reassured that we were sisters on the same exact page.

(Jake, there will always be days in your life, even if you can't remember me, that you will miss me. That you'll need me. A person never stops needing his mother.)

Allie and I turned our attention from the computer, from the lake. We looked at each other; we each had her eyes, and in them we found solace.

4

The next morning you were playing Angry Birds on my iPhone when it rang; you picked up, even though you weren't supposed to. "Oh, hi," you said, speaking too loudly—for all your pleasure in picking up, you didn't really have any idea how to talk on the phone. "Yes, I know who you are . . . Yes. Seattle. Yes." Then you dropped the phone on the bed and lay down next to it.

"Jake—" Holy shit—was it your father? I lurched, my heart hammering. "Is someone on the phone?"

"It's Ace."

"Jesus, Jake." I picked up the phone, a weird tingling in my fingers, either anxiety or nerve damage. "Ace, sorry, my kid likes phones."

"He's spunky, that's good," Ace said. "Listen, you know anything about France? That's where we're going. I want to make it to Normandy, see the D-day beaches, but Jillie wants to go to some castles. Do you know if they got castles in Normandy?"

"I'm your campaign manager, not your travel agent."

"I know, honey," he chuckled. "I just wanted to hear your voice."

"Oh," I said. "Well, here it is."

"Everything okay by you? You feeling all right?"

I told him I was. I don't know, Ace was a decent-enough guy. He cared about me, in his way. He even loved his wife, despite his inane and pedestrian betrayals.

"Listen, Karen, the real reason I'm calling, my daughter found some Hernandez family videos on YouTube. She thought you should watch them. Hernandez isn't the most polished gal, but she does have a certain, I don't know, authenticity. She's got one of those inspirational my-father-was-a-shepherd stories. You know how people like that."

"Really? Her father was a shepherd?"

"I'm speaking broadly," Ace said. "I'm wondering if we should send out a little biographical mailing, tell everyone who I was too. You know, she's not the only one who came from a farm."

"Wasn't your father a teamster?" I asked. "Listen, it doesn't matter—this isn't about biography. It's about results, right? Who can bring city dollars to the district. Who can represent the people. You've been doing that for four years. You'll keep doing it."

"Yeah, but I got 2017 to think about."

"2017 is four years from now," I said. "The mayor's race is tomorrow's problem. Let's do one thing at a time."

"This is my last chance to make a name for myself before the mayoral primaries."

"Ace, we've got this," I said, but I knew he wasn't satisfied. "I'll look for those videos."

"Thanks, honey."

"Go to France and have fun."

Despite the pins and needles that were now traversing my palms I found my laptop and opened up YouTube. Beverly Hernandez, Beverly Hernandez—I had to click past several videos of a Colombian teenager singing pop songs before I got to a shot of our particular Beverly Hernandez sitting on a couch under a hideous oil painting with a girl who looked to be about eight. I pressed Play.

"Hi," said the girl. "My name is Monica O'Neil, and today I am interviewing my grandmother Beverly Hernandez about her life journey for my project about American immigration."

The girl drew a breath. Dark curls framed her face; she was wearing a pink sweatshirt and hoops in her ears. "My grandmother Beverly Hernandez grew up on a sugarcane plantation in the Dominican Republic before the evil dictator Trujillo removed the farmers from the property."

Although she seemed to be reading from cue cards, she pronounced *Trujillo* in flawless Dominican. "Her mother decided to escape with her children and go to the Bronx, in New York. I am now going to ask my grandmother what she remembers about being an American immigrant."

Beverly smiled at the camera and adjusted her necklace, a fat silver cross. She looked even better in motion than she did in her Facebook stills—her face was so soft and expressive—but the video must have been shot while she was still undergoing treatment, because she was clearly wearing a wig, and not a great one. The fibers looked like nylon.

"Hello, third graders. I'm happy to speak to you about my

journey." She had a thick borough accent, a hint of Spanish in the vowels.

"So as you heard, I was born in the Dominican Republic, which is a very small country on an island in the Caribbean Sea. I lived in a little village, and my house had no electricity, which might be hard for you to believe. We did have lots of family, though, and I remember that I loved to play outside with all my little cousins.

"When I got to New York City, I was six years old. I was very scared. This place—it was nothing like my small village in the Dominican Republic. I had never seen so many people or such big buildings in my whole life. I remember being terrified of everything, the cars, the people, even the other children—I didn't want to leave my mother's side. And then that first day, when I started school, I couldn't speak English, not a word. Not only did I have no friends, I didn't even have a language to *make* friends!"

"Wow," said the girl, in a tone that said she'd heard this before.

"That's why, Monica, when people want to have the ESL classes, or teach classes in Spanish, I think this is a very bad idea. You don't learn by being catered to that way. You learn by being thrown into the classroom! I learned English in six months. If they had separated me into an ESL class, I might never have learned. And then I wouldn't be the person I am today. I'd probably be living on welfare or something, unable to get a job because I couldn't speak the American language."

Okay, so she was an English-only welfare fascist—well, she *was* running as a Republican.

"And you had to work while you were in school, right?" Monica asked.

"*Mami*, I feel like I worked from the day I was born." Beverly adjusted her necklace again. "Even when I was having my babies, I was working two jobs sometimes. People would say, How could you work when you have those babies? But I loved working and I loved my girls. I *needed* to work and I needed my girls." The shot pointed at the floor for a minute and then came back up, and it occurred to me that one of those daughters was probably holding the camera. "I loved them both. There was no way to choose."

"And you went to college?"

"I went to college, yes, and then I went to graduate school, which is what you do when you want to be something in this country. That is what makes this country so special. Anyone who chooses to get educated, to work hard, anyone who takes responsibility for success, they can do that if they go to college. And now I am a senior administrator at Roosevelt Hospital, which is the biggest public hospital in New York City. I have come very far, very far, because I chose to be educated and I chose to work hard."

Bev smiled at the camera, big and toothy, and for a second I was a little concerned. She could take that smile all the way to Congress if she wanted.

"So what I want for you, and for all your classmates, is to work very very hard and to know that if you don't give up, if you keep studying, if you don't let yourself off the hook, you can succeed just like I did. Don't allow for making excuses. If you're tired, so what? Everybody's tired. If you're broke, so what? I was broke too. Work hard and save your money. You won't be broke any more, you know? And that is the very simple way to success in this country. People think it's hard, like you need to figure out a special secret, but it's really not so hard. Study hard. Work hard. Don't make stupid choices."

Oy, usually I hated this Republican reductive bullshit, but the way Bev was looking at the camera, earnest, her granddaughter nodding along, I found myself, without meaning to—nodding. For just a second. Listen, if Bev could appeal to me, she'd appeal to voters. She seemed friendly and she'd survived cancer and her story really was that perfect mix of inspirational and relatable. Even I could relate to it. Did I ever tell you this, Jake? I took three weeks maternity leave and then it was right back to the office.

"And if you do right by yourself, working hard, improving yourself," Bev was saying, "chances are you'll do right by your family too."

I didn't even think twice about it: I'd just take you to the office, let you nap in your Pack 'n Play while I ran meetings. The first time I took you on the campaign trail, back in 2008, I'd hired a nanny to watch you in hotel rooms while I traversed various counties in congressional districts along the mid-Atlantic. My major candidate that year was Lacey in New York's Eighteenth— a tight race, a first-time candidate. Whenever we needed a baby for a photo op, I'd race up to the hotel room, wrap you up in something fleecy, and haul you to the nearest stump speech or Walmart opening. You posed in a hundred propaganda shots that year and looked adorable in every one of them.

My parents were still living in Rockville Centre then, and

when the nanny needed a break, my mother would drive upstate to watch you while I coached Lacey through the day's travails. I remember one night I'd caught some sort of bug and all I could do was lie in bed and moan and tap out emails. This would have been fine, except I had a speech to write for a fund-raising dinner, and I was so nauseated that I couldn't even sit up, much less write something incredible.

"Here," my mother said, sitting at the flimsy hotel desk, "give me the computer."

"You already have the baby."

"I can handle two things at once."

You were such a gorgeous baby, Jacob, really—all rosy cheeks and soft blond hair. I remember looking at you in my mother's arms and feeling jealous that she had the strength to hold you. "What are you going to do with my computer?"

"I'm writing your speech."

"Mom, stop."

"What, you think I don't know how to write?"

"You don't know how to write one of these things."

"I've heard every last speech any of your candidates has ever delivered," she said. "I know how this works."

Well, that was true—she was so proud of me that she'd become a sort of groupie, tagging along to any rally or fund-raiser where she knew a politician would read a speech I'd written. Weakly, I pointed out where I kept my different templates. You've got to thank all those people in that list, I said. And you've got to include personal details.

"I've got it," she said. Then I fell asleep.

The Eighteenth was so ridiculously tight that year—Republicans were scrambling to stop their hemorrhage in the House, and they thought they could flip the district, tap into working class resentment of the new money "elites" buying lakefront property in the lower Hudson Valley. The Democratic National Committee was panicking, throwing lots of resources our way. I knew that if I blew Lacey, it would look really bad. But what could I do? I shivered then burned, shook with fever, slept in some sort of sweaty delirium. My mother escorted you to the fund-raiser, where she handed Lacey the speech she'd written and then spooned you mashed sweet potatoes in one of the private rooms. Back at the Holiday Inn, I'd gain clarity for a moment, realize I'd abdicated my professional responsibility to my mother, then lapse once more into hallucinatory sleep.

That was October 20, 2008. October 21, it was like the whole thing had never happened—my head was clear, my stomach settled—and our finance guy reported that my mother's speech helped earn an additional $175,000 that night. A month later, Lacey won the district by six points, and the Democrats took over the House by an additional twenty-one seats.

A pretty great story, right, Jake?

Bev's story was pretty great too, though. Ace was onto something. If she managed to put together a decent campaign, she could have a fighting chance at this thing. Ace and I would have to work harder than I thought we would for our legacy. As you know, Ace wanted to be mayor one day. And this would probably be the last campaign I'd ever run.

LET'S RETURN, FOR a moment, to my mother, who recognized what was happening to my father long before the rest of us caught on. In 2010, she packed up the house on Long Island, sold it for a song as the housing market crashed, and moved to the house my sister built for her on Mercer Island. I remember, while she was packing, going through my father's clothes, his beautiful suits, his hats. I remember being aghast that she was planning to give so much of it away. You were three years old then. You know that picture of you as a toddler with the fedora on? That's from that time, when we were packing. And the ring—that's when she gave me the platinum ring my father had worn around his wedding finger every day for decades.

"Why are you giving this to me?"

"Daddy almost let it fall down the drain the other day," my mother said. "He'd be heartsick if he lost it."

"Why not give it to Allie?" I asked, although already I had fitted it around my thumb.

"I thought you'd love it more," she said. (I think she was right. I haven't taken it off since, except for surgeries, and the day I had you.)

For seven months they lived together in Seattle in this very guesthouse, sleeping in twin beds in the bedroom where you sleep now. My mother did a lot of nannying for Allie's kids during those seven months, even though Allie already had a nanny, a fat Slavic lady my mother didn't like. Allie kept telling my mom to relax, take it easy, but my mom didn't know how. When she wasn't ferrying the kids to school or baseball or dance or soccer, she was cooking dinner or folding laundry. The only thing she didn't do was take dad to his doctor's appointments; she said it was because she didn't like to drive on the highways, so Allie did it, and let the issue rest.

And then one afternoon, in the guesthouse kitchen, she dropped dead of an aneurysm. She'd been making my father lunch. He was asleep in his wheelchair when she fell to the floor; Camilla found her several hours later. And now we were living in the house where my mother died. We ate there; we slept there. I did all my writing in the room where she did her crosswords. You'd think I would have found it upsetting or at least a little creepy. But what a comfort it was—to know she'd lived in these rooms, and to still feel her there unexpectedly, when I turned my head or caught the sight of something hazy from the corner of my eye.

THE LAST THURSDAY in June, you and Dustin started summer camp on the Bush School grounds. Your hours at camp felt like a little too much time apart, since I'd just as soon have had you home, chatting with me as I tried to figure out how to bury Beverly Hernandez. But I knew camp was good for you, the running around. The normalcy.

I'd just taken some vitamins and was attending to paperwork, planning a few speaking engagements for Ace, when an email came in from your father. "July 4" was the subject line.

Christ. July 4 was seven days away.

"Karen, please let me know if this is too soon, but I can't stop thinking about Jacob, and if it's possible, I'd really like to come to Seattle over the holiday weekend. We do not have to spend that much time together—I'd settle for even an hour. Please let me know at your earliest convenience."

My earliest convenience? Was he demanding *my* earliest *convenience*? From there my line of thinking dissolved into a simple no no no no no. Not now, why right now? And not on his terms, whatever those terms might have been.

On the other hand, it probably had to happen sooner or later. For you, I mean.

"Sure," I typed back, not letting myself outthink myself. "That would be fine."

We were supposed to go to the house in Friday Harbor, but Allie and the kids could go without us. Or we could meet them there the next day. No reason to let your father ruin the whole weekend.

He was still online, wrote back immediately: "Really? You mean it? Oh, you've made me so happy, you have no idea. I already booked a room at the Westin. Thank you, Karen, thank you."

And at this I clicked off without a response because no matter how much resignation I felt about seeing your father I really didn't like making him so happy.

JAKE, I DO realize at this point in the book that I'm not giving you as much advice as I meant to—in fact, when I originally started planning this project, I was thinking in terms of something that would intertwine autobiography and advice, so not only would you learn all about me, but you'd also learn whatever wisdom I have to pass on to you. I suppose, when I started this, I thought I'd have more wisdom. But here it is now, six in the evening, a long day, dinner almost ready in the house across the lawn, and I'm right where I was two weeks ago. There you are, once again playing hide-and-seek with Dustin somewhere near the water (don't fall in, Jesus Christ, you know that, right?) Allie is grilling chicken on the patio and Camilla is standing next to her, gesticulating wildly, and Ross is in all likelihood phone-sexing with Asha, depending on what time of day it is in Mumbai, and I'm just now worrying I have no wisdom to give you at all.

Two weeks ago when I started this, your father was a bad memory and a dim idea. Now he was on his way. July 4 weekend. Happy birthday, America.

I wanted you to think he was fine but not better than fine. I wanted you to like him but not love him.

But also I guess . . .

Well, you should know you were conceived (Is this something you want to know? Probably not—you can skip these pages if they gross you out, but just in case . . .) in a happy place. I mean, your dad and I had only six months together, but I believe they were very happy months.

We escaped sometimes to the Maryland shore or drove together to Delaware.

One night, we ate crabs and drank beer in a barn somewhere between cornfields and the Atlantic and then danced to country music till midnight. We line danced—we had no idea how to line dance! Another time we went to an Orioles game. Another time we had a righteous New York City date, kissed on top of the Empire State Building like tourists. There was that one time we saw three movies in one day.

The day after Griffith won his primary, I did two minutes of postgame analysis on MSNBC, and then your father met me at the studio—which was, conveniently, just down the road from his house in New Jersey—and took me for breakfast at a Korean joint in Fort Lee, the kind of place that served kimchi with its eggs. He would have made me something at his house, but the only thing he knew how to cook were pancakes, which I was sick of.

Anyway, I was wearing too much makeup, a terrible plum-colored blazer, but I was so high off the victory that I didn't care what I looked like, and your father—he thought I was beautiful. He told me so.

"I was watching you on the monitor when you were talking," your father said to me as I was forking up my eggs. "You looked beautiful. You are beautiful."

I put down my fork, embarrassed. Was he teasing me? I'd let myself grow too comfortable around him. I'd told him I was sick of his pancakes. "No," I said.

"Really."

I shook my head. There was a bright pendant light swinging over our table. I could see a faint trace of veins in your father's broad forehead, and a smattering of freckles, like your freckles, on his pale skin. "You are, Karen," he said. "I don't know why you don't believe me."

I kept my gaze on his forehead so I wouldn't break. "Because nobody ever told me that," I whispered. Allie was the pretty one.

"Then let me be the one to tell you."

Your father, Jake. Let me tell you. Your father.

We didn't see each other as much as I wanted—my work, his schedule—but we did see each other an awful lot, and if it wasn't love like I thought it was, it certainly—well, it was something. And not just tender moments in Korean restaurants either. Your dad loved to laugh. If you asked him what his favorite movies were, he'd say, in all seriousness, *Airplane* or *The Naked Gun* or *Harold and Kumar Go to White Castle*. He had no patience whatsoever for serious movies or grim television; the very idea of *Mad Men* drove him crazy. Who needed weird set pieces about the sixties when the world was so full of weirdness and lunacy and sadness and anger? I tried to argue for the artistic value, or maybe just the cultural obligation, of art to examine human out-rageousness and anger, but he would wave me off. He was not a simple guy, your dad, but he liked his pleasure simple.

I wonder but I am trying not to wonder what he would have thought if I told him you'd been born. He liked his pleasure simple and you being born would have made his life less simple. Maybe that's why he didn't want kids all those years ago. He wasn't afraid of global warming; he was afraid of *complication*. He somehow understood more than most people that having kids means losing control. I thought I knew him, but I guess I knew only one part of him, the part that was easiest for him to show.

It seems to me, Jacob, that when the time comes for you to pick a life partner, you should pick someone who behaves well in a crisis. It's very easy to think you know someone—it's very easy to think you know *yourself*—when life is calm and orderly, movie dates on Saturdays, chicken dinner at seven. But people become their truest selves in emergencies. Selfish people jump into the life raft first. Cowards sneak out the back door. Liars say whatever it takes to get out of trouble. Craven people walk away from what they've wrought. But good, morally sound people take responsibility for their actions and stand up for the people they care about, even if they put themselves at risk. Even if they put their own desires second. I want you to choose someone who is good and morally sound. Make that your first priority when you decide who you want to spend your life with. I promise you, Jacob, that person will be out there, and you will be happier with that person than you ever would have been on your own.

I'm not saying your father should have immediately changed his mind about children when he found out I was pregnant. But at the very least I think he should have tried.

I COULD SEE across the lawn that the grill was closing down, and sure enough my phone buzzed; I was being called for dinner. Camilla was setting the table on the patio—the sky was gray but the drizzle seemed to be holding off—and in a few minutes we'd all assembled, you and Dustin, Ross and Camilla and Allie, and Bruce, home unexpectedly early. He kissed the ladies on the cheek, ruffled the boys' hair, even Ross's, even yours.

"How'd you get out of work before six?" Allie asked Bruce, passing around a big salad. Your aunt was not exactly a domestic goddess—she didn't get too freaked out about dirty laundry, say—but she did a nice job of putting together dinner: grilled vegetables, grilled chicken, salad, a big loaf of bread. It looked like the sort of thing a magazine would call an "easy weeknight supper" but that would have taken me, at home, hours to figure out. I'm sorry to say that you and I ate way too much takeout in New York, way too many sandwiches. You'd eat better once you moved here, I was sure.

"Ross texted me. Said he wanted to have a chat." Bruce poured white wine for the grown-ups while Ross picked a nail. I wanted Bruce to pour him some too, but he didn't, because Ross wasn't really a grown-up. "So what's going on?"

"Just . . . I don't know." He was doing that thing teenage boys do, gunning his foot up and down under the table.

"You don't know? You said you wanted to talk."

"Here," you said to Ross, and extracted something from the pocket of your sweatshirt. It looked like one of those shriveled skulls from old adventure movies: your power gourd. "This'll help."

"Thanks," Ross said, taking the gourd from your little hands. We were all quiet for a minute, assessing it. Ross put the gourd on his plate, thought better of it, held it aloft.

"I've been sleeping with it," you said. "Like you told me to."

"You have?" said Ross and Allie and I at the same time.

"What the hell *is* that?" Bruce asked.

"It's a ceremonial power gourd from Guatemala," you said, and I couldn't believe you remembered what it was called or that the country was named Guatemala, even though of course you remembered that, you remembered everything. "I've been sleeping with it so I don't get bad dreams."

"Does it work?" Ross asked.

"Have you been having bad dreams again?" I asked.

You shrugged, ripped a piece of skin off your chicken with your grubby hands. I should have made you wash. "Only sometimes. Not like before."

"Are you sure?" I asked.

"Yeah. Before was worse."

Before referred to that terrible time after we met with Dr. Susan and she explained to you what was happening to me because I couldn't find the words. And even though she did it in the most clinically approved way, and even though we both emphasized that I would be here for a long time and that the doctors were going to work as hard as they could to keep me healthy, you started having screaming nightmares every night and ending up in bed with me, where you would kick me in the scar and thrash, but still I did not have it in me to put you back in bed. I didn't have the physical strength; I didn't have the will. That was a year ago now, when you were just five, and I don't know what the hell we were thinking. Why, again, was it necessary to tell a not-quite five-year-old his mother had cancer? Just because it was true?

"What are you dreaming about, Jake?" I asked.

"I keep thinking that you won't be able to find my dad," you said with those little guilt-making eyes of yours, and I gulped my wine to keep from slashing my wrists with my knife.

"I found him," I said after I put my wineglass down.

"You did?" you asked. "When? Why didn't you tell me?"

"He wants to come see you," I said. "July 4 weekend."

"July 4?" you said. "How many days is that?"

"July 4?" Allie said. "Aren't we going away?"

"That soon, huh," said Bruce. "That seems a little soon."

"How many days is that?" you demanded, and suddenly I felt like the cruelest person ever born, to keep you and your father away from each other when you were both counting days, but then I reminded myself of my righteous rage and set my lip.

"Mommy!"

"Seven days," I said. "It's seven days from now."

"Seven days! That's not far!"

"He's flying here?" asked Camilla. "From New York?" I really didn't want to get into the details with you there so I just nodded noncommittally, but you had already grabbed the power gourd back from Ross and were squeezing it between your hands. You had a look I'd seen only a few times before: when I got you the Batcave you wanted so desperately for your sixth birthday, when we brought home Kelly the hamster from the pet store. You were looking determined to make the most of what you'd been given: you were half-smiling, you were bashful and ecstatic.

"Seven days isn't even very long," you said to the gourd.

I pinched the bridge of my nose. What was I doing? What had I done?

"So that's great, Karen, it's great he's coming," Ross said. "Also I wanted to just say I'm thinking about going to India next year instead of U Dub, okay? I want to move to Mumbai."

"What?" said Allie.

"Why?" said Camilla.

"That's not what we planned on," said Bruce mildly, cutting his chicken. "I thought you wanted to stay close to home."

"I'm kind of rethinking that."

"Is it your girlfriend?" Camilla asked; Ross sent her death glares.

"Is Mumbai the same thing as Bombay?" Allie asked. "Is that what they call it now?"

"Yes, Mom," Ross said. "It's the same."

"Watch your tone."

"Wait, aren't we still talking about July 4?" Dustin said, looking at you. "Jakey's dad?" You were still in your blissed-out trance, you and your gourd.

"Whoa there," said Bruce. "Just—whoa there. Who said anything about Mumbai? Who's this girl?"

"Asha," Ross said. "From Guatemala. I told you?" he said, with a tone that suggested he didn't actually tell his father anything but wanted him to believe that he had.

But Bruce hadn't gotten this far in life by being a fool. "I don't think you did, Ross."

"No, I definitely—" Ross let his voice get small. "I definitely did."

"Jakey," Dustin said, "aren't you excited to meet your dad?"

You rolled your eyes at him. "Um, *yeah*," you said.

"What do you think he's like?"

"I think he's awesome."

"Why do you think that?" Dustin asked, having shoved half a chicken breast in his mouth so that he was talking through a pasty bolus.

"Because," you said, "he's my *father*."

"Yeah, but it's not like you've ever met him."

"Dustin," Allie said.

You seemed unbothered, gave Dustin what I suspected was the first superior smile I'd ever seen on your face. "Um, I have so met him," you said. "In my *dreams*."

"In your what?" I said, and you turned that same withering smile on me.

"That's crazy," Dustin said. You didn't respond, put the gourd in your lap, and began to cut your chicken nicely, like I'd always asked you to, like you'd never done.

"So anyway, if it's okay with you guys," said Ross, smelling another opening, "I'm just going to go ahead and tell U Dub. I'm going to withdraw—"

Bruce shook his head. "I don't think so."

"But *Dad*—"

"Ross, cool it." He was a nice guy, my brother-in-law—I'd known him since high school, although I often forgot that. I was a senior, Bruce was a junior, and Allie was a sophomore when they began dating. He picked her up for a date once in his father's Jaguar and his nerdiness was instantly forgiven. He'd placed a rose on the Jaguar's front seat.

"Dad, listen, if you would just—"

"Ross," Bruce said, warmly, warningly. "I said cool it."

The years had worn on Bruce gently enough—he kept himself trim like all Seattle executives did, and although he'd lost most of his hair, he neatly groomed what he had. He wore fancy European glasses and a Rolex, but otherwise (if there could be an otherwise) he dressed plainly. He valued his children, education, reliable cars, medium-risk investments, his boat, local politics, good coffee, early morning runs, and most of all, your aunt Allison. Even now, when he was putting on his Father Knows Best, he still reached out to touch her hand.

"Is this the same girl who suggested you get a tattoo?" Bruce said.

Ross was wearing his sleeves rolled down.

"Maybe we should talk about this later," Bruce said. "In private."

Ross shrugged. You took the power gourd from your lap. "Use it," you said. "It will help you. It helps your dreams."

"Thanks," Ross said, and smiled at you like he was really grateful.

And this was where I started crying, which was of course no use to Ross or to you, but people here had become used to my strange bursts and nobody looked at me funny.

"Anybody up for dessert?" Allie asked.

"I'll get it," Ross said, jumping up. It was possible he could go live a life that nobody expected for him or planned out: he could go to Mumbai, not go to Mumbai, find himself with Asha or another beautiful woman. He could become someone he didn't yet know how to be. Is that what happened to your cousin, Jake? I must admit, my guess was that he'd end up in Seattle, down the road from his mother. Ross didn't seem like he had the fortitude to live on his own for too long.

Do you have that fortitude, Jacob? Will this book give you any fortitude? To go off into your own life?

"Aunt Karen, you want ice cream?"

I nodded my head, even though I didn't.

We cleared the table, Ross brought out the ice cream, and all of us sat there, eating quietly, and when it started to rain we pretended not to notice.

JAKE, IT'S BEEN occurring to me, as I write this, that the future you I'm writing for is someone I'm conjuring out of the barest hints. Clues you don't even know you're leaving me. When I imagine the future you, I imagine a quiet young man, since the present you is quiet. I imagine someone who loves the Yankees, loves new toys, is a good and loyal friend.

But the most insistent part of the future you I imagine are the things about you that remind me of me. The you I imagine came from me and nobody else—that's the you I think of even now, although I know that makes me seem like a total narcissist. Still, over the past several years, whenever you've done something that reminds me of your father (discovered Star Wars, grown taller and more freckled) I've thought of it as a quirk, a surprise appearance by a rogue gene. Because the you I see is so essentially me, Jake. The you I know appreciates sarcasm, handles hardship with grace, travels well, is dignified, occasionally pouty, just like me. The you I know needs at least ten hours of sleep. Prefers hot to cold. Sweet to salt. The you I know couldn't be anyone else, because I am who I am, and you are mine.

And so as I write for the future you, I am writing for someone who seems a lot like the person I am now. The future you sees the truth about people and is essentially unsurprised. The future you understands that I was your sainted mother but not always such a saint.

I do enjoy imagining the future you, by the way—the you that I am writing for. You are someone I'm certain I would like very very much, were I going to be around to meet you. I'm pretty sure we'd still be going to movies together, spend Christmas eating Szechuan. At some point you'd get me to finally try rock climbing. I'd introduce you to my favorite books, all of them, the mysteries and the philosophy and the biographies. We'd have the same politics. Your girlfriend would annoy me, but I'd try not to let on. You'd know she annoyed me, but you'd still move in with her and her cat.

But you'd spend holidays in your old bedroom. You'd invite me over for coffee.

I guess what I'm saying is, I think you would have liked me too.

THREE WEEKS AFTER you started kindergarten, I officially entered remission: the end-of-chemo tests confirmed my CA 125 was normal, my CT scans were clear. Sure, there was the weakness in my extremities, the hair loss, the scarring, and let's not forget the sudden and devastating menopause, but besides all that: remission! Even my doctors sounded jazzed. I danced out of their office at two thirty and realized I was just in time to go collect you from school, so I waved off Julisa and showed up myself at the gates of PS 199, where the crowd of moms and nannies gossiped until dismissal. I didn't really know any of your classmates' moms yet; it occurred to me that I should introduce myself. Suddenly I felt like there was time to get to know new people. Remission! The world was once again a little bit mine.

"Hi," I said to a cheery-looking brunette in glasses. "I'm Jacob Neulander's mom. He's in Mrs. Crane's class."

"Natalie Kennedy," she said. "My daughter's in Mrs. Hook's." And we stood there amiably and talked about nothing, and I was filled with the glee of being just like everyone else. For the first time in months I felt like I had a real appetite. I decided I would take you to Serendipity for an early dinner, those awesome burgers followed by ice cream sundaes the size of your head.

A big group of kids emerged from the exit: adorable, multicultural, high-end sneakers. A little too tall to be kindergartners. Then the next class emerged, also adorable and multicultural, and this time just the right size to be you, but I didn't see you.

"Is that Mrs. Crane's?" I asked Natalie Kennedy.

"Sure is."

I scanned harder. I promised myself I wouldn't say anything to you about remission because I didn't want you to confuse it with a cure, but still I wanted you to celebrate with me. We finally had something to celebrate! For the first time in so long I was an approximation of a healthy person. I wondered if you'd be able to tell. Then suddenly there you were, in your Lego Star Wars backpack, your curling-at-the-edges hair. You were talking eagerly to another kid, not even looking my way. I waved at you, but you didn't see me. It was nice, in a way. A bit like spying.

And then you looked over at me and instead of smiling, your face seemed to—well, not exactly fall, but sort of settle. You trudged over. "What are you doing here?"

"I wanted to see you!"

"Are you okay?"

"Yes! Yes, I'm so okay. I wanted to take you to Serendipity! Ice cream!" My voice was scaling up like a teenage girl's.

"Now? Why?"

"We're celebrating!"

You looked suspicious. "What are we celebrating?"

I didn't want to explain it. "Just life," I said.

"But it's Tuesday."

"We can't celebrate on a Tuesday?"

"Tuesdays I go to Aiden's to play Pokémon."

"You do?" Did I know that? I wasn't sure I'd ever heard of Aiden.

"Julisa is friends with his nanny," you said. "His older brother has like five thousand Pokémon cards. He's teaching us how to use them."

"I didn't know," I said. "You can go next week."

"But . . ." You looked crushed. "But I want to go *now*," you said. "Aiden's waiting." I looked up and sure enough, the kid you were talking to before I interrupted was standing a little behind you and to the left. Right next to him, the nanny. They were waiting for us to finish our chat.

"You don't want to go to Serendipity?"

You kind of slumped, shook your head. "Maybe some other time?"

"But we can get ice cream!"

"I'd rather play at Aiden's."

Jake, it's a little embarrassing telling you this now, but I felt, at that moment, like I'd been dumped. I wanted to kill Julisa—how could she not tell me you had this Tuesday routine? Except that maybe she had. It's possible she had. My attention had become so scattered.

"Okay for him to come?" asked the nanny. It turned out Aiden lived on Seventy-Fifth, a block away, and the nanny had no problem walking you home, and you really wanted to go, please please please, so how could I say no? I didn't say no. Instead, I stayed rooted to my spot in front of the school and watched you leave, and then I dawdled home by myself after the crowd had dispersed, you, the nanny, Natalie Kennedy, just like I used to all those years ago when I walked home from my own elementary school. In my head, I was writing you an angry letter: Don't you see this is a movie where I'm dying? And the doctors pressed Pause? We don't know how long the pause will last,

Jake! We have to celebrate every fucking second of the pause!
Cancer might press Play any second!

And then I took a breath and erased the letter.

How good it was that you were making friends, and how
good it was that you were starting to feel comfortable with new
people. And how good that you didn't feel overly protective of
me, like you could never leave my side.

But I never wanted you to ever leave my side. I sat on our
stoop for two hours, until I saw you bouncing up the street, the
nanny and Aiden a few steps behind. And the sight of your face
mended my heart and felt like enough of a celebration.

THE PAIN WOKE me up at four in the morning. Sharp,
in my stomach. Right there, right below my stomach. Not my
stomach. Or was it? They said, after the debulking, this wouldn't
migrate to my stomach. Metastasize. They said it wouldn't. Not
there—please, I still wanted to eat, I couldn't bear a colostomy
bag, please God, please, I thought, I know I don't believe in you,
please someone, please don't let me scream in pain, please don't
let me wake up Jakey—please, oh God —I would type. Sometimes that helped.

I stood. That helped. I sat down to type. The pain now came
and went in waves. I remembered the instructions: *Hold your
breath at the top of the wave, let it out at the bottom.* It was
okay. Typing made it better.

I will write this down, I will write this away, I will let you
know what this was like. I will pass on this wisdom. I will let
you witness what this was like. Your mother at the end of her
life. If you don't want to know you don't have to read it.

This was me. *This is me.*

Please don't let me wake you up. I will not wake you up. I will not wake you up. Please please please please please—typing helps. I will type this.

I called Allie. She didn't answer. Thank God. I didn't want go to the hospital.

Then it hurt more. I stood, then sat. Didn't help. I called her again. She woke up, groggy. "You okay?"

"I'm not okay."

"I'll be right there."

I HAD COME to know these aches and pains, had told myself that's what they were. Scar tissue. This was not metastasis. This was old hat. I was in remission, wasn't I? But I was writhing on the bed when Allie came. "I'm calling an ambulance." I looked at her, my I'm-gonna-kill-you look.

"Codeine," I managed.

"Karen." Was she really going to fight me on this one? I gave her again my death look, but it was dark in this bedroom, she might not have been able to see it. She picked up the phone.

"Codeine," I hissed, and she relented, put down the phone, went to the bathroom. Returned with a pill and a Dixie cup of water.

"Karen, come on." She held me up as I took the pill. It was almost four thirty and the relentless Seattle day was about to break. We were so far north here, almost Alaska. I thought about everything I needed to do, track down Ace, finish some Power-Points, check in with everyone in New York, and there was you, quality time with you. There was a private tennis coach at the camp; I wanted to sign you up for lessons. I wanted to take you to the toy store in Pioneer Square for the Playmobil pirate ship you'd been inquiring about.

I gagged on the pill but got it down. Allie lay down next to me in the big soft bed. She put quality mattresses in the guesthouse. She had never stinted on a thing.

"Are you okay?"

I was not. The codeine worked fast, but I still had twenty minutes to wait. "I won't be able to take them to camp," I said.

"Karen."

"You'll have to—" It was so unfair so unfair so unfair. I wanted to take you to camp. I wanted to meet your tennis instructor. I did not want to be high on codeine I did not want to miss breakfast I did not want to miss you Jakey.

"Karen, after I get the boys to camp, let's go to the doctor, okay?"

"I have to work today."

"The doctor," she said again. "Please, Karen."

"Let's see," I whispered, "if the codeine helps."

"Please."

"Let's see." It was already helping. It worked fast.

Allie and I lay there in the same bed the way we used to when we were little, in that house on Long Island, the grandparents asleep upstairs. As I drifted, I remembered feeling their heavy unsettling sadness even in their sleep. I remembered the way the sadness would permeate the night, and the way Allie's flaxen hair would fall against the pillow in our shared bed. I would look to see patterns in her swirls of hair. I knew she was faking sleep just like I was. I would close my eyes; she would open hers.

I saw her now. She was faking sleep now. Her hair was still long and blonde against the pillows. Her mouth drawn tight.

I rolled over, stuck my hand in the cool space between the mattress and the wall. There was something lumpy there. A dried avocado? Why would—I pulled it out, inspected it through my medicated haze.

You'd left me your gourd.

Jesus Christ, Jacob. How would I live without you?

I clutched it in my hands for a long time as the light grew brighter outside. I listened to my sister's breathing deepen. She was no longer faking it and neither was I. I could feel my own breathing start to grow longer, deeper. I would be asleep very soon. I tucked the gourd to my chest, clasped my hands around it. I closed my eyes and fell asleep and soon I knew I would dream sweet dreams.

5

One of the pleasures of being a six-year-old is that you find farting one of the most expressive of human activities, and occasionally, when you have a really substantive specimen building up, you quiet us down in the room so that you can perform. "Shhh, guys, check this out!" But as I'm sure you now know, once they hit puberty, most women no longer find public displays of flatulence entertaining. In fact, most women start pretending they never fart just around the time they start realizing boys always do. Which is to say, I was embarrassed before I was worried about a persistent and noxious gassiness that hit me right around my forty-first birthday and refused to dissipate or even, sometimes, be relieved. (What I mean is that I wanted to fart all the time and half the time I couldn't.)

Well, probably this is what it means to get older, I thought, and tried to stay away from roughage. When the *Times* did that piece on me, the one where it called me "equal parts sweet and tough" (which I loved), I looked notably bloated in the accompanying photo. But we were wrapping up a busy 2011 and I was on my usual autumn diet of pizza and Tums. Who wouldn't have been bloated? Then, just after Election Day (DiFierro won by six points, Johnson by four, bonuses all around), my back started aching and also I had this scratchy voice and—well, there's no need to get into the whole story. What's there to say about the story? Ovarian cancer is called a silent killer, but unlike what it says on the internet, that's not because it's asymptomatic. I was doubly, triply, quadruply symptomatic. It's just that my symptoms were the sorts of small or embarrassing annoyances that were easy to ignore or to blame on myself.

Within days of my diagnosis, I met Dr. Steiner, who was going to do something called a debulking, a surgery that would remove many of the organs I had previously considered crucial to my staying alive. Exactly how worried was I supposed to be?

"We're going to find out what's going on inside you," Dr. Steiner said, which wasn't really an answer.

"Will I at least get skinny?"

"You will get very skinny," Dr. Steiner said, half-frowning; he did not seem to realize I was joking.

The debulking took nine hours, I was told, and was not optimal (they couldn't get all the cancer out without damaging my distal aorta) but not too terribly suboptimal either (they managed to get a lot of it out, they thought). This was the good news, such as it was.

"But then there's bad news," I said to Dr. Steiner, because I was getting used to his half frown.

"Well, mixed bad," he said. He was scratching his nose. Despite his nebbishy demeanor, Dr. Steiner had kind eyes, and in my foggy imagination, I thought maybe he too was trying not to cry. I thought that was sweet of him, not to cry. Allison had come out for the surgery and she was in the room with us, holding my hand. Her own was cold.

The mixed-bad news was that this was stage IV cancer. The mixed-bad news was it had spread to lymph nodes in my pelvis. The mixed-bad news was that they weren't able to scrape out every bit of tumor.

The bad news was that I would not live to see you turn ten.

The good news was that they would be able to slow it down, if I were willing to endure periodic rounds of chemotherapy, if I were willing to endure living, knowing how soon the end would come.

"And that's the good news?" Allison said.

"Mixed," Dr. Steiner said. "She's young, she's healthy."

"I'm not healthy," I said. "It sounds like bad news to me. Just bad. Not mixed."

"No, really," said Dr. Steiner. "Really, it could be so much worse. I've seen it worse. And there are new therapies that are being developed, therapies that might extend your life span."

"Clinical trials?" Allison said. "Can we get her on some clinical trials?"

"First," Dr. Steiner said, "first let's just go with what we know works."

"And what works?"

"Chemo," he said. "Chemo and surgery. Standard protocol."

"But you just said there are new therapies that—"

Dr. Steiner looked exhausted. "Your sister needs rest," he said. "We can talk more tomorrow."

So how much time, exactly, did I spend thinking about the mixed bad news? More time than the social workers hoped. More time than Allison wanted. Enough time, actually, to think about just ending it all right away, to forget about the good fight and the long game and—I'm sorry, Jake—deciding to die right then, while you were at school, while Julisa was in the other room, doing the dishes. While Allie was running in Central Park. A gun, a rope, pills. All of the above. That felt like the brave choice to me, even braver than living. But I didn't know where to find a gun, and I didn't really want to die (I still don't want to die).

Maybe there still are alternative therapies, clinical trials. Maybe there are other things I could be doing right now. But instead I've been doing what the good girl does, just following orders. Chemo, surgery. More chemo. Writing my will. Writing this.

Anyway, while I was in the hospital, Allie and Julisa divided and conquered, getting you to school, making sure the house was clean and the hamster was fed. Allie fed me ice chips while I blinked in and out of consciousness after the debulking, thought about bringing you to visit me, took you to the movies instead. After I got home, she shuttled me back and forth to my chemo appointments, kept me well stocked in the food I felt like eating (pureed soups, cantaloupe) new issues of *People* and *Us Weekly*, Julia Roberts movies. I thought about how grateful I was to her, how much I hated being grateful to her. She had left her own kids across the country, her husband, her life, and moved in with me. Without blinking. She had done this, even though I'd been so mean to her in high school, even though I teased her behind her back and even to her face about her life of tennis and yoga and float planes to the summer house. She stopped her life to come save mine. She wouldn't let me say thank you. She got you to school five minutes early for the first time in your life.

Do you remember the first time you saw me after the surgery? You were barely five, but you were worldly. You said, *You don't look as bad as they said you would*, and snuggled up in bed with me, unafraid to wrap your arms around me, even though Allie had told you not to, that it might hurt me. Of course it hurt me; of course I didn't let you go.

Six weeks after surgery I started chemo, which took place in a weird-looking office-type room with beds and televisions. Four or five days after chemo I'd feel good enough to work again, to live again, and that's when Allie would take you to the museum or soccer or swim lessons, Julisa would go back home to Queens, and I would spread out my documents or get on the phone or even powwow with Chuck spread out on the apartment floor over pizza, like we used to back when we started the business. He pretended not to notice when I didn't eat the pizza. We were starting to get ready for the 2012 races, had taken meetings with McClear in New Hampshire and Fussell in Rhode Island. So we talked about that. And we reached out to the people we knew on the Democratic National Campaign Committee, to talk to them about their 2012 plans. But our work meetings also had a sort of Potemkin feeling about them, as though we were proving to outsiders (our clients, our consciences) that everything inside was just fine.

One night, Chuck asked, gently, if I thought we should consider expanding our hiring in light of my inevitable absence. Not a replacement, he said, there couldn't be a replacement—but just some reinforcement. I said I didn't think it was necessary yet. We didn't hire anyone.

I went into remission after eight rounds of chemo. Before she flew back to Seattle, Allie treated me to a long brown wig of Jennifer Lopez heft and luster, and I started wearing it around the house. Do you remember how you admired my hair and remarked on how quickly it grew back? Once I realized you thought the wig was real, I decided I would never take it off, not even while I slept. I wanted you to think I looked healthy. I wanted you not to look afraid the way you did when you saw me in my headscarf.

Then one Thursday—do you remember?—I took you to free swim at the JCC. You begged me to get in the pool like I used to and I didn't know what to do—I had my swimsuit in our locker, but no swim cap—but you kept begging. You wouldn't take no for an answer. Did you want to see if I could still do it, could still swim? Did I want to see it? I still had some weight on, the swimsuit still fit. But I knew I shouldn't get that wig wet, or at least I thought I shouldn't, and what if it fell off? In front of your friends? In front of you?

"Please, Mom?" You'd started swimming at the JCC when

you were just a few months old, for a Mommy and Me swim class. And we'd kept it up, for the most part—swim lessons in the spring and fall, swimming during the free swim sessions on Sunday, swimming on vacation in Florida, in Puerto Rico. Both of us together, not just you. Remember that sweet Russian teacher, Tanya, and the way she kept her meaty arms around you and said, kick, kick, and it sounded like "keek"?

"Please get in?" It was strange for you to be in the water and me to stand on the side; you didn't like it. You so rarely said "please" of your own accord. So I maneuvered in, kept my head above water. The water felt warm and calming against my agitated skin. We splashed around for a little while, and I just stood there in the shallow end. But soon enough you were bored.

"Shark, Mom!"

"Honey, I can't."

"Please, Mom! Just a little?" Do you remember shark, Jake? You'd doggie paddle, and I'd swim after you deep in the water, as stealthily as I could, and then, just as I got close to your legs, I'd jump up and yell, "Shark!" and you'd either race away or get tickled, depending on how fast we both moved.

"Please?"

But I just couldn't play shark with you in my wig, and you were disappointed and didn't understand why, and I almost told you it was my hair, but I think just as I was about to speak, you understood and you didn't want to understand, so instead I stood with you in the water and let the chlorine splash at the two-thousand-dollar wig (Allison insisted) and decided not to care until the burning in my eyes became too much. "I think we should go now, Mom," you said. "You look tired." I was tired, I suppose, but also felt the edges of the fabric of my life in my fingers.

It was such a pleasure to watch you swim, Jake—it was then and still is. You're so good at it, a natural, a fish. Are you still swimming? I hope so—it's very good exercise, light on the knees, and it builds those kind of broad shoulders that make men seem more powerful, like they can carry the entire world.

Dr. Steiner told me I would eventually need more surgeries for a variety of reasons (mixed news), only he couldn't tell me exactly when I'd need those surgeries, nor could he tell me what exactly for. The possibilities were endless and horrifying. And all this could happen while I felt like I was still in remission, and all this could mean that the cancer was back, and that it was more virulent, and that it might still be best, all things considered, to figure out how to buy a gun.

Remarkably, the year after the debulking went pretty well. But this past March I checked in with Steiner and the other nebbishy members of his practice, who chalked up my (highly relative) good fortune to youth and decent health, the fact that I had never been a heavy drinker or a smoker, that vanity had caused me to keep my weight in check via a grown-up apportionment of clean diet and hard exercise. I was doing so well, in fact, that when I suggested to Steiner (and the social workers and Dr. Susan) I wanted to spend a few months in Seattle with my sister, as long as I was in remission, he didn't blink. They did patch me in with a few doctors at Hutch, just in case, but overall everyone seemed to think it was a very nice idea for me to have this time with family, and with you. I could get my scans. I would be sure to take naps.

But then, of course, from the second we landed at Sea-Tac, I'd been nauseated, tired. The pain in my side came and went and came back. I was never more than a room away from my codeine. And it had become impossible to hide all this, and insane to try to lie. Allison dragged me to the Hutchinson Center, and she would not let me become the worst version of myself, the version who begged to be left alone to die.

"You promised me at least four years, Karen," she said to me this morning, forcing me out of bed. "I'm not letting you go any sooner."

And so I'm sitting here typing away on my iPad waiting to be told the results of this morning's PET scan, which will tell me what's happening inside me and whether the cancer has spread sooner or farther than they thought, and whether I have indeed already spent my final months in Seattle, and you're at camp right now, and here's the doctor, and soon I'll know more. Soon I'll tell you more. In front of me I see my sister's anxious face, Steiner's mixed-news face. I feel the thorns on the potted plant in the corner of the room. I am sitting, even though I feel like I can't sit.

I was really hoping I'd be able to finish this book for you, Jakey. Please let there be enough time at least to let me finish this book.

So for a few hours I thought about editing out the above paragraphs because they make me look histrionic, don't they? I don't want you to remember me as histrionic, the sort of person who would rather shoot herself than go through any more chemo. Chemo really isn't as bad as all that—I mean, yes of course it's bad, but it's only bad for a little while, and then after you can sit in bed and watch dumb movies and feel pleasantly sorry for yourself. Or perhaps it was because this morning's news was "good" that I felt so chirpy. Our test results came back: the cancer hadn't metastasized. Instead, the pain was being caused by a partial bowel obstruction—scar tissue that was dragging on my intestine and causing intermittent agony. Dr. Horchow, my Seattle doc, thought we could and should operate on this—the operation was, in his words, "no big deal" and would increase my quality of life, such as it was. I, on the other hand, had no interest in getting sliced open again and did not wish to subject my poor intestine to any more ignominy than it had already suffered. Plus, I was terrified of a colostomy bag. Anyway, the surgery for one obstruction could cause another: a pointless surgical catch-22.

But then the pain came in wretched waves and I reconsidered.

Drs. Horchow and Wang at the Hutch Center here in Seattle were very well regarded, just like Dr. Steiner, and they had all been in consultation with one another, Steiner and his minions from the East Coast team, Wang and Horchow from the West, and they had agreed that considering my relatively good prognosis (So young! So healthy—sort of!) and the increasing level of pain, I should have probably just gone ahead and had the surgery in Seattle, where I'd be looked after by family, where you would be distracted, where all the pine trees and fresh water would certainly aid my recovery or, at the very least, give me something new to look at.

But I didn't want to have another surgery. I didn't care what they said: when they opened me up I didn't know what they'd find, and I didn't want to know. I wanted to keep the illusion that I could keep going like this. I wanted to order pizza and eat it on the floor. I wanted to look at my lustrous wig and pretend to see my own hair.

6

On July 3, Allie decided we needed to visit Dad before the holiday. She was right, of course: on the small chance our father could remember us, he had to be wondering where we'd been hiding.

As I've said, you would have liked my folks—they were really terrific grandparents, much more joyful than they were when I was a kid. Although even when we were little, they had their happy moments. My dad, for instance, got great pleasure out of sharing his work with me, showing off the textbooks he used in college classrooms. The dissertation he never finished was about the eastern European wars of the twentieth century; my suspicion is he found the subject too endlessly fascinating to ever stop writing about it. He kept a beat-up map of Ottoman-era Europe on our dining table and referred to it as often as people in other families might have referred to the *TV Guide*.

Upstairs in our Long Island duplex, my grandparents were big into Reagan, kept a glossy framed picture of him by their fridge. Meanwhile, downstairs, my mother tilted liberal, and my grandparents' Republican leanings drove her crazy. Caught in the middle, my dad explained to me why his parents believed what they believed, the horn blasts of history: World War II, Stalin, the annexation of Hungary, Soviet breadlines, the way that Reagan seemed, to people like my grandparents, the embodiment of moral clarity. And though I didn't know it then, my father's lectures in front of a beat-up map, drawing pencil lines in great arcs across Eastern Europe—I think those moments were what first got me interested in politics. My dad taught me that political power matters more than even financial power. That people with political power make history for every other person in the world.

I owed my dad a lot—I probably owed him my career. I couldn't believe how rarely I came see him.

"He really doesn't know the difference," Allison said.

He was sitting up in bed when we got there. Olga, the lovely nurse Allie paid to sit by his side, was immersed in something on her iPad. "Oh, there you are!" She looked up as though she'd been expecting us. "We were just talking about you!"

God, we were the worst. "You were?"

"I was showing Mr. Gil pictures from his albums, right, Mr. Gil?" In a broad bookcase by his window were nothing but photo albums and Olga's romance novels. "We especially like to look at the ones from your high school graduation, Karen. Mr. Gil loves those."

"Hi, Dad," Allie said, kissing him; I did the same. He was sitting up straight, wearing blue-striped pajamas, looked clean, smelled clean, like baby shampoo. He'd been shaved recently. He was thin, with watery red-rimmed eyes and a prominent Adam's apple, and hair that remained luxurious and thick, white and combed back in the style he'd worn since he was twenty. He followed our voices with his head but didn't make eye contact. Occasionally he licked his dry lips. His hands were cracked, lizardy. Allie picked up some balm from his nightstand table and began to massage them, which he let her do, unresponsive.

"Has he said anything recently?" I asked. I didn't even know where to stand. The room was so small, just one extra chair for Olga. I leaned awkwardly against a wall.

"Not much," she said. "You've been quiet today, right, Mr. Gil?"

My father looked at her, moved his head, an indiscriminate gesture.

Olga smiled. "Some days, he says something, but most days not a word."

Jacob, the truth: this was why I didn't come. I didn't have the foggiest idea what to say to my dad. I had no language. I would never have been able to sit here and show him photo albums and explain to him which person was his wife, which was his mother. How could Olga do it when he so rarely said anything back? Was she some sort of dementia savant? Was she just wired totally differently than I was? (Although maybe it was easier to do this for someone else's father. Maybe, were it her own, she'd never be able to sit there all day and remind him of his past.)

I'm telling you, Jake, my dad was not always like this. When you were born, he was still the warm, comforting, loquacious father I grew up with. When Dave and I broke up, when Dave kicked me out that morning—there were so many hours left in the day and I didn't know what to do with any of them. How would I get through that day, much less the rest of my life? I went home, showered, wanted a drink and knew I couldn't have one; I was two months pregnant. I called my father. He was at my apartment within an hour. He'd brought me flowers.

"What am I going to do?" Because he was there, I allowed myself to become inconsolable. While I wept he put the flowers in a jar, put some water in the jar.

"They're pretty, aren't they?"

They were pretty. Daisies.

Then he sat down next to me on the couch and I sort of cuddled against him like when I was little, like when I thought his very presence made me safe. I cried for just about forever. "So this is what you're going to do," he said when I had tired myself out. "You're going to put on something nice."

I nodded out of weariness.

"And then we're going to go have a bite to eat."

"I'm not hungry."

"You have to eat," he said. "For the baby."

I sniffled, nodded again.

"And then we're going to the movies."

"I can't go to the movies."

"You have to go."

"I can't," I said, but he shook his head at me. I could. "What are we going to see?"

"I have no idea, something funny. Or exciting. And then we'll go out for dessert. And then tomorrow you'll go to work."

"But what am I going to do after work tomorrow?" I was a loose thread away from crying again.

"You'll call me." He pulled a flower from the jar and handed it to me. "We'll do something together."

Because my father had given me a plan, I had to follow that plan. I put on something nice. We went for Chinese food, then out to see *Snakes on a Plane*, and the next night, as promised, we went for dinner again and then to see the new James Bond. And then the next day I had to head back to Maryland and was pretty busy throughout the rest of the campaign, and then you were born, and then—and then my dad was still there for me. In that room. Dancing with you in his arms.

For as long as he could have been he was there for me. Why had I not been here for him?

"Daddy," I said. I took out a photo album and made room for myself by his side on the bed. I showed him pictures of us when we were kids—remember this? Grandpa and Grandma? Remember the trip to Virginia Beach? The Catskills? Allie took out her phone and showed him recent pictures of our kids, you and Dustin being silly together, Cammy pretending to push Ross into the lake. And it did seem to me he was able to follow our chatter and all the pictures, even though he didn't say a word.

After about fifteen minutes, he started to close his eyes.

"I think he needs his rest," Olga said. "This was very exciting to see your girls, wasn't it, Mr. Gil?"

Allie leaned down to kiss his soft cheek. "Here," Olga said, picking up her iPad. "I'll take a picture of you together and later on we can talk about your visit." Allie and I stood next to our father with our arms around him and smiled when Olga said smile, but when we looked at the picture our father's eyes were closed; it turned out he was already asleep.

WE RETURNED FROM Bellevue to a surprising moment of domestic instability. Ross and Bruce were going at it over Ross's ability to make his own choices regarding his own future. Camilla met us at the door. "I'd avoid the kitchen if I were you."

A long, strangled "I'm eighteen, you asshole," echoed from down the hall.

Allie dropped her purse and went charging like a fullback, Camilla and I following from a nervous distance. "What the hell is happening?"

In the sprawling kitchen, Ross was standing, fully extended, red with anger. Bruce was sitting at the counter, both hands wrapped around a coffee mug, somber but unagitated. In all the years I'd been visiting Allie, in all my time in Seattle, I had never heard anybody call anyone else an asshole. In fact, their life had always seemed one of almost comical tranquillity.

"Would someone tell me what the hell is going on?"

"I am eighteen years old," Ross growled. Had he really grown so much overnight? I'd never seen him so big, so broad. "I can vote. I can drive. I can work. I can make my own decisions."

Bruce's face remained placid, but he was clutching that cup for dear life.

"Is this about Mumbai?" Allie asked.

"You are not going to go hang out in India for a year," Bruce said, icy calm. "You're starting college. That's it. I'm not having this discussion anymore with you. I am finished."

"Jesus Christ, if college is so important to you, I'll fucking go to college in India," Ross said. "Okay? Is that okay by you?"

"How is that going to happen, exactly?" Bruce said. "And if

you curse at me one more time, Ross, every privilege I've ever granted you—"

"You're on the fucking board of Columbia University! You can get me in somewhere!"

"Ross, what did I just say to you?"

"Do you think I can't handle it? Is that the problem? You think I'm stupid?"

"Oh Jesus Christ," Bruce said, finally releasing his coffee cup so he could bury his forehead in his hand.

"Then what. The. Fuck."

"Ross!" Allie said, and Bruce stood up and suddenly lost it, yelled at Ross to get the hell out of this room, out of his life, he was a spoiled shit, a stupid child, and suddenly the two of them were barking at each other like wild dogs, and I couldn't help but notice how much bigger Ross was than Bruce, especially when he was in his face. And then Allie was behind her son trying to pull him away from her husband, not that they'd come to blows, but I guess they could have come to blows, and that's when I looked down and saw you standing next to me, your eyes wide like quarters.

"Mom?" you said, reaching for my hand.

"It's okay, sweetie," I said.

"Is it?"

"Sure. They'll get over it in a little while."

But you'd never seen a father act like this toward his own son before.

I hoped you were paying careful attention.

BY THE NEXT morning, however, all seemed relatively calm; Allie and Bruce and the kids headed off to the float plane without any mention of yesterday's scene. "All good?" I whispered to Allie on her way out the door, and she made a sort of what-can-you-do gesture, but she looked tired.

I myself had been up half the night with worry, although a Xanax did eventually knock me out. The plan for the day was simple: at eleven, you and I would go to Tully's Coffee by the Pike Place Market and we would seat ourselves in a corner booth. Your father would meet us there. We'd stay for one hour. If all went well, we could go to the park for one more hour. Then you and I would get into the Hyundai and drive to Anacortes and make it there for the five o'clock ferry. We'd be at the house in Friday Harbor in time for cocktails. This was nonnegotiable. The cocktails.

After my sister and her family left, we trooped upstairs to the kitchen for breakfast, where you found the wrapped Playmobil pirate ship on the table. "What? It's not even my birthday!"

"Well, almost," I said. Your birthday was in six months.

"No it's not, and also"—you looked at me suspiciously—"does this mean I'm not getting the Lego Millennium Falcon?" The Lego Millennium Falcon was the toy that you'd decided, after much weighing of the options, to select as your primary gift upon turning seven.

"It doesn't mean anything. I thought you'd like it."

You were still suspicious, but soon enough you'd gotten over it, and we tore open the nine million different parts and pieces of the pirate ship, spread them out on their kitchen table. There were cannons, torches, a tiny parrot, pin-sized gold coins. Huge flags that needed to be tacked up to the boat with twine, and a tiny plank off which to walk our tiny prisoners. It was 10:05 a.m.

If we tackled the job the right way, we could have been there all afternoon.

"Mom!" you said, amid the plastic squalor. "Mom, the clock! We can't do this now! We have to leave!"

"We don't have to leave. It doesn't take an hour to get downtown."

"Yeah, but . . ." You looked at me warily. "What about parking?"

"It won't be a problem," I said. "It's a holiday."

"We can't be late," you said, pointing at me with a wee Playmobil cannon.

Right. Well. "Why don't you stay here and start putting this together and I'll go get some makeup on."

As I tromped across the grass toward our guest cottage, I thought that maybe this was the first time in your life you'd ever been alone in a house. I turned and saw you through the window, standing at the kitchen table, staging a battle with some pirates. You were swooping them through the air, high-diving them back to the table. You were singing out loud, I could tell.

AND SUDDENLY IT was 10:40 a.m. and we were sailing over the Murrow Bridge toward downtown, I-90 miraculously free of traffic, sailboats clogging up the waterway on either side of us. The day was Seattle gloomy, but hell, it was still a holiday, and along the shoreline I could see Mercer Islanders relaxing on their docks, setting out in their skiffs. At that very moment Allie's family was descending on the San Juans, and I wished with everything I had we were with them.

Instead: I'd spent the better part of the past seven sleepless nights figuring out what to wear for today's meeting and had settled, rather glumly, on an Eileen Fisher getup that made me look middle-aged and polite. Flowy pants, cashmere T-shirt, a nice scarf. When your father and I were dating, I was prone to a lot of Eileen Fisher, since it travels well and coordinates, and when you're running a campaign the last thing you have time for is the dry cleaner. Still, if I were healthy, if I still had a figure, I probably would have gone for something a little foxier, for self-esteem's sake.

My chemo hair was in a tiny ponytail. I was wearing enormous sunglasses and I didn't plan to take them off.

As for you—although I stopped picking out your clothes at least a year ago, I tactfully suggested that you wear a shirt with a collar and clean jeans, and you were fine with it, since you never cared too much about what you were wearing. For a while you were against anything with zippers, but now you owned a small collection of Dustin's hand-me-down hoodies that you wore with zeal. You also liked superheroes on your underwear; on this, I was happy to indulge you. So there you were, in my rearview mirror, in a blue shirt and blue jeans and a gray Bush School hoodie, looking like a real Seattle boy. You had assorted Playmobils in your lap, plus the power gourd. You were thrumming your feet expectantly on the back of my seat.

"Knock it off," I said. You didn't.

Weirdly, I wasn't as nervous as I would have predicted. I think I'd gotten all my nerves out already, or maybe simply calling your father in the first place was the hard part, because this, I thought, this was like going in for surgery, this was like waking up in the recovery room, this was like rehab and buying a wig and tending to the dressing on my side and learning how to eat again. It was like the shock of the diagnosis was over and then it was just a series of long and tedious steps. We'd see your father. I knew how to drink coffee.

But I would be lying if I said my stomach wasn't tight as we walked down Second Street toward Tully's. You were racing ahead, your pockets bulging with your toys and your gourd, and I screamed at you to stop, but you were deliberately not hearing me. You would get there first if I didn't catch you. "Stop!" I screamed as loud as I could, and passersby stopped to stare, but you didn't hear me. Hadn't I trained you to hear me? Not to run away from me on city streets? And now as I ran after you—all that was happening in my abdomen, it really hurt to run—I realized what a fool I was to plan it this way. Why were we both meeting him at the same time? Why didn't I meet him first, just to lay down some ground rules, just to make sure he understood what was happening?

Because by the time I reached you, it was too late.

He was right there, outside of Tully's. He was bending down, looking at you. He had a shopping bag on each side, wrapped presents peeking out. I had not seen this man in almost seven years. He looked exactly the same. He was kneeling. You were showing him something. I slowed down to gather my breath. Whatever was happening ten feet away from me, it was too late to stop it.

I walked slowly. I was still walking slowly as he leaned in to give you a hug. Usually you didn't like being hugged. Usually your arms hung stiff at your sides. This time, though, you hugged back.

"Dave," I managed to say. I had practiced this at home, what I'd say, how it would come out. If I remember correctly, I thought I'd memorized some pretty good lines. But I couldn't remember a thing correctly.

He stood, reached out to me, so I let him hug me. It felt good to see that I didn't think I was in love with him anymore. He smelled strange, like Pine-Sol, and he'd developed a bit of a gut. He was softer than I remembered. And not quite as tall.

"Karen, hi," he said. He took a step back but was still holding on to my elbows. I wondered if he could see that my muscles were desiccated. I wondered if he could see that I had chemo hair. Could he see the way my face had gone ashy?

"You look great," he said. Perhaps he could not.

I swallowed. "I see you've met Jakey."

You and Dave were standing next to each other and you had your Playmobil pirates clenched in your hands. Of course you had the same expressions on your faces. Of course you looked exactly alike. "He says he has presents for me," you said.

"Tully's is closed," he said. "The holiday."

"What? Shit," I said, and then I blushed, because did he really need to know I was the kind of mother who cursed freely in front of her six-year-old? And also clearly I wasn't on top of my game anymore because if I were I would have checked to make sure that Tully's was open on July 4, I never would have assumed. I pulled on the door once just to double-check and he was right.

"Maybe we should take him to our house?" you said. "So I can show him the pirate ship?"

"What?"

"Well," your father said, pulling out an enormous wrapped

something from one of his shopping bags. I was furious, of course, that he brought you all this crap like he was trying to buy your love, but then again I'd be furious if he hadn't, so I didn't know what to do exactly. Right there on the wide Seattle sidewalk, you started to shred open an enormous present. "Skull Island!" you said with as much enthusiasm as you'd ever said anything in your life. Skull Island was a Playmobil set designed to go along with the pirate ship. It cost $120 and there were at least three other packages in your father's bags, and they were all just as big.

"How did you know?" I asked your father.

"Facebook!" he said with a dumb grin, and I realized that I bragged way too much about the day-to-day shit I did on Facebook, like I needed approval for everything, the gifts I bought you, the gifts I promised. I'd put a picture of the pirate ship online, and in the thirty spare seconds I had to get dressed this morning I'd posted another of you opening it joyfully.

And now you had met both your parents and it looked like both your parents were going to bankrupt themselves trying to buy your love. This seemed unfair. I shouldn't have had to buy you stuff to make sure you loved me more than you loved him. You were now reaching into the bag to pull out more booty and I felt this was unseemly. "Jake, not now."

"But—"

"You can't open all this stuff on the sidewalk."

"So where should we go?" Dave asked, jauntily.

"Please can we just go to the house, Mom, please? I want to show him all the other stuff. The pirate ship."

Dave put his hands in his pockets. "I don't know if your mom needs—"

"Oh come on, Mom, it's okay, right? Can't he see the pirate ship?"

I swear to God I could have killed myself over that pirate ship. "We could just go to Starbucks."

"No!" you said, and you looked so stricken, your little face. "I hate Starbucks! We don't even live that far! I want to show him my stuff!"

"Whatever you're comfortable with, Karen," your father said softly, and it occurred to me that perhaps we were having a parenting discussion, and perhaps it wasn't going well, and perhaps you were about to have a temper tantrum on the sidewalk and I would do anything I could to avoid that. I might curse in front of you, but really, as a mother, I wasn't as bad as all that. My six-year-old did not still have temper tantrums.

"Please!" you said, hysteria in your voice.

"Jake, I don't think—"

"*Please.*" You had dropped the Playmobil. "Mom?"

Do you remember what meeting him felt like? The street in front of Tully's? The way the rain started to fall? I bent down to look you in the eye; you looked down at the street.

"Okay," I said, straightening up. "Let's go to the house. Jake, you can show Dave some of your toys. But remember, we have to leave at two, okay?" I looked at my watch. It was only five past eleven. "So Dave can't stay very long."

The block and a half to the car you and Dave walked next to each other, with me a half step ahead; you two chattered away about Skull Island, and twice you asked Dave to reveal what was in the other boxes, and he wouldn't, and he asked you all sorts of stuff about where you lived and went to school and who your friends were, and you told him about Kelly the hamster and your best friend, Kyle, and you told him about Mrs. Crane, your old kindergarten teacher, and how you'd be starting first grade in the fall. You'd have Mrs. Dubrov, who supposedly loved music, who supposedly made her kids sing a new song every morning. You were talking so fast! You told him about camp and how you were in the camp play and I had no idea you were in the camp play, which evidently was *Peter Pan* and evidently you were going to be one of the Lost Boys. And then we got to the Hyundai and you got into your booster and your father looked at me funny.

"He still has to sit in a booster?" he said, not like he was accusing me of having done something wrong, but maybe I'd just been a little overprotective.

"Up till eighty pounds," I said. "It's the law."

"Is that just a Seattle thing or is it everywhere?"

"It's everywhere," I said, and added "dummy" to myself, although of course if it weren't for you I wouldn't have known a thing about booster seats or pirate ships or skull islands or *Peter Pan*. But then I thought, Isn't he an ambulance chaser? Shouldn't he know these things? And then I saw that he was leaning back to help buckle you in, even though you knew how to do it yourself. And you, of course, let him.

Then we were all in the car, our first family car ride, back out to I-90 and home toward Mercer Island. Dave Kersey was in the seat beside me. I turned the radio on and then I turned it off.

"Away we go," Dave said. I forgot how he used to say stupid shit like that.

I explained that it was my sister's house, and that her husband did quite well, and then I realized I sounded like I was apologizing for my sister's success, so I shut up and looked out the window. In the backseat, you were ripping into Skull Island. I told you not to lose any pieces and you ignored me. Your power gourd was rolling around on the seat next to you.

"So how are you feeling, anyway?" your father asked me. His Pine-Sol smell was filling up the car and making it hard for me to breathe.

"I'm fine," I said. "How are you?"

"No," he said. "I mean with the cancer."

"I'm sorry?"

"Facebook," he said. "I read that—you've been writing about ovarian cancer."

"Oh," I said. Facebook. "I'm fine."

"Are you in treatment?"

"Remission," I said. For some reason there was traffic—what were you people doing, assholes? *Didn't you know it was a holiday?*—so I had no choice but to slow down, although it occurred to me I could just plunge us all into Lake Washington and be done with it.

"That's great. You working?"

"I'm managing Ace Reynolds. Remember him?"

Dave chuckled. "Ace Wastes Pace Case," he said. "How could I forget?"

"It's reelection time," I said. "He'll win."

"Good for him," Dave said—why should he have cared about Ace? "You look good, Karen, you really do."

I sighed. I did not. "Tell me about yourself, Dave," I said. "What have you been up to?"

"Well, as you know, I'm married," he said in this dumb declarative way, as though he just wanted to warn me in case I had any ideas. As though I would ever have any ideas! I clenched my fists around the steering wheel and kept driving.

"I saw," I said. "She looks very nice."

"She's great," he said. "She works in banking." He paused. "We can't have children."

"Well, you did have a vasectomy," I said. *Dummy.*

"We reversed it."

I felt something prickle my eyes, refused to blink.

"I don't mean . . . It's been . . ." He looked out the window and began thrumming his fingers on the armrest the way you thrummed your feet on the ride over here and again Lake Washington beckoned to me, the icy plunge.

"Do you like Star Wars?" you asked Dave from the backseat.

"Of course," he said. "Didn't your mother tell you?"

"I didn't ask her," you said. "I didn't think she'd know."

"He likes Star Wars," I said. "I should have mentioned it." Dave kept his collection of vintage Star Wars figurines lined up according to value along three shelves in his bedroom.

"Which one's your favorite?" you asked. "Of the movies?"

"*Empire Strikes Back,*" he said. "They're all good though. I even like the prequels."

"I'm not allowed to see *Empire* yet. Only the first one."

"That's a great one too," Dave said. "*Empire Strikes Back* is a little more violent."

"I have to wait till I'm eight," you said. "I'm only six."

"Six is an excellent age," Dave said. "I remember six very well."

You were making the residents of Skull Island shoot each other in the face. "How old are you?" you asked him.

"I'm forty-eight," Dave said.

"Wow," you said. "My mom's only forty-three."

"I know," Dave said. "And her birthday is April 18."

"She's an Aries," you said.

"I know," said Dave.

"What's your birthday?"

"I'm April 4," he said. "An Aries, like your mom."

"Is that why you liked her?" you said. "When you guys met?"

"It's one of the reasons."

I was still clutching the steering wheel. There needed to be a different subject, something else I could stand, but I wasn't sure what. Dave and I broke up just after my birthday. I remembered that birthday, my thirty-sixth birthday, in my old apartment in Chelsea. Griffith had just sent us a check for $120,000; I was going to use my cut as a deposit for a new apartment. A two bedroom on the Upper West Side. In a good school district. I had just found out I was pregnant. Chuck and I were ramping up the business then; he didn't know that I was pregnant and he didn't even know it was my birthday, but when he came to the apartment with takeout so we could go over some business plans, he found me on the floor, in my T-shirt, staring into space.

The thing is, Jake, of course I never wanted to be a single mother. Raising you has been the best thing I've done in my life, but it's not how I would have planned it. I always left the domestic daydreams to Allie; growing up on Long Island, she was the one who would analyze other people's houses and cars and decide she'd want this one when she was a grown-up—no, maybe that one. And she'd have three children by the time she was thirty and a handsome husband who went to work every day and that's pretty much what she got. But while she was so focused on being supermom, I focused more on being successful at work. I didn't make meeting someone a priority.

(That's what I used to tell myself when I felt sorry for myself—it would have been different if I'd had different priorities.)

But I suppose the truth was that he just never came along. I thought your father was it—I thought he was the man I'd been waiting for—and in some ways I guess he was, because he's your father. But then it turned out that he wasn't the right man either.

And then once you came along—some of my friends told me I should keep dating, that of course there were men out there willing to take on a single mother in her late thirties, but I never found any. Once I had you I didn't really feel like continuing to look. And my shell ossified; I didn't want anybody else in our little life. Our apartment on West Seventy-Fourth. *Our* hamster, *our* vacations, *our* piano lessons. Nobody else's. Ours.

Then I tuned in and you two were discussing somebody named Boba Fett.

Thank sweet Jesus the traffic on I-90 started to move.

DAVE, TO HIS credit, didn't seem overly impressed with Allie's estate. He raised an eyebrow and said, "Nice place," and when I explained that Bruce had a fancy job with Starbucks, he nodded and said, "That'll do it."

Jake, it wasn't just the Star Wars and the pirate ships and Skull Island. It's that . . . Honey, you are exactly like him. It's not only what your face looks like—I've always known you *resemble* him—but your expressions! Your laugh! Your lanky body, your thin shoulders. Your heartbreaking smile.

I excused myself to hide in the bathroom for a minute and do my breathing exercises, breathe in, count to five, breathe out, count to eight. I wanted to take another codeine, but then I wouldn't be able to drive your father back to his hotel. I breathed again to five. Maybe I could drink something? I used to keep an airplane-sized bottle of Malibu rum in my purse; maybe it was still there? But my purse was in the hallway. I breathed out, eight. I had my phone, checked my emails, Facebook. Nothing. It was a holiday. I checked the *New York Times* website, Huffington Post. I called Dr. Susan. Answering machine; it was still a holiday.

Please, eighteen-year-old Jake: I ask you when you read this to look back at me and the choices I made with a little bit of sympathy. If you're reading this—I'm trying to picture you now, in your dorm room, maybe there's music playing, maybe there's a cool roommate, maybe you're working on some sort of holographic computer, God knows what the future looks like. If you're reading this in the year 2025, please think back to what you know of 2013, and how limited we were. We put the most important things we knew on Facebook. We snooped, but we didn't talk. We assumed, but we didn't ask.

I'm so sorry I kept your father from you. I'm so sorry I won't be able to give you more of him now. But perhaps by the time you're reading this you won't care so much. Your father will be just another story. Your family will be a new and different thing, something you've chosen for yourself, not this fucked up thing I left you with, an absent father who knew only how to be Santa Claus because that's all that I allowed him to be.

HOURS LATER, THE kitchen table looked like the vitrine of a European toy store, an expertly assembled pirate ship pulling in to Skull Island's harbor, with a castle, a pyramid, and an unexpected veterinarian's office lurking in the distance. The trip to Anacortes was going to take almost three hours and we should have been in the car already, but I hadn't found the heart to pull you and Dave away from each other. You worked in silent concentration, snapping Playmobil pieces together, threading twine, hanging small plastic coconuts off plastic palms.

Neither one of you had even paused for lunch, and usually you were both so hungry.

I took our bag to the doorway. I made and drank some tea. Eventually I decided to get out my laptop and start working, and the three of us spent another half hour on our projects. Finally, your dad looked at the clock. "Oh man—it's almost three."

You looked up, panicked. "I don't want to go!"

"Jakey—"

"I don't want to go on a stupid ferry! It takes too long! I want to stay here with him!"

Dave looked from you to me, saw my expression. "Jake, your mom and you have plans, and I don't think—"

"No!" you said, turning red.

"Dustin's going to be so disappointed if we don't get there tonight. And we have to get to the ferry."

"I don't want to go on *the stupid ferry*! I want to stay here and *play*!"

"What if we take some of your new toys?"

"No!" you said, murderously stabbing some miniature cannonballs into their cannons.

"Jake, please."

You didn't look up. "Dad?" you said. "Please?"

What was wrong with me that everything about this whole afternoon seemed like the worst possible surprise? It never occurred to me you'd call him Dad.

"You should listen to your mom, Jake."

You slammed the cannonball down on the table.

"Honey, why don't you go play some Wii in the den for a second so I can talk to your father?"

"But then do we have to?"

"The Wii," I said. "Whatever you want to play."

You looked suspiciously from me to him, but the siren call of the Wii was irresistible, so after another huffy breath you left Dave and me to the Playmobil landscape and ourselves. I sat down at the table and cradled my head in my hands. My whole body hurt and I hated this stupid Eileen Fisher outfit, I really did. It was the only cashmere I'd ever felt that *itched*. If I took a codeine, I could make this go away. Maybe on the boat. I could probably take one on the boat. Once we got off the boat, we had to drive only a little way.

"He's an incredible kid," your father said softly. He was sitting next to me, fiddling with a figurine.

"Most of the time," I said. "You need a ride back to the Westin?"

"Will I be able to see him again?" said your father, the man who realized he wanted children six years too late.

I shrugged. "I have cancer, you know."

"I know."

"I mean, I'm dying."

He didn't respond. Perhaps he thought I was joking? But when I looked at his face he just looked confused.

"Like I don't have very long to live."

"But—" He looked taken aback. "But I thought you said—"

"I was diagnosed with stage IV ovarian cancer at the end of 2011," I said. "I was given four years, more or less," I said. "Things have been going relatively well, so I'm hoping it'll be more. There haven't been any uncontrollable metastases as far as I know. And I had an initial surgery after the diagnosis that removed a lot of the cancer. But remission never lasts forever. It will come back—it's just a waiting game."

"Oh, Karen," your father said. He looked artless, truly. He did not know what to say. "Karen, I'm so sorry."

"After I die, Jacob will move here, to live with my sister and her family. We've been spending a lot of time out here so that he can get used to it."

"Ah," he murmured. "Well, I guess that makes sense," your father said, his eyebrows knitting.

"So my point is that Jacob is going through a lot right now. Much more than any six-year-old should go through. More than any kid should go through. In a year or two he's going to get uprooted from everything he knows and move to a different part of the country. Obviously I want this to go as smoothly as it possibly can for him."

"Obviously," your father agreed. He took up again with the figurine.

"So therefore I'm not that interested in introducing new variables into his life. We've set up—I mean, my sister and I have set up a plan that seems like a good plan. We're going to get him acclimated. We're treating her family like a natural extension of his family. His cousins are like his brothers and sister. And when I get really sick, we'll come out here. I'm going to be buried here. This is where Jakey's going to live."

I stopped talking so that I didn't risk crying. I took off my stupid scarf and folded it in my hands.

"Can I—" he said. His voice went soft the same way yours did when you wanted something. "Can I help?"

"I don't see how."

"I could—I could do this sometimes. Just, you know, just come play some games or something. I wouldn't . . . I wouldn't interfere. I know you have a plan, I don't want to change your plan."

"So then don't."

"But maybe I could just come hang out once in a while?"

"I'm not sure that's a good idea," I said.

"But what if . . . what if he wanted to?" We both let this hang in the air. I didn't have the energy to explain to your father that it was bad practice to let a six-year-old get everything he wanted.

"It just seems like . . ." your father said.

"Seems like what?"

He didn't answer.

"Listen, my treatments are very hard. Jakey has seen me very sick sometimes, and he knows what's going to happen to me. And I'm the only parent he has." I shot Dave a look. He was looking at his hands. "And what I want for him is stability. I want him to have predictability. I can't just invite new people in to play huge roles in his life. Especially not you. You're a very fraught figure to him."

"I don't have to be," he said. "Fraught."

"Well, you are," I said.

Your dad was quiet for a while.

"I guess this must be convenient for you." It just slipped out.

"I'm sorry?" he said.

"Well, here you are, right, pushing fifty with this hot little wife and everything's great except you realized way too late you want a kid because, you know, global warming, and then all of the sudden your biological son gets dropped in your lap."

"Karen?"

I hated how I sounded but I couldn't stop. "And I'm sure infertility hasn't been fun, it never is, and maybe it's even ruining your marriage, I mean maybe that's why she's on the road all the time, trying to get away from you and your disappointing barren life together, but now all of the sudden you can call her up and say, 'Guess what, honey, I found us a kid! He even looks like me!' And you don't even have to hate yourself any more for all those years you thought you didn't want children. Because now you do and presto—you have one!"

"Karen, stop."

"It won't work that way," I said. "Jacob is not going to save your marriage."

"I didn't think he would."

"Jacob is not going to make you feel better about yourself or your terrible choices or anything like that."

He wrinkled his eyebrows. "That's not fair."

"Really? You want to talk about fair?"

"I want to talk about—" Your father's brow remained wrinkled, like he was confused. "Karen, he's my son. You reached out to me—"

"He's a little boy. He won't save you."

"Save me?" your father said, after waiting a minute to make sure I was done. "I don't want Jacob to save me. I don't want him to do anything at all. I mean, I don't need him for anything. Or if I do—my marriage is fine, Karen." He stopped for a second. "I just want to get to know him."

"Why?"

"Even though you kept him from me—look, he *is* my son."

"I *kept* him?"

"Karen—"

"You didn't want a son!" I might have been hissing.

"Karen," he said, "I just want to know him now." He paused. "See him grow."

"I've been seeing him grow every day for almost seven years," I said, and suddenly I was crying into my scarf. Jesus, Jakey, does it seem like I spent most of your life just crying? Believe me when I tell you I am not a crybaby! I never was! The campaigns I lost, the failures I suffered, my mother's death—I rarely cried, Jacob. Honestly. But now my body is no longer my own. Half my clothing has become useless, torn or slopped upon or shat on or snotted or sweat-stained. I am not myself, I suppose, is what I'm saying. But I was powerful once, I swear.

"Karen, look . . . I was a different person then. I had different ideas. But I would really like to spend time with him now. And I think . . ."

We were both silent as I finished snotting into my scarf and took a deep, raspy breath.

"I think he'd like it too."

"You do?"

"Yes," he said. "I think he'd like to spend time with me too."

I would have liked to rail against this except that I couldn't. It was true. You wanted to spend time with him too. Nobody had ever played with you for three hours so beautifully. I'd never seen you play with anybody like this before. Not even Kyle. Not even Dustin. And even if your father were only playacting here, only putting on his best show to worm his way into our lives—he wasn't. I knew he wasn't. The motherfucker fucking *loved* plastic figurines.

"Can I think about it?"

"Sure," he said.

We sat there and looked at each other. I once loved this man so much I couldn't eat.

"Mom?" you called. "Can I do Winter Olympics on the Wii?"

"We should actually get a move on," I said.

"Now?"

"Five minutes."

Dave looked at me. This seemed like the part in the conversation where he should have stood up and we should have all gotten in the car and then waved good-bye—fuck the Westin, I'd drop him off at the Park and Ride to downtown, or he could call a fucking cab, I just wanted to leave this place, get out of there immediately, but he didn't stand up. He wanted more from me. "Can I call?"

"Dave," I said.

"Please?" he said, and this was like you too, the pleading, the relentlessness.

"I'll call you," I said. "Let me see what Jake makes of this first, okay?"

The pleading look.

"Okay?"

"Okay," he said, and finally he stood and wiped his hands on his knees. "I've never felt like this before, Karen."

"Oh?" I was getting a headache.

"I just . . . I don't know if you could imagine this, what it would be like to meet him when he's already formed. You've done such a good job with him."

I shrugged. What other kind of job could I have done?

"I can't wait to see him again. I hate how much I've missed."

"Let's not talk about that, okay? I don't think I can talk about that right now." But I would let the record show that he had regrets. "Jake!" I called. "Let's get going. Your father's leaving."

"Don't we have to take him back downtown?"

"Jake, get in here."

"I can walk to the bus. There's probably a bus, right?"

"I'll drive you," I said. "It's not a problem."

So we piled back into the car and drove into Seattle, and then we were going to turn around and get back on I-5 toward Anacortes, which was fine. I mean, the drive was fine. This time I turned on the radio and kept it on. Our bag was in the car and we'd packed up Skull Island. We were definitely going to miss the five o'clock ferry and probably even the six, but the seven would be okay. Holiday traffic had eased. And when we got there, it would still be cocktails.

"So when can we hang out again?" you asked Dave as we pulled up to the Westin.

"Let me talk to your mom, okay? And then we can figure it out."

"We get home at the end of July," you said.

"Your mom and I will figure it out." Your dad got out of the car, opened your door, ruffled your hair. "Be nice to her, okay? She works hard." But you'd already burst out of your booster seat and thrown yourself into his arms.

"Hey," your father said.

"I love you, Dad," you said. It sounded like something you'd always wanted to say, that you'd practiced saying, but maybe it had just burst out of you the way so much burst out of me.

"Oh, Jake," he said, "I love you too."

And then he buckled you back in, and I sped the fuck out of there, your father standing next to the Westin doorman on the sidewalk, holding out his hand in an extended good-bye.

7

You were silent on the ferry, which was fine; so was I. We left the car on the ground floor and took a booth in the upstairs interior cabin by the window to watch the horizon leach out toward China. I was so tired I could barely think. You were reading one of the Jedi Apprentice books Dustin had lent you and pulling french fries, idly, from a McDonald's bag. Under normal circumstances I never let you get McDonald's, but on the drive up you were hungry and my defenses were shot.

"Do you want to talk about him?" I asked, after a long silent while. I'd been reading the Friday Harbor tourist brochures, the words melting on the page.

You shook your head, ate another fry.

"You sure?"

Your eyes flickered upward. Today you had grown older, and the age showed in your posture, your half-annoyed expression. You seemed tired too, and you didn't like to be interrupted while you were reading.

"I'm going to go get some coffee."

You nodded at me, went back to your book.

The ride was placid, not too many kids running around. A couple sitting at a table near us was playing Scrabble on a big magnetic board. Another woman, behind them, listened to headphones while nursing a baby. I stood up to head toward the snack bar in the middle of the cabin, holding on to the backs of other people's chairs in case the boat swayed. I knew the boat wouldn't sway, but I held on anyway, tightly. Too tightly. I'd been doing my breathing exercises all afternoon. *In, five. Out, eight.*

I was dizzy and my joints felt poorly welded together. I stopped again, breathed; I wasn't sure I'd make it, and if I did I wasn't sure I'd make it back while holding a cup of coffee. I considered whether I could manage the ten paces between me and the coffee. If I made my way through the obstacle course of chairs and booths, I thought I'd be okay, but if I couldn't, if I went down, I didn't know what would happen next. You'd be frightened. More frightened, I thought, than if I returned without coffee. That you might not even notice. So maybe I just wouldn't get the coffee.

"Are you okay?" A man about my age was gazing at me with concern. I must have looked even worse than I felt.

"Yes, thank you," I blurted. "I'm fine."

"Are you sure? Can I help you with something?" Oh these fucking Northwesterners. I'd just said I was fine! But then I saw the guy was wearing an official-looking uniform and discerned that it was his job to help me, so I told him I was working off a leg injury and that I would have loved a cup of coffee but I was afraid my legs still weren't working too well. I might have even said something about a triathlon. He said not to worry and helped me back to my seat, then disappeared to fetch me some coffee, and I felt not even slightly guilty that I lied and was just delighted to have someone serve me, and I wondered if this was what it was like to be old. When I offered him two dollars for the coffee he said, again, not to worry, pointed his thumb at you, said, "Cute kid," and then made his way off to see to other passengers' comforts, like a male Florence Nightingale in a Washington State Ferries cap. I loved him. The coffee was good.

"It's freaking me out that you won't talk about him," I finally said.

"Why?" you said.

"Look up at me when I talk to you," I said. "It's rude to read while I'm talking to you."

"It's rude to talk to me while I'm reading."

"When did you turn seventeen?" I asked.

"I'm not seventeen," you said, but you put down the book and you smiled. You loved it when I accused you of behaving like a teenager. "I'm not even seven."

"But you will be soon."

"I know," you said. You put the book down on your lap and shoved the last of the fries into your mouth. You had ketchup on your chin, you were missing two teeth, you were my little boy again. "I think I decided what I want for my birthday," you said.

"The Lego Millennium Falcon," I said. "We settled that weeks ago."

"Well, you can get me that," you said. "But Dad should get me the Rancor Pit and help me set it up."

"Dad?" I said. "You mean Dave? Hasn't he gotten you enough stuff?"

"He's my dad," you said. "He has to get me a birthday present."

"That's not all dads do," I said. "Their job isn't just to get you stuff."

"I know," you said, but you said it sadly. You loved stuff, you just loved it. Are you still like this in the future, or has the odd nexus of loss and privilege you've lived with made you more monastic? I think, if I may insert a little advice here, Jacob, I think it's a nice thing not to attach yourself to too much stuff. First of all, the environment, as I'm sure you know, cannot support the endless manufacture and discarding of American crap. As I write this, global warming seems to have reached its tipping point; we're no longer looking suspiciously toward some weird weather some day but living the weirdness. There have been hurricanes and tornadoes in *New York City* recently, along with the hottest summers on record. We don't know whether to burn or to drown. Maybe we'll have achieved some small progress by the time you read this, I don't know, but I'm not hopeful. Ace, in one of his finer moments in City Hall, campaigned to build a multibillion-dollar seawall to protect lower Manhattan from the inevitable, but it's still the inevitable.

The other thing about stuff that I've learned over the years is that the more of it you have the more of it you want. Stuff breeds stuff; you buy stuff and you have to take care of it—let's say you buy a car, then you need to buy insurance and gas and new tires and oil changes, and if you're still in New York, there's parking: it's a nightmare. Rent cars, borrow when you can, don't overpurchase, and don't succumb to the adrenaline rush that might accompany purchases. Or try not to. A trick I use when I'm shopping is just to say under my breath stuff stuff stuff and suddenly that beautiful set of Heath dinnerware I've been lusting after is just more crap to take care of.

I tried to teach you that trick this year, but you were like, "Mom, it's not stuff, it's a Lego Death Star," which I guess made sense. You were six.

Now that I'd taken your attention from the Jedi Apprentice, I felt like I should have something wise to say about your father, but instead the only thing I wanted to ask you is why you told him you love him. But I didn't expect you to be able to explain. I expected you didn't even know, really. What was love to a six-year-old? You looked down in the bottom of the McDonald's bag and were saddened to see there were no more fries. I asked you what you wanted to do in Friday Harbor and you wanted to do what you always do, go swimming and eat ice cream and see the seals, all of which sounded good to me. I tilted my head back and closed my eyes, and in the blink of an eye, the split of a second, the horn blared and there we were, at a harbor on an island at the end of the world.

"Are you going to be okay, Mom?" you asked me.

I opened my eyes. I stood up steadily. "I promise," I lied, and took your hand.

ONE OF THE books Dr. Susan recommended, *A Mother's Light*, suggests making a list of all the things you want your family to do when you're gone so that they can check things off the list periodically and have an excuse to talk about you. The author advises including such things as see the Christmas tree in Rockefeller Center! Climb the tallest mountain in your home state! See the *Mona Lisa* in the Louvre! Although I cannot imagine, personally, instructing you to climb a mountain in my honor, I think about this list more often than I'd like to. What sorts of things would I like you to do in your life? Not necessarily so you'd have a chance to talk about me (which I can't figure out how much I'd like you to do—do I want to be a lingering memory or will that just make me a millstone?). But what sorts of things do I think the good life requires? I've come down to just a few things: Be tolerant of other people. Life, I've learned, is just too stressful when *every single person* you meet annoys you. When people are mean to you, remember something is probably lacking in their lives, not yours. Check for lumps. Try to get eight hours of sleep at a stretch as often as possible. Be thoughtful about money, fall in love with the right person, read a lot. Know that your family—Allie and Bruce and Ross and Camilla and Dustin— they think of you as one of theirs. You belong to me and you belong to them and when you grow up you'll belong to the world.

Try not to do too many stupid things when you're a teenager if at all possible.

I don't really care if you ever climb a mountain.

It was almost midnight, and I was on my second codeine.

Nights on this island were so black they reminded me that I only rarely saw night; my nights in Manhattan were merely grayish, since so much light spilled out from the streets, and even on Mercer Island the light pollution from Seattle, or just general cloudiness, kept us from seeing many stars. But here the sky looked like some lunatic artist sprayed it with glitter. The Milky Way splashed out across the black. You were asleep and

Allie and Bruce were asleep and I was sitting outside on the deck, thinking of you and also my father, and how he named all the stars when I was a kid, showing me them in the encyclopedia. I pointed them out to myself, Orion the hunter, the Big and Little Dippers, the Dog Star. I remembered that I wanted to tell you the names of the stars before I went. I wasn't sure Allie knew them.

The names are really beautiful, Jacob. Cassiopeia, Triangulum. Vulpecula.

It felt good to put some distance between your father and myself, and even better knowing he'd be on a plane tomorrow. I kept myself from looking at Facebook to see if he'd recorded any assessments of the afternoon. The internet connection was pleasingly dodgy on Friday Harbor. The pain in my side came and went, and so did the fogginess in my head. I wondered if things were progressing more quickly than the doctors said they would, if they knew this, if they lied to me to keep me from total despair. If the surgery I needed was actually the last intervention of my life. It was okay, I thought, if they'd lied to me. I would have lied to me. I was not doing well in those early months and maybe the right approach, therapeutically, was to lie.

Why did Dr. Susan insist on telling you, anyway? I'm still working on that one. Do you remember sitting in her office, the way she leaned forward in her own clinical Eileen Fisher outfit? The way she said that I was going to get sick and then sicker, the way I might have to go to the hospital? That someday I would no longer be with you in person but I would be standing next to you in spirit?

You weren't even five. You had no idea what she was talking about.

"You're sick?" you asked me. "What kind of sick?"

"Cancer," I said.

"Doesn't that make you die?"

Kyle's grandmother had recently died of pancreatic cancer.

I looked away, half-shrugged. Dr. Susan tried to interject more nonsense about my spirit and how there would always be someone to take care of you and etcetera but you weren't listening. It was like having one of those horrible dying mother books come to life, spouting out nonsense about how I'd be there in the rainbows.

"When?"

"Not for a very long time," I said. "Not soon."

"Like how old will I be?"

"Eight at least."

"So that's three years," you said. You've always been good at numbers. "And then I'll live with Aunt Allie and Uncle Bruce?"

"That's right," I said. "But not for a very long time."

"Okay," you said, and didn't say anything else, and when we left Dr. Susan said that she thought it had gone pretty well, generally speaking, but she wasn't there for your nightmares that night, or the wet bed that morning, or how I walked into your room two days later and overheard you telling Kelly the hamster that you were sorry but you were going to throw her out the window because it was time for her to die.

"You want some company?"

Ross and Camilla didn't hang out together too much on Mercer Island, but here they were best friends. And though I didn't particularly want company, I smiled and said sure, because Ross had already pulled up a deck chair beside me and Camilla had sprawled out at our feet. She was a pretty girl, my niece, although a more prosaic beauty than her big brother, and although she had no idea how to let well enough alone. Her blondish-brownish hair was dyed an icy shade of yellow, the color of peed-on snow. She wore too much eyeliner, too many necklaces, and talked her parents into getting her a nose job last year. Yet for all these efforts, she was still a pleasant-looking kid, and artsy, tacking images of Frida Kahlo paintings on her walls and reading books by Kerouac and Jeannette Winterson. She didn't seem to resent Ross for all the attention he stole.

We were quiet for a while, watching the stars emit light that, if I remembered correctly, was almost three million years old.

"Anybody mind if I smoke this?" Ross asked, interrupting a silence that had almost lulled me to sleep. He was holding a small joint, perfectly rolled.

"Spark it," Camilla said lazily, and I was flattered. The cool kids were smoking around me. Ross lit the joint, inhaled, leaned his head back to blow smoke toward the sky. I closed my eyes. I had a small supply of medical marijuana back home, but I rarely used it, preferring the full-body fog of codeine. Also it felt weird getting high around you.

"You want?" Ross asked, passing me the joint.

I took it from his hands, thought about saying something like, *I shouldn't be doing this* or *don't tell your mom*, but said nothing, put the joint to my mouth, tried not to smell the sickly herbaceousness of it (this was bargain-basement weed, for sure), and inhaled. I coughed for the tiniest second, but neither of your cousins said anything derisive to me. After a minute, Camilla took the joint from my hand.

I waited for a minute to feel groggy or paranoid or anything at all, but there was nothing, really—just a sort of delayed peace. Cutting through the smell of the joint was the memory of the smell of your father and the way it felt to hug him. He was on a plane and I was on an island and so I let myself think of him, what it was to see him, how his arms were still strong around me and how he still missed that spot right under his lower lip while he was shaving. I used to run my finger on that rough spot, a place nobody else would touch or see.

If you were curious about my love life before or after your father (I have no idea if this is the sort of thing you'd be curious about, and if it's not, feel free to skip this passage), but before your father I dated two men significantly (Howard, 1994–98, and Jim, 2001–4) and afterward no one. I had a few flings, I suppose—men I met on the campaign trails, once a reporter, and for a few lovely weeks, Haven Singlebury's dad (Do you remember Haven? Redheaded girl from your kindergarten class?) when he and Haven's mom were on a trial separation. This started happening right after drop-off—it was October, still warm, and Haven's dad and I bumped into each other at the Starbucks on Amsterdam and Seventy-Sixth. He mentioned in that casual-direct way that men have when they want sex that his wife had just left for an extended stay at the Kripalu yoga center in the Berkshires. She was going through something, he said, and needed time away.

I was only half-listening. "That's nice," I said, "that your wife's a yogini," as being into yoga was one of those things I had always planned on.

"My apartment's empty," he said, and looked down into his latte as if he were surprised with himself, although I'm sure he wasn't. "I'm working from home today. I have no idea when she'll be back. If," he said, ominously, "she'll be back at all."

Before this, I had exchanged maybe twenty words with Haven Singlebury's dad (it must be the THC afterglow, but as I write this, I can't even remember his name). I do remember that he was tall, squarely built, square face, kind of a potbelly. Blue eyes. I think he was a screenwriter or something.

"I'm working from home too," I said, which was true—it's what I usually did. Chuck and I had a small office in Chelsea, but that was mostly where we kept our interns.

"Want to come over?" Haven Singlebury's dad asked.

"Sure," I said, all casual. And for the next two weeks, every morning after drop-off, I would meet Haven's dad at Starbucks, engage in refreshingly little chitchat, then go home with him to his messy classic six on Seventieth Street and stay there till the housekeeper arrived around noon.

And then, as October started to finally cool down, Haven's mom came back from Kripalu, having decided to give it one more chance under certain conditions; soon after that, the Singleburys moved to Connecticut. You probably have no idea who Haven Singlebury was, the name doesn't even ring a bell, but there were moments when I was so dreamy with possibility (and I barely even knew her father, wasn't sure if I even liked him all that much) that I thought maybe one day she'd become your stepsister.

And then Haven's mom returned and I never saw him again or even thought about him much.

I guess the thing I want you to know, Jacob, is that there was nobody I loved like your father.

Sitting under the stars, getting stoned with your cousins (Don't get stoned with your cousins! Or, if you do, please don't drive anywhere after), I allowed myself to think about Haven's dad a little and your dad a lot, until Camilla rolled over and looked at me and said, "Holy shit, Aunt Karen, are you okay?" because I was crying. But it seemed hilarious to be getting stoned with someone who still called me "Aunt Karen," so I started to giggle, and then Ross and Cammy joined me giggling, even though they probably didn't know what was so funny and weren't even as high as all that. But it felt good for all of us to laugh. I laughed enough so that I confused my tears with tears of laughter and I wiped them off my cheeks with my sleeve.

"You can finish this," Ross said, handing the end of the joint to Camilla. I was sad he didn't hand it to me. I got out of the deck chair and lay down on the thick green lawn next to Cammy, and Ross lay down next to me, and I remembered how once they were both so little I could carry them in my arms at the same time, and then I decided to stop remembering things.

"Wow," Ross said. "Those stars."

"I always think I'll get used to them, but I never do." Camilla held the very end of the joint between her fingers like a guitar pick. She squinted through the last drag, then pushed it out on the grass.

"You know their names, right?" I asked. "Your mom taught you their names?"

"That's the Big Dipper, isn't it?" Ross said, pointing at Perseus.

"Not at all," I said.

"What's that one?" Cammy asked, stretching an arm dreamily toward the sky.

"That's Leo," I said, even though I wasn't certain what she was pointing at. "If you look to the left a little, you can see his tail."

"How do you know?"

"Grandpa taught me," I said. "We used to drive out sometimes to eastern Long Island, where it was much more rural—we'd go to the beach and then we'd wait for it to get dark and my dad would give us his binoculars and tell us about each of the constellations. He knew all of them. His dad taught him when he was a kid."

"Actually, I kind of remember," said Ross. "He had all those books about myths, remember? Greek myths? He taught me about the different gods and how you can see them in the stars. Their chariots. I remember sitting on his lap when I was little," he said.

"I remember that too," said Cammy.

I felt a pleasant buzzy feeling in my muscles from the joint. "I can't believe what's happened to him."

"It's still locked in there somewhere," Camilla said. "He just can't access it anymore."

"You think so?" I asked.

Cammy shrugged. "We're always the people we were, aren't we? Just because Grandpa doesn't seem to know what's going on doesn't mean things aren't still somewhere inside him. Doesn't mean he isn't still thinking. It's just different now. He can't talk to us anymore."

I didn't ask her to elaborate. Ross said, "You're high."

We were all still gazing at the stars. I coughed. Then I lifted my shirt to the cool air, ran my hand over the landscape of scars, some keloidal, some mere traces, that ran across the lower part of my belly. I felt them hold together the leftover pieces of me, like solder on stained glass. Another surgery, then more of me to solder back together. I kept my eyes closed. The stars were so bright and eternal I couldn't face them.

You know we're made of stars, right? That every atom in us was made in the burning crucible of the explosion of some long ago star? You may have already learned about this in physics class, although my favorite scientist on the subject is Walt Whitman: *I celebrate myself, and sing myself, / And what I assume you shall assume, / For every atom belonging to me as good belongs to you.*

"My tongue, every atom of my blood," I said out loud as I traced my scars, 'form'd from this soil, this air, / Born here of parents born here from parents the same, and their parents the same. / I, now thirty-seven years old in perfect health begin, / Hoping to cease not till death.'"

It felt weird and lovely to recite Whitman, on a summer evening, on a beautiful island, lying on the grass. *Leaves of Grass*: read that as soon as you can if you haven't already.

"But you're forty-three," Cammy said. "Not thirty-seven. You're two years older than my mom."

My eyes were still closed. I knew what my belly looked like. Pale, shrunken, with leftover stretch marks (I put on sixty pounds when I was pregnant, grew as swollen and unmanageable as a tick). Some of the skin was still stretched out. The scars from my surgeries were a pale rosy pink, the shade of a lipstick I favored in high school. The scars inside me were adhering to the sides of my empty abdomen. I pressed down on them, tried to feel my way inside, pushed harder, even though it hurt. I wanted to reach inside and rearrange it all. Maybe I could fix this all myself.

Cammy looked over at me. "So how was it with Dave today?"

"Exhausting," I said.

"Was it weird to see him?" asked Ross. "Did Jake like him?"

"Jake loved him," I said. "It's not hard to make a kid love you when you bring him enough toys to stock a toy store."

"That was smart, bringing toys," said Ross.

"What else?" asked Cammy, after a while.

"There's not much more to say, really," I said, only half-lying, because while someone more articulate in these arenas might have been able to explain my Jackson Pollack of feelings (rage, heartbreak, longing, sadness, patience, grief, sweetness, murder), I didn't know how to even begin. "He was a nice guy then. He's a nice guy now. Has more patience with Legos than I do. He seemed really into Jake."

"Will you see him again?"

"I don't know," I said. "I'm sure Jake will want to." I wished I were more stoned.

"Well, it was nice of you to do that for him," Ross said.

"What else could I have done?"

"Anything, I guess," Ross said. "Right? You could have told him anything?"

"Like what?"

"I don't know, like his father had gone missing. Or that you tried to find him but you couldn't." Ross paused. "You could have said he was dead."

"Ross," I said, more sharply than I meant to. "He's going

to have a dead mother soon enough. I don't need to kill off his father too."

"No, you know—" Ross said. "Just so that you wouldn't have to see him."

"I would never have done that to him."

"I know," he said. "You're a good mom."

I was a good mom. I was a good-enough mom. "Speaking of dads, how's everything with yours?"

Ross groaned. "I just don't think he can handle having an adult kid. He still wants me to be a baby."

"That's how it is for a lot of parents. It's hard to face that your kid is growing up. That one day you won't really need him anymore."

"You're not like that, though. You're smarter than that."

I smiled at the stars, flattered. But then, as though a glacier was carving through me, I froze from the inside. I was smart, maybe—but I wasn't smart enough. How did it not occur to me sooner? What was wrong with me?

I was realizing that your father could sue me for custody. That was his job, suing people. He could figure it out. He could sue me and take you away. To have the kid his wife wanted. The kid he suddenly wanted. Jake, I know how this might sound—but that's when I suddenly realized that your father might be a monster.

Was he? Underneath that nice-gee-aw-shucks persona, was your father a monster? He might have been. People changed.

"Guys, I need you to do me a favor."

Of course, they said. Anything.

"I need you to keep an eye out for Jake," I said.

Of course, they said. Of course they would.

"No, not just the big-sister, big-brother stuff," I said. "I mean you need to keep him with you. Keep an eye on him. And you need to be very careful about his dad, okay?"

"Okay," said Cammy, but she sounded confused.

"Like he cannot go live with his father. He cannot even spend too much time with him. Like he can see him maybe once a year for lunch or something. His high school graduation. But otherwise, nothing. Protect him."

"Got it," Ross said.

"Why?" Cammy said. "Why can't he see him more?"

"Because those are my rules," I said. Jesus, how could I not have seen it? *I* was the dummy. "Before I die. After. Especially after. His father cannot take him."

They were quiet, absorbing this. "But I don't think you're really dying," Cammy said. "I think they're going to figure out a cure before and it's going to turn out okay in the end."

"In Guatemala, they see traditional healers," Ross said. "I don't know if you've ever tried that?"

"Ross," I said, "in Guatemala they believe gourds are magic."

They both giggled a little, and then we were quiet. I waited until the glacier of ice receded from my insides. I took my hands off my stomach, reached for each of their hands. Behind us, someone flipped a switch in the house and cast a block of light down toward where we lay. Bruce, getting some water in the kitchen. Allison, popping an Ambien, wondering where we were. We were on their lawn, holding hands, paper dolls.

"Listen, I'm asking you guys to please protect Jacob when I'm gone. Please teach him his constellations. Please make sure he reads good books. Please see that he keeps up with his swim lessons. And please, don't let his father manipulate him, or you. Okay? Don't let his father worm his way in. His father wasn't there before and he doesn't get to be there now, just because it feels good to play Dad."

They didn't say anything.

"And even if it sounds like I'm being unfair, I don't care."

Cammy squeezed my hand. "Okay," she said.

"Okay," said Ross.

And we lay there like that, on the grass, for what felt like a long time, until Allie opened the back door of the house and yelled that for God's sakes it was two in the morning and time to come inside.

And then we lay there for a while more, for even longer than that, but I could feel the ice inside me, preparing to return.

TWO

Manhattan

8

It was a strange and terrific thing, walking back into our apartment after so many months away. Mercer Island is big, spread open—the people there fetishize their space, claiming as much as they can of it for themselves, waste it on things like front lawns. New Yorkers, as I'm sure you know, are different: we like to squeeze into small places, make the most out of hidden corners. I've never met a Manhattanite, no matter how wealthy, who has a single empty kitchen drawer. My sister has an entire row of drawers containing nothing but packets of duck sauce.

As I turned the key in the downstairs lock, trudged up the stairs, turned the key in our door, kicked off my shoes by the door: I exhaled, finally. I remembered why I wanted to come home. The renegade heat enveloped me (closed windows, no central air, ninety degrees outside), and I dropped our suitcase and you scurried in, and outside a car alarm started to wail, but I was so happy I could sing, and started to. *Who let the dogs out? Who? Who?* For years, this was your favorite song.

"Mom," you said, warning. *Who? Who?*

Our apartment, as you may or may not remember, was actually pretty big for Manhattan: nine hundred square feet, two real bedrooms (each with two closets), a bathroom and a half, and a roof deck we shared with our neighbors. We lived on the top floor of a four-story converted townhouse; I would tell you what I paid for these nine hundred square feet, but it might not seem like that much to you in the future, and therefore you will not be suitably impressed (God knows what this place will go for in the future, unless of course Manhattan's underwater from global warming, in which case I guess it won't matter).

Julisa was on vacation, closing out her summer in steamy Puerto Rico, but before she left she'd come by to dust, change the sheets, and return Kelly from her house in Rego Park to her rightful place in your room. You were so excited that even though the flight was miserable and you were exhausted and Jesus Christ it was hot, you streaked across the living room into your bedroom, squealed loudly, and emerged having broken House Rule #1: Kelly Stays in Her Cage.

"Jacob," I said wearily, "put Kelly back."

You said, "Nuh-uh."

I turned on the air conditioner full blast, but it was a window unit and capable of only so much. I turned on the fans too, one in every corner of the room.

"Did you miss me? Did you?" you asked, snuggling the rodent. You were sitting on the shag rug in the middle of the living room, a rug on which Kelly reliably defecated every time you violated House Rule #1.

"Jacob," I said, over the whirr of the fans.

You ignored me, lay on your back, and let Kelly run across your face, which was disgusting. Then you picked her up and tossed her gently from hand to hand.

"Get her back in her cage," I said.

"Look, Mom, she missed us!"

"I see." She had missed us so much, in fact, that she had already urinated a tiny yellow dribble on your arm.

Jake, do you remember Kelly? How I let you pick her out for your fifth birthday from the pet store that used to be on Ninety-Sixth Street? You wanted a dog, and I think in happier days I would have let you get a dog, but I was weak from chemo and I thought I wouldn't be able to handle it. But now I wasn't so sure—maybe a dog would be a good thing for you to take with you to Seattle. The co-op allowed pets under fifty pounds. Maybe I'd ask Allison, see what she thought.

"Mom, Kelly peed!" you said, delighted.

"Wash your arm," I said, "and put her back," but we both knew better than to expect you to listen.

Anyway, besides a little hamster piss the place looked good—noisy, off-smelling, hot, but good. Our kitchen bled into our living room, where we'd stashed a dining table, a coffee table, a pullout couch, a television, your video games, our family desktop, three bookshelves, your bike, your soccer balls, your backpack, your board games, and again it astonished me how much space my sister had on her Mercer Island compound: three different structures *for five people*. The guesthouse we lived in was bigger than this apartment.

"Can we order dinner?" you asked, immediately a city kid again. Generally speaking, you and I used to get takeout at least every other night. When I asked you what you wanted you said Carmine's, so I called and ordered a platter of rigatoni with broccoli, which would feed us for the next three nights. I thought about how great a shower would feel, wondered if I had time to take one before the food got here, and yelled at you one more time to put the hamster back in her cage.

"Five minutes, Mom."

Five minutes.

I sat down on the shag rug, opened our suitcase, and started to remove the dirty laundry—we traveled light, having left most of our stuff at Allie's. Dirty underwear, socks. I had my laptop; while you played with Kelly, I typed some notes. It felt good to be industrious. And then suddenly the pain in my side hit me so hard I gasped.

"Mom!" You flew to me and I wanted to tell you not to worry, but I couldn't speak, I couldn't do anything, I felt like I was being ripped apart, shredded, by something unspeakably hot and sharp.

"*Mom!*" you screamed, and I motioned to the phone—I wanted you to call 911, but instead you attempted to call Julisa in Puerto Rico. Allie was right—even lifting that pathetic little suitcase was too much. Dragging it up four floors. For what? Socks and underwear and a cheap laptop.

"Mom, what should I do?"

There was codeine in my purse—I managed to gasp the word *purse*, and you brought it to me and I motioned to you and you dug through it and found the pill bottle. You knew it was what I needed, I wasn't as secretive as I thought I was, and then I realized I was on the floor and my six-year-old was finding my codeine and my eyes welled up, but still I couldn't speak. "I'll get you water," you whispered. My six-year-old got me water. You got me water, Jakey. You got me water and helped sit me up, but you could not open the childproof pill bottle, which was, I guess, a good thing—but I was too weak to do it. Another spasm sent me down, my face against the shag. I wondered if my bowel was perforating. I wondered if this was my punishment for my hubris, my stubbornness: to die in front of my son.

"Mom!" you said, and then you disappeared and I could not scream after you—I only lay there, wondering when I would shit myself or when I would die. I would almost certainly foul myself, the floor, the apartment I hadn't seen in so long. Kelly had gone somewhere. You had pee on you and I was almost certainly going to shit myself. Where had you gone? Where had you gone? Would I ever see you again?

Despite what they said, I'd thought the surgery and the medicine would keep me alive forever.

(Jake, from the hospital room where I'm recollecting my memory of this night, it occurs to me that it's possible I got it all wrong. Perhaps the night went differently, perhaps you weren't gone for hours, perhaps you remember it in another way. I wonder how you remember that night, and the look on my face. What I looked like. You were more and more conscious of what I looked like as I got sicker and were always gauging my color, my hair, what I was wearing. You liked it when I wore my old semistylish clothes. You hated it when I wore sweatpants. For my forty-third birthday you colluded with Allison and had three-hundred-dollar boots delivered to our doorstep.

Anyway, that's how I hope you remember me. You will not

remember me in a hospital gown, you will not remember me like this.)

"Mom!"

On the floor of the apartment, I closed my eyes. I was hot and cold at the same time. My head was swimming, but I felt strangely at peace. It was okay if it was over for me. I decided that it was okay. I'd lived a longer, better life than most people had ever have lived in the history of this awful world.

And then the next thing I knew our neighbor from downstairs, the lady who was always in yoga pants, I forgot her name, she had my face in her hands. "Karen, Karen, are you okay? Karen, I'm going to call an ambulance."

"Medicine," I sputtered, or something like it, and she took the codeine bottle and twisted off the top for me and handed me a pill and the water. I had to sit up to take the pill and I could not sit up.

Yuki, her name was Yuki. I'd known her for years. "I'm okay," I exhaled. I looked around; I hadn't shit myself. And the pain wouldn't have been receding if I actually had torn my bowel. So I thought I was going to be okay again. I could feel it, the relief, which felt something like ecstasy. Of course, I was still on the ground.

"I have an emergency list on the wall."

"Karen, I'm going to call 911, okay?"

"On the wall by the fridge—"

"I'm calling now, Karen."

"Kyle's mom—her name is Ann—she's my backup when Julisa's away. They're two floors down—"

"I'm calling 911," and I tried to say no, but she had already dialed, and while I could fight with Allison, I couldn't tell this neighbor I hardly knew to go away. Across the floor darted something: Kelly the hamster. We'd broken House Rule #1 within minutes of getting back home. We would never see Kelly again. And that open suitcase, full of dirty underwear and socks. Your backpack spilling open, your iPad, your gourd. And me on the floor, sweating, so sweaty my T-shirt was translucent. I could smell myself: I smelled like a New York City trash bin in the sun. I wanted to sit up, but I couldn't sit up.

Jacob, where had all my dignity gone?

Yuki was holding my hand. Suddenly I didn't see you anywhere. Yuki was kind-looking, pale skin, a smattering of freckles on her nose. I had assumed we were the same age, but I could see that she was younger. "Babe, everything all right?" A male voice at our open door.

Babe? Was it for me?

"We're fine," Yuki said, not turning, not looking at him. "An ambulance is coming."

"I'll wait outside," said the man. He must have been Yuki's boyfriend, I hadn't known she had a boyfriend. I'd been away for too long. Did my neighbors know I had cancer? Had I told them? Did they remember me in my scarf, in my wig? Could she see it now in my short fried hair and my yellowed skin and the lines around my eyes?

"Mommy?" you said. There you were: sitting next to Yuki, cross-legged. "I put Kelly back in her cage."

"Thank you," I whispered, and soon enough the ambulance

arrived, followed closely by the delivery guy from Carmine's. Just before I passed out, I heard Yuki's boyfriend pay the guy, tell him to keep the change.

FORTY-EIGHT HOURS LATER, I was still in the stupid surgical center of stupid Memorial Sloan Kettering, and I wouldn't be allowed to go home until—you ready?—until I farted. There's just *so much farting* involved in ovarian cancer. My guess is that you'll think that's just as funny when you read this as you did then. Twice Kyle's mom brought you to see me and twice you asked, "So, Mom, fart yet?" and then fell down on the floor with hysterics (which seemed, frankly, a bit too hysterical to me—which seemed like the gestures of a boy who thought his mother was going to die in front of him just a few nights before).

My adhesions, it turned out, weren't yet perforating the bowel, but they were blocking about half of a section of my intestine. Evidently this was a situation most medical professionals wanted to fix quickly. Evidently this could cause the sort of pain that even codeine couldn't mitigate very well. In fact, the next morning the surgeon said he was surprised I'd managed to keep a normal routine with the agony I must have been suffering—this, of course, made me feel like a hero. The doctor was young, handsome, a resident I think, although capable-sounding. He said that from the looks of things inside, there weren't any new tumors in any unexpected places. From the looks of things, anyway, he said. He wore a wedding ring on a chain around his neck. "So I think that's some good news, Karen," he said, and I admit I felt elated.

Good news! Mixed news! Then yesterday Dr. Steiner stopped by just as I was attempting to work up a nice fart. He was a little disgusted with me for waiting so long to get the surgery—evidently I was playing with hotter fire than I knew—but he too was relieved that we got out of this one okay, nothing but a few new scars and a burgeoning opiate addiction. He wanted me to come in for some scans next week. I told him I was busy, I was working. He raised a paternal eyebrow at me. I told him I'd make time.

So I decided to try to get some work done with my laptop on this dumb hospital tray, having pushed aside the food I had no interest in (although the nurse did remind me that if I didn't eat, it was unlikely I would fart) and already taken my required ambulation up and down the hall, holding on to the IV pole like a goddamn senior citizen. Back in bed, I sketched out a proposal for our new direct mail for Ace; I couldn't believe that this was all I had to work on these days, and I couldn't help it, I was worried about my inability to give it my all. I was also a little bit worried about the company. Or about my role in the company. When Chuck and I started Neulander-Davis, we were a fifty-fifty partnership. I was a founding partner! But I hadn't talked to Chuck in ten days. And when I did, he seemed awfully busy and a little bit impatient. I picked up my phone and called, told him I was back in New York, didn't mention that I was in the hospital. "Karen!" he said. "Glad you're back!" But then he started talking fast: he was going to be in meetings for the rest of the day, he didn't tell me with whom, and I hung up feeling even farther away than I did when I was across the country.

I pressed the morphine button, dialed the phone one more time. And he picked up! "Ace, it's me, Karen," I said. "I'm back in town. Let's schedule a meeting." I would be out of there soon, in plenty of time for a meeting.

"Great," he said. "Karen, great. You're gonna want to talk to Amani about scheduling." I knew, of course, you always talk to the assistant, but I was feeling so totally impotent in the hospital bed, I felt like I needed some direct chitchat.

"How was France?"

"A second honeymoon! Incredible, really. Utah Beach, Omaha Beach. Chilling. You gotta get there."

Maybe I'd get there.

"How's Bev?" he asked.

I clicked a few buttons. "Looks like she's raised fifteen thousand dollars. Working with a campaign manager named Jorge Grubar."

"Never heard of him."

"It's her nephew."

"Heh," Ace chuckled, dryly. "So what are you going to need from me?"

"A little face time. Just to plot out some coordinates. You around next week? Can I come over?"

"You planning on any neat tricks? Inhospitable ties in the Dominican Republic?"

"Ace, get out of here," I said. I looked down at myself. There was nothing I could do even if I wanted to. "The only trick you need is to keep up the good work in City Hall."

I clicked over to Facebook, to Bev's page. She'd posted some updates, including a few from her campaign. She did a fund-raiser at someone's house, fifty bucks a plate for a Spanish-looking dinner, and I'd felt sorry for her—fifty bucks?—but the food looked good. There was a nice shot of a huge foil container of flan.

"We're gonna kill her, Karen?"

I was as weak as a freshly hatched chick. "We'll kill her," I said, and hung up.

I wondered if Bev was going to want to do a debate or some kind of forum, and if Ace would agree. I found Jorge Grubar online, emailed him that I'd like to schedule something if they were interested. Then I scrolled over to her platform: lower city taxes, school choice, fewer business regulations. Bev, what was this, Texas? She was also "fervently pro-life," had a yellow cross on her homepage in memorial to the "babies we've lost to abortion." Usually this sort of thinking made me hate a candidate on principle, but I don't know, I was still kind of sweet on Bev.

Three kids, five grandkids. She was only fifteen years older than me.

I wanted to tell you that I was so sorry for collapsing on the floor like that (I told you this a million times in the past two days, and you always said that it was all right, but I couldn't stop telling you). I missed you so much.

Also you were now a little bit in love with Yuki, and I suspected she was a little bit in love with you too. That first night after the ambulance came, Kyle's mom wasn't able to get there till midnight, so evidently Yuki and the boyfriend ate the Carmine's with you and stayed up playing Wii until Ann came. And the past two nights Yuki had been visiting you at Kyle's after she got home from work.

And this morning she sent me flowers.

All of which leads me to something I've been meaning to say to you in this book: it's important to know your neighbors. One of the things that bothers me about the way Americans act—even in Manhattan, this crowded little island—it's that we act like we don't have any responsibility toward one another. Everybody's so atomized these days—each person on her own little device, each of us tuning out that which doesn't interest us. We might not even know the names of the people who live right downstairs from us! And that lack of connection leads us to feel lonely. It's not human to not know your neighbors.

So my advice to you is, whenever you move somewhere or someone moves in close to you, go meet that person. Go say hi. I'm not saying you have to bake a cake or anything (although nobody's ever turned down a nice batch of cookies or, if that's too much, maybe a bottle of wine). But just say hi to the people who live near you, check their mail when they're away, walk their dogs when they're sick. It's a good thing to do, to be neighborly, and I think it's one of the values that's most gotten away from us during my lifetime.

You told me that Yuki's boyfriend's name was Tom. They'd been together for almost a year. Evidently he was in our building all the time, but somehow I'd never even noticed him.

Incidentally, I think one of the reasons Ace was such a good city councilman was that, deep down, he was just an incredibly good neighbor. He liked them all, the 9/11 widows, those kids with the asthma at the hospital clinics. He liked the PTA members at PS 304 and 19, he liked his bus drivers and dry cleaner—he genuinely wanted them to be happy. He got into service in order to serve them, is what I'm saying. And because it was so clear that his interests in his constituency were heartfelt—it wasn't like he was in this for the money—his constituents liked him. They reelected him. They couldn't have given a shit about his dalliances with twentysomethings. That was just their old friend Ace, that's what they thought. And it wasn't nice to stick your nose too deep into your friend's business.

And there you were! Your beautiful face! It was three o'clock already and I really had to get out of there. I wondered what it was like outside. Weather.com said eighty-three degrees, low humidity, but that sounded a little too perfect for Manhattan at the end of July. Bring on the ninety-degree 90-percent-humidity hideout in the movie theater all day miseries! Bring on the summer! Bring on my son!

"Hi, Mom," you said, coming up shyly for the hug you knew I couldn't wait to plant on you. You were trailed by Yuki, which was a surprise, but I was happy to see her. Just like I couldn't stop apologizing to you, I couldn't stop thanking Yuki. I'm sure she found it wearisome.

"Where's Ann?"

"Her husband had to go to the cardiologist." Shit—Kyle's dad was an overweight diabetic.

"Oh dear."

"I hope you don't mind, but she asked me if I'd take over. I was working from home today so I said sure."

"How could I mind?" How could I have minded beautiful Yuki in her perpetual yoga pants and tight shirt and neon sneakers? What did she even do that she never had to change out of that outfit?

"Yuki, are you a yoga instructor?"

"What? No," she said. "I'm an architect. Anyway, Ann didn't

want to bother you, so I said I'd keep him for the afternoon and then his father's going to get him at six, when he's done with work. He said he'd bring him home to New Jersey."

"Who?"

"Jake's dad," she said, smiling, but a slightly worried look cast across her face as she met my eyes. "Jake said he was the person to call, so I figured—"

"Jake said—you said to call your dad, Jakey?"

You shrugged, gazed toward the empty bed in the other half of the room. I had a roommate yesterday, but she was gone now, healthy or dead.

"You said to call your dad?" I repeated.

You nodded. "Yes," you said. "I wanted to see him."

I was immobile. I was in a hospital bed scanning Facebook and calling it work. I was ruminating about Bev fucking Hernandez. I'd had scar tissue sucked out of the space in my belly where I used to have organs. I was as impotent as the Jell-O quivering on the bedside stand. I was nothing anymore, nothing nothing.

"I didn't know who else to call."

"Jake, we have the emergency list," I said in a low tone.

"I wanted to call him."

"But our list—"

"Karen, I'm sorry—" Yuki couldn't help but hear. "I thought it would be fine—"

"No, of course. It's his father," I said weakly. I could not yell at you for this; I could not yell at Yuki. I could not even yell at your father. What had gone wrong here, exactly? I was sick, the nanny was in Puerto Rico, so the boy went to his father. Didn't that make sense? Wasn't that the right thing?

But not this father not now and not ever. God, I prayed, give me the strength to get healthy please right now and take you home.

"He said he'd just pick him up at the hospital," said Yuki.

"But we have"—I could hear how lame my voice sounded—"we have an emergency list. It's in the kitchen. I have . . . If you find me my cell phone, we can call some of the people on the list." Kyle's parents. Julisa's sister. Even Dr. Susan if there was a true crisis. "We can call Julisa's sister. I'm sure she'll get you. Julisa told me—"

"*No!*" You let out a wail so fierce that Yuki took a step back. You could tell now that she wanted out of there, wanted to walk back her steps in our neighborly direction. "*No I'm going to my dad's house, he's coming to pick me up!*" You finished this up with that horrible grunting sound you made when you were really enraged.

"No, Jake," I started. "We have an emergency list."

"*No!*"

"Come on, kiddo, don't yell at your mom like that," Yuki said. She put a firm hand on your shoulder. How quickly you two connected: how quickly you let people into your life. I had prepared you for nothing.

"I want my dad."

"Okay," Yuki said, hand on your shoulder, looking at me, apologetic.

You were crying now, you were pathetic, your face tilted toward the floor. I tried to take your hand, but I couldn't reach that far. The bandaging around my middle. "Jakey, please," I said. You just stood there, the tears dropping like slow rain on the floor tiles. I wanted to grab you and pull you to me and kiss you and tickle your collarbone, anything to make you happy again—I wanted to buy you ice cream and new games for your Wii.

"It was a bad divorce?" Yuki asked, quietly, her hand still on Jake's shoulder.

"We were never married," I said, and Yuki nodded as though she understood.

You shivered; you were still crying.

"Well, Jake's dad said he'd be happy to keep him for as long as you needed. If you needed time to recover. He sounded happy to help." Yuki was rubbing your shoulder gently. "He sounded nice."

"He's nice enough."

You stopped crying at this, looked up at me pleadingly. "He is, Mom. He's nice. He's really happy to help," you said. "It's not a problem for him."

"Jacob."

"It's not," you repeated.

My cell phone was on my bedside tray and the bedside tray was wheeled away when it became clear I wasn't going to be able to down my Jell-O. Without my phone, I could not call Kyle's mom or Dr. Susan, I couldn't call Allison. I was trapped there and would be for as long as I couldn't eat my Jell-O, couldn't kick my digestive process into gear, couldn't retrieve you from your father, who I could now see was going to treat my illness with a predatory zeal. Just steal you away while I couldn't stop him. Just swoop down in: hey, what a nice guy! A nice guy like a fucking vulture.

(A beautiful six-year-old boy gift-wrapped and presented on his doorstep. A good hand at tennis. The same shade of hazel eyes.)

"Well, thanks for your help, Yuki," I said, to give her permission to leave.

"I'm sorry, I just didn't realize—"

"No, no, please don't apologize. It was great of you to step in. I really appreciate how much you've done for us" (although the gift certificate to Per Se I was planning to send had just been downgraded to Hunan Balcony). Yuki ruffled your hair and tiptoed out in her yoga pants and you slunk into the chair in the corner.

"I'm going to get a roommate soon," I said after a minute or so, during which the clock ticked loudly.

"Okay."

"So you won't be allowed to scream like that. We're in a hospital. People are trying to get healthy here. Screaming is like the opposite of healthy."

"Sorry," you said, petulant—the sort of sorry you delivered when you didn't mean it. "Can I play with your phone?"

"Really?" I said. "I haven't seen you in twenty-four hours and all you want to do is play with my phone?"

"Sorry," you said again, and then you just stared at me glumly. I wondered what you would do at your father's house. If I remembered correctly, there was a huge deck off the third floor of his complex, with a big pool, a few diving boards, a slide. It looked out over the Hudson and New York City beyond. I'd be in a hospital room. You wouldn't think to wave.

"Jake, how did you have his number?"

"He gave it to me in Seattle. He said in case I needed it." That vulture.

"You didn't tell me that."

You shrugged. "Are you mad?"

"I don't like you keeping secrets from me."

"I didn't really think about it," you said. "It wasn't like a *se-cret* secret. I wasn't trying to lie to you."

"Do you even feel comfortable going over there? You've never been there before." Historically, you didn't like new places, nor the houses of people you didn't know. Once when you were four, you chose to wet your pants rather than go inside Kyle's grandmother's apartment to pee.

"He said there were a lot of games at his house, like board games. He has chess," you said. You'd been angling to learn how to play chess. "And a bedroom I can have to myself. It's not like I'm going to have to sleep on a couch."

"You're planning on spending the night?"

"Well, I can't stay in the apartment by myself, right? And Kyle's mom needs to be with his dad. He has to go to the cardiologist."

Kyle's fucking dad.

"Will Dave's wife be there? Is she traveling?"

You shrugged. How should you know if the wife would be there? Did you even know he had a wife? "Please can I play with your phone?" you said.

"Why don't you climb onto the bed," I said. "We can watch TV."

"There's nothing on the TV here," you said.

But after a minute of stare-down you climbed into the bed

next to me, and we watched some nitwit *Nick at Nite* show and I typed. I wrote down as best I could what I said to you, and what you screamed at me, while we waited for your father to arrive. This would be my gift to you, Jacob. The truth about who we both were.

AT FIVE FORTY-FIVE, just as I was starting to feel a pleasant accumulating sensation somewhere in my middle, your father arrived. He strode in quickly, as though he'd taken a cue from a medical show and might need to save somebody's life. He was wearing rolled-up sleeves, Dockers, glasses. A hospital visitor's badge. I twisted the platinum ring around my thumb.

"Dad!" you said, and burst out of the bed, hitting me a little in my side. I absolutely had to fart now—of course I did—and of course now was when I had to squelch it.

"Hey, Jake," he said, and hugged you briskly, then moved to my side with a look of concern. Jesus, I couldn't even imagine what I looked like. It hadn't occurred to me to try to look any better, not that I could have. I was in my hospital gown, the morphine running into one arm, the catheter running out beneath me. This was so humiliating, Jacob. When I met your father, I was a nice size 8, curvy. I'd always wanted to lose ten pounds, but now I'd lost too many and I was wasted. I was ripe before. Ripe or whatever the word is for young and healthy and fertile and dumb.

"Karen, are you okay? What happened?"

"Small bowel obstruction," I said. "I'll get out of here tomorrow, I think. It's a complication from an earlier surgery." He sat at my bedside, took my hand in his. Oh Jesus, his big strong hand. I didn't look at him. I looked at the needle taped into the top of my own hand, I looked at the blue veins tracing my own white arm, a pattern that could decorate a mosque. Swirling lines, indigo against alabaster.

"I wish I'd known," he said. "I could have done something sooner. I could have taken Jacob home." He wanted to take you home.

"There's no need for you to take Jacob," I said, "it's really not necessary," but then I caught your eye and you gave me that look that said you were going to start shrieking, so I didn't continue. I wouldn't have you shrieking in front of your father at the end of visiting hours.

"Look, I know it's not—I mean, we've only just reconnected, but we've got a lot of room, Jake will be fine. Is he in camp or anything? Do you need me to take him to camp tomorrow?"

"He's not in camp," I said, suddenly feeling neglectful. I should have enrolled you in camp for August, but I wanted you with me. "In fact, if you just want to take him to a diner or something, I can probably arrange for one of my neighbors to take him in tonight."

"But it's not necessary, really."

"Mom?" you said. "Please?"

I could not win this one, but I was lousy at losing. "Don't you like Yuki? I'm sure you could stay with Yuki." I wasn't sure of this at all.

"If you're worried about anything—I'll leave you all my numbers," your father said, his hair flopping in front of his face and his mouth set tight as he tried to figure out how to prove his ability to take care of you. "Are there food allergies I need to worry about? That sort of thing?"

You were holding his hand.

"No," I whispered. "No food allergies."

"Okay," your father said. For a moment, then, we were all holding hands: you holding your dad's, him holding mine. But then he let go of mine.

"Ann Brown, Kyle's mother, has a car," I finally said. "She lives in our building. She'll get him tomorrow." Although I had no idea if Ann could get to New Jersey tomorrow.

"Karen, he doesn't have to stay with anyone else tomorrow. He can stay with me."

"You have to work," I said.

"I can take a day off," he said.

"It's not necessary," I said quickly, looking up somewhere near the television, where the end credits of whatever horrible show we were watching started to roll. "You're kind to be so helpful in a pinch, but after this I'll secure more stable emergency plans. I just really didn't think we'd end up like this. Ann is usually very dependable. Her husband was ill, that's all."

"Karen," he said. He was looking at me with those eyes that were so uncannily like yours, I don't know why it still surprised me how much they were like yours. And his blondish-brownish hair curled like yours, around the edges. And his mouth—almost seven years I'd kissed your mouth, and in a weird genetically magical way, I'd also been kissing his. (Yes, Jake, I kissed you right on the mouth, I did, I didn't care, you were mine, my baby boy.)

"I'm happy to be helpful here. It's more than that—I mean, to tell you the truth, I'm thrilled. I'm thrilled I can, I mean I'm not thrilled that you're sick, that's not what I mean, but I'm grateful I can be of use."

"That's kind of you," I said dully, but I could feel the ice creep into the spaces where the morphine was a minute ago. He was going to take you. And then he was going to try to keep you. "It's nice of you to be helpful," I said as casually as I could, "but I have all my systems set up here, Dave."

"You know, if you want, I could even take a week off, I could take him to Quogue."

"Please, Dave," I said. I was freezing. The ice—I was freezing to death. "Please. That's not necessary." I turned to you. "Jake, I'll be out of here tomorrow or the next day, and you'll come home." The urge to pass gas, so elusive, had now disappeared, but it would come back. It had to come back. I would fart and I would leave and I would never let you near another phone. "Kyle's mom will be around tomorrow. There's no need for you to stay at Dave's house for more than the night."

"Are you sure?" Dave asked.

How could a person change so much in so few years? Not to drag up difficult memories, Jacob, but if you could have only seen the look on his face when I found out I was with child—and now suddenly it was all Playmobil and the house in Quogue. Why, Jacob? The wife? Marriage? Was that really all it took? Or was it the looming mortality apparent in a receding hairline?

Or was it, simply, the magic of you?

"I'm sure," I said.

"Or maybe"—he said—"I mean what if, if you're feeling better, I mean—what if you and he come out to Quogue in a week or two? It's a huge house, you'll see, we've got tons of room. And you can see what it's like so you can feel comfortable with him visiting."

He wanted me to go to his house in Quogue.

"Can we do that, Mom?" you asked.

"We cannot," I said. "I'm sorry, Dave. But we cannot."

"But, Mom, why?"

"Because—" I said, and I was suddenly so faint I could barely remember what we were talking about. I maybe had been pressing the morphine button again and again.

"Mom?"

Did I mention to you how much I had loved this man, Jacob? Did I make it clear? It wasn't just a fling, Jacob. It wasn't just six months and see you later, gator. I loved him. He had broken my heart. "You can't have him, Dave."

"What?"

"I mean he's not—" What did I mean? I meant you were mine. Only mine. It was amazing to me that your father didn't seem to understand this or understand how compromised I was at the moment. He could not take my son. I would kill him first. I would die in jail, relieved. "He has to come back home."

"As soon as you're ready," he said.

"I'll be ready tomorrow."

"But—"

"Dave, this is not the time to fight with me."

He nodded. He finally got it, as much as he could get anything. And then a new television show began, and the chirpy theme music filled the room, and we all turned to it to gaze at the pretty lights, the pretty dancing teenagers on the screen, and then the nurse came in to take my vitals, and before I could stop her she asked me—

"And have we passed gas yet, Karen?"

And your father had the good manners to pretend he hadn't heard what the nurse just said and you'd already scooped up your backpack, you were so eager to get out of there, and some part of me wanted to remind you about the nightmares and the bed-wetting and how once upon a time the thought of my death meant that you'd be an orphan and now it just meant you'd get to spend time in Quogue with your really cool dad, this guy you just met who bought you toys.

"I'm trying to eat," I muttered as she wrapped the blood pressure cuff around my arm. "Jake, don't leave yet."

So you and your father watched stoically as I got cuffed and temperatured and the nurse began to remove my blankets to check my bandages (and, Jesus Christ, my catheter), but I asked her to please hold off until my child and my former boyfriend left. "Are they going soon?"

"No," I said.

"Yes, let's get out of here," your father said. "I mean, is there anything else, Karen, that you need?"

"I want you to call me when you get there. Jacob, you call me." I knew you knew how to use the phone.

You both nodded, same nod, same expression.

"And I'll call you to say good night tonight. Dave, his bedtime is at eight thirty. I don't want him up later than that, okay? Leave me all your numbers. House, cell, all of them."

I could not believe he was taking my son. I could not believe I was letting him take my son. My heart monitor was beeping faster. The nurse looked at it for a moment, then slid her eyes to you and Dave. Dave scribbled down his numbers on a pad on the bedside tray, next to the uneaten Jell-O. "Your address too," I said, although I remembered his address.

"Ann will be there in the morning. I'll ask her to get there by eight so you can get to work."

He nodded. You looked disappointed but had the good sense to be grateful for what you'd gotten. We were all quiet then.

"So I guess that means we're off?" Dave said, with the courtesy to sound uneasy.

I felt faint again. "I don't think I'm forgetting anything. He'll need a toothbrush, of course. Jacob, did you pack a toothbrush? And pajamas?"

You nodded. "Yuki helped me."

Dave came to me, gave me a kiss on the forehead. "Thank you, Karen. I know this isn't easy for you."

"You know nothing," I spat. Then you came and I squeezed you to me despite how much it hurt—despite all the morphine, Jesus it hurt—and then I watched as you and your father, same bearing, same cowlick, same expression, same nod, walked out the hospital door to a place I could not follow.

"Away we go!" said your father as you disappeared.

The nurse had the courtesy to change me quickly and hum a little bit while she did it. "Don't worry," she said to me softly, handing me a tissue for my cheeks. "He'll be back. Don't worry. Your son will be back soon."

"But what if he takes him forever?"

"How could he do that, sweetie?"

"He's a lawyer," I said.

"Why would he take your son from his sweet mama? What good would come from that?"

And I wanted to tell her about how he wasn't just a lawyer—how he was a vampire, a shape-shifter, one of those mythological characters that started out as one thing but had become something entirely else. And once upon a time I would have known how to defame his character so hard that no judge would have ever let him *near* a six-year-old boy, much less parent one, but those days were over, and now I was as powerless myself as a child.

9

Now, Jacob, I want to tell you a story.

Eighty-four years before you were born—eighty-four years to the very week, in fact—a banker's wife delivered a son, her first child, in an upstairs bedroom in a tall brick house near the Danube, in Budapest, Hungary. The banker and his wife had wanted a child for many years, but by the time their son was born in 1923, they were shocked, as they were both past forty and had been married for almost two barren decades. They were also slightly frightened. What would they do with a little boy? At that point, they had settled into their childlessness, had filled their lives with art and music (she was an amateur pianist; he played the cello). Moreover, according to rumor, the banker was also an insatiable philanderer, spent his lunch hours with alternating mistresses, although from what I know of the couple their domestic life remained tranquil. (One can never really know what happens in another person's marriage, Jacob, and one should never expect to.)

They named their baby Janos. He grew up to be smart and independent, played chess, learned English courtesy of a British nanny (evidently British nannies were all the rage in bourgeois Hungary between the wars). After school and on the weekends, in between strictly enforced piano lessons, Janos played with other children in the beautiful parks of Budapest, and as he grew older he established himself as the leader of a crew of other well-heeled boys, and together they would prowl the avenues and side streets of their lovely city. In his early adolescence, he developed a crush on a girl named Lina, who was the leader of her own crew of girls, each one uglier than the last. Janos admired Lina's strategic thinking—why surround yourself with ugly girls if not to make yourself more beautiful?—her tinkling laugh, and the way she could smile with her mouth while frowning with her eyes.

At night, after dinner with his parents, Janos would do his homework, crawl into bed, and dream of living in his own tall brick house in Budapest one day, with Lina and their strategically minded children.

Although no photographs of Janos's parents survive, we do have a large oil portrait of the family, which was discovered in the basement of a New York gallery in 1974 (how it got there remains as much a mystery as life itself). The portrait shows a tall, patrician man standing behind his wife, who wears pearls and a fox stole; she is seated on a piano bench, and he rests his hand on her shoulder. On his fourth finger you can see, glimmering, a wide platinum ring. Between them is a boy, their son, with his mother's blonde curls and his father's severe stare. He is thirteen years old. Scribbled on the back of the portrait is

"Neulander family, Budapest, 1936: Sandor, Eva, Janos." There is also a dashed line of Hebrew and the artist's smudged name.

The Neulanders were intellectual atheists, more invested in gardening and poetry than religion, but they must have felt sentimental enough to celebrate the bar mitzvah of their only child and to commission a portrait on that occasion.

So okay, Jacob, here's some history for you: even though Hungary formed an alliance with Germany during the war, its (otherwise corrupt and fascist) government allowed, for a time, certain Jews to remain in the country unmolested. Therefore, the Neulanders survived the first several years of World War II in declining but still acceptable levels of comfort. True, Sandor was removed from his position at the bank, but he was ready to retire anyway. And true, the Ladies' Gardening Society of Buda and Pest replaced Eva as head of the Newcomer Committee, but she'd been getting sick of all those old crones and their dahlias. The Neulanders spent much of the years between 1939 and 1944 indoors, playing music, reading English literature, and using whatever pull they still had to protect their son from the draft.

When Germany broke its alliance with Hungary in March of 1944, the Neulanders felt safe enough in Budapest not to try to escape—not that there was anywhere to go. All of Europe was in flames, and they'd lost so many of their connections with the outside world. Besides, they barely practiced Judaism; besides, they had once counted among their closest friends the mayor, the mayor's wife, and the director of the symphony orchestra. If connections like that couldn't keep you safe, what were connections for?

Sandor and Eva and Janos were rounded up in October of

1944: mother and father and son, lined up and sectioned off like livestock. Just before they parted for what they knew to be eternity, Sandor took the platinum ring off his finger and handed it to Janos. Go! his father said. Go? Where would he go?

Janos knew the streets of Budapest like he knew his father's voice; a guard turned his head for a moment, and Janos went.

WHAT HAPPENED NEXT is hazy: food stolen from farmers, occasional shelter in a barn or a church, and winter nights spent in a hole dug out of the floor of the half-frozen forest. Janos ate squirrels and acorns and drank his own urine, hid from soldiers in trees, and found out the European war had ended from a drunk Russian soldier. He returned to Budapest, but there really was no more Budapest, or no more of the Budapest he'd known; the only home he'd ever lived in had been bombed to its frame, and his parents were figments of another time. He started walking, came upon a group of Allied soldiers, was placed on a convoy to Enns, a displaced-persons camp just over the border in Austria. The Americans who ran the camp at Enns put Janos to work immediately, as his English was excellent and he seemed relatively sound in mind and body. It was his job to help welcome and settle the refugees who were streaming in from Mauthausen and Birkenau, from Romania and Hungary and Czechoslovakia.

He enjoyed the work, and because he felt useful, because he knew he was truly helping other people, he grew to like musty Enns. Families were sheltered in cramped one-room apartments, but there was usually enough heat and enough food, and there were rumors, every so often, that soon the British would allow them all into Palestine.

In early 1946, a young woman arrived at the camp on her own. She heard Janos speaking English to someone from the Joint Committee and asked him for help in her own British-inflected English. She too had once had a British nanny, she said; she too had once lived in Budapest. She looked familiar to him, or maybe it was just her voice. Or maybe he had known her in another life? He was busy, though, so he didn't ask, and she was so shy she didn't say.

He helped her get settled in a dormitory with other single women, and although it wasn't kind of him, he hoped no family would come to claim her. For weeks, they circled each other at Enns, on the grounds, in the dormitories, walking past each other along the nearby river, looking across the border into Hungary, a country whose air neither of them would ever breathe again. Finally the girl spoke to him at the commissary on a freezing February morning.

"You really don't recognize me, Janos?"

He looked at her closely: the frowning eyes, the unsmiling smile. "Lina?"

"Ha," the girl said. "Lina was shot with her entire family by an Arrow Cross guard. I'm Berthe. Remember?"

He sort of remembered: one of Lina's ugly friends, although now she seemed as beautiful as summer. She'd been taken in by a Catholic dairy farmer and spent the war taking care of his remaining cows. It could have been worse, she said. For most people it had been.

Three years later, in a tiny Bronx apartment, they embraced their new life with whatever gusto they still had in them. They opened a music school and taught their students in fluent English.

Still, moved by sentiment or memory, sometimes they would say a few words of Hungarian to their young son, Gil, and sing him Hungarian songs. Now almost seventy years later, Gil sits by a window in Bellevue, Washington. He almost never speaks, but when he does, the word he seems to say most often is *szerelmem*, which is Hungarian for "love."

ANOTHER STORY NOW. A love story of my own.

Maybe six weeks into my—fling, romance, whatever—with your father, I returned for a night to my old apartment in Chelsea. I'd told your dad I'd be home for about twelve hours to water the plants and get my mail. In the morning, I'd be shuttling back to Baltimore.

It was winter, a New York City winter, gray and dark more hours than not, everyone hiding behind burkas of coats and scarves. If Christmas was in the air, I couldn't smell it. I had interminable meetings the next few days and was hoping to schedule some New York fund-raising events, and maybe California too. Were there any celebrities we could get behind Griffith's cause? Maryland celebrities? Griffith was the biggest client I'd scored so far. If we lost, it wasn't going to be because I hadn't worked my ass off.

So that was mostly what was on my mind when I returned home that weekend: Griffith, money, polls, work. Still, your dad was also on my mind. Like I said, we'd been emailing each other a lot. I had something called a BlackBerry then, which was like this phone you could use to email. It was sort of primitive, but in those days it was an impressive thing. People saw me with one and knew I was somebody who mattered. I liked whipping it out whenever I sensed I was being underestimated. I sent emails during meetings—behavior that I would never condone anymore.

So anyway, I was on my twelve-hour furlough, waiting there by my building's elevator, roller suitcase, wrapped in a coat, checking my BlackBerry, not even looking to see where I was headed. I got in the elevator, pressed the button. I marched down the hallway, fished for my keys in my purse. And then someone said "Boo!" and I almost keeled over from the fright. Dropped the BlackBerry right there on the floor.

It was your father. He was holding flowers.

Never had someone waited for me on a doorstep, with or without flowers. "What are you doing here?"

"Are you hungry?" he asked. "I made us reservations. But if you're not hungry, I can cancel them."

I wasn't hungry.

But then, hours later, I was very hungry indeed, and so your father and I walked down to a place I hope is still there, this bar on Jane Street where there were famously good hamburgers and decent beers. We got a table in the back room and ordered burgers and beers and sat at the table across from each other, holding hands. There was a football game on television, I remember, and people crowded around us cheering on whichever team was playing, and I remember thinking, This will be my life. Your father, some beers, the crowds around us and us not even seeing them. Work and then breaks from work. Your dad's strong hands, a football game. I had put his flowers in a vase in the kitchen except for one, a small tiger lily, which I had bobby-pinned behind my ear.

"I couldn't wait to see you," he said. "I can't stop thinking about you. Is that crazy?"

"It's not crazy," I said. "I can't stop thinking about you either." I felt myself blushing and knew that I was giving up embarrassing or dangerous material about myself, even though your father was also giving up embarrassing truths about himself. Your father was the one who had made himself vulnerable first. In Maryland, a few weeks before, we had gone to a Ravens game together (Griffith had been there too, in better seats, close to the field), and we had been to Ocean City; in New York, we had already eaten at a few good restaurants. But still I felt like I didn't know your father too well—not nearly well enough to know if I loved him. Did I love him? I thought about that as we sat there. Love, to me, was something akin to habituation: I know your smile, I love your smile. I know what you'll say in response to this question, and I love that I know how to predict your response. Your predictability and your familiarity are, to me, what make me able to love you—they are, in fact, inseparable from love.

What I mean is that I identified what I felt for your father that night as something more like a crush. Something a teenager might feel.

We held hands and ate and drank and then walked around the city in the dark for a little bit. I had only six or so more hours before I had to catch my train back down to Baltimore, and there didn't seem to be much point in sleeping. The night seemed to be warming up a little, or maybe I was just warm from the beers and your dad—so we just started walking, directionless. I don't know. At one point we passed a mirrored length of wall and I paused so that we could look at ourselves together, see what we looked like next to each other. I was just about as tall as his shoulder. We looked beautiful.

There's so much to see in New York at night, all night, which might be something you know or maybe isn't, since you've now probably lived most of your life in Seattle. The primary reason for this, and the reason New York City has survived its various seasons of misfortune, is because of its subway system. Because of the subway, New York City's economy is able to run in every corner of the (vast) city, every hour of the day; people can work around the clock, people can eat and travel and come home and go out again. Because of the subway, New Yorkers are more productive than people in other parts of the country (no lost time in traffic, no lost time spent parking) and healthier too, because they die in fewer traffic accidents and because they have to walk a little more to get where they're going. And the subway, especially in your lifetime, is clean and safe. It's almost a miracle, but it's a miracle people don't think about enough.

Anyway, at four in the morning we took the subway and went to the Battery so we could take a ride on the Staten Island Ferry. We did this because I had mentioned, casually, that I had never done it before, and your father was dismayed. He said I'd missed one of New York's best adventures, and that much like the subway, the ferry ran around the clock, so there was really no excuse.

And because we were lucky that night, we made it to the ferry terminal just as the boat was about to leave, and we boarded and glided off into the night, New York City's sequined skyline looming above us. And your father stood behind me with his arms around me, and rather than look out toward where we were going, we stared at where we had just been, the glow of the harbor, the blue and white and yellow lights of Lower Manhattan.

That's when I realized we were, in fact, going to Staten Island, and I felt a little bit nervous about that—what would happen when we got there? For a moment I thought: we will leave Manhattan and the scene of this magical night and all this magic will vanish. Your father would see me for what I was, an exhausted woman in dirty clothes pushing forty, a wilted flower behind my ear. I imagined Staten Island would be all fluorescent lights and truth serum.

But that's not what happened at all. We stayed in Staten Island for a total of five minutes; we had to get off the boat, walk a circuit through the terminal, and then reboard. And it was there, in that bleak, silvery terminal, that your father took my hand, whirled me around to face him—the flower escaped my hair—and said, "I love you, Karen."

"You do?"

He nodded. He was smiling broadly, as though he had just pulled off something heroic. Was I supposed to say it back to him? Would I even be telling the truth? Did I love him? Did I know him well enough to love him? Would it be an automatic giveback if I just came out with it too? Wouldn't it be a better thing to just have the power for a little while, whatever I could take of it? He loved me, but was there a law that said I had to love him too?

(Oh, but of course I loved him, Jacob. He was mysterious to me, but I loved him so much it felt like my heart had built a new chamber.)

We stood there kissing for a while under the ferry terminal's bright lights—it was still so dark outside—and then we reboarded the ferry, where it was freezing.

Do you know that poem, Jacob?

We were very tired, we were very merry—
We had gone back and forth all night on the ferry;
And you ate an apple, and I ate a pear,
From a dozen of each we had bought somewhere;
And the sky went wan, and the wind came cold,
And the sun rose dripping, a bucketful of gold.

Okay I know how cheeseball it sounds, but that's what happened that night, Jacob. A poem. He took me to Penn Station, and just before I got on my train, I told him that I loved him too.

Anyway, until the night you were born, a little more than a year later, this night qualified as the best of my life. And then— wait, shit, Jacob, I just broke a rule. This Big Formless Project of Mine's Rule #1, which is, I've just realized, to always be honest. No matter how much it hurts, no matter how embarrassing—I need to tell you the truth. I will not lie to you from beyond the grave. And I was just not being honest there; I mean, I was saying what I felt like I was supposed to say but not what I meant to say. The night you were born was *not* the best night of my life. I was in pain, I was terrified, I was tired, I was sad. I missed your father and I wanted to kill your father. I looked at you and started to shiver all over. My mother had to hold me in bed while I cried. It was not the best night of my life, nor was it even a very good night at all.

No, the best single night of my life was the night your father took me to Staten Island to tell me that he loved me.

I have known more happiness since then, of course, but never so fleetingly profound.

A THIRD STORY: the nurse came in a little while ago to take my blood pressure. It's a little high, she said. You feeling okay?

By then you were asleep at your dad's house, probably in the guest room, which was, last time I checked, furnished with a double bed, an incongruous poster print of a Renoir painting, and plastic crates of your dad's old crap. The sheets were grimy; your father never washed them nor asked his cleaning lady to do it.

Maybe there was better stuff in there now. Maybe he cleaned it out for you, maybe he thought to furnish it with a stuffed animal or a children's book. Maybe he knew to leave a night-light on, and another light to guide your way to the bathroom.

(I tried to imagine you there, sleeping on his old grimy sheets. I wondered if you would know where you were when you woke up. I wondered if, for a moment, you'd be frightened—or if you'd know instantly where you were and feel thrilled.

I missed you so much, Jacob. I missed you like I'd never see you again.)

I LOOKED AT the clock; it was only five in the morning. I of all people knew better than to wish away time.

Dear God, when would this spiteful sun rise?

10

But I must have fallen asleep, because in the morning the first person's face I saw was Allison's. She had taken a red-eye the night before, got into Newark probably just as I was finally passing out. She'd been sitting in the corner of the room drinking coffee when I opened my eyes. I gasped. "Shhh," she said. "You have a new roommate," and she pointed theatrically to the bed on the other side of the room. "Diverticulitis," she said, and I thought she meant me, but then I realized that she meant the person on the other side of the curtain, and I relaxed.

"What time is it? Did you get Jacob?"

Allison nodded. Evidently she'd rented a car as soon as she'd gotten off the plane; now you were ensconced at the movies with Kyle, and it was almost three in the afternoon.

"Did you see him? Did you ask about Dave? What he did all night?" I knew, by the way, that instead of making demands I was supposed to start thanking her for schlepping out all this way in the middle of the summer when she was supposed to be at Friday Harbor with her gorgeous family, but luckily she was my sister, so I didn't really have to thank her.

"I think he had a nice time. His apartment looked very nice. He made breakfast."

"Breakfast? You had breakfast with him?"

"He made pancakes." Of course.

"Did he feed him anything else?"

"I assume he gave him dinner."

"Junk food?"

"I didn't ask," Allie said.

"I bet they had McDonald's—you really didn't ask?"

Allie was starting to look more annoyed than tired. "No, Karen," she said. "I didn't."

The needle in my arm was pulling at me. I took the platinum ring off my finger, palmed it. Put it back on.

"Are you feeling okay?" she asked.

"Allison, did he say anything about keeping Jakey?"

"What?"

"Did he act like he wouldn't let him go?"

"He said he'd be happy to help out again—"

"Was he reluctant to let him leave? Was he trying to hold on to him?"

"I don't know what you mean. He seemed a little sad. But nothing crazy."

"He let him out of the apartment?"

"Well, what were you expecting, exactly?"

"That he was going to take him from me," I whispered, but Allie just wrinkled her nose like I'd said something insane and I decided that was good: she thought I was being insane. She did not think Dave was trying to take my baby.

"Seriously?" she said.

I shrugged. Slid the ring up and down my finger.

With her there, I felt a renewed determination to eat, digest, and get the hell out of there. I knew there were new things for me to worry about—Steiner came in to discuss new potentialities, inflammations, adhesions, side effects, and whether I might need new medication. And when and where we expected my tumors to metastasize, although that was mostly me asking the questions. First things first. Mixed good news. They were going to run a few more tests. I wasn't even sure what he was talking about.

But like I said, I felt renewed in spirit and vigor. Allie was going to stay in your bedroom on the bottom bunk, because she didn't want to stay in a hotel in case of an emergency. Jesus, I was sick of emergencies, but I was also glad she'd be able to stay. I couldn't risk another round with your father. Or even, frankly, with Yuki.

So one more day in the hospital during which I ate and—huzzah!—digested, and then I was discharged Saturday morning. It was raining out, gentle New York City rain. Before I got into the cab, I tilted my head up and let the rain wash down over my face.

AND THEN IT was Sunday and I was in my own home. Allie took you and Kyle to the park, and I was relishing all of your absences. I was relishing being alone in the apartment. I was in my bathrobe. I had just changed my bandage and was not feeling anything bad. In fact, I had an appetite. In fact, I had some energy. I hadn't realized how the pain in my side had been dragging me down or how I needed it to disappear, but now that it was gone I felt almost like a person. I was not that worried anymore about your father suing for custody or about having the strength to fight him.

The *Times* had been delivered. I was going to sit there in my bathrobe and read the *Times* and eat half a bagel like a normal New Yorker, like the person I was. I poured myself a little decaf. At three o'clock I was settled in on the couch with the Styles section and a *Law and Order* rerun on television. I was gazing endlessly at my toenails, which needed painting. The bum-bum of *Law and Order* periodically lured me to the screen. Then the phone rang, an unknown number.

"Karen Neulander? This is Jorge Grubar, Beverly Hernandez's campaign manager, returning your call."

Grubar! I muted the television, flipped open my laptop, started taking notes. "Glad you called, Jorge," I said. "I'm wondering if Beverly wants to do a community forum with Ace, maybe at PS 19, sometime in October? If so, we need to get that on the schedule now, and if there are any other joint appearances she's interested in, I'd like to—"

"Of course," Jorge said. "We would, in fact, like to plan three joint forums, including one at the Roosevelt Hospital and one in territory where your candidate has a natural constituency."

"I'm sorry," I said, so happy, too happy, to be back in the game, "but if you think I'm going to let Ace do a debate at *Roosevelt*—"

"Listen, Ace doesn't have to worry about—"

"That doesn't mean I have to do you guys any favors—"

"Although, candidly, I'm not sure if you've noticed there are new rumors starting to surface . . ."

I paused.

"Rumors," Jorge repeated. "Which I realize are usually your stock in trade."

"What?"

"Dealing with rumors," Jorge prompted. "Isn't that how you usually operate?"

"I really have no idea what you're talking about."

"Just some whispers about our councilman's extracurricular behavior."

"Honestly, Jorge, all that's a million years old."

"Another round, Karen," Jorge said. "Another round."

But if there were another round of rumors, I would have known about it. "You know how these things go, Jorge," I said. "Ace was shamed once before and nobody cares."

"Yes, but this time? A trip to France with an intern from his campaign?"

"He went to France with his *wife*," I said. "It was an anniversary trip."

"Hmm," Jorge chuckled. He had a very suave voice, a very suave chuckle. "You don't have to sandbag me," he said.

"What are you talking about?"

Jorge chuckled again. What a jackass. "Well, evidently his wife had to leave France early, and instead of going back with her, Ace stayed around for a couple of days and had a visitor from his campaign fly in. Briefly. A young visitor. A recent Hunter College grad. One of his constituents, I've been told."

Oh fuck. The empty space in my stomach flooded.

"You have proof of this?"

"No," Jorge admitted. "There are only rumors."

"Where do these rumors come from?"

"Come up to the Bronx and ask around," Jorge said.

"Jorge, listen, even if this stuff *is* true, it doesn't matter." But suddenly I was spinning, and I knew he could hear the spin in my voice as loudly as I could. "Ace was busted for this once before and was still elected by eighteen points. The public just doesn't care what a city councilor does in his private life. It's not illegal. If it even happened, which I have to say I doubt. Rumors swirl around the Bronx all the time."

"Perhaps," said Jorge. "But it is also possible that his district has grown just a bit tired of his extracurricular proclivities. I mean, after all, this was his *anniversary trip.*"

While Jorge talked, I did a series of rapid-fire Google searches, trying to see if Ace's name came up in any recent news reports in conjunction with the terms *infidelity, intern, Hunter, anniversary, France.* It didn't. Then I went wide on an image search, but there was nothing, a few old photos of the tabloid covers but that was it. My heart was still pounding, though.

"Jorge," I said, "I don't see what good it's going to do us going back and forth over rumors. Why don't we pin down a date for a community forum at the school and then I'll ask Ace what he thinks about any other meetings."

"Fine," Jorge said, and we went over some dates, and meanwhile I was still clicking around Google just to calm my nerves. Really, there was nothing. An old shot of the Pace soph Ace boffed. She wasn't even that pretty. I felt a tiny bit assured.

"By the way," Jorge said, before we got off the phone, "you're feeling better? I heard that you were in the hospital."

"How did you hear? I'm fine, by the way. It was just a stomach thing."

"Ah, well," he said. Then: "I'm Beverly's campaign manager. It's my job to know things about her opponent." A cough; he had a hard time delivering this line. I Googled Jorge Grubar. Jesus Christ, this kid was like twenty-five. "Anyway, I'm glad to hear you're doing better."

As soon as we hung up I called Amani, but she didn't pick up. I called Ace's cell: nothing. I called his home number, even though he hated when I did that. But honestly, if my candidate had been banging some intern on his *anniversary trip with his wife*, then clearly, even if I believed in Ace's politics, which I supposed I did, I had serious doubts about his ability to make sound judgments. The phone rang a few times and then an out-of-breath woman answered and at first I thought, Oh Jesus Christ, it's the intern, but then I realized it was his wife. Jill.

"Oh hi, Karen. You looking for Ace? He went golfing. He should be back in an hour or two. He didn't pick up his phone?"

I could have just hung up, but instead I pressed my luck. "You know how he is when he's golfing. How was France?"

"Oh, God, it was amazing. Incredible. Normandy—have you been there, Karen?"

I hadn't.

"Well, you wouldn't even believe the place we stayed, like this eight-hundred-year-old castle. There was a chapel in the back where Joan of Arc supposedly prayed! Can you even believe that?"

I told Jill I couldn't believe it, but it sounded great, and just as I was about to hang up, she said, "Ace really liked it too! I mean, usually he's so eager to be back home in the Bronx, but this time he really took to it. I had to get home to help my mother with her house, but Ace stuck around for a few days. He wanted to get a closer look at the Normandy landing sites."

"He did?" My heart sank.

"He did! You know how he's just a history buff at heart. And it's pretty shocking up there, all those graves lined up by the sea, white crosses. American soldiers. You can't help but be moved."

"I'm sure," I said. "How long was he there for?"

"Just an extra two days. He took some great photos, though. You should ask him to show you."

I really should, I thought.

I hung up the phone wondering about damage control, even though I wasn't sure what the damage really was. There were photos? Of what? Would Ace really have been dumb enough to fly in an intern for forty-eight hours of French nookie? And if so, could I get him to confess?

In campaign crisis management, I always believed that anything was fixable if you got out in front of it and that the electorate didn't truly care about anything besides their sense that someone was, deep down, a decent person. Would they have a beer with this guy? Would they be happy to hang out with him at a ball game? Ace was a beer and ball game guy, a fixer and a schmoozer, and one of them—a little bit better dressed but basically one of them. He rooted for the Yankees; he played golf at Van Cortlandt up in the Bronx. And even if he had been unfaithful—hell, who among us couldn't understand the need to have sex with cute twenty-year-olds?

But your candidate needed to tell you the truth. You needed to have strong and open lines of communication at all times. You needed to have a bond of truth like steel. So it really didn't help when you couldn't even get your guy on the phone. When I made the questionable choice to leak those abortion records, at least I knew my guy was behind me, 100 percent.

"Amani, it's Karen, pick up," I said to an answering machine. Ace oversaw a constituency the size of half the population of Wyoming. He was a member of the council of the most important and dynamic city in the world. Why did he have to bang an intern? Again? And get caught? Didn't he love his wife?

I stood up, but I moved too quickly; my sutures pulled. I was also starting to get that woozy feeling I got sometimes on codeine, and for a moment it crossed my mind that I should not be doing this right now. I leaned against the wall for support. It was a Sunday afternoon in a New York City summer. Nobody else was working—why should I have been the only one?

Still, I brought the laptop to bed and did a deep dive into the recent media, all through my incipient headache. I still couldn't dig up any photos. There were no whispers on the inside–New York City–politics blogs. Was it possible that Jorge was trying to psych me out? Twenty-five-year-old Jorge with his Montalbán suaveness and the deft chuckle?

Back on Facebook, I sussed out Jorge. My, but he *was* handsome, dark hair in a thick brush cut, nicely tailored suit at Bev's recent fund-raiser. Tan skin, an easy smile. Reflexively, I wondered if he was single. He seemed to be. Was he gay? His interests included politics (duh), the Yankees (duh again), cooking, and meringue. Cooking and meringue! Jorge was either gay or a catch. I wondered if there was anything about Jorge worth sharing with the world? Fight fire with fire? But no—the most cursory internet examination came back clean as bleach.

Could Ace have really been so stupid? My heart was no longer pounding, and I could think clearly about the possibility. Would he have? Could he have? I feared I knew the answer.

I checked to see what Bev had been up to, but her Facebook page showed only one new photo, from a distance. She looked like she'd lost weight. She'd also included a link to her campaign website, which was finally up and running but contained no new information except for a list of local appearances, which I made a note of. As soon as I was up to it, I'd go do a little recon in the Bronx. It would be nice to see Bev in person, go eyeball-to-eyeball. If I needed to protect Ace from himself, I would need to get to know his opponent. I'd do it when I had a few more resources. When I'd recovered a little more of my old gusto.

Since I was on Facebook anyway, I clicked over to your father's site, both hopeful and terrified I'd find a picture of you. I didn't want him to be posting pictures of you. I didn't want the world to see him with you and expect to see more of him with you. But there were no pictures, no new bits of gossip. There was only one line, liked by five people, commented on by nobody: "Having the time of my life."

I knew enough then and slept away the rest of the afternoon.

THAT NIGHT, I gave Allie clearance to take herself to a movie—she'd been running around with two six-year-olds all day—and took on the bath and bedtime duties by myself. We hadn't done nighttime alone in the apartment in a long time and the rhythms of it felt creaky to me, especially because I didn't want to move too fast. I'd tried to put Ace out of my mind, but I still felt a little worried. Regardless, at 8 p.m. I ran your bath; at 8:15 I began to nag you about getting in. At 8:23 you acquiesced and stripped down to your underwear with an admonishment that I should not look at your butt. Then you got into the bath and I kept my eyes averted until your private bits were submerged under the bubbles, at which point I took my place on the floor so we could chat. This was how we'd done bath time for the past year or so, ever since you became aware of your body and my body and how they were different, and my scars became things I wanted to hide.

"What did you do all day?" you asked, which was sweet. "Did you feel healthy?"

"Yes," I said. "I dealt with Ace, mostly."

"Our old friend Ace," you said, mimicking me. I handed you a soapy cloth so you could wash yourself.

"Hey, you never told me how it went at your dad's house."

You paused for a little bit. I guess I'd already taught you to be cagey. "It was fun," you said, splashing a little at the sides of the tub. "We ate spaghetti."

"What was his apartment like?"

You shrugged. "It was pretty nice. It was bigger than our apartment."

"That's because it's in New Jersey."

"I guess."

"I heard you watched Spider-Man," I said. "Which one?"

"*Spider-Man 3*," you said, a bit mournfully. You knew what was coming.

"Jacob, what's that rated?"

"PG-13," you said. "But it wasn't scary! It wasn't! And my dad covered my eyes!"

"He covered your eyes?"

"When it got scary!"

"I thought you said it wasn't scary."

"But just in case."

Goddammit. "Jacob, you know you're not allowed to watch those movies," I said. "You know you're not thirteen. If you get nightmares, you only have yourself to blame." Which couldn't have been less true.

You splashed the water against the side of the tub, not looking at me. "I know," you said, but already you were playing me against Dave. *My dad covered my eyes.*

"Duck your head," I said, and after I've washed the soap out of your hair, I asked you if his wife was there, which was a question I'd wanted to ask earlier but didn't, afraid of how I'd seem.

You shook your head. "My dad says she travels a lot. To tell you the truth, I think he's kind of lonely."

"He might be," I agreed.

"Do you think that's why he wants to hang out with me? Cause he's alone all the time?"

"No," I said. "I think he wants to hang out with you because you're a cool kid and he likes you a lot. You're fun to be with."

"And I'm his son," you said.

"And you're his son."

You took some of the Playmobil figures from the edge of the bath and started making them dive in and out of the bubbles. Occasionally they stopped to shoot each other. After a few minutes you seemed to forget I was there and started providing your figures with voices, strange accents, high whiny voices for the characters who were dressed as farmers and athletes and deep growly voices for the pirates. I thought about all the toys we had left at Allison's and wondered, if Ace lost the election, if he really had shagged another bimbo, whether we should move to Seattle sooner than we'd planned on. It had to be harder to wage a custody battle with someone in Seattle. I mean, worst case, we could always run to Vancouver.

"Did I hurt your feelings?" you said, and for a minute I thought you were talking to the dolls before I realized you were talking to me. "Did you want me to stay in the hospital with you?"

"No, honey, of course not." My abdomen was starting to ache. I thought about what I'd eaten today: half a bagel, hardly enough.

"But you were mad when I left."

"I was just worried whether you'd be okay with Dave."

"You looked mad."

I didn't say anything.

You floated your plastic figures above the water and then watched them drop below the surface. "Are you closer to dying now?"

I felt my heart pause, then double beat. "No," I said. "In fact, when they looked inside me they saw that the tumor hasn't spread much. The chemo's still working."

You were quiet then, swirling your toys around in the water. I wondered if I really should have been talking to you all along in these frank words: chemo, tumor. Dr. Susan, as you might remember, was all for honesty and direct language, but it still seemed strange to me that a six-year-old should know what chemotherapy was.

"Do you think they're wrong?" you asked, looking up at me. "Maybe you're not going to die after all?"

Despite my aching body, I reached out into the tub and touched your sweet soft face. "I don't know, Jakey," I said. "I don't know." This is what I said to you when I didn't want to tell you the truth.

"I think they're wrong," you said. "Or at least they might not be right."

I agreed with you, they might not be right, and then I staggered up and helped you out of the bath and wrapped you in the hooded towel you'd gotten for a gift when you were born; it used to drag on the floor after you, and now it hit your knees. You were growing every day, my son, and in different ways, so was I.

Before bed we decided to read the first chapter of *Harry Potter and the Sorceror's Stone*, which I'd gotten you for Chanukah and you'd had no time for. But you mentioned that Dave was a big Harry Potter fan and was surprised you don't know much about it, so we decided to get started right away, to make up for this deficit and any others. You cuddled into the corner of your bed. The air-conditioning was high; the lights were low. Your hair was wet. You were mine, baby, you were mine. Nobody could ever take you from me. I opened the first page and started to read.

BY THE TIME Allie got home, it was ten and I was mostly asleep. She hadn't gone to the movies after all; she'd gone shopping and then out to dinner, which was funny because in Seattle

Allie would never go to a restaurant by herself: What if someone saw her alone and jumped to conclusions? But here, in New York, we were all free to be whomever we wanted.

"Look what I bought you!" she said, handing me a bag. Inside was a leather jacket.

Jesus, Allie. "You've got to be kidding. Why would you get me this?" I could see the price tag, four hundred dollars. Allie was both generous beyond measure and an enormous show-off.

"It was fifty percent off, out of season. I already have two. I couldn't get it for Camilla, she's so spoiled. And it was such a bargain, I couldn't let it go."

I groaned, let her help me sit up. "Allie, you've got to stop buying me stuff. I can't take it with me, you know."

"Shut up," she said. She helped me out of bed and I turned on the light, stood in front of the full-length mirror. I didn't look at myself until I'd put the jacket on (I couldn't look at myself at night, I looked so awful). But with the jacket on, I looked much better: it was gorgeous, soft and black, with a wool insert inside to keep me warm. I was glad to be warm; I had the air-conditioning turned up too high. I kept it on and got back in bed. She got in next to me.

For a while, we said nothing, letting the air conditioner hum at us. "I called Daddy today."

"That was nice of you," I said. "Any news?"

"He said hello. At least it sounded like hello."

"What did Olga say?"

"She said everything's basically the same."

I wished I could tell him about you, everything we'd been doing. I had no idea how much he could understand, so why couldn't I just assume he could understand all of it? That like Cammy said, he just had it all locked away? Still, the idea of spilling out my guts to a man who couldn't tell us where he was, what his name was, or even that his wife of forty years was dead (Did he know this? At her funeral he stared straight ahead even when we pointed to her coffin)—it seemed unnecessarily cruel. If I told him I was dying and he didn't say a word—that would be cruel for both of us.

Jacob, did I ever tell you my mother cooked dinner for my grandparents every night? She'd get home from the law firm, trade her heels for sneakers, and start pulling things out of the fridge or the pantry. Twenty minutes later she'd have two plates made up on a tray, and she'd send either me or Allie upstairs to feed my grandparents. They'd open the door, say, "Thank you, dear," and take the tray. Half an hour later one of us would go back to pick it up. And all that time, all those years, barely a word passed between us.

"Do you remember how Mom made dinner for Grandma and Grandpa?" I asked Allie, because suddenly it felt like a forged memory, like something that was too strange to have really happened.

But Allie remembered. "She respected them. What they'd been through. She wanted to do something for them."

"I should have been more grateful," I said.

"We were so young, though."

"I was ten," I said. "That's old enough." Outside our window, people were laughing loudly.

After several minutes, Allie said, "Bruce says he and Ross are

at it again. Evidently Ross stayed out till two in the morning
Saturday. Didn't text, didn't pick up his phone. Bruce went crazy
on him, took away his car. And of course they're not talking to
each other."

"Shit," I said.

"It's never been like this, not even when he was thirteen, four-
teen, the age they're supposed to be brats."

"Is he still talking about India?"

"He thinks if he pouts enough it'll happen," Allie said. "Eighteen years old, the kid is walking around like he gets to make his
own decisions, like he's in charge of his own life."

"He sort of is," I said.

"He's in charge of some things," Allie said. "He can decide
what he wants to study, what he wants to do with his time. But
he can't decide he's going to move to the third world for some
person we've never met."

"Is India the third world?"

"For Ross it would be. For Ross some parts of Seattle are the
third world."

"He'd probably come home again," I said, mildly.

Allie dragged a pillow over her head. Muffled by the pillow,
she said, "I'm just not ready to let him go."

Sure she wasn't. I said, "I know how you feel."

In the dark, from her hiding space under the pillow, Allie
squeezed my hand, and the old platinum ring on my thumb, and
we fell asleep pondering the condition of being mothers, which
was, of course, the condition of helping the people you love most
in the world leave you.

II

Sometimes I wonder if you think politics is irrelevant, or if I spend entirely too much time wrapped up in poll numbers or my candidate's personal life. I hope you don't—I mean, I hope you know it's meaningful. I hope you're registered to vote. You are, aren't you? And you vote even in the years that end in an odd number?

My own political awakening stemmed in part from my father's history lessons and in part, I fear, from being the poorest kid in Rockville Centre. I mean, I wasn't really the poorest—I was never on free lunch, never went without a winter coat—but I was the only one I knew who didn't go to camp, didn't wear Guess jeans or Reebok sneakers. This privation led me, in my adolescence, to a strong identification with the poor and meek and unpopular. Every year I grimly ran for student government on a platform of banishing the homecoming court; every year I lost badly. By my senior year of high school, I understood that someone like me (mouthy, occasionally impolite, unafraid of confrontation) would make a better campaign manager than candidate. And that seemed perfectly all right; candidates live or die by the voter, but campaign managers always live to fight another day.

As I hope you remember, I went on to college at SUNY Binghamton, graduating with a degree in poli-sci in 1992. It was a presidential campaign year, and there was considerable excitement around a candidate named Bill Clinton. He was a youngish dude from Arkansas with a proclivity for fast food and loose women, a good talker and very smart. On the whole, people liked him. Earlier in the primaries, I'd been a fan of a guy named Paul Tsongas but—and at the time this seemed no more than a distant sadness—he was a metastatic cancer patient who really never stood a chance. So once Tsongas lost in the primaries, I became a Clinton girl, defending him against charges of hillbillyism and sexual predation and admiring him for his stand on reproductive rights and the way he played the saxophone. (Is Bill Clinton still alive when you're reading this? I hope so. He's a complicated figure but on the whole, I believe, a force for good, and these days I think of him as a much-improved version of Ace.)

Upon my graduation, one of my poli-sci professors hooked me up with a barely paying job at Clinton's DC campaign office, where I spent most of my time sending faxes (do they still have faxes in the future?) and ordering pizza. I lived with three other girls in a small house on Avenue U, near the Metro stop, and spent about fifteen hours a day at the Clinton office feeling enormously pleased with myself for working such an important job. I remember calling my parents back on Long Island on Sundays and acting as if I was in charge of Clinton's entire campaign, and them being quite impressed and bragging to their friends.

What was nice about that campaign—before *Citizens United*, before super PACs and superconsultants—was that there was a feeling of real camaraderie, and a feeling of belief in our candidate. It's harder and harder to find that kind of belief in a national candidate these days. We've become jaded by the internet and by the things we now know and by Clinton himself, who, regardless of the fact that nobody seemed to care much (when he left office after his second term, his approvals were at 66 percent), did introduce blow jobs into the national conversation.

(Sorry I just mentioned blow jobs.)

(Jesus Christ, what did Ace do?)

After Clinton won (the most incredible night, and I'll never forget the way we gathered around the television and cried, all of us, as he gave his midnight speech) a contact from the campaign found me a job as an assistant at a political consulting firm, a small one that did regional work in Maryland and Virginia. It was called Harley Political Consulting, and it was there I met another barely paid assistant, a Georgetown grad named Chuck, who was both a devout Catholic and a homosexual and made up for his work in liberal causes by attending mass every Sunday and donating a small portion of his tiny earnings to the church.

(I had a pretty big crush on Chuck back then. I liked boys who were self-abnegating and well dressed, and I didn't find out he was gay for quite some time. I just thought he didn't really like me.)

I stayed at Harley for five years, at which point I did the math and realized I could make more money if I went out on my own—although I was not even quite twenty-nine yet, I was very self-assured. I knew that I could live on next to nothing, since that's how I'd lived my entire life, and that I could work harder than anybody else I knew, since I'd done that too.

I asked Chuck if he wanted to come with me. Chuck was sick of DC and had lots of family money; he agreed to my offer without taking nearly enough time to mull it over. We decided we'd be called Neulander Davis, because the firm was my idea. We also decided we'd be roommates, and we rented a very tiny apartment in Queens and used the kitchen as our initial head-quarters. We would divide the place along the usual lines for a campaign consulting shop: Chuck would take on long-term projects for nonprofits and unions while I'd hold the hands of whatever candidates we took on. Meanwhile, his parents gave us the money we needed for things like letterhead and an accountant and direct-mail lists, and within two years Neulander Davis was a blooming company with a reputation for playing hardball. I traveled up and down the East Coast managing candidates, while Chuck met the man who would become his life's partner, adopted a child, and formed very friendly relations with the teacher's union, Greenpeace, and half a dozen other companies that hired us to promote their agendas.

My relationship with Chuck was a bit funny: although I'd known him almost half my life, even though we'd lived together for a while, we'd never been super close. I'd never met his parents. I'd never met his siblings. The most I saw of his husband or their kids was on their annual holiday card, or the rare occasion when we decided it was time we really did get together and went out for family pizzas. But this happened maybe every eighteen months. Otherwise, Chuck and I were like the two axles of a car: when we were both rolling we made the thing go, but we never had to touch each other, or even speak.

Which is all a long way of saying I was surprised when I got to the office for a long overdue visit to find that Chuck had ordered in breakfast from Murray's, and Starbucks coffee. "Welcome back, Karen," he said, and we hugged, which was another thing we did rarely. The air-conditioning was, as usual for the building, turned up way too high; I pulled a cardigan from the closet and checked out my workspace: dusty-looking and empty. Well, I'd been working remotely lately. And of course I hadn't been able to take on as many clients.

But the rest of the place looked sharp and busy: lots of papers and folders lying around, a few new workspaces crammed into corners. We had taken our decorating cue from the bull pen Bloomberg used as New York's mayor: open spaces jammed with desks, open lines of communication (via yelling across the room), and a fridge in the office kitchen filled with snacks. Although it was only seven thirty, a young woman I didn't know followed me into the office, nodded at me, then sat down at a workspace and started to type away.

"Chuck, who's that?"

"Nina," Chuck said. "I hired her to help me with the clean energy ballot initiative, remember?"

Had he told me about Nina or about the ballot initiative? I couldn't remember and I was embarrassed I couldn't remember. I was feeling tired and wanted to sit down, but I didn't want to admit to feeling tired or needing to sit.

"Nina," Chuck said, "this is Karen." Nina looked over at me and nodded. "Karen Neulander."

"Oh!" she said, and jumped up. "Oh! I didn't realize—I mean I thought you weren't coming back in for a while." She came, shook my hand. She had long dark hair and lovely skin. She was maybe twenty-three. She would look good, I thought, on MSNBC: I used to look good myself when I was a guest on MSNBC. Maybe Chuck had mentioned her, or someone with a master's degree in something who he was going to hire as a contract worker, or maybe part-time, or maybe full-time, I couldn't think.

I closed my eyes for a second longer than what probably seemed normal, perched on the edge of a desk. One of the lingering effects of chemo was that I still sometimes felt both forgetful and dizzy or, as Allie put it, elderly.

"It's nice to meet you," I said to Nina after I opened my eyes. "Are you enjoying your work here?" Jesus, I sounded elderly.

I saw Nina shoot what looked like a worried glance toward Chuck and wondered what on earth it was she had to be worried about—why would she worry?—and then she answered my questions and we chitchatted a little bit about the ballot initiative's polling while I faked remembering what the hell the ballot initiative was, and then Chuck ushered me into the kitchen, where our Murray's and our Starbucks was waiting. He had ordered me a skinny vanilla latte, which was what I used to drink before I got sick and my taste buds changed. I pretended to be grateful for the drink and the food.

"She seems nice," I said. "Is she smart?"

Chuck stood and closed the kitchen door. "Very smart," he said. "Very organized and creative too. I like her."

"Good," I said. "I'm sorry I haven't been able to be more involved in hiring," I said. I tried to take a sip of the latte, but even the smell made me feel nauseated. I put it down, leaned my head against my hand. I hoped Chuck couldn't tell just how worn out I was. I hadn't told him I'd gotten out of the hospital four days ago or that even this morning I felt worried I wouldn't be able to make the meeting, worried I was going to fall over or fall apart. Allie had to help me into the cab, and it took me way too long to get out. My abdomen was still bandaged. Tomorrow I was supposed to report back to Steiner at Sloan Kettering.

"It's fine. Obviously you've been dealing with a lot."

"I guess," I said. "But at least the tumor seems to be behaving itself for now. I mean, it's responding to the treatment. Well, it responded to the last treatment."

"Good," Chuck said.

"My team is optimistic."

"That's great," Chuck said with that note of sympathy and condescension I'd grown used to from doctors, and he reached out to pat my hand gently, awkwardly, and that's when I realized that Chuck had invited me here not to talk about business but to talk about me.

"What's going on?" I said, summoning my old ball buster voice. "Is there something I need to know about?"

Chuck busied himself with a bagel, buttering it in his precise, counterclockwise way; I had eaten maybe one thousand bagels with him over the years and knew his procedure the way I knew how he signed his emails ("Best, Charles"). Chuck had the softening body of a married man in his forties, but his face was still handsome and his eyes were still gentle, and he still dressed very well. He had grown a little goatee to take some attention away from his bald spot, and started wearing glasses with interesting frames. And though I felt enormous affection for him, considering all we'd shared over the years, I also felt furious, because I knew he was about to betray me.

"Chuck, what the hell."

"Karen—" He put down the bagel, put down his knife. For a moment he touched his hand to the top of my hand, the same spot where just the other day an IV had emerged. "I think we need to hire a new principal."

"We need to what?"

"Look," he said, "I'm not saying you shouldn't work anymore, but we need reinforcements you're not providing right now."

"Chuck, it's not up to you whether I work or not."

"Right, but—" He managed to look me in the eye. "Karen, you know that recruiting clients was never really my bag. That was always what you brought to the table, but during the past several months—"

"Did you just say *your bag*?"

"—you have to admit you've been out of the office *a lot*, and we're starting another election cycle, and there hasn't been anyone around to bring in new clients or to work with the DSCC or the DCCC. I mean we have the ongoing stuff with the teacher's union, but the coordinating committees are hiring again, and I don't have anyone to talk to them. You know that's not what I do . . ."

"It's what I do."

"Right," Chuck said, looking relieved, as though his slow student was catching on.

"So then why aren't they calling me, Chuck? It's not like I have to be in the office to be working—"

"Right, I know," he said. "But you've been so sick that I haven't wanted to—"

"Chuck, it's not like I'm dying," I said. We both let that hang in the air for a minute.

He picked up his bagel and then put it back down. "Karen, this company needs more than you're able to give."

"That's not fair," I said. "I know I've been sick, but I don't think we need a new principal to take my place. You can't penalize me because I've been sick, Chuck. You can't try to force me out because I have health problems."

"Karen, I'm not forcing you anywhere. I'm just giving you the room you need to take care of yourself while our company continues to thrive."

Nice, Chuck. Make it like you're doing this for *me*. "If you feel strongly about it, maybe we can hire a client management specialist or something—"

"The thing is, though, without an active principal, I'm not sure we're bringing in enough business. I mean we need another name to shore up our operations."

"This place is called *Neulander* Davis. Neulander. We can't just bring in another name without calling this place something else. I'm the Neulander in Neulander Davis. This has been my shop for fifteen years—"

"It's been *our* shop," Chuck said.

I gritted my teeth, which hurt my jaw. The pain felt good. I gritted again.

Chuck said, "I'm not telling you to leave."

"You *can't* tell me to leave."

"But," Chuck said, "I'm just saying that it's clear you're indisposed. The whole world knows you're indisposed."

"The whole world, Chuck?"

"We need someone who can do some of the high-energy work right now that you're not able to do. We've gotten calls from the Sunday shows and I've got nobody right now. When the Anthony Weiner thing broke we had nobody to go on camera. We're not keeping our name in the conversation."

"Jesus, I could have talked about Weiner," I said.

"You were in treatment, Karen. You didn't have any hair. You couldn't get out of bed."

"I have a fucking wig, Chuck—" I said, and then there was a knock on the door and lovely Nina walked in, smiled at us, pulled a Luna bar from a basket on the countertop and smiled again at us as she left. She must have heard everything we were saying. The walls in the office were paper thin.

"Chuck, this is my company. This is *my living*!"

"Nobody's taking your living from you, Karen. But you're no longer in any position to be the principal of the firm. You have to see that."

"My health insurance, Chuck, Jesus Christ! I need my health insurance!"

"Karen, nobody's firing you."

"You can't fire me!" Dave, Chuck, all these men trying to take what was mine!

"Karen, I need to hire someone and I need to do it soon."

"*You* need to?"

"The firm needs to," he said. "I'm setting up interviews with a few people," Chuck said. "If you'd like to sit in on them—"

"You cannot make these decisions unilaterally."

"We need to plan for the future."

"You think I'm not planning for the future?" Because I didn't want lovely Nina to overhear, I lowered my voice but was still seething. "That's all I'm doing! That's all I do! I plan for my son's future, I plan for my own future, I plan for my client's future."

"The firm, Karen. I'm talking about the firm. At least till you get better."

"Fuck you. You know I'm not getting better."

We were quiet. The elevator clanged somewhere in the building's depths.

"And you should know I fucking hate lattes now."

Chuck nodded. "We can switch drinks if you want," he said.

I stood up, rubbed my eyes, wondered where I was going. My cell phone buzzed and I hoped it was Amani, but it was Allie, checking in the way she did in the morning, to tell me everything was fine. They were going to the park.

I sat back down.

"How's Ace doing?" Chuck said tentatively.

"He's doing fine," I said. "Because I'm his campaign manager."

"Of course," he said. "I know."

We both stared miserably at the plate of bagels in between us. I don't know why Chuck and I weren't closer, why we'd never become better friends. I think there was always the fragility of political life between us, the fact that things could change on a dime: winds and fortunes and so forth. Or health. Paul Tsongas, the candidate I admired back in 1992, before I jumped on the Clinton bandwagon—Paul Tsongas lied about the recurrence of his cancer. He said, in 1992, that he'd been cancer-free since a bone marrow transplant in 1986. It came out later that the doctors had discovered more cancer in a lymph node in 1987. And then, soon after Clinton won the election, he announced that the cancer was back. And then he died five years later. He was a diminished man.

Political winds, political fortune. *Winds of War.* Have you read that book, Jacob?

"My name is on the lease of this place, Chuck," I said. "So I'm going to stick around and do some work this morning. Are you okay with that?"

Finally, Chuck had the manners to look ashamed of himself. "Of course," he said.

Sagging, I went to my computer and thought about calling Ace again, or Amani, but instead I wrote a few pages of this book—these pages, actually—and then I thought about the truth, which was that Ace didn't really need me. He didn't need me. My last client ever, and I was running the barest shell of a campaign, utterly hollow. He'd win by a landslide even without a campaign manager—that's the way these elections went. And the rumors about Ace were just hearsay, because if there had been anything to them, I would have already known. So therefore, he didn't need me. And Chuck didn't need me. I had no work left. There was no longer any point. But just before I could jump out the window my phone rang: Ace's office. Thank God.

"You want to schedule a forum with Beverly Hernandez?" Amani said.

"Amani, what have you been hearing about Ace's extracur-riculars? And where is he? And why won't he call me back? We were supposed to have a meeting."

"I'm not sure what you're talking about," Amani said. "Right now he has most of October free."

"Where is he, Amani? I've heard some disturbing reports and I just need to make sure they're not true."

"I'm supposed to speak to him later today—"

"Amani—"

"And I'll have him call you. I'll ask him about the meeting, and put the forum in tentatively for October 14. If that doesn't work for the Hernandez campaign, let me know."

With that, we hung up. I felt dizzy and a little bit nauseated and was afraid, for the tiniest moment, that I might throw up on the floor. Jesus! To throw up on the floor in front of Chuck. I decided right then not to get too sentimental about leaving our crappy office in Chelsea—what was it anyway but some grimy carpeting and particleboard partitions?—and hobbled to the el-evator to take a cab home. I'd be back when I felt better. I still had a campaign to run. As I left the office, Chuck tried to smile at me, but I did myself a favor and didn't return it.

I suppose, Jacob, that right about now you're starting to think of the person you want to be as an adult. If you're lucky, like I was, you'll discover a particular passion for something (Tennis? Video games?) and you'll be able to translate that pas-sion into your life's work. If you're a little less lucky—but still lucky enough—you'll find a job you enjoy and be able to do this thing you love during your free time. I know people in their

forties who still rock out with their bands on the weekends. Your
school nurse at PS 199 is also a poet. My hope for you, Jacob, is
that, like them, you've found a real passion.

I try to imagine you at eighteen, where you'll be, what you'll
look like. I assume you'll be tall, since you already are. My guess
is that you'll wear glasses, since I started needing them when I
was eight. I have no idea where you'll go to college, but I like to
envision you in some liberal arts college somewhere in Massachu-
setts or Vermont, where the students wear long woolen scarves
and play lacrosse and get drunk on the weekends because there's
nothing better to do. Anywhere you want to go, Jake, you can go.
I've put away money. Get in somewhere good and go there and
love every minute of it. That's my advice for you. Oh, and learn
a foreign language. I'm thinking probably Spanish or Mandarin.

The next morning I was asleep when Steiner called.

"You awake?" he said. I lied and said that I was.

Some of the lab reports they did at the hospital were back, he
said, and they were a little troubling.

"How little?"

"Just a little."

He began explaining and I heard him and then I didn't; I said,
"I don't think that's right." But, he said, from some samples they
took it was possible that, well, anyway, not to get too worried,
they were just going to change the medication a little, put me on
a more aggressive regimen.

"What does this mean?"

"It means we're going to be more aggressive. That's all."

"But why do we need more aggression?"

"To keep you going as long as possible."

"But what—"

"That's all, Karen. We just want to be aggressive. Outsmart the cancer."

"But what's different now? Did the cancer get smarter?"

"You should tolerate this new medication well," he said. "Most people find the side effects to be minor."

"I don't mind side effects."

"Good," he said. "So I'll see you in the office tomorrow?"

"Yes, but—" I said, and then, "You will," and then, because I was still in those golden seconds before he hung up, I said, "This doesn't change my prognosis, does it? I still have the time you promised?"

"It's hard to say, Karen. But it doesn't necessarily change anything. It's hard to say."

"But what would you say?"

"It's hard to say." My golden seconds were over. "I'll see you tomorrow. We'll talk some more."

Well.

Jakey, this sounded more like bad news than mixed. Didn't it? I mean, what would you have said to that? More aggressive? Hustling me on the phone? I could do nothing—what could I do? It was nine in the morning and you and Allie were watching television; I could hear the animated squawk of something infernal, *Lego Ninjago*. I allowed myself five minutes of crying, three hundred seconds and no more.

"Hey guys," I said at 9:08 as I creaked to the door. You both looked at me with concern. Did I look that bad? Sound that bad? It was only five minutes of crying.

"Mom?"

"I'm going to work," I said. Did this change my prognosis? Yes, it did. I was going to work now.

"Working where?" you asked.

"The Bronx," I said. I still had one client left. I still had one campaign. I would win this campaign with everything I had. If Jorge Grubar thought he had some dirty tricks up his sleeve, he had no idea what he was up against. I had dirty tricks up my entire shirt.

"How are you getting there?" Allie turned down the volume on the television, as though we were having a big-deal discussion, even though we were just talking about me going to work, which wasn't a big deal. I was a working mother. I worked. I touched my face. It was hot and puffy.

"Cab."

"Can you handle it?"

"Why couldn't I?"

Her expression was bleak. I should have pinched my cheeks before I left the bedroom to make sure I looked nice and rosy; I should have put on my wig. "I can go to work."

"You look tired," Allie said. "Or something. Who was on the phone?"

"Nobody."

"Can Aunt Allie take me to FAO Schwarz?" you asked.

"FAO Schwarz is for tourists."

"Aunt Allie's a tourist."

"I grew up here," Allie said, eyeing me like she didn't trust me.

"You can go, but no candy," I said.

"Who was on the phone?" Allie said.

"No candy?" you repeated, uncomprehending. You liked FAO Schwartz only because there was a gigantic and overpriced bulk candy department on the ground floor, a treat for when you were good or I was wiped out. "Please, Mom? Just a little?"

"No," I said.

"*Please?*" you whimpered as though *you* were the one facing mixed-bad news.

"I have to shower," I said. "I have to go."

"Mom, *please can we go to the candy floor?*"

"Not now, Jacob," Allie said.

"Please?"

"Jacob, leave your mother alone."

"*Please! You said we could go!*"

Did I? The medication made me so foggy, and I'd been promising you everything lately, Yankees games, pizza, the moon and stars, that it was quite possible I'd promised you a trip to the FAO Schwarz candy floor, but that didn't mean that you got to go now or that you got to whine your way into it or take advantage of the opening you clearly saw. I was twine-haired and stooped, older than the universe. I was holding on to the back of the chair.

"Jacob, give your mom a break," Allie said.

"*Mom!*" And then you threw yourself on to the floor. Where had this come from? You'd stopped throwing temper tantrums months ago, maybe even years. I touched the scraggly hair on my head, my puffy face. I thought I might faint.

"*Mom!*"

"Jacob, if you don't stop right now, you're locked in your

room for the rest of the day," Allie said. The television was off, and she had her arms crossed on her chest and a don't-fuck-with-me look on her face, God bless her.

"But you said!"

"Now," Allie said.

"You're not my mother!"

"Now," I whispered. You looked from her to me and back again and saw no soft place to land. You went to your room and slammed the door, but there was an iPad in there, so I knew you wouldn't suffer. We were quiet as we listened to you freak out, scream at your pillows, and then stop freaking out.

"I'm sorry," I said after a few minutes of quiet.

"For what?" Allie said. "Who was on the phone?"

"Steiner's changing my medication."

"Why?"

"Cancer's stronger now."

She stood, began picking breakfast plates off the coffee table. You'd been eating peach yogurt and English muffins. "Is that what the doctor said?"

"He said he wasn't sure."

"So then you don't know—"

"Allie, I know."

"If the doctor didn't say—"

"I know what he was implying."

She didn't look at me, began bustling. There was crap everywhere, magazines, your toys. She put them in their bins along the wall. I listened for you in your room.

"But if he didn't say—" Allie said.

"He said it was troubling."

"Why?"

"He didn't say."

She rubbed her hands up and down her arms, just looking at me. Then she blinked. "Can I make you something to eat?"

"I'm not hungry." I watched her ferry plates to the kitchen sink, come back to wipe off the coffee table. She was wearing a gray U Dub T-shirt and exercise pants, blonde hair in a ponytail, looking like a mom in a commercial, but she still wouldn't look at me. "Okay, an English muffin," I said, even though I had no idea how I was going to eat it.

"Okay," Allie said. "Good."

From your room, the blips and bleeps of Big Win Hockey on your iPad.

"Sorry he's acting like a shit."

"He's just being six," she said from the kitchen, where she was slicing me a muffin, pouring me some coffee. "Believe me, it's easier than dealing with a teenager."

I would be leaving her to deal with one more teenager.

"Do you want me to stay?" I asked, helplessly.

"Go to work," she said. She was trying to smile.

And of course I felt bad because (a) I didn't want to worry my sister and (b) she shouldn't have had to do this for me yet. I mean she shouldn't have had to be your mother yet (and you were right, she wasn't your mother, but soon enough she'd be the closest thing you had, and at some point you might even refer to her as mom, and that would be okay with me, that's what I wanted, for you always to have a mom, and for that mom to be Allie if it couldn't be me), but also she was healthy and I wasn't, so she had to suck it up and deal with you and I was going to go take a long hot shower for as long as I could stand it then get in a taxi like a person who wasn't dying and go to work.

ROOSEVELT MEDICAL CENTER was the opposite of the swish Manhattan hospitals I was used to—Sloan Kettering, NYU—with hushed hallways and cafeterias that could double as executive lunchrooms. Roosevelt was loud and grimy and smelled powerfully of cheap disinfectant, which brought me back in a not-unpleasant way to my years at SUNY Binghamton. There was no cafeteria, only a snack bar filled with vending machines. Outside there were smokers.

Like a lot of borough hospitals, this one dated from the fifties, when New York's postwar population exploded and so did the idea of acute care. Roosevelt originally served a middle-class population, but in the seventies it was known as one of the few hospitals in the city whose doctors cheerfully took Medicaid, whose staff spoke languages from Portuguese to Farsi, where someone in the ER would probably see you within twenty-four hours or faster if you were clearly in labor or bleeding to death, and whose bill collectors wouldn't chase you down for money they knew you didn't have.

I had the cab leave me off at the entrance, in a scrum of traffic and wheelchairs and security people staring passively at all of us like UN peacekeepers. It took me an embarrassingly long time to maneuver to the hospital's broken sliding doors. But I must have looked pretty sick because eventually people let me pass.

Slowly, I traversed Roosevelt's long and cluttered hallways, every so often landing in a small lobby filled with people in wheelchairs or filthy toddlers running freely. All the televisions were playing dismal talk shows. There were more women in full Muslim dress than I was used to seeing; more people on stretchers. Every so often I would try my luck at a broken drinking fountain. I could have asked someone where to find Bev, but I couldn't find anyone to ask.

After about fifteen minutes of meandering, I ended up by Oncology, which was at the end of a hallway on the second floor that I wasn't even sure how I found—I didn't remember any elevators or stairs. I stood at the doorway of an infusion ward, which even from the perimeter seemed sticky with nausea. People were sleeping with their mouths open; the place smelled like rotten bananas and the small televisions were old and the nurses looked bored. Spanish newspapers lay about. At Sloan Kettering I had a choice of wonderful magazines and satellite television. In the corner of this room I spied a woman my age, staring at me, a tube in her arm. Or maybe she was younger than me. Her skin was bluish gray.

"Can I help you?" asked a nurse after I'd been standing there, just watching—Watching what? Lives less privileged than my own sad dying life?—for quite some time.

"Are you scheduled to come in today?"

"I'm sorry?"

"Your name?"

I was in my healthy drag, the wig was on, the makeup, but still there was no concealing what I was. I wondered if Dr. Steiner would keep me alive longer than a Roosevelt doctor would. I wondered what this new aggressive medication was going to do to me. Someone was groaning in the corner and was ignored.

"I'm not a patient. I'm looking for the executive offices," I said crisply. I had my briefcase with me, although it was empty. I held it up a little.

"Ground floor," she said. "You need a visitor's badge if you're going to walk around. Security will escort you out otherwise." She looked at my face and felt pity. "Just a minute, I'll get you one."

With a white sticker stuck on my lapel, I found my way to the ground floor. Then I found the executive offices, Bev's office, where her secretary listened to R&B music in a cube covered with baby photos.

"Can I help you?"

"I'm here to see Beverly Hernandez."

"Do you have an appointment?" The secretary had long nails painted in a checkerboard pattern.

"It's about the campaign," I said. "For city council."

"Do you have an appointment?"

I shook my head.

"Your name?"

I didn't want to tell the secretary who I was because I didn't want Bev to think I was the enemy. "Karen."

"Just a second," said the secretary. She picked up the phone, spoke quietly in Spanish, and then said, "If you can make it quick, you can go in. She's got a meeting in five minutes."

I stood. I felt obscurely embarrassed. I was thinking of the woman with the bluish-gray skin, the one who was my age. "Go on," said the secretary. "You only have five minutes."

Bev's office was small, the size of our kitchen, or maybe smaller. There was one chair for visitors, but it was jammed into the corner of the room by a filing cabinet, and there was a purse on it, so I stood.

"Just a sec—" Bev said, holding up a finger at me without looking away from her computer screen. Her office was cluttered in a friendly way, papers on the desk, a wall of framed photographs and diplomas; it looked out on a Bronx streetscape of fruit vendors and buses. Bev herself looked just like she did on Facebook (and why should she have looked any different?): dark close-cropped hair, no visible gray, slightly yellowish-tan skin, a broad face, rimless glasses. Maybe the yellowish tan was jaundice? Maybe she was sick again? "Okay," she said, looking at me. Her voice was familiar from her video. "You want to talk about the campaign? Your name is Karen?"

I stood by her desk, my briefcase in both hands. I realized suddenly how tired I was.

"May I sit?" I croaked.

"Chair's over there," Bev said, but a fleck of worry creased her eyebrows. "Are you okay?"

"I—my name is—I'm Karen Neulander." I felt enormously foolish. "I'm here—I wanted to meet you."

"Karen Neulander?" The crease of worry deepened. "You're that shark Ace hired?"

All you had to do was look at me to see I was no shark.

Bev sighed heavily, picked up the phone receiver again. "It's not appropriate for you to just show up at my office without an appointment."

"I just . . . I wanted to say . . . I'm not here for any real campaign purpose. I just honestly wanted to meet you." If it was true Ace was in trouble, maybe I could learn something about Bev, enough to go back on the attack. If I needed to. Would I even need to? I supposed I could have raised questions about her health.

"Meet me?" She hadn't dialed a number on the phone yet. The photos on the wall behind her, interspersed with the diplomas, were all of bright-eyed young women and their children. Bev's family. I recognized Monica, the granddaughter from YouTube. Ace's office was festooned with pictures of him playing golf with other politicians, radio hosts, celebrity restaurateurs.

"We haven't had any events yet, so I haven't had a chance . . ." Bev just raised an eyebrow.

"You were diagnosed with stage III cancer four years ago?" I said. It slipped out.

She gave me a look. "That's right," Bev said, crisply. "But I've been cancer-free for more than two years."

"Are you sure?"

"What is that supposed to mean?"

Her computer made a beeping noise, which we both ignored.

"I have ovarian cancer," I said. This slipped out too. "It's spreading. The doctor called—the doctor called me this morning."

She put down the receiver. "You weren't diagnosed this morning," she said.

"No," I said. "I've known for almost two years. The doctor just had more bad news for me today. Stronger medication. The cancer's changing. I'm not sure how much longer I have."

"Nobody is," Bev said. She turned off the beeping noise on her computer. For a moment we looked at each other. I was using my cancer to gain her trust, so that she'd tell me she was sick too, and then, if we needed to, we could use that and win. I felt my adrenaline coming back. That's why I was here! That was the reason.

"Does Ace know you came here?"

I shook my head. "I was on my way up to the Bronx and I asked the cab to stop here. I would have told you I was coming, but I didn't know myself."

"Surely you know other cancer survivors besides me," Bev said. "You didn't need to come all this way to meet someone else who's had cancer."

"Of course," I said, although the truth was my contact list wasn't thick with cancer survivors, and the few I knew had escaped the relatively toothless ones, thyroid, early stage colon or breast. A handful of basal cells. Nobody with ovarian; almost nobody escaped that bitch alive.

"So then what can I do for you?"

"Did the doctor ever tell you it wasn't working? The drugs weren't working? Did you ever lose hope?" I kept slipping.

"No," Bev said, steely. She was a candidate for public office in New York City. "Not once."

"I have," I said. "I think right now I'm losing hope."

Bev sighed. She looked away from me, scratched her neck, and for a moment I was terrified she was going to tell me to leave. "Actually—well, sure, I remember that feeling."

"You do?"

"Oh, honey, of course," she said. She looked at me bleakly. "It wasn't really that long ago."

I closed my eyes. All he'd said was that they were changing the drugs, I reminded myself. He hadn't said the cancer was back, just that things were a little bit troubling.

"I remember the day they told me it was cancer," Bev said. "I was supposed to go to a meeting, but I just went home instead.

Didn't call anyone. Hid in bed. Let myself be terrified all day. The next day I got up and started fighting."

"I'm so scared," I said.

She looked at me. Those eyes, they were warm and melting, cow's eyes. "Listen, can I ask you something?"

I shrugged.

"What do you want more than anything else in the world?"

"What do I want? I want to live."

"Of course you do," she said. "But if that's not what you can control—if that's not what you're in charge of—what else is it that you want? That you can achieve?"

I shook my head, unsure what she meant.

"Listen, when I had cancer, I remember that I had to figure it out. It took me a while, but I realized . . . there were many nights when I was up late, my youngest daughter was still at home, I'd look at her sleeping and I'd think, all I want is for you to grow up happy. All I want is for you to be okay when I'm gone. Even more than I wanted to be healthy, I wanted her to be okay. I knew she needed me more than my other girls. That's what I wanted most."

"I know that feeling," I whispered.

"I realized that, and then I had something to focus on. Something to live for. To prepare her to keep going."

If I focused on the mess on her desk, I would not cry.

"Sometimes I knew my daughter would come into our bedroom when I was napping, or she thought I was napping, and I'd pretend to be asleep so she wouldn't think I was up worrying. It was sort of funny, this charade we put on for each other. Not like with my husband. He was just, 'Okay? You feeling okay, sweetheart?' And then off to work. But my daughter—she was so tuned in. I was so scared for her. More than even saving myself, I wanted to save her."

I looked at Beverly's warm wide face. It would be okay if I cried. I closed my eyes again and put a finger under each to catch the tears. Wordlessly, Bev handed me a tissue.

"Do you believe in God, Karen?"

I deflated, shook my head.

"Me neither," she said; I reinflated a little. "I'm a Catholic and all, sent my girls to Catholic school, but I never could believe in an actual guy with a white beard up there looking down on me. I sort of wished I could, though. It might have helped."

"I'm the same," I said, fingers still under my eyes. "The same way. Jewish, though."

"They want you to believe, don't they?"

"Who?"

"The message boards. Facebook. The priests."

"I only have a therapist. And my sister."

"Are they helpful?"

"If it weren't for my sister, I'd be dead already." Bev handed me another tissue.

"I'm glad you have her," she said. She waited for me to blow my nose. I crumpled up the tissue, stuck it in a pocket. I was pitiful. "So what did the doctor say today?"

I could barely get it out. "Troubling numbers."

"So that could mean anything."

"New medication," I said.

She nodded. "What I decided to do, when I was really sick—I didn't have God, I kept having to put on a front for my kid, I was absolutely terrible at taking things one day at a time—"

"Me too," I said.

"I decided to trust myself. Just trust that I was doing the right things. That I was getting the right care, had picked the right doctors. That I was taking care of myself, that I was preparing my daughter to live the best life she could. That helped me be optimistic. And being optimistic, I think, helped me live. Just, you know, having faith in myself and the world around me that it would be all right."

"I have no faith," I said.

"Well, get some," Bev said. "You wouldn't be where you are if you weren't smart enough to make the right choices. If you have no faith in God, have some in yourself."

"My son's father wants to take him away from me."

"No," Bev said, "he can't. He won't."

"He's going to try."

"While you're sick?"

I wiped my cheek with the back of my wrist. "He thinks I'm weak."

"Oh, c'mon," Bev said. "Anyone who knows anything about politics in this city knows how tough you are."

"How tough I used to be."

"Karen, listen," Bev said, and now she changed her tone, became steelier. "Ace needs you. That's why he hired you. Because you're tough. Nobody can take anything from you."

For the briefest of moments, she reached across the desk and touched my arm. In the quiet, cheerful office, I could almost not think about the infusion ward above us, the woman with the bluish skin, the fact that I was there to do the recon on the opponent.

Bev took a breath. "Listen, can I tell you something? Your man, no offense," she said, "your guy is a terrible guy."

"You think?" I said.

"I know," she said. "Someone should put that son of a bitch out of office, and I'll tell you, Karen, it might as well be me. Listen, I'm a woman, the mother of daughters—I can't stand being represented by that man. Twenty-year-old girls! It's such a cliché. And frankly, the fact that he barely bothers to hide it—that's what's most upsetting, I think. He doesn't even bother to hide."

"He's going to win," I said, trying to get in gear.

"He might not," Bev said.

"You know the polls?"

She made a pshaw gesture with his hands. "I think he won't," she said. "Look, I've beaten long odds my whole life. I was born"—she sounded like a seasoned candidate now—"to an illiterate farm worker and his fifteen-year-old wife. I came to America, went to college, got a graduate degree. I've been married for thirty-nine years. How many odds are that? I'm a Dominican woman with my own secretary."

"That's not bad," I said.

"And I haven't even gotten to the cancer. So when people ask me what I'm doing, how I think I can win, I tell them that I've always been a winner. Why would I stop now? Besides, I can drop a bomb on Ace whenever I want. There was another twenty-year-old, you know."

"Nobody cares," I said, but I did, in fact, feel energized by Bev's threat. "Incumbents are reelected about ninety percent of the time in city council races."

"Doesn't sound like one hundred percent to me."

"It's close enough."

"When the public finds out about his latest—"

"There's no proof."

"Not yet," she said.

I glanced up at the pictures behind her. Her daughters all looked like her, same big brown eyes. Her husband was bald with a mustache. Bev caught me looking. I wondered which one was the daughter that she loved the most.

Bev smiled at me, and the fraught air of competition dissolved. It was all an act anyway.

"What am I going to do?" I asked her. I fingered the name tag on my lapel with my fingertips. She should have called security or the psychiatry ward. What the hell was I doing here? I was a lunatic.

"You're going to keep living," Bev said. "You're going to keep working for your son of a bitch. You're going to keep living until you're dead. You're going to fight for your son. You're a mother," she said. "You have no choice. And you're going to trust yourself, that you're a hell of a campaign manager. It's going to be okay."

I didn't respond.

Her phone rang. "I've got to take this," she said.

"Thanks for talking with me."

"Good luck," she said.

"Good luck to you," I said, and I meant it. Then I made my

way out of her office, as behind me, Bev said, Hi sweetheart, I'm here, just some campaign business, and I felt good because I had just done another morning's work.

THAT NIGHT, YOU woke up screaming.

"Jake! Jake!" Allison was already by your side, already shushing you; she was sharing your room. "Jacob, baby."

I hadn't heard you shriek like this in the night since Dr. Susan explained to you my diagnosis.

"I had a dream," you said, when you could finally speak, "about Venom."

"Who is Venom?" I said at the same time Allie said, "Venom from Spider-Man?"

You nodded pitifully. "He's the bad guy in *Spider-Man 3*." Your voice was hoarse; you were shaking. "Can I sleep next to you?"

"How scary is *Spider-Man 3*, exactly? Just who is the intended audience for *Spider-Man 3*?"

"He had it at his house," you said.

"How scary is it?"

Allie said, "It's scary."

"Mom, he didn't know—"

"You weren't allowed to see it?"

"Don't yell at him," you said.

Your fucking father. I could not fucking believe it. As though you didn't have enough legitimate reasons to have nightmares? And now you had one more? It was everything I had not to pick up the phone right that second and lose my mind on him.

"Mom?"

"Come on," I said, taking your hand and walking you to my bedroom. I could not fucking even deal with this. Your father, giving you nightmares.

"Mom, please? I told him it was okay."

"But you know it's not."

"I wanted to see it."

"We'll talk about this tomorrow, Jacob."

"Just please promise? Don't yell at him?"

"Jake—"

"Please?"

"Okay," I sighed. I needed you to go back to sleep and I knew you wouldn't if you thought I was going to go ballistic on your father. "Okay."

"Thanks, Mom," you said. In five minutes you were back asleep, because you were a child and had a gift for it. I, on the other hand, was up for the rest of the night, waiting for the sun to rise so that I could call your father and freak out at him. Except that by the time day finally broke, I was so tired that I realized I wouldn't even be coherent, and also you looked so still and sweet in your sleep, that I decided I'd keep my promise to you and, for the moment, spare your father my righteous wrath. Also, of course, I was the tiniest bit glad this happened. It would be proof in court, if I needed it, that your father was entirely unfit to be your legal guardian.

12

Ten fifteen, on my way to Dr. Steiner's, I spied the man himself, your father, walking down the street with a shopping bag in his hand. At first I thought it was a coincidence; how many years had it been since I'd seen him and now, suddenly, he was everywhere?—but then I realized that, no, he was heading for our apartment and that the shopping bag probably tolled for thee. Jesus, Jake, how much shit did a six-year-old need? Fortunately he didn't know that you were at Chelsea Piers with Allie and that whatever goodies he was going to dispense with were bound for an empty home. Reflexively, I wanted to hide. I almost made it to the Starbucks on the corner. But then he saw me and smiled that I'm-married-now smile, and I knew I'd look like a fool if I ran. I smiled back.

"I was in the neighborhood," he said, by way of greeting. It was the first time I'd seen him without you around to shield me, and my heart immediately hurt, my stomach hurt.

"Okay," I said.

"Getting coffee?"

"Going to the doctor," I said.

"Everything okay?"

"Sure," I said. I wanted to bring up *Spider-Man 3* but held my tongue. "It's great."

"Time for some coffee before you go?"

A coffee date with your father. I looked down at what I was wearing: grubby black pants, a loose T-shirt. "No," I said. He looked disappointed. "But you can walk me to the bus stop."

We walked to the block in silence that was not at all companionable; if I'd known he was coming, I would have put on lipstick. Who did he think he was that he could just show up in our neighborhood like this? Was he stalking you? Was he stalking me? Did he want to see if I was still sick, if I was any closer to death?

"What's in the bag?"

"Some of Jake's clothes," your dad said. "He left them at our house."

"He was just there for one night."

"He overpacked," he said. "He brought three bathing suits."

"I see." You'd brought every bathing suit you owned. We reached the bus shelter and I scanned the schedule posted to the side. Eight minutes till the next crosstown. "You could have mailed them."

"I had some stuff to do in the city today anyway. It's a nice walk up from midtown."

I didn't say anything, looked down the street to see if maybe a bus would show up early.

"Anyway, I was thinking—"

"You let him watch *Spider-Man 3*."

"What?"

A Vietnamese girl I recognized from the nail salon joined us in the bus shelter.

"He had nightmares last night. Screaming nightmares. Because you showed him a deeply inappropriate movie. Why would you do that? What's the matter with you?"

"I covered his eyes during the scary parts."

"Are you joking?"

"No, I . . . He said he wanted to watch it."

"Do you have *any idea* what the thirteen stands for in PG-13?" I was hissing. "He's six, you idiot."

"I didn't—"

"Like he needs anything else to be afraid of right now."

"I didn't—" He honestly looked abashed. "Is he okay?"

"Of course he's okay," I said. "It was just a nightmare."

"Yeah, but—" He gripped his shopping bag, looked down. "I'm really sorry."

I shrugged. I wondered how my cheeks looked; this morning they looked sallow so I slapped myself a few times, lightly, to get the blood running. I couldn't look sick in front of your father—or any sicker than naturally I must have looked.

"But otherwise we had a good time," your father said, his moment of mortification passing in the breeze.

I slapped my cheek lightly, quickly, like I was slapping a bug. "Bugs," I said.

"Actually, I was thinking," your dad said, "some of my clients have box seats at Yankee Stadium. They never use them. And the Yankees hardly ever give anyone nightmares." He tried a grin.

"Right," I said. The morning was muggy and smelled like trash, even inside the shelter.

"I'd be happy to take Jake some time."

I watched the traffic for a moment, counted nine yellow cabs. But the bus wasn't coming. I breathed in five seconds, out three. I had to ask him. "Dave, what do you want, exactly?"

"I want to get to know our son."

"Our son? Really? *Our* son?"

He gave me a curious look. "Yes," Dave said. "Jake. Our son."

"Give me a fucking break." A few other people joined my manicurist inside the bus shelter, so I wasn't able to speak as loudly as I wanted to, but I managed to get enough growl into my syllables to make my point. "He's not *ours*."

"I'm not sure what you mean," Dave said. Gone was the slightly confused look; now he sounded peeved. "Jacob is our son."

"Jesus," I said.

"I don't understand why you're so angry at me," he said.

"You don't *understand*?" and I realized that in fact I was angry. I was furious, which was much easier than being scared.

"Karen, you tell me that you're pregnant and then you disappear—"

"You *kicked me out*—"

"That's actually not true."

"Excuse me?" We were both loudly whispering, like actors.

"Karen, I called you that afternoon and I called you again the next day and the next day. You led me to believe you were getting an abortion and you never wanted to see me again."

"That, friend, is bullshit."

"That, friend, is not." Dave wasn't whispering anymore; in fact, he was almost yelling. "You said something along the lines of how you'd never bring an unwanted baby into the world, that it was your right as a woman, you could do whatever you wanted. You didn't need me, you never needed me."

"You fucking Catholic, all you hear is abortion, you never called me."

"Karen," your father said, and he wasn't quite yelling, but he was dragging my arm so that he could get me out of the shelter and away from the pricked-up ears, even the manicurist was listening, and I thought fuck I'd be late for Steiner unless I got a cab. I wanted him to pay for my fucking cab.

"Karen," he said again, once he'd dragged me to a fire hydrant four feet away from the shelter.

"Dave," I said. "Please don't touch me."

He didn't let go. "I am not going to keep playing he-said she-said with you, but I am going to tell you that for six years I had a son I didn't know about. For six years you kept the biggest secret from me I can imagine anyone keeping. I am not going to let you keep him from me again."

"What does that mean?" I shrieked, fear intruding on rage.

"It means I want to see him, Karen!"

"You can't take him from me!"

"I know him now and I will keep knowing him."

"He is *my* son! *Mine!* And if you think you can—"

He was still holding my arm. I don't think he knew how easily I bruised. "He is *ours.*"

I pulled my arm away, wiped my eye with it.

Jacob, he never called. Your father was remembering what he

wanted to remember in order to make himself feel better. Your father wanted to remember himself as the kind of person who called. But still, believe me—I was the one with the broken heart, and I'm the one who remembers every second of my pregnancy like I remember every freckle on your face.

"I am just asking," your father said, "to be part of his life."

"You can't take him from me," I said.

"I'm not talking about taking him," your dad said. "I'm talking about knowing him."

"You don't even know what movies he's allowed to watch."

"So I'll learn."

"You're too stupid to learn."

"Jesus, it's no wonder you stayed single."

"Fuck you."

He paused. "You cannot keep me from him," he said. "You just can't."

I wiped my eye again. I thought about losing you, how I had once lost your bastard of a father.

No bus. No taxis anymore either.

"Dave, I'm dying. Okay? I'm dying. What else do you want from me?"

"I want you to say that I can see him."

I had a vision then of you squeezed in between him and Megan, the Megan I knew from Facebook, pert little blonde, on some holiday card, a *Christmas* card, they would never raise you Jewish, those fucking papists, and I knew that I was crying there on the sidewalk next to the grimy bus shelter. I was crying in front of your father, who was winning or who had already won.

"I have *cancer*, Dave."

"I know," he said. And nothing else. At the hydrant, a dog stopped to pee. I looked down Seventy-Second.

"I'm not talking about taking him," Dave said. "I just want to get to know him. Please."

"Why should I believe you?"

"Why shouldn't you?"

"There are too many reasons to count," I said.

Dave shook his head, blew out through puffed cheeks, but if he was going to say something, he thought the better of it.

"My bus is here."

"Do you need company?" he asked. "At the doctor's? I'll go with you."

Did he want to meet Steiner to find out just how quickly I'd be out of the picture? "I'm fine, thanks. Give me the bag and I'll bring it home."

He looked down at his Trojan horse of a shopping bag, his little pretext full of your clothes. I took it from him as the bus pulled up. The bus would make me late, but it didn't really matter; Steiner always made me wait at least twenty minutes.

"Thanks for dropping it off," I said.

"I'll call you," he said.

"Sure you will," I said, as though he'd called me all those years ago, as though he'd been waiting to call me ever since. I watched him standing there as the bus pulled away, keeping his eyes on mine, a poor facsimile of a big romantic scene.

BUSES RAN A little faster in the summer since the streets were a little emptier, and I made it to Steiner's office right on time. I'd managed to pull myself together on the bus and was finally wearing lipstick by the time I checked in with the receptionist. To my surprise, Steiner was ready for me. Because I was in a scared mood I took this as a scary sign.

"Are you okay, Karen?" Steiner asked. His tie was decorated with tiny hot-air balloons. "You seem distressed."

"I'm fine." I was sick of being in other people's offices surrounded by other people's diplomas; I missed my own.

"Listen, don't look so scared."

"I look scared?"

Steiner nodded. He wanted to confirm some numbers, have his nurses take some more blood, which was curious since I had just been in surgery and surely could have donated all the blood the labs would ever need while I was under, but no, that wasn't the way it went, my veins had to be being strip-mined like a West Virginia coal deposit. "Are you rethinking my prognosis, Dr. Steiner?"

"Why would we do that?"

"Because of what you said on the phone."

Steiner picked up a sheaf of papers, dropped them on his desk. Shuffled through them. Avoiding my gaze. "There are some cancer cells recurring on your intestine," he said. "Surgery isn't really an option for this, so we're going to start you with Avastin and Taxol infusions."

"Am I still in remission?"

"Technically, no," he said. He looked apologetic. "But we'll get you back there soon. I promise."

My heart was pounding like a series of gunshots. "I'm not in remission."

"Karen, I told you that was a possibility."

"You did? When did you say that?" Jesus, I was so sick of men telling me they'd already told me things they'd never told me.

He flipped through his papers again. "There was always a possibility this would happen. But this new drug will help stave off growth."

I'd loved remission. I'd been so proud of my remission.

"We'll need to get you scheduled for an infusion next week," Steiner said.

I stared glumly at his stupid hot-air balloons. I could have just let that bus run me over.

"Karen, have you been seeing Susan Reed? Has she been helpful?"

Dr. Susan. "She's in Martha's Vineyard for the summer."

"I'm sure she'll take your calls."

"I haven't felt like calling," I said.

Steiner sighed. "You working? Are you able to work?"

"I hate my candidate," I said.

"We'll go after these rogue cells," Steiner said. "We'll get you back into remission. In the meantime, try to focus on the positive. Really, it helps. Studies prove it."

"You need studies to prove that being positive is helpful?"

Steiner patted me on the back as he ushered me out toward the examining room for the nurses to draw my blood. "I thought you'd feel better if I put it like that."

WHEN I WAS thirty-five, long before my diagnosis or even my bloated belly, I woke up one day to see that I was old. I felt as shocked as Gregor Samsa must have been the day he woke up a bug. Gray hairs had appeared along my temples overnight;

my hands were suddenly lumpy with veins. My back twinged when I stood up too quickly. What was shocking about this, in retrospect, was that various women's magazines had led me to believe that I wouldn't start aging until I was at least forty-seven. You can imagine my surprise.

I was unmarried, even though I'd always assumed I'd get married before I was old; I had no children and it seemed possible to me that I might never have children. I guess what I'm saying is that I'd always thought I'd have more time, and then suddenly, when I was thirty-five, I realized that I didn't have more time. Does this seem silly to you? Perhaps you've grown up in a more rational generation; perhaps American life expectancy has started to decline after years of increased longevity—what I mean is that perhaps, for you, youth isn't as protracted as it was for me, for people born in the 1970s. I hope that's the case and that when you're thirty-five you don't think you're still kind of closing down your twenties.

"Well sure," Chuck said to me when I confessed to him that I was old and that I was only going to get older. "If you were living during the twelfth century you'd be considered ancient if you weren't already dead. Age is a construct. Feel however you want to feel." I'd noted that Chuck, like a lot of men from wealthy families, seemed to get only more handsome as he got older.

"I feel decrepit," I said.

"You look the same," Chuck said. "Maybe get a haircut?"

I got a haircut, but the depression continued and deepened; Chuck recommended a therapist he liked, but she didn't take insurance so instead I did what I'd always done: I turned to books. From the Barnes & Noble in Chelsea, back when there was a

Barnes & Noble in Chelsea, I stocked up on things I'd always meant to read: *Les Misérables, Eichmann in Jerusalem, Band of Brothers.* Fiction and nonfictional war, suffering greater than my own. Stuff my dad had liked. It usually did the trick. When I'd been depressed right after college, I'd found great comfort in *The Rise and Fall of the Third Reich.*

But the books didn't enliven me the way I'd hoped, and neither did the purchase of several new pairs of shoes, and frankly I'm not sure even having you did it, since I was geriatric *primigravida* and subjected to about nine million genetic tests. (In the end, you know what did it? Cancer. Forty-one is like a child when it comes to ovarian cancer. Everyone choruses, all the time: but you're so young!)

Anyway, I mention this now because I've been thinking about you and your youth, and even my own relative youth; we are young until we decide to be old. We are alive until we decide to be dead. The pile of books that I bought during that bout of depression almost a decade ago is still here. They're all good, if ponderous, and if you're going to read any of them (you should probably read all of them), I'd like to recommend *Eichmann in Jerusalem.* This is not only so that you can feel a connection to certain historical events, but also because it's a curious meditation on a time—the 1960s—and place—Israel—and because Arendt is very smart about death and dying. She quotes a German who says that the reason more Germans weren't willing to help Jews was because they knew that if they were caught, they would die anonymous deaths. They'd just be taken out and shot somewhere and buried in a pit with all the other traitors to the

Nazi cause. And to the German, an anonymous, pit-of-corpses death was even worse than dying itself.

I kind of understand that German guy: to a certain way of thinking, even death isn't so bad if it means people will really make a whole deal out of you. Sometimes that's what I think about: that I will die with the comfort of knowing I'll be memorialized. After my funeral, there will be a catered luncheon at the Columbia Club, courtesy of Bruce's membership and seat on that university's board. If you don't want to go, I told your cousins, they should take you anywhere you want. Yankees games, pizza, anything.

I'm going to pack these books up and add them to the crates we'll take to Seattle. When I unpack your bookshelves I'll add these to the top, and tell Allie that they're there, and that you should read them when you're ready to. Not when you're depressed, necessarily. Just when you feel like remembering.

"You left all this stuff at Dave's house," I said when you came home from Chelsea Piers, showing you the bag.

"I was going to leave it there," you said. "For when I go back."

I waited for a moment to see if I felt stabbed, but for some reason I didn't.

"I guess that makes sense," I said.

You nodded. Of course it made sense. He was your father and you were certain you'd be seeing him again. I kissed you on the forehead. The next day I headed off to my first Avastin infusion with Adolf Eichmann in my arms.

As Steiner promised, the side effects really weren't so awful, and after a few days of pukiness, I started to feel like my old disgusting self again. At ten o'clock on Sunday, I declared that I was ready for (gentle, geriatric) action, and then we kind of lazed around the apartment, deciding what to do. My instinct was to lie in bed and wait to barf, but that didn't seem like the most productive way to spend a warm weekend morning in New York.

"We could go to Jones Beach," Allie said. "Remember how we did that as kids?"

"You hated Jones Beach," I protested, so I didn't have to admit I had no energy. "Those gross changing rooms? The jellyfish?"

"The *Times* says it's nicer now."

"I could go to the beach," you said. "Or Coney Island." Oh my God, no, I couldn't face Coney Island—the rides? The hot dogs?

"I've never been to Coney Island!" Allie said, clapping her hands. "Oh totally, let's do it."

"It's like hours away on the train," I said.

"One hour," you said. "I went with Kyle."

"You hate being on the train for a whole hour."

"No I don't."

I escaped this one when the phone rang. Ace. Finally. I took the phone into my bedroom.

"You're a hard man to get a hold of," I said, sounding peevish despite myself. "I spoke to someone on the Hernandez campaign who's been spreading rumors about you."

"Beverly's dead," Ace said.

I half-sat, half-collapsed down on the bed.

"I just found out," Ace said.

"When?"

"Just now. You're the first person I called."

"But I just saw her."

"You saw her?"

"For the campaign," I said. "Two days ago. What happened?"

"Stroke," he said. "Not much need for a campaign now, huh? They're not going to find someone to take her place for an election that's in—what, four months? I guess I'm running unopposed." Christ, in his mind he was already installing his furniture in the mayor's office. Meanwhile, I was tingling all over. Bev. Who lived until she died. Three children and five grandchildren that all looked like her. Her office, her own secretary. Illiterate father and look at me now.

Bev was cancer-free. Paul Tsongas was cancer-free.

"Do you know anything else?"

"Just that she died at work a few hours ago. In her office on a Sunday, the poor broad. A guy I know at Roosevelt told me. I don't think it's public yet."

My laptop was on the bed; I flipped it open and went to Bev's website, but there was nothing there, nor on her Facebook page. Nothing on the Roosevelt Medical Center site.

"Are you sure?" I thought of her crowded little office, the photographs.

"Positive."

"Stroke?"

"Evidently it's some kind of complication from the medication she was on. That's what my friend said. But I don't know, what do I know? I'm not a doctor."

"She was healthy," I said. "She said she was healthy."

I could practically hear Ace shrug.

"Where are you now?"

"In a car on my way from City Hall," he said. "I've got a meeting tonight, then dinner with a few of the guys from the precinct. Photo op, not that I'll need it, I guess."

"We'll need to put out a statement."

"Get something to Amani."

"I will," I said, then let the conversation sag. I could hear sirens passing Ace's car on the highway.

Beverly. She'd touched my hand and told me it would be okay.

"Anything else?" Ace asked.

It was beside the point of course, but I still wanted to know. I didn't hear any gloating or satisfaction in his voice—he wasn't cruel enough to wish his competition dead. But he sounded nonchalant, undisturbed. A good woman in her fifties dead of a stroke and he was in a car on the West Side Highway and his life would go on undisturbed, unchanged.

"Ace—"

"I'll still pay you your fees," he said. "You'll still be the head of my campaign."

"Ace," I said, flushing—I didn't want to talk about money, but also *of course* he was going to pay me my fucking fees; it was in the contract—"Ace, you didn't do something indiscreet in France, did you?"

"What are you talking about?"

"I spoke to someone on the Hernandez campaign—"

"There is no more Hernandez campaign."

"Who said that you . . ." I couldn't even get the words out, which was surprising. In the past I'd been much better about confronting my clients. "Who said that you flew one of your interns to France after Jill left. A female intern."

Ace paused.

"Ace, that's true?"

"Girl had never been to Europe before. Had hardly left New York State. I gave her a history lesson. You know, Karen, once upon a time I used to teach American history."

"You brought one of your staffers to France to teach her a lesson in American history?" That cocksucker. But although I tried to muster some indignation, all I really felt was heartbreak. Bev, poor decent Bev. She called it like she saw it: Ace was a son of a bitch. I wondered where her memorial service would be. Would they do something at Roosevelt Medical? The grandkids, her young grandkids. The one from the video. Her husband with the mustache, the daughter she was so worried about.

"Listen, Karen, I appreciate your concern, but there's nothing more to say about it. It was perfectly innocent."

"I'm not an idiot, Ace." But even I could hear the resignation in my voice. "You don't have to lie to me."

"She was there for a day and a half on her way to meet friends in England."

"France isn't on the way to England."

"It can be."

"What's her name?"

"You don't need to know it."

"If Jorge Grubar knows it, I need to know it."

"Who's Jorge Grubar?"

"He manages the Hernandez campaign."

"There is no more Hernandez campaign."

I was so tired. "Jorge called me to report that an intern of yours went to France to meet with you after Jill left. Ace, if Jorge Grubar knows, don't you think that Jill will find out?"

"There's nothing for Jill to know."

"Are you kidding me?"

"You keep my wife out of this, Karen. There is nothing for her to know."

"How could you do this to her, Ace? Again?"

"Listen, if I tell you it was innocent, it was innocent." His voice turned hard. He paused again, then attempted to sound jocular. "What does it say about me that my own campaign manager finds me so hard to trust?"

I lay back on my bed; I was melting with exhaustion. I didn't trust Ace because he was one of the least trustworthy people I'd ever met, and he was lying to me, the only person he really wasn't supposed to lie to. But Bev was gone, and soon enough I'd be gone too, so I guess he thought he could.

"Ace, if this comes out, it'll be very bad."

"There's nothing to come out, Karen. Honestly. You don't have to sound so concerned."

"I'm not *concerned*," I said. "I'm furious." Although what I really was, was grief-stricken.

"This is nothing," he said. "And if it were something, it would be your job to make it go away."

"Is there something I need to make go away?" Silence. "Ace?"

And this was where our line got disconnected. I knew I should call him back, but I didn't have the energy to beg for the truth.

I didn't have the energy to play this one like the player I used to be. I waited for the phone to ring; it didn't.

And honestly, Jake, how lucky for him that Bev was out of the picture, that he was essentially running unopposed, that Jill would never know, and maybe the whole world had conspired to work in Ace's favor, the inconvenient women either oblivious or dead. The convenient woman winning a trip to France for thirty-two hours of *fromage* and fucking.

And Bev dead. Of course, this sort of luck on the part of my candidate never used to bother me.

If the world found out, Ace would issue a statement or a denial and smear the intern's credibility, and that would be that. He would be left with only his wife to appease. Surely she'd agree to be appeased. Why did I begrudge him his good luck?

I clicked again on Bev's website and found a statement:

It is with great sadness that we announce the passing of Beverly A. Hernandez, mother, grandmother, daughter, wife; dedicated development director of Roosevelt Medical Center for twenty-one years; and candidate for City Council in 2013.

I took a breath; I was aware of the bandage on my abdomen.

In lieu of flowers, Beverly's family asks that donations be made to the O'Malley Breast Health Center at Roosevelt Medical Center. Dates for a public memorial service will soon be announced.

And I knew it was true. When I'd heard it only from Ace's mouth, I hadn't felt the imperative to believe it.

13

Even though I told her she was free to go home, Allie insisted on staying. She claimed it was because she wasn't sure how I'd handle the new medical regimen: a day in the infusion ward every three weeks, nausea in the morning and dizziness the rest of the day, and my hair thinned to the point where I was back on the wig. (Do you remember this Jake? Did you notice?) But actually I think she stayed because it was easier to take care of me than it was for her to go home. Bruce and Ross were at each other's throats all the time. Camilla had gone ahead and pierced her septum, and Dustin had been keeping a medium-sized collection of garden snakes in the pool house, which scared the shit out of the groundskeeper when he found them. So maybe life in our slightly cramped apartment seemed good to her too.

In the following days, I started working again, at low levels of intensity and duration. I wrote a moving statement about Bev for Ace to release and told him that in the meantime he was to keep his neck clean. "That's what I pay you for," he said, and he was right—in the absence of any real competition, that was all he paid me for. He was in a preposterously good mood all the time now, thanked me for all my terrific work.

I called Jorge Grubar to leave my condolences. He didn't call me back.

I also spent a good part of every afternoon with you, doing all the things we liked doing: the Central Park Zoo and movies and even a schlep one afternoon all the way out to stupid Jones Beach. Thoughts of Bev would float through, and I would remember her warm voice and feel grateful that I'd met her. It felt like an odd bit of luck that I'd gotten there right in time.

August was turning out to be surpassingly mild, which was a relief, and at night we opened the windows and turned off the air. You had a long list of first grade reading to prepare for, but I also read you some of the books I loved when I was your age, and you were patient with me when I reached for *The Phantom Tollbooth* and *Just So Stories*. You and I would read until you were practically asleep, and those were the best parts of my days by far.

I hope you remember them, Jacob.

And then, four days before Allie was finally due to depart, your father called. "Hey," he said.

I knew who it was, but I acted like I didn't. "Yes?"

"It's Dave," he said. "Dave Kersey."

"Yes," I said. I allowed the quiet to fester. Late at night, when I couldn't sleep, I'd been working on this book for you, and trying not to reread the parts about Dave, but sometimes I couldn't help it and it would make me fall apart, the way that you looked when you ran into his arms. I kept rereading those pages. I'd thought about erasing them, they made me feel so raw.

"How are you feeling?"

"I'm great," I said, although actually what I felt was the sudden onset of all that ice. It was two in the afternoon and you and I were planning a trip to Fairway for groceries. Allie was digging around for our reusable bags.

"No more . . . Nothing bad happening? On the medical front?"

"Dave, what can I do for you?"

"I, um—" He cleared his throat. "I'm wondering if you'd like to bring Jacob over for dinner this weekend if you don't have plans."

"I have plans," I said.

"Mom! We're ready!" You and Allie both stood in my bedroom door, each holding colorful grocery bags. Fairway. I had my list.

"You have plans both nights?" Dave asked. "Megan's back from Brazil and she'd really like to meet you both."

My stomach clutched. Megan.

"Maybe," Dave said, "maybe you could do brunch?"

"Mom! Come on, we're going!"

"Is that Jake?" Dave asked.

I allowed that it was.

"Can I say hi?"

"We're on our way out, Dave."

"It'll just be a minute."

"Dave? Is that my dad?" You dropped the bags and rushed to the phone. "Hey! I got to level five on Rabbit Invasion."

Noise on Dave's end.

"Yeah, I like totally crushed the garden level and then I got to the part where the baby bunnies blow up the farm."

Three minutes later, you handed me the phone—even with your father, you weren't much of a phone person. "Can we go, Mom?"

"What?"

"Dave said we were invited to have lunch at his house this weekend. All of us. Can we go? Please?"

Going through you to get to you. I took the phone back.

"I'm sorry, Dave, we just don't have the time this weekend."

"Karen, don't do that." Allie stood next to you, looking disappointed in me.

"Allie, we're really busy," I said to her, loud enough so your father could hear. "You're leaving Sunday."

"What does that matter?"

"Mom! I want to see him!"

"Karen?" your father said tentatively on the other end of the phone. "It doesn't have to be a big thing. I mean, just lunch. We can go out somewhere if you'd be more comfortable at a restaurant. But, you know, we'd love to host. You could see the place."

"I've seen it."

"It's different now."

I said nothing.

"You could see where Jake slept when he came over," he said. "I know you were concerned."

"*Mo-om!*" you wailed from the other side of the couch, and I knew Dave could hear you.

I sighed, petulant. "What time do you want us and what should we bring?"

He wanted us at noon on Saturday. That meant Allie would be there, which was a relief: I didn't know if I could face this without her, even though she had a son who was at war with her husband, a daughter whose septum ring she had to remove. And our father—someone had to take care of our father. But still I wanted my sister with me, only me.

"Thanks, Karen," your father said.

"Stop thanking me," I said.

I stomped around Fairway throwing pointless things in our basket: the kind of cereal you'd never eat, the runny sort of cheese I could barely stomach. I still had some hair underneath my wig, so my scalp felt scratchy.

"Karen?" Allie asked as I plowed my way through the poultry (ground, whole, organic, kosher). "Karen, what are you doing?"

I didn't answer her, just barreled around the corner, Allie in pursuit, and loaded up on strange multicolored salsas. You had shuffled away toward the chips and cookies, and I shouted at you—too loudly—to reel you back in.

"Karen, you're buying duck legs?"

I looked down into the cart. I could throw a temper tantrum if I wanted to; it was my prerogative. "Yes," I said. "I'm buying duck legs. Is there a problem?" There were people all around us, moms with their jumbo packs of juice boxes, single women with their yogurts, food snobs with their galangal and lemongrass. Fairway was like a gigantic hangar where it was easier to find exotic fruits than it was Lean Cuisine. I grabbed you by the sleeve, slammed my cart in the other direction, went back to poultry and threw two more duck legs in the pile.

"Jesus," Allie said, and I did not respond.

At checkout I paid for upward of three hundred dollars worth of crap. "Karen, what are you going to do with all this?" Allie asked gently, and I wondered if she was judging me for poor spending choices or if she was only judging me for my temper tantrum.

"I'm going to eat it."

"Hmmm," Allie said.

We needed to take a cab home because of all the bags and that was another ten dollars you would never see. On the other hand, you and Allie gave me the space to calm down by going to the movies without me that night; I spent my quiet time stalking Megan on every available social network before finally falling asleep in my wig.

Two mornings later I met Ace in the Bronx for breakfast at JJ's, a diner that sat squarely in the shadow of Yankee Stadium. We would head from there to Beverly Hernandez's memorial service at St. Boniface, up the road, the Catholic church of the Bronx political and administrative class, to which Ace made a hefty donation once a year in order to keep the priest and staff quiet about his pro-choice stance. I was looking forward to seeing Beverly's friends and acquaintances and also giving Ace the opportunity to pretend to be a mensch.

He was already waiting at JJ's when I got there; this was a surprise because Ace was almost never on time. He looked handsome—nice navy suit, maroon tie, thick hair pomaded back, crooner-style. But I could see him startle when he looked at me, and I knew it was because we hadn't seen each other in many months.

"So how you holding up, anyway?" he said, his voice more gentle than it ever was on the phone. He took me by the arm, kissed my cheek. He smelled like leather and pine, a fine gentle-man's cologne.

"I'm okay, Ace."

"That a wig on your head?"

I touched my hair reflexively, sat down on my end of the booth.

"I thought you said you were doing all right," he said.

"I'm on a new medication. It thins my hair more than usual."

He leaned across the table, patted my hand with a sort of fatherly ineptitude. "What are your doctors saying?"

"They're saying I'm fine."

"Are they really?" He sat back, assessed me critically, the wash of concern lingering on his face. Jesus, how shitty did I look? I'd spent extra time on my makeup this morning, and usually the wig brought a veneer of health to my otherwise spotty complexion. And I was wearing a nice purple dress and my new leather jacket!

"Ace, you're giving me a complex."

"I just . . . I don't think I realized . . ."

"You didn't realize?"

The waitress came by and dropped off two coffees. "Anything else you need, Ace? I got your eggs cooking."

"You want something?" he asked, gesturing to me with his coffee cup. I had no appetite, but I didn't want to give Ace the impression I was about to keel over, so I ordered some toast.

"That's it?" Ace and the waitress said at the same time.

"That's it," I said, ashamed.

JJ's was a very Bronx hybrid of a Greek diner and Dominican gentleman's club, with feta omelets and a bunch of *abuelos* in the corner hunched over their *cafés con leche*, chatting in Spanish. There was 1950s music on the stereo—Dion, Gerry and the Pacemakers—and stout waitresses in faded pink outfits. Ace conducted most of his Bronx business meetings there, since half his constituency ate at least a meal a week in the place and liked to recognize him at his usual table.

"So," he said, dumping three minicartons of half-and-half in his coffee, "you guys are still going to send out the direct-mail piece?"

"Can't hurt," I said. "You've already paid for it."

Ace nodded, smacked a few packets of Sweet'N Lo's against the side of the table. Then he tucked a napkin into his shirt like he was some kind of trencherman. "You know, part of me is sad I don't have an opponent anymore. This doesn't feel like much without any competition. And what a shitty way to die too. A stroke at your desk on a weekend. I mean, come on."

"At least she wasn't in a hospital bed," I said. "She was living her life."

"Yeah, but—"

"She lived until she died." I didn't want him to say anything bad about Bev—I wouldn't let him. The air-conditioning was turned up too high and I felt the chill penetrate my jacket. "Still seeing that college girl?" I asked.

"Really?" Ace laughed, swirled his spoon in his coffee. "We're back to that?"

"I just don't understand how you could have," I said. "Especially after all you've been through."

The waitress circled back with our food and plopped it on the table, then gave her hips a little shimmy as she turned away. Ace

266 | LAUREN GRODSTEIN

looked on appreciatively. "It's over," he said softly, his eyes still trailing our waitress. "You don't have to worry about it."

"Such a stupid risk."

His expression grew pointed. "Karen, enough. In four years, I'm running for mayor. I'm going to serve the city of New York for four more years as a councilman and then I will be running for mayor. That's what's important. I'd like you to stop carrying on about this crap. This is not your job."

But he couldn't bully me. "Of course it's my job. I'm trying to look out for you."

"Look out for my campaign," he said. "Not my personal life."

"You know they're the same thing," I said.

He scowled.

"Just tell me why," I said. "If you tell me why, maybe I can help—I can rationalize it. If I need to. If I need to make it go away."

"There's nothing more to say."

I found myself buttering my toast in the OCD Chuck style, just to have something to do with my hands. "You love your wife, though, don't you? I mean—I know it sounds old-fashioned, but—"

"Of course I do," he said. "Don't be stupid."

"So then why . . ."

He didn't respond for a good long while. Then, finally, "life." He paused again. "Do you know what I mean?"

"Explain it to me," I said, to see if he could.

"Young women," he said, "and I know how this might sound, but I need that energy. That enthusiasm. They give you that. It's not like with Jill. Jillie is history, my entire life story. But young girls, they make me feel alive."

"Why can't you get energy and enthusiasm from something less scandalous?" I asked. "You're a New York City councilman. You're a *grandfather*!"

"I'm old," he sighed.

"That's it?"

"Does there need to be anything else?"

Christ. "Do you know how lucky you are to get old?" I said, and he looked at me, perplexed for a moment, and then his expression softened into pity. The worst.

"You never think about it like that," he said.

"How did Grubar know?"

"She was from the neighborhood once upon a time," he said. "Everybody knows everything up here."

"Jesus," I said, but nothing more. What was the point? If it came out, we would handle it, but it probably wouldn't come out. We could have sat there arguing about it, but I was afraid we'd be late for Bev's funeral, which I didn't want to miss. "Her obituaries were pretty lame," I said.

"Whose?"

"Bev's," I said.

"You read the obituaries?"

"You didn't?"

"What's there to know? Dominican hospital administrator dies of cancer after half-assed half run for New York City Council. Leaves behind bereaved family. Donations should be made somewhere. I told Amani to make a donation."

"Could you try to be more charitable for a second?"

"I said I made a donation," he said.

"We have three and a half months before the election," I said. "Be a gentleman."

"Karen, come on," he said. "You know me."

I knew him. As we made the quick drive over to St. Boniface, I noticed that Ace had become more cautious behind the wheel—when I first met him he caromed around the Bronx thoroughfares like a race car driver, but now he sat closer to the dashboard and kept his hands at ten and two. He was, indeed, getting older. But that didn't make me feel sorry for him.

We were late when we pulled up to St. Boniface; already a crowd had gathered in the vestibule and on the stairway leading up to the church.

"Come on, let's go," I said.

"What are you so anxious for?" he asked me. "It's just a memorial service." Still, he relinquished his keys to an attendant, took my arm and led me up the stairs, a chivalrous gesture that was second nature. There was a reporter and photographer from the local paper, the *Bronx Times*, guys who looked familiar; Ace gave them a big smile as we walked into the nave, the photographer clicking away. He said he'd catch up with them later. "No problem, Ace," the reporter said, because my candidate was beloved.

Inside the church, I took a program and a memorial card from a kind-looking lady in an ugly suit. Beverly Annuncia Hernandez, on the cover of the program, over a picture of an angel hugging a cross. Jews don't go in for this kind of decoration, FYI. No angels, no crosses. No heaven or hell. I hope you know that. I hope Allie sent you to Hebrew school with the money I set aside.

I sat down next to Ace at a pew toward the middle of the room; he'd been shaking hands as he walked in, dispensed a few hugs. Pancake breakfasts and hospital openings and school graduations and memorial services—they were all opportunities to him, and he was terrific at them all. He was wearing his professional political face and frowning down at the program and the card in his hand, at the angel and the cross and the goopy bio.

Beverly Annuncia Hernandez was born on a beautiful winter's day in San Cristóbal, Dominican Republic, in 1952 and moved to her beloved Bronx with her mother when she was six. She was the first person in her family to go to college (Hostos Community College and Mount St. Mary) and the first to get a graduate degree (Hunter College in the City of New York). Beverly married her dear husband, Jaime, in 1980, and together they raised three beautiful daughters, Mariana, Catalina, and Rosanna. Anyone who had the pleasure of knowing Beverly knew that her husband, her girls, and her five grandchildren were the loves of her life.

In 2007, Beverly was struck by breast cancer, which she fought valiantly to remission two years later. Determined to make the most of whatever time she had left, Beverly decided to run for city council to help make her part of the Bronx, and all of New York City, a better place to live. Unfortunately, this terrible disease, against which Beverly waged the battle of her life, was not done with her, and on August 10 Beverly suffered a stroke that ended her life.

We ask all mourners at this celebration of Beverly Hernandez's life to consider wearing something pink tomorrow in her honor and to make a donation, no matter how big or small, to the O'Malley Breast Health Center at Roosevelt Hospital. Brave and resourceful physicians at O'Malley are doing everything they can every day to save amazing women like Beverly Hernandez, and we know that with more financial support, and the faith of friends like you, the battle against the disease of cancer will be won.

(Jake, I just refuse to wear pink. I'm sorry, Bev. I'm sorry, women of the world, breast cancer survivors and unsurvivors alike. I look fucking horrible in pink. I always have.) (Although if memory serves me right, ovarian cancer's color is teal.)

I felt sure Bev had been more interesting than these few dim facts of her life: it was all there on YouTube, after all. I made a note to myself to edit my own bio for my own memorial program; I wanted to include a list of my favorite books, for instance. Maybe some of my core political values.

The service began with an invocation from a priest, and I seemed to be the only one who didn't know all the words—we did a Christian song and then something that sounded like the AA prayer; I mouthed along. Then, after the priest stepped aside, the friends and co-workers trooped upstage to talk about Bev, again in the most anodyne platitudes. I'd been to enough funerals in my time (my own mother's, even) to know that a good eulogy is about as rare as a good steak, but still I was a little troubled at the fact that nobody could talk about Beverly without using words like *tough*, *struggle*, and *loving*. I was also dismayed that nobody could talk about her life without talking about her death.

I was tuning out, refining the list of speakers at my own funeral

(Chuck? Would he say anything good?) when Beverly's daughter Rosanna approached the podium. It was getting hot in the pews, and I'd been sitting too long, watched over by a hundred stained-glass saints. But when Rosanna came to the lectern the whole audience seemed to sit up in their seats, for here she was, one of the daughters, one of the grief-stricken, and so poised (as they say) and so lovely (she was lovely enough), and the people all around me stretched their necks to get a good look at her and her sadness. This had to be her, I thought. The favored daughter.

She ruffled the papers in front of her.

"The thing is," she began, as though she'd been talking to us for hours already, "it's so hard to eulogize a woman I never thought would die. I never thought my mother would die." She coughed a little, cleared her throat. She looked to be maybe twenty-six or so. She was slender, with glossy black hair she kept tucked behind her ears. Her face was mottled, as though she'd done more than her share of crying lately.

"And what I just don't know is how I'm going to live every day without my mother," she said. "I don't know—" Her voice echoed through the packed pews of the church; the other speakers' words had melted, but hers bounced against the corners of the room.

"I don't know how I'm going to get married one day. I don't know how I'm going to have my own children without her to hold my hand through the pregnancy and all that. For every one of my nieces and nephews, when they were born, my mother was there in the room, telling my sisters you can do this. You just keep breathing. You will do this. And then they brought their babies home, and it was my mom who sat up with them at night when the kids wouldn't sleep. It was my mom who took over when my sisters needed to nap. It was my mom who taught them how to mash up baby food and what to do when those kids had fevers. My mom was there and I know my sisters would not have been able to do it without her." I remembered Monica from the video.

Someone—perhaps her—let out a frightful sob from the front pew.

"How are you supposed to live without a mother?" she asked. "How am I supposed to live and keep living without her?"

I hadn't even noticed the tissues tucked in the pockets behind the pews until people started reaching in and pulling them out.

"I know . . . I know that I should have been prepared for this. I knew that she was sick and that she was never completely cured. And I know too that people live without their mothers all the time. I grew up with people who never really knew their mothers and people whose mothers left them when they were kids.

"But not her. My mother was there. No matter what else she had to do that day—and she was a very busy and successful woman—but no matter what else she had to do, my mother was there. She was there for school projects and sports games and graduations. She was there for no reason at all. Just to go out to lunch or something. And when I think about the fact that my mother is no longer here, I don't feel brave or courageous, like I will be strong because of the lessons she's taught me. I don't feel like I'll know how to go on because of her example. And I'm sorry, Mamá, because I know that's how you'd want me to feel.

You told me that, that I should remember you and feel strength because of your memory.

"But right now I cannot think of you at all, because when I think of you, all I can think about is how much I miss you, and then I can't think of anything else." Rosanna stopped looking down at whatever she'd written, was now gazing upward, toward the painted Jesus above her with a lamb in his arms. "I am so angry that you left us, Mamá. I don't want to be angry with you, but I can't help it. I'm so angry. I wish you had fought just a little harder, Mamá. I wish the doctors at O'Malley had done a little more. I know I'm not supposed to say that—that this wasn't your fault, that you *wanted* to be here, that you wanted more than anything, but still, you left, Mamá, and now I don't know who will help me live the rest of my life."

No, no, no, I wanted to say. This is not what she wanted. This is not what she prepared you for! She wanted you to be okay. More than anything! That's all she wanted.

I felt myself frozen under the petrified gaze of all those saints, and the audience, now equally horrified and moved. And as Ace reached out to (I think) squeeze my hand, I stood up and edged out of my pew, thinking Jake Jake Jake please don't hate me Jake. I'm so sorry, I can't help it, I'm fighting as hard as I can.

"The only thing I can say is that I've been cheated and my mother was cheated. We were cheated of even being able to say good-bye to her. We'd practiced saying good-bye to her so many times when she was sick, but then she has a stroke and dies at work. At work! So who does she say good-bye to? Her desk? I don't know, Mamá. Why did it have to end like this? Why couldn't you have waited just a little longer? Except I know that even if you waited a little longer I still wouldn't have known how to say good-bye to you, Mamá."

Rosanna would not be okay. I was so hot. I shuffled out of the church, sat down on the steps, and took off my jacket and then my wig and sat there, exposed, while the photographer on the stairs snapped away. I must have made a great mood shot, bald and sobbing.

"Could you stop that, please?"

"I'm sorry, ma'am," he said, but he didn't stop.

"I'll call the fucking cops," I yelled, which felt good. It felt good to yell. I did it again. "Fuck you I'll call the cops!"

"Okay, ma'am, okay," said the photographer, backing off.

Of course, I now knew why I was so eager to get to Bev's funeral. It felt like the closest I was going to come to previewing my own, and it was awful. I sat on the steps with my head in my hands. The Avastin's side effects were manageable most of the time but also irregular, seeming to come and go of their own accord rather than any sort of timetable. I closed my eyes against the sun. The sweat traced patterns down my back, between my breasts. The metal clasp of my bra felt like it was burning me. If Ace fired me, if I had no more work—and why shouldn't he fire me? Despite my contract, what was really left for me to do anymore? He was right, the race was as good as won.

I felt a presence next to me: my last candidate. "You holding up?" he asked.

"Funerals get to me these days."

"Understandable," Ace said, and patted my back, and I turned to look at him, feeling unexpected softness toward the old goat.

But instead of looking at me, his eyes were trailing the backsides of two young women walking along the street in front of us in short shorts. Ace made a low noise.

"Did you just whistle?"

He moved his hand from my back. "It's possible," he said. His eyes remained trained on the teenaged ass parade.

My mouth felt metallic with rage. "Ace," I said. "Go back inside."

"You'll be okay?" he said. I didn't answer, and after a second he was gone.

Moments later, the reporter and photographer danced back in my line of vision. Kit Rannells from the *Bronx Times*—I recognized him from last year's congressionals—scratching feverishly at his notebook.

"Kit, hey." He looked up blankly; I put the wig back on my head. "It's me, Karen Neulander."

"Oh hey, Karen. Didn't recognize you."

A weird little shot of adrenaline burst in me like when I leaked those abortion records all those years ago. I still felt the heat of Ace's lecherous hand on my back, the metallic taste in my mouth.

"I want you know to know there's nothing to those rumors," I said.

"Excuse me?" Kit was maybe twenty-three or -four, a puppy straight out of J-school. "Rumors?"

"There's nothing there," I said.

"Okay," Kit said. He looked confused for a split second, then got a little closer. "Are there specific rumors you're talking about?"

"C'mon, Kit," I said. "Do your own job."

He had a reporter's notebook stuck in his back pocket. "Right," he said.

I patted my wig down, put on some lipstick, and made my way back inside the church, leaving Kit to his cell phone and his imagination. When I saw Ace, I waited to feel angry again, or even guilty, but instead all I felt was a sort of righteousness. And then, again, the sorrow.

14

Saturday morning the rain came down fierce, woke us all up with its pounding on the windows. I stayed in my bed for as long as I could, listening to Allie get up with you, make you breakfast; I popped a Xanax and lay there while the television went on and a show's opening theme started and a little while later its closing theme started and then a new show came on. I heard you ask Allie if she thought I was still sleeping. She said that I probably was.

Finally, after listening to two more rounds of cartoons, I desperately needed to pee. The last of the bandages had been removed the day before and I was left with raw skin and achy bones. I toddled out of my room like a child, nodded at you and Allie, made my way to the bathroom.

"Mom! It's almost time to go!" You were still wearing your pajamas, had yogurt around your mouth. You had pulled all the pillows off the couch and had been sitting on them, beanbag style. Allie looked up at me apologetically from her coffee and her *Times*. She was leaving tomorrow, but I was trying not to think about that.

"Go where?"

"Mom! *To Dad's house!*"

"Jake, how can we go," I asked, "if you're not even dressed?"

You looked down at yourself, surprised to find yourself in your pajamas.

Oh, Jakey. "Give me two seconds," you said, and bolted into your room.

"I'll go pick up the car in a few," Allie said as I poured myself coffee, took a sniff, poured it out. She'd rented a car to go visit your father, since she didn't want us to be stuck at the mercy of New Jersey Transit, and there was no way I could ask your father to pick us up or even meet us at the bridge. It was ludicrously expensive for the day, but Allie said she'd cover it. That, plus the tolls—it was going to be almost $150. I felt stupider than I had before about my Fairway spending spree. I pulled a cherry-ginger-flavored Swiss yogurt from the fridge to make amends.

"You really going to eat that?" Allie asked.

I nodded bravely, got about half of it down.

An hour later, we were stuck in moderate traffic on the West Side Highway, heading up to the George Washington Bridge and thence to Englewood Cliffs. At every stop and start, you banged your little frustrated fist against the window. I would have been content to stay in traffic forever. I had decided, after a certain amount of carrying on, to wear the wig, although I was afraid that its lushness made the rest of me look even more fragile. Allie said I was overthinking and that, anyway, they knew I had cancer. I knew they knew, but I didn't want that to be what they were thinking about.

"You know they have an iguana, right?" you asked from the backseat.

"I didn't know that," I said.

"Yup. It's name is Friendly."

"Better than a pool house full of snakes," Allie said, snorting. She merged into the traffic heading toward the bridge, and I felt sad for a second that she didn't clip anyone and so we had no choice but to keep going. Soon enough there was the bridge, with its skyscraper-sized American flag hanging down from the highest beam (like any good liberal, I found ostentatious displays of American jingoism grotesque), and then we were following my phone's GPS out toward the low-rises overlooking the Hudson. I found myself sweating, and wasn't sure if it was the Avastin or the nerves or the rogue cancer cells or maybe just the heat; I turned the air all the way up.

"Mom, I'm freezing!"

"I don't care," I said. Allie had rented a big old SUV and the air-conditioning was like frost. I wiped my face.

"You nervous?" Allie asked.

"No," I said.

"You don't look nervous," she said.

"Good." Then we zoned out onto the Palisades, the thin shelf of cliffs facing the Hudson, across which lay civilization. Off exit 1, we headed south a little, then took a short road through a surprising patch of woods.

It was exactly as I remembered it. We rounded a circular drive, where a uniformed doorman (who looked familiar but whose name I could not remember) took our keys and said not to worry about parking. He would take care of it. I thanked him. Allie thanked him. I tried not to think, or remember anything, as we marched through the lobby. I tried not to remember anything as we stepped into the elevator.

"It's the sixth floor, Mom. The penthouse."

Only in New Jersey would the penthouse be on the sixth floor.

My heart was beating so fast by the time we got to Dave's door that I honestly wasn't sure I'd be able to keep moving, but the abject humiliation at the mere *idea* of passing out kept me strong. I knocked on the door; you pounded it. Allie stood just a little behind me as if to catch me when I fell. She even put her hand on my back for a second to prop me up.

The door opened. The old apartment. The smell of that old apartment. You'd think that years later, a woman moves in, you get yourself married, you buy new stuff, you install a few rugs, you get a plant, an iguana—you think all that changes and so the smell of your apartment changes too, but no, it didn't, it smelled just like I'd remembered it—a very distinctive sort of apple air-freshener smell, and it hit me hard like it did when I was pregnant with you, in those few weeks before I knew I was pregnant with you. When all the smells were so intense. When I felt your heart fluttering inside me and didn't even know what I was feeling.

"Dad!" You rushed past me and into Dave's arms. He picked you up and flung you around in a circle. How was it that he loved you so much? He'd spent all of two days with you? Wasn't that right? The day in Seattle, the day when I was in the hospital— and yet the look on his face and the look on yours, and the way he was spinning you around—

"Wow," said the woman who had opened the door. I hadn't even looked at her yet. But there she was. Wifey.

The ice was back. It was invading every part of me.

"Those guys really hit it off, huh?" Wifey said, big smile, big teeth. Calista Gingrich hair. "I'm Megan. Come on in."

We shook hands all around, me and Allie and Megan, and Dave and Allie, and Dave semihugged me and I semihugged him back, even though being there in that fake-apple-scented apartment almost destroyed my ability to hug or move or do anything at all. I could barely speak. I thought for a second I would choke. And then I thought to myself: Karen, Jesus Christ, grow up.

But at least (and despite the smell) the apartment *looked* completely different; an expensive-looking Indian rug was on the floor, and the black leather couches had been traded in for some hip-looking midcentury versions, and there was a Noguchi coffee table and an Eames lounge chair and eccentric lamps. The open kitchen had been remodeled too, and furnished with all sorts of expensive looking appliances. Webbed leather barstools lined up against a granite island. The dining table looked like it had come straight from a farmhouse, although surely it came from a pricey design store, and on it was laid an assortment of goodies and an ice bucket stocked with two bottles of champagne.

I took a seat on a midcentury sofa before anyone invited me to.

"Karen," Megan said, sitting down opposite me. "I'm so glad you were able to come. I know it's been a tough time, but I really wanted to meet you and Jacob."

Close up, I saw that Megan wasn't quite the beauty that she seemed to be in her (obviously well curated) Facebook photos, but she was still attractive and slim, with a wide, if thin-lipped, smile. She was wearing a loose black T-shirt and black leggings, an outfit both studiously casual and carelessly chic. I was wearing a long linen skirt and a white top, which made me feel eight million years old and frumpy, but the linen was cool and my legs had turned veiny and bad. I needed to keep them comfortable. And Allie had lied to me and told me I looked like I was a character in a Graham Greene novel.

"It was kind of you to have us."

"Of course!" Megan said. "I mean Dave is so excited to get to know Jake, and he sounds like such an incredible little boy—"

"He is," I said. "He's incredible."

"That's what I hear," Megan said, and for a moment something uncomfortable passed across her face, the briefest look, which was good. It made me feel better.

"Mom, you want to meet Friendly?"

I wanted to not talk to Megan and thus to meet Friendly; I followed you into the second bedroom. That whole room had been totally redone as well—redone in a way that exactly suited you and your interests. On the left-hand shelves were Lego models of Yankee Stadium and the AT-AT cruiser; on the right-hand shelves were sets of elaborate Playmobils. There was a laminate desk just the right size for a six-year-old and a double bed outfitted with Star Wars sheets and blankets. A bookshelf stocked with kid's books. The iguana lived in an oversized cage on the matching laminate bureau (a bureau that looked brand-new, that seemed certain not to have any clothes in it, since Dave had brought all your clothes back).

"Dave, how long have you had Friendly?" I asked as you reached into the cage to bring him out.

"We got him the night I was here!"

"You did?"

Why hadn't you told me? Or had you told me and I'd forgotten? An iguana? Would I have forgotten? Dave shrugged. "I'd been thinking about a pet. I thought it would be fun to let Jake help me pick one out."

He'd gotten Friendly for you.

"Dave, this is a really nice room," I said. I meant it to come out as an accusation, but of course it just sounded like a compliment.

"Thanks," he said. "I wanted to make it comfortable for Jake to stay."

So he was going to try to take you. He was! Here it was: the fucker admitting it! He was going to try to take you! Well, he couldn't. I'd sue the life out of him. I'd sue him with every penny I'd saved up for you. I'd defame him so hard his own mirror wouldn't be able to look at him. I remembered how.

I tried to exchange glances with Allie, but she was just gazing approvingly at the Playmobils, and at the view of the George Washington Bridge from the bedroom's window.

And then I realized: they had planned it together. There had been some sort of grand conspiracy. Allie didn't want you, she wasn't going to take you. She'd told Yuki to call your father and your father was going to take you from me with everybody's consent. Because your father didn't even need to sue me—all this time, I'd been thinking he would try to take you, but why? Why would he?

He could just wait for me to go.

He could spend the next two years finding a path through some bankrupting legal house of horrors or he could just—wait.

And then I'd be gone. And then he could take you. I held on to the desk.

"Karen?"

You'd be his.

"Are you okay? Do you need to sit?" Your fucking duplicitous father. "Do you need to lie down? Our room is right down the—"

Lie down in your father's bed! I shrieked at the thought of it, but fortunately I could pretend I was shrieking because you'd placed an iguana in my arms. "Isn't he cute?" you said.

I took a breath. I would not—I just would not let myself fall apart. The scaly horror I was holding.

"Mom? Isn't he?"

Deep breath. It's fine. You're alive every day that you're alive. "He's not as cute as Kelly," I said, even though I hated Kelly.

"I wasn't so sure about him myself," said Megan, taking him from my arms and putting him back in his cage.

I took another deep breath, but I still felt faint. All this and an iguana.

"Come on, Karen, let me get you something to drink."

"I'm fine," I said, but Megan had taken me gently by the arm—how fucking sick I must have looked, that she was touching me, thought she had the right to *touch* me—and we all trooped back into the living room, which, the more I looked at it, seemed like a clear and unimaginative rip-off of a million HGTV renovation shows, and I wondered who this Megan was in her leggings and her granite countertops—who could she really be? Who lived like this? Who got Dave Kersey to live like this? Who was okay renovating a room for the long-absent child of your husband's son by another woman? Who was okay waiting out that woman's life so you could bring that child into your home?

"That's a nice room," I said. "Did Dave just put it together?"

"Well, obviously we added a few things for Jakey," Megan said.

"Jake," I said. "Just—he's just Jake. I'm the only one who calls him Jakey."

"Right, of course," Megan said, smoothly. "Jake." She removed a bottle of champagne from the ice bucket, withdrew the cork smoothly. "Mimosa or straight up?" she asked.

"He's not going to move here," I said.

"Of course not," Megan said. "We know that. This is just for when he visits."

"But even after—even after I die. He's going to live with my sister," I said. "With her."

"Oh, Karen." She handed me a glass of champagne. "Nothing is imminent, right? You're here now, aren't you?"

What did she mean? "I just need you to know—"

"Megan, I just love this print," Allie said, pointing to something on the wall, and I thought about how I was starting to sound unhinged and how I had to pull it together for the rest of the afternoon. I could call the lawyer as soon as we got home; I could start making provisions in my will. Even after I was gone, he wouldn't get you without a fight.

You and Dave had bopped off somewhere else—the den, I surmised, because in a few seconds I heard the beep and clang of a video game. You knew you were supposed to ask permission before you played video games!

Allie and Megan returned to the couch, smiling, holding mimosas. "She has a Francis Bacon lithograph!"

"It's tiny," Megan said. "It's the first thing I bought when I started making money. Some people buy cars or go on vacations. I bought art."

What did she want, a fucking prize?

"It's so beautiful," said Allie, the traitor.

"So what was that room like before? The room Jake stayed in?" I asked. "I mean, the last time I was in this apartment"—*That's right, Megan, I was here long before Dave had even heard your name*—"it was mostly just storage."

"Well, we've had it as a guest room for a while," Megan said. "My parents sometimes come stay, other guests come by."

"Where are your parents from?" Allie asked.

"Tacoma, Washington," Megan said. "I grew up there."

"You're kidding!" Allie said. "I live in Seattle."

"I know," Megan said. "Dave told me you live on Mercer Island. He said it's a gorgeous house."

Allie blushed. I thought, Jesus Christ, they'll follow you to Seattle, they'll follow you everywhere. Words were crowding in my brain: LegoStarWarsFrancisBacon.

"We really love the location," Allie said.

"Are your parents still alive?"

Megan blinked at me. "They are."

Allie, giving me a quick look, deftly moved the conversation to the Pacific Northwest—skiing, hiking, Friday Harbor, all that shit—while I thought about my breathing exercises, which I tried to do subtly, so as not to look like I was having problems. I replayed the mantra: *None of us know what the future holds.*

None of us can control the future. I get to live every day I'm alive. I will not melt down and humiliate myself.

I thought of the codeine in my purse. I still kept codeine in my purse. It would help me get through this. If only I could stand.

"And then when I was a kid, we'd spend summers in Yachats, on the coast in Oregon," Megan said, still musing on her childhood. My purse was in the corner of the room. I could have probably gotten there, and would have, but Allie kept flashing me warning looks: sit down, sit down, relax, it's going to be okay.

Could I still believe anything she said? The bedroom, the iguana, the toys: clearly your father planned to keep you in his life in a serious way. I thought about the codeine and how I could create a provision in my will limiting the amount of time he'd get to see you. I was pretty sure I could do something like that. Like a sort of permanent restraining order. I could figure out how to do that, or someone could.

"Have you ever been to the Shakespeare festival in Ashland?" Allie asked.

From the den, I heard a series of loud beeps and then an alarming crash.

"Are they okay in there?" I asked.

"Oh, that's just NHL hockey," Megan laughed. "Dave wanted to get him Spec Ops and I was like, are you kidding? He's six years old! But you know boys."

"Spec Ops?" I slumped. "Dave thought that was—appropriate?" *Spider-Man 3.* I had lost, I had completely lost.

"Oh, you know, he's just so excited," Megan said. "He's been learning everything he can about six-year-old boys, but sometimes I think he forgets himself. He doesn't remember how violent these games can be."

"How has he been learning about six-year-old boys?"

"My kids weren't allowed to play Spec Ops till they turned ten," Allie said. She took a sip of her mimosa.

Megan had already downed hers. "He's doing his best," she said, and looked at her hands.

"I have to say I just love this view," Allie said.

"Thanks." Megan perked up. "It's pretty great, isn't it? It's the reason we've stayed here. And the commute isn't bad. How long did it take you guys from the Upper West Side? Twenty minutes?" She stood, went to the fridge, messed around with something in there, came back to the table empty-handed. So she was nervous too? But what did she have to be nervous about? She had won and I had lost.

"Karen, Dave told me you're a political consultant. That must be fascinating."

Oh shit, we were going to do this now. "Sometimes," I said.

"What are some of the campaigns you've worked on?"

I took a breath, then I told her about Griffith, and I told her about some of the other big ones—the congresspeople she'd pretended to have heard of, the various statewide elections. I found that the more I talked the easier it was to breathe, and the easier it was not to panic. I had to stop panicking if I was going to get through this. It would be okay. I'd talk to the lawyer tomorrow. I had codeine in my purse.

Allie mentioned that I had single-handedly saved Ace Reynolds's career four years ago and that I was working for him again, and of course Megan remembered Ace—who didn't?—and asked if it was hard saving candidates from the brink of their own self-destruction.

"Not for Karen," Allie said. "It's what she's best at. She makes sure her candidates look superhuman. Infallible. By the time she was done with the Griffith campaign, people wanted to vote for him to be God."

That wasn't really true, but Megan nodded anyway. "I can imagine. You seem like you'd be great at that."

"Why?" I asked. "Why do I seem like that?"

"And you're a banker?" Allie said.

"Sort of," Megan said. "I'm more like a researcher. I travel to South American markets to find out more about industries Citi might want to invest in."

"What sorts of industries?" Allie poured herself more mimosa and topped my glass full of orange juice, and I took that opportunity to get up, pop one of my codeines, wait for the soft flood of nothingness to take over. I felt bad that I'd resorted to it but knew I'd feel better soon and would also forget that I'd felt bad. Which was one of the nice things about codeine, as opposed to Xanax. And I took only thirty milligrams.

While Megan babbled about steel and industry and Brazil and manufacturing, you and Dave came to the table, and Dave poured you some orange juice, and then you grabbed a bagel from the bowl and Dave cut it for you, and I just watched. The codeine wasn't even really kicking in yet, but just knowing it was inside me gave me a feeling of calm, a feeling of floating away from myself, like I could just watch this and see what it looked like when you and Dave hung out. What did it look like for him to cut a bagel for you? Did he know you preferred butter to cream cheese? He did not, but you corrected him. Did he know you liked a slice of tomato on your buttered salt bagel, the only time you would ever let a fresh tomato cross your little lips? He did not. You draped the tomato on your bagel, sat down, across from me.

"Hey, Mom," you said.

"Hey, Jakey," I said. "You having fun?"

You nodded, stuffed your mouth full of bagel. Dr. Susan said that one of the best things I could do at any time but especially when I was feeling panicky—*Jake I'm dying*—was to just concentrate on the actual sensations around me. What was around me? The air, the feeling of the linen of my skirt. The wooden seat I was sitting on. The smell of apple air freshener and mimosa and the salty briny smell of smoked salmon. Capers. My sister's perfume. The sight of your half-chapped lips, the exact slope of your nose. The thick black lushness, the absurd lushness, of your eyelashes. The sandy wavy brown of your hair. The way your ears curved like shells. The yellow around your irises. Your smooth white neck, and the point of your left clavicle under the skewed collar of your New York Yankees T-shirt.

The chomping noise you made as you ate your bagel.

I felt the codeine splash up against my insides like water. It took away the panic but not the pain.

I DON'T REMEMBER much about the rest of that afternoon except that we stayed for what seemed to be way too long, and at the end I needed to plead exhaustion so that we could get out of there. Allie and Megan seemed to be on very good terms; every time there was a pause in the conversation, one of them would reel it back to the Pacific Northwest and all the wonderful things to do there, to eat there, all that fucking salmon.

At one point, Dave asked you when school started, and you said the Tuesday after Labor Day, wasn't that right, Mom? It was right, and it sent me into a spin because the Tuesday after Labor Day was really only nine days away, and we still had so much to do: doctors' forms and new sneakers and lunch boxes and the rest of it. We would get your supply list any day now, and the dates for back-to-school night. I wondered if this would be your last year at PS 199. Maybe next year at this time we'd have already moved to Seattle. I had the strangest sensation of wanting to see my father.

On the way out, Megan pressed a bag of salt bagels in my hand and said she looked forward to seeing us all soon. Then Dave said he wondered if they allowed iguanas on the subway and you started to laugh, and there was some noise about bringing Friendly in for a visit, and I tried to crack a joke about Friendly the iguana eating Kelly the hamster and you said, *Mom, everyone knows iguanas are vegetarian*! And I said how silly I was to forget.

Then everyone hugged everyone. I tried not to feel anything when I hugged Dave, and think I pretty much succeeded, but I couldn't help but feel Megan's soft skin, or smell her pretty hair. The last hug administered was between Megan and you, and she folded you into her arms like she really was very fond of you and you were fond of her. I didn't know why that should have been the case, really. You two barely even knew each other.

And then the car came around and I promptly fell asleep in the front seat, except that wasn't what it was, I didn't fall asleep,

I passed out because I had taken another codeine in the bathroom around the same time you and Dave and Megan started talking about all the fun there was to be had in Labor Day in Quogue. Can we go? you asked. We cannot, I said, and for once Dave didn't push it. "Next time, bud," Dave said to you, and I ignored him.

At home, Allie started packing up. I was in the living room and she was in your bedroom, trying to break the laws of physics by cramming everything she'd bought over the past three weeks into her Samsonite. I went to the doorway and watched her for a while. Tomorrow Julisa would return; tomorrow I had to go to the clinic; tomorrow I would not be able to take her to the airport.

"Are you going to let Dave have him?" I whispered.

"What?"

"When I die," I said. "Will you let him take Jacob?"

"Karen," she said. The light in the bedroom was dim and my sister looked older.

"Please don't let him take my son."

"Karen, I won't," she said.

"Do you promise?"

"I promise," she said. She returned to her packing.

"Really promise?"

"Karen, you have to stop."

"Please?"

"I really promise," she said, but she was jamming underwear into the corner of her bag and therefore not looking at me and I wanted to believe her, but I couldn't entirely believe her, nor could I ask her to keep making promises to me about how she'd act after I died when I couldn't force her to accept that I was going to.

She put her head in her hands for a moment, then continued her packing.

"I wish you weren't leaving," I said.

"I can be back in days," she said.

"No, you can't," I said, because it was true—she had a life in Seattle to attend to. She had her family. A daughter with a septum ring!

"I can figure out something," she said. "I think I can."

"Like what?"

"I don't know," she said. "But I'll be back here in a week or two. Somehow. I've been thinking of things I can do to get back here."

"Allie, you can't."

"Don't tell me what I can't do."

I'd been half-consciously doing my breathing exercises all afternoon and I found myself doing them again now: in through the nose, out through the mouth. I wanted to tell Allie how scared I was for her to go, but I didn't want to say it like that, I didn't want to make her feel worse than I'd already made her feel. And also I was the big sister: I was the one who should have been taking care of *her*. Wasn't that how it was supposed to be? How it had always been? When she was little—I'm talking three or four years old—she used to get nightmares, these horrific nightmares. She would sit up screaming in her bed, this blank look on her face, she was still asleep, and I'd smack her to wake her up and then just hold her there while she cried. She would try to tell me what she was dreaming about, but the horrors were so vicious and true she couldn't even describe them. Usually I'd end up falling asleep with my arms around her. She looked like a little doll, with her blonde hair and her nightgown with the frilly collar. Screaming like someone had plunged a knife in her throat. I'd hold her, put my arms around her. Don't cry, sissy, I would say—not sissy like a scaredy-cat, but sissy like my sister. Which is what I called her when we were very young.

Sometimes our grandparents would say, in the morning, that they had heard her screaming, and could she please try harder not to scream? Because it reminded them of their suffering, you know. Of the war.

"She can't help it," I'd say. "Just because you had bad child-hoods my sister can still get nightmares." Then I'd get smacked in the head for being rude.

"Allie—" I said, but didn't finish the sentence, cut myself off before I could ask her not to go.

"Yeah?" She didn't look up at me. Neither one of us was going to cry, but in order to pull that off we couldn't look at each other's faces.

"You want to eat something?"

"No," she said. "I'm not really hungry."

"Me neither," I said.

"Maybe in an hour? Or when Jake eats?"

"I'll check on him," I said, and backed out of the room. She had her head bent in a pile of new shirts; she still wouldn't look up. She was folding and refolding a T-shirt, artfully.

My mother and my father and now me. Was it better to be the last woman standing? Or was it easier to go down in the opening round?

You were dancing around with the Wii in the living room, playing the NHL hockey game, which Dave must have given you. I watched you play for a while, clumsily; the opposing team kept scoring on your underresourced defense. You didn't seem to mind very much that you were losing. The effects on the game were really good: the cheering crowd sounded like a real cheering crowd, and the play-by-play was being narrated by someone who sounded eerily like a professional sportscaster. I picked up the game's case. The price sticker was still on it: forty-eight dollars, brand-new.

After you lost, I clicked off the Wii. "It's time for dinner," I said. It was actually past dinnertime—it was already seven—but we'd noshed all afternoon.

"I'm not hungry," you said. "I want to play."

"First you have to eat."

"But I'm not hungry!" you said. You reached for the controller; I held it out of your way.

"Mo-om! Give me that!" You dove for it, playfully, and I darted out of the way so you couldn't connect with my ribs, but the darting pulled on my skin and hurt.

"Jake, you know you can't jump on me. Enough with the vids—you've been playing all day. You want spaghetti?"

"I said I'm not hungry!"

"Meatballs? Pizza? Come on. I'll make you a peanut butter and jelly."

"There's nothing I want to eat!" you said, and you went from whining to anger. "I ate all day!" I used to have these same fights with my mother, I remember, when I was little. All those delicious foods she would offer me: baked chicken with lemon, mashed potatoes, noodles with butter and cheese. All I wanted was to be left alone.

"Can I make you noodles with butter and cheese?"

You shot me a look, then plopped backward on the couch.

"If you don't eat dinner, you're going to wake up starving in the middle of the night and it'll be too late."

You gave me another look, still unimpressed, then moved to turn the Wii back on, which you were not allowed to do—only I could, which was one of the rules I insisted on when we bought the Wii. Only I could turn that thing on, and I decided when it was going to be turned off.

"What do you think you're doing?"

"I want to play," you said.

"You're done playing. It's time for dinner."

"I'll eat *later*."

"It will be too late later."

"Why?"

"Because I'm not going to get up to fix you something at two in the morning, Jacob!"

You were looking at me with something like calculation in your eyes. Your hand was still on the Wii controller. You mumbled a few words I couldn't hear.

"Excuse me?"

"Megan would."

I took a breath. I grabbed the Wii controller from your pudgy little hand.

"If I were staying at dad's house and I was hungry in the middle of the night, I bet Megan would make me something to eat. She wouldn't let me go hungry."

I found myself leaning against the wall, pointing the Wii at you. You were standing by the couch, a palm out, as if to accept it.

"Megan would?"

"Yes," you said again, but you looked away.

"Megan?"

Now you kept your mouth shut.

"Megan is *not your mother*," I hissed. "She will never be your mother."

"I know," you said.

"She will never be your mother."

"I know," you said, and suddenly the defiance was gone from your expression.

"She is not your mother."

"Right, mom, I know."

"She is NOT YOUR MOTHER. SHE IS NOT YOUR MOTHER. SHE IS NOT YOUR MOTHER."

"Mom! I know! I'm sorry, I know!"

"SHE DID NOT RAISE YOU! I RAISED YOU! I AM YOUR MOTHER! I AM YOUR MOTHER." Allie burst out of the bedroom. You started to cry.

"I AM YOUR MOTHER! NOBODY ELSE IS YOUR MOTHER! I RAISED YOU ON MY OWN! I DID THIS ON MY OWN! YOU ARE WHO YOU ARE BECAUSE OF ME! DO YOU UNDERSTAND ME?"

"Karen, stop it—you're screaming!"

"DO YOU UNDERSTAND ME?"

"Mommy! Stop it!"

"DO YOU FUCKING UNDERSTAND ME? I AM YOUR MOTHER!"

The room was swimming and my vision was swimming. You

were crouched on the sofa, crying, holding a pillow over your head. "I'm sorry," you said. "I'm sorry, Mommy."

"*I AM YOUR MOTHER!*" I screamed. I was so flooded with this feeling I didn't know I could ever feel. "*DON'T YOU EVER, EVER—*"

"Karen!" Allie now had her arms around me, as though to hold me back.

"*I AM YOUR MOTHER!*"

"Karen! Stop!"

"*ONLY ME! NOBODY ELSE! YOU WILL NEVER TALK ABOUT MEGAN THAT WAY!*"

"Mommy!" You were hysterical.

"*NOBODY ELSE! I AM YOUR ONLY MOTHER!*"

"Please, Mommy!"

"*NOBODY!*"

I didn't know who I was. I was standing, rigid, standing over you with the game controller, Allie holding me back. Was I going to hurt you? How could I have hurt you? You? My beautiful boy? And yet I was gripping your arm with my free hand.

"Mommy, please?" You tried to free yourself from my grasp. Allie pulled me away from you, pulled me back.

"I'm sorry," you choked.

"Never," I whispered hoarsely.

"I'm sorry," you said again. You were free and hiding now, all of you, on the couch, under the pillows.

"Jacob, it's going to be okay. Go to your room," Allie said. "I need to talk to your mom."

"Mommy." You were shuddering under the pillow. "I'm sorry, Mommy."

"You don't have to be sorry, Jacob," Allie said. "Just go to your room now. I need to talk to your mother."

She was still holding me back, but I shook her off. Was I hurting you? Could I have hurt you?

"Mommy." You were reaching up from the blanket, pale and teary and snot-spackled. I had never screamed at you in your entire life. My beautiful boy. I had never hurt you. I took you in my arms. I might have hurt you, Jacob.

I am writing this down now, hours later. I am writing down everything. The truth.

If Allie hadn't been there, I might have just ended it all.

15

Later that night I had the strongest urge to talk to my father. I knew we wouldn't have a conversation—it's not like I expected him to be able to really *talk*—but there were moments, every so often, when he would wake from his catatonia to respond to questions in grunts or make little noises of his own. I wanted to hear his voice. It seemed to me that night, as the ambulances howled on West Seventy-Fourth Street, and you and Allie slept in another room, and I sat on the couch, listening to the way New York City was never quiet: it seemed to me that I would soon be out of chances.

It was two in the morning, which meant it was 11:00 p.m. at Bellevue, but that didn't matter. Time meant nothing to dementia. I dialed the number, was put through. "Is he sleeping, Olga?" I asked.

"No," Olga said. She sounded gentle, spoke gently; I felt unworthy of her gentleness. "Would you like to talk to him?" I assented. "Mr. Gil, your daughter is on your phone. Your beautiful daughter Karen, from New York." I heard a sort of gurgle from the other end. I had picked the right night—a good night to call. "Here, I put you on speaker."

"Daddy?" I said.

There it was, unmistakably, a gurgle. He could hear me.

"Daddy, I need to tell you something. It's Karen. Your daughter. Can you understand me, Daddy?"

Silence on the other end. I wondered if Olga was listening or if she had disappeared into her pile of *Us Weekly*s.

Another gurgle, which I took as a cue to go on. "Daddy, I did something terrible tonight. I yelled at Jacob, Daddy. I screamed at him and I almost hurt him. I feel so terrible. I don't know how I'm going to keep living with myself. I can't believe what I did."

A car alarm started and stopped outside. A drunk girl cackled. Saturday night.

I wanted him to tell me it was okay. I wanted him to tell me we all make mistakes. I wanted him to tell me you'd forgive me. That you'd still love me in the morning. That he still loved me. That I was still his little girl.

"And I need to tell you something else. I'm dying, Daddy. Not because I yelled at Jacob. I'm just—I have cancer. I have ovarian cancer. I have another two years, maybe. If I can last that long. The doctors think it might be getting worse."

There was nothing. "Do you understand me? I'm dying."

I waited for a gurgle, I waited for anything. I thought about you, and how grateful I was that this was something you would never say to me.

"Daddy, I need you to live, okay? Just—I need you to keep living. For Allison. For your other daughter. She can't be alone. She is saving me and I need you to save her. Okay? Just hold on. Hold on as long as you can. I'm going to try to live as long as I can, but I need you to do that too. Okay, Daddy?"

I imagined him there, his stiffened face, staring out into the dark calm waters of Lake Washington. In his striped pajamas. Still a full head of hair. "Daddy?"

"I think he is hearing you, Miss Karen," Olga said. "He is blinking his eyes."

"Daddy? I need you to live as long as you can."

"Oh, he will keep living," Olga said. "He's a tough old guy, aren't you, Mr. Gil?"

"Daddy, please," I said.

Finally, I heard him make a noise. A strangled gargle, a choked-off something.

"You hear him, Miss Karen?"

"Daddy?"

"He is speaking, Miss Karen."

"Daddy?"

We were quiet then, all three of us, and New York City, and the continent between us. Then: *Szerelmem.* I heard him say it.

Someone still loved me.

"I love you too," I said, and I listened for a little while longer, and the noises began again. I listened to the street, the creaks of the old apartment, the pacing of the neighbor upstairs, the whining of the people downstairs, and out across America, the strained whoosh of an old/young man's breathing, and the still dark waters of the lake, and the entire rest of the world.

WHEN IT WAS time to lie down to sleep, I found I still could not. I went into your room. You were on the bottom bunk, Allison on the top. You had an old navy blue rug on the floor—Yankees navy blue—and it hurt to lie down on it, and the pain felt right. I took one of your stuffed animals from the floor, placed it under my head, and imagined it was one hundred thousand years ago, and we were all in a cave somewhere, and it was my job to protect us all from whatever raged outside, and whatever raged inside me. And when that didn't work, I prayed for my jetpack.

THREE

In Another Country

16

And suddenly it was the Tuesday after Labor Day. It was time for you to start first grade. First grade! I remembered my own first grade clearly: My teacher's name was Mrs. Penny. She had red hair and a pretty singing voice and wore colorful macramé vests and I loved her. She was the first person to tell me I was smart.

It felt good that I could remember first grade, because that meant, in all likelihood, that you'd be able to remember it too, and that maybe you'd even remember today, when you wore your new Sith Lord backpack and your Derek Jeter T-shirt and the light-up sneakers that, after much debate, you decided you preferred to the blue New Balances I favored. In the morning, we got up early, ate eggs and English muffins, and talked about the different things you'd learn at school this year: definitely addition and subtraction but probably also science, and if you wanted, you could take the Spanish-language program after school, which you thought would be too much work but I thought would be terrific preparation for life in the middle part of this century.

We never really talked about what happened the night before Allie left. I tried to apologize, but then you ended up starting to apologize again, and I told you please not to, that it was my fault, and I felt myself start to cry. Which scared you. But please know, Jake of the future—please know, if you read this, how ashamed I am of what I did. I am keeping this in the record, both what I said to you, and that I'm afraid I'll never get over it. I want to let you know that I remember it too.

But we must keep living. And so in order to keep living, after breakfast we fed Kelly and combed out your hair, and I checked your backpack one last time to make sure you had all your supplies. Mrs. Dubrov had emailed a very comprehensive list of things you need, different kinds of pencils, a zip drive. A zip drive! Back in my day it was a glue stick and a pile of folders. But you had your zip drive, your various pencils, and in the front compartment, your power gourd. Because you never know.

And this was how we would keep living.

At twenty of eight, we walked down our four flights—you bouncing ahead, me trying not to feel dizzy—and onto Seventy-Fourth Street, where a parade of children in new backpacks and new sneakers bounded toward PS 199. Kyle and his folks were half a block away from us, but you did not run toward them. You held my hand.

At the corner I had to stop. I pretended to sneeze so you'd think I was stopping so I could sneeze.

"Mom?" Your cheeks went pale.

I fake-wiped my nose with my wrist. "I have a surprise for you," I said.

I had meant to keep it till later, when you deserved a treat, but I'd have said anything to get that worried look off your face. Of course now you looked even more worried. "A good surprise?"

"Yes! A good surprise. I signed you up for tennis lessons. Private. Twice a week."

You didn't smile, but your color did return.

"This teacher's the best, I asked around. A bunch of kids from your school go to him."

"Like who?"

"He told me an Emma? I think in second grade?"

"I don't know her."

"You'll improve your game really fast with a private teacher," I said. "Not like in group lessons. It'll be better."

"Cool," you said. You picked up my hand again, and we rejoined the parade, behind a family of four and an old man walking his dog.

A few seconds passed. "Do you want to keep playing tennis?"

"I guess," you said. "Can I still do soccer too?"

"Of course," I said. "Soccer's only on Sunday afternoons. Tennis is on weekdays."

"Cool," you said again. When did you start using the word *cool*? There was a pain in my side and I didn't know what it was about, but I decided to chalk it up to emotion. I was dizzy. My son was growing up. He was in first grade now. I thought he'd like playing tennis. If he didn't want to do the Spanish program, I guess he didn't have to.

When we got to the front door of your school, you dropped my hand like a grenade and raced in. The school was buzzing. All the first graders were running around like they owned the place, while the kindergartners stood back, shyly, their parents looking traumatized, and the second graders, already too cool, moseyed on to their classrooms with their parents ten steps behind. It was a blur of primary colors and cinderblock walls and brightly lettered posters and teachers standing outside their classrooms, smiling, come in, come in. I took a deep breath and walked slowly, geriatrically, following the yellow arrows to Mrs. Dubrov's classroom. Just under a year ago I'd been in remission. I was not anymore.

Your first grade classroom was big, with cubbies on the wall. I found your cubby; you were already there. Jacob Neulander. You had the best cubby.

"Do you need help unpacking?" But you waved me off, private with your stuff.

Mrs. Dubrov had red hair, just like my first grade teacher did, so I liked her immediately. "Welcome, welcome!" You first graders looked so big, so assured, compared to where we were last year. The boys wore soccer jerseys and baseball T-shirts; the girls wore dresses and leggings I recognize from the Boden catalog. Mrs. Dubrov took family pictures with what was probably the last living Polaroid in New York, and the little girls posed prettily, and the boys just stood there and looked embarrassed.

"Jacob!" She knew it was you without my having to introduce us. "Is this your mom? Mrs. Neulander?" We shook hands. She looked at me searchingly for just a moment. Then she put the camera to her eye.

A click, a flash: you submitted to having your photograph taken. Mrs. Dubrov handed us the photo, and together we watched as it assembled into an image: your freckles emerged, your half-curly hair, my hand on your shoulder. Finally, my face, ghostly, so much older than I had ever looked before. Was that what I really looked like? I knew that nobody looked good under fluorescents but—man. Even in my wig.

"Thank you," I mumbled to Mrs. Dubrov. I wanted to sound like I meant it.

She smiled at me again, then patted you on the shoulder. "We're going to have a great year, Jacob."

"You can call me Jake."

"We are going to have a great year, Jake." You were looking down at the picture. I took it from you, left you to your friends. You didn't have to see me captured like this.

There were other parents around, milling by the cubbies, and I could see a few that I sort of knew, and we discussed our various summers—the Hamptons, the Catskills—and nobody asked me anything about how I was doing. Maybe I didn't look as terrible as I thought I did, as I knew I did. And then Mrs. Dubrov told the children to say good-bye to their parents, and we all went for our last hugs, and some of the kids would have us and some of the kids would not. I was glad that you still would have me; I wrapped you in my arms. I ruffled your hair, I kissed your forehead, and then I was gone.

THE WALK HOME took hours, Jacob. I hate telling you this, but it's the truth. The walk home took me at least a million years.

AND NOW IT'S cooler, early September—not quite sweater weather yet, but the sidewalk ginkgos are changing color, and I'm opening the windows rather than relying on the air conditioner at home. I've never really been one for symbolism—in my line of work, if you've got something to say, you should just say it—but I do feel like the changing of the leaves, the coolness of the evening, I don't know, maybe it *portends*. The geese in the sky all seem to be flying in one direction these days, their Vs marking arrows to a country I can't see.

I was diagnosed two years ago, in 2011, when I was forty-one years old. The doctors told me that I would live for four or five more years, and now I am halfway through those four or five more years. I am supposed to have two or even two and a half left. I have counted on having every single day, every single hour of those four to five years. Every second. But now I'm not sure what I should be counting on.

If you want to know the truth, Jacob, about how I've lived since my diagnosis, how I've planned and how I've considered, and how I've managed to raise you—even how I've written this book—it's that I've always suspected, in the back of my mind, that maybe I would be the miracle. The woman who defied the odds. I didn't expect to do it with any grand shows of strength, running a marathon five years after my diagnosis or getting hired to run a presidential campaign. I just thought, maybe they'd find something that would keep me alive for six more months. And then six months after that. And then, before you looked too hard at it, it would turn out I'd stuck around for seven years, eight, it would turn out I saw you graduate from high school, and go off to college, and get married, and if I didn't yell too loud, if I didn't make my little miracle known, then nobody would catch me having what I wasn't supposed to have. All those extra years, a little secret treat for me, a brownie I nibbled on after I was supposed to have gone to bed.

I mean, if someone got to be a miracle, why couldn't it be me? Ten months after my diagnosis, after surgery and chemotherapy, I went into remission. The doctors told me that although they couldn't get all of my tumor, they got most of it. They expected further rounds of chemo to keep those last bits of tumor contained. They expected that my body would respond well to treatment, as young and relatively healthy as it was. They seemed so cheerful about me! The bowel obstruction was just a complication. The exhaustion was just a normal part of treatment. The grayness and the sorrow were just normal parts of cancer. And that I should talk to Dr. Susan if I was feeling sad.

Steiner promised me—didn't he promise me?—that the long, slow disgusting infusions would stop the cancer from growing. But now I wonder if it's just that the tumor isn't growing where he was looking for it to grow. But it's in me, Jacob. It's in me, it's watching me, it's waiting for me to become too exhausted to be vigilant so it can start growing again and take me away from you. I don't know what I did to deserve this. I don't know why I have to try to sneak in the years that should be rightfully mine. I don't want to live whatever time I have left full of grayness and sorrow. But the hope that I would be a miracle is dimming.

Jacob, my beautiful boy. Look: you are in first grade today. Together at least we made it this far.

AND ALSO, AT least I had my work. It was the heart of campaign season, and my candidate needed me. I'm telling you, kid, thank God for Ace, stupid, incorrigible Ace. After I dropped you off at school, I made it back up the stairs to our apartment, a rest on each landing, then headed to the bathroom to wash up, put on a little more makeup, nicer shoes. In a few hours I had to be in the Bronx for an emergency meeting. The phone was already ringing. And therefore I could not be gray or sorrowful today. I could not be exhausted today. I had too much else to do.

In the days after Bev's funeral, Kit Rannells dug just deep enough into Ace's fidelity to bring the problem back into the spotlight. His first piece—"A Wrap for Reynolds?"—showed up the Friday before Labor Day weekend, a little sidebar on a slow news day. We might have ignored it, but then he wrote another piece, above the fold, for the Sunday paper, and that one was scary enough to catch Ace's attention. Kit didn't name any names; he didn't make any specific accusations. Just picked up on the "rumors floating around Riverdale" that you can't teach "old dog Ace Reynolds" any "new tricks." The Sunday *Bronx Times* had a readership of about eighteen thousand, but the bigger papers picked up on it, started calling me for comments.

Deny, deny, deny. Crisis management.

Still, Kit had no comment, no name—just some unsubstantiated stories from old guys in the Bronx with bones to pick and lies to tell. Right? Right?

Ace had called last night while you and I were having dinner. "Who is this reporter? A twenty-year-old kid? Get him fired!"

You looked up from your spaghetti. "Is that Ace?"

"Sure is," I mouthed. We could both hear him sputtering over the receiver. You laughed, shook your head, watched in amusement while I tried to soothe Ace's nerves.

"Have you told the girl to keep her mouth shut? Is she going to go public?"

"What girl? There was no girl!"

"Ace, you already told me—"

"Nothing! There was nobody! Nobody's saying anything!"

"Jeez, Ace," I said while you giggled. I made a crazy gesture, a circle around my ear.

"He won't find her, will he?"

"Not if there's nobody to find," I said. (I actually had a feeling Kit was going to find the girl, but there was nothing I could do about it if Ace wouldn't tell me her name.)

Then, after I put you to bed, Ace's daughter called me from South Carolina. She was a sweet girl, late twenties, worked as a golf pro and tried to keep her distance from her grasping father. She asked me to please please kill these rumors. For the sake of her mother, who really couldn't take any more of this crap.

I was lying on the couch with a heating pad under my back. Listen, I told her, I can manage the relationship your father has with the public, but I can't do anything about his relationship with your mother.

"She might actually leave him this time," said Ruth. "And he'll be devastated. Even after all this, he really does love her." She sounded sniffly. "I don't think he understands how serious this is."

"He understands," I said, thinking if he loves her so much, why couldn't he keep his pants on? Why couldn't he have honored his wedding vows like they actually meant something? Why couldn't he find life with his wife of thirty-five years and not some twenty-year-old nobody?

"Do you think he did it?" Ruth asked.

"He says he didn't."

"Right, but do you think?"

"The press hasn't found the body yet."

The daughter sniffled again. "What an asshole," she said. "And he still wants to be mayor some day."

"They all," I said, "want to be mayor some day."

Before I went to bed, I looked at you asleep in your bunk bed, your hand loosely clenching your sheet. I thought, You, my son, you can be mayor one day, and then I kissed your forehead and went to sleep.

I STOOD IN the bathroom heaping on more eye shadow and the phone started ringing again, and I picked it up and said, "There's no story," before I even knew who was calling, because I guess I was feeling a little flustered—I hadn't had to put down a good crisis in years.

"That's good," said my sister. "It's better when there's no story."

I should have known it was Allison—she called me every three hours, and if I didn't pick up, she called back in a half an hour. She wanted me to buy you a cell phone so she could check in on you too but I'm sorry, six-years-olds don't get cell phones, not even on the Upper West Side.

"You feeling okay?" she asked.

Allie had not held my fury against me; when I'd tried to apologize to her, she said she understood, that she was surprised it had taken me so long to snap. When I apologized again, she said that she noticed I was on new medication and that it probably made me a little moody. And then she wouldn't let me mention it again.

"Karen? Are you okay?"

I would not mention the ache in my side. "Great," I said with enough oomph that she'd believe me but not so much that she'd think I was acting.

On her way out the door to the airport, she had turned to me and said she didn't have to go. She would miss her flight, she didn't care, she could stay. I told her that of course she had to go, that she had a family to take care of on Mercer Island, and a peace to broker between her husband and her son. She said she'd be back in a few weeks. I told her she didn't have to. She didn't have to be a martyr or anything. Which was just a pissy-enough thing to say that it got her out the door and into the cab.

"You have an infusion on Thursday?" she asked.

"Are my doctor's appointments still in your calendar?"

"All of them," Allie said.

I looked at myself in the bathroom vanity. Better with the eye shadow on. "How's everything at home?"

"Well, Dustin keeps collecting snakes. We found some in the garage the other day."

"Dead or alive?"

"Dead. He overestimates a snake's ability to live in a sealed plastic box."

"Oh my God," I said. "What about Bruce and Ross?"

"You know, surprisingly, they're doing a lot better. I guess Ross decided to enroll at U Dub after all, since he found an apartment near campus with some friends."

"Just like that?"

"Just like that," Allie said. "And now that he's leaving soon—I don't know. They're getting along a lot better. I think they just realized there's no time left to waste fighting. He's going to be gone so soon," she said. "Why waste a second of it on bullshit?"

"Exactly," I said.

"Well," she said. And then, after a few moments, "You sound okay. Strong."

"I have a lot of work to do right now," I said. "Ace fucked up again. So I have to deal with that. And I just dropped Jake off at school."

"That's right! Today's the first day!"

"I told him about the tennis lessons. He was psyched."

"I'm glad!" she said. "The next round's on me."

"You don't have to pay for everything, Allie."

"It's all I can do from here," she said.

The call-waiting beeped; it was the car service. "I better go," I said. My makeup was only half on, but I could finish in the back of the car.

"I love you," Allie said. I knew she did, but it made me sad that she'd started saying it when she got off the phone, as though she was running out of chances to tell me.

"I'll call you later."

"Please," she said.

"I promise." So for her, I pretended to be my old self, swiped on a little lipstick, grabbed my briefcase, and bounded out the door, not pausing to consider the pain that was now radiating up half my side, not pausing to think about her or you or even myself, just my candidate and my job and the car that was waiting downstairs to take me to my crisis, which I could not have been more grateful for (as I was for you, and her, and my job).

THE DRIVE UP the West Side Highway was jerky—traffic that came and went without any particular rhythm. Although I wanted to be sharp for Ace, I popped a codeine; I was so used to the narcotics flowing through me that I doubted he'd know I was drugged. It was going to be him, me, maybe Amani. No family or surrogates—not yet. Until we knew for sure what anybody knew, there was no need to rally the troops.

My phone rang and it was Ace—suddenly, he was always available. "I just don't understand where this came from! How did he find out?"

To my left, the Hudson River sludged toward New York Harbor, steel-colored and dreary. "Ace, you of all people should know there are no secrets in politics."

"But it meant nothing!"

"Oh, Ace, come on."

(Look, I know what you're wondering.)

"But how did he find out?"

(I can't give you a good answer.)

"How, Karen?"

Why did I tell Kit Rannells the truth—was I on some sort of quest for justice? Did I want a little revenge and for Ace to stop acting like such a smug asshole? Or did I do it for Bev? Or because I just wanted to keep working a few more months? (Without a crisis, really, I'd have had nothing to do today but go to the emergency room.)

We pulled through Ace's gates at 10:30 a.m., the sun dappling through the trees on his property. The window shades were all drawn shut. I looked around the street for any reporters waiting to pounce, any TV vans, but there was nothing. I tipped the driver, kept the receipt, and walked up to Ace's house with the codeine coursing through my veins. The door opened before I rang the bell.

"Karen, oh thank God."

"Jill, hey," I said, surprised. I hadn't expected her to be there. She crushed my hands between her own.

I knew I looked like shit, but between the two of us, I still came out the winner. The Jill I remembered was handsome in an art-history-professor way, with a reddish-gold bob and chic glasses. This Jill was puffy, her hair a mess, smelling faintly of tobacco. She wore a stained T-shirt and Fordham sweatpants. She didn't blink at my appearance. I suddenly felt pretty horrible. I had done this to her. I mean obviously Ace had done this to her—but if it hadn't been for me she might never have had to find out.

"Mom, is that Karen?" Ruth appeared at her side. Must have taken an early morning flight. How could I have been so reckless with someone else's life?

"Just tell me he didn't do it again, okay? Because I can't—I honestly just can't. I can't stand by his side one more time. I cannot play the forgiving wife again, okay? Just tell me—Karen, be honest with me. Please."

"Is he here?"

"Karen, I'm asking you, did he do it?"

The codeine was giving me a tingly feeling in my fingers and along my spine; perhaps I'd taken a few milligrams extra.

"Jill, of course not."

She started to cry, and her daughter held her by the shoulders, removed her from the doorway. "Come on, Mom. Let Karen in."

I wanted to hug her, but it wasn't my place to hug her. Jesus, for a second I really hated myself. I coughed a little, felt worse. "Is Ace here?"

"He's hiding in the study," Ruth said. "A reporter showed up at the house late last night, asked for a comment. My father screamed at the guy and my mom's been like this ever since."

"Don't talk about me in the third person," Jill snapped.

"Mom," Ruth said.

"Jill, I promise it will be okay." She didn't even look at me, waved a hand in my face.

Inside, the house was warm and smelled a bit like dog; a terrier yapped in the kitchen. (Remember the Checkers speech, Jake? Is that something they still teach in history class? It's one of the best political speeches of the twentieth century, and the main reason all politicians should own dogs. Dogs make people seem more human than they are.)

I followed them to the kitchen table. "Where was the reporter from? Who showed up?"

"Does it matter?"

"As long as it wasn't the *Times*," I said. "As long as it's not in the *Times*, it's not real news."

"Do you think it's real news?" Jill sat down heavily at the table with me; her daughter lifted the terrier in her arms and disappeared. "Do you think he could have done this again? In France? After our anniversary trip?"

"No, Jill, of course not." The tingling.

"Because I will not go through this again. It was the most

humiliating thing I've ever had to do, to stand there with him while he admitted he's made *mistakes* in our marriage. Mistakes! Forgetting to turn off the oven is a mistake. A fender bender is a mistake."

"Jill, come on."

"As though I'd forgiven him. As though I supported him! And the whole time when I wanted to kill him." Did she? I remembered her as very compliant, very cordial. I remembered being impressed.

"I know, look—"

"And if he's done it again—how could he do that to our family? We have two daughters! Ruth is engaged to be *married*. What, are we not going to walk her down the aisle together? Are we not going to stand together with our daughter when she gets *married*? Are we going to act like marriage doesn't even matter?"

"Jill, come on . . ." I considered offering her a codeine. Maybe a Xanax. "Do you want a Xanax?"

"I already took two," she said. She looked up sharply. Ace was standing in the kitchen doorway.

"Jillie, come on," he said.

She turned rigid, shot daggers through him. "I'm going out," she said.

"Where you gonna go?"

"I can't be here right now." Then she stood, brushed past him, a cloud of rage in her wake. Somewhere in the house the terrier yapped. Ace wore jeans, a white V-neck T-shirt, as casual as I'd ever seen him. Bags under his eyes. His hair was still perfect, though. After a minute or so, he sat down at the table with me.

We were quiet. In another minute, we heard the garage door open, Jill's car pull out.

"Jesus," I said, but without her in the room, I felt better.

"I know." He leaned back in his chair, rubbed his mouth. He didn't look tormented, exactly, but he looked wary. "I just don't know . . . I don't know how I wasn't . . ."

I waited for him to finish, but he didn't. "How you weren't what?"

"I wasn't thinking," he said.

"That's true," I said.

"Can I get you anything?" Ace asked me. "Coffee? Anything?"

"I'm fine," I said, but Ace stood and poured two coffees, then pulled some bourbon out of a cabinet and added a slug to one of the mugs and then, after a pause, the other. With all the drugs I was on I couldn't drink bourbon, but I did like the smell.

Ace's kitchen was nice: skylights, a big Wolf range. From what he'd told me, Jill was a really good cook. He'd always been proud of her cooking. They hosted Thanksgiving dinners for half the Bronx, and she'd welcomed dozens of New York City dignitaries to their dining room: Bloomberg, Koch, Cuomo. Lots of Italian stuff, lots of baking.

Ace sat down, pushed a mug at me.

"So what now?" I asked him.

"You know I was a history teacher a million years ago. You know that, right?"

"I do," I said. Birds chirping outside. You'd never have known you were in the Bronx.

"Right after college, after Vietnam, I get educated on the GI bill, first one in my family, the whole thing. Meet Jillie freshman year, first day of classes. Somehow get up the nerve to ask her out. Somehow get up the nerve to ask her to marry me. Me! An idiot from the Bronx, and here's this beautiful girl from Manhattan, and I get her to agree to marry me."

He drummed his fingers on the table. Did he want me tell him he wasn't an idiot?

"I get an education degree from New York University, start teaching in Westchester. American history. Revolution through the Depression, every year. And every year I talk about the same people making the mistakes, King George III underestimating the American colonists, Calvin Coolidge underestimating the financial crisis. Woodrow Wilson. Treaty of Versailles. Same mistakes, again and again. Not even hearing myself. Meanwhile, Jillie's raising the girls, keeping up the house, and then her father dies and she gets all this money and what does she want to spend it on? A nice house for our girls. Good schools for our girls. Jill never does anything for herself. She wants a nice kitchen, we get a nice kitchen. So she can feed us, that's why she wants a nice kitchen. So she can cook for her family."

"Okay." I was certain he wasn't half the history teacher my father had been.

"Ach," Ace said. He drank from his mug, a little too much. "So then I decide I want more than that, just being a history teacher, so I go into politics. I'm an assemblyman, I'm Bronx borough president. Then I'm a city councilman. And the whole time I'm just taking for granted that it's all about me, about what *I* want, and that what I want will be good for my constituents, good for my family. Good for my wife. How could it not be? It's what *I* want. And I'm a good guy, so the things I want must be good. Right? I mean, I would certainly never hurt anybody. I would never take bribes, anything like that. I'd never be corrupt. I do the right things by the people who elected me to office. I do right by my family and right for the Bronx."

"You've always done right, Ace."

"Not always, Karen."

I looked at the table.

"Sometimes at night—that time when you're supposed to be most honest with yourself, it's just you and your God—I knew I wasn't doing right. And I did it anyway."

I didn't really know how to answer that. I sniffed my coffee, resisted taking a sip.

"And then, that one time I got caught, I got saved—you saved me, Karen—and I started to think I was invincible. If I weren't invincible, why was I still alive? I learned nothing. I was a good boy for a couple of years, but then I couldn't help it, I did this stupid shit again. And I still thought I was going to survive it because nothing really bad had ever happened to me, and even when it had . . . it really hadn't."

"These things happen," I said, witlessly.

"I've gotten away with shit I never should have gotten away with."

"Yeah, but—"

"My life isn't just about me, Karen. Just because I don't get hurt doesn't mean nobody else in my life is hurting."

I sighed, sniffed my coffee.

"I'm fifty-nine years old. I don't know why it took me so long to figure that out."

I took a sip of the coffee and immediately the bourbon hit my brain, made me blink hard.

"I'm dropping out of the race, Karen."

It took me a moment to hear him. "You're *what*?"

"I can't do it to Jill. I can't make her go through this again. I love my wife, Karen."

"Ace, they're never going to find out!"

"They'll find out," Ace said. "They always find out in the end."

Jesus Christ. "Ace, all you've talked about since I met you is running for mayor one day." I felt slurry and deranged, and I didn't know if it was from the bourbon plus the codeine or just from what Ace was telling me. "Don't let a sudden bout of morals change your entire life goals."

"It's just what's right."

For fuck's sake. Didn't he know this was my last campaign? I was flailing, panicking: How could I be myself without a job?

"I've put her through enough," he said.

"Oh, don't be such a melodramatic baby. These are just some stupid rumors in the *Bronx Times*. They're bullshit!" I hoped my voice was as clear as I wanted it to be. "You don't have to throw yourself on the sword just because of a dumb mistake."

"It's more than just a dumb mistake."

My poor heart started pounding, thrumming against the bourbon, the codeine, all those depressants. As sorry as I felt for Jill, I feel even sorrier for myself. "What about your responsibility to your constituents?" I asked. "To the people who elected you?"

"They'll elect someone else. Or they won't. What do we get, thirty percent voter participation up here?"

"Ace"—I could hear it, I was slurring—"Ace, I *strongly* encourage you to reconsider your position. You have no opponent.

You're running unopposed. Even if Rannells somehow manages to expose—"

"I made up my mind. Last night, I'm sleeping on the couch—it's four a.m., I can't sleep. You know what that feels like?"

Of course I knew what that felt like.

"And that's when it was time for me to finally be honest with myself. If I couldn't be honest with anyone else, then I could at least be honest with myself. I tiptoed upstairs, I peeked in on Jill—she was fast asleep, tissues piled up around her, she'd been crying. And I swear to God I saw the same beautiful woman I married thirty-five years ago. Like not a day had passed. And I thought to myself, how could I do this to her? How could I keep doing what I need, what I want, instead of what she deserves? This is my wife, you know? This is the woman who keeps me alive."

Last night, I kissed you on the forehead in your bunk bed while you slept. Your beautiful long lashes. The sheets clutched in your fingers.

"I know."

All Ace ever wanted was to be mayor, and all I ever wanted—well, most of what I wanted—was to be a good mother to you.

I excused myself, went to the bathroom. I looked shot. No more campaign. No more work. I splashed water on my face, took a deep breath in, a deep breath out. And slowly my heart relaxed into its usual pace.

You see, Jacob, it's just that I'd been working since I was in high school. At the dry cleaner's next door to our house. At the Binghamton cafeteria during the lunchtime rush. At Harley Political for five long years. At my own shop every year since. And just like that, my work was gone, leaving me with nothing but myself.

But also leaving me with you. Without Ace, I would have the time I needed to have with you.

I had given myself the gift of time with you without even realizing what I was doing.

My face was dripping. I toweled off, headed back to the kitchen table, sat down next to Ace. For a long time we didn't bother saying anything. What was left? After a while, Ace stood, poured the remains of our coffee down the drain, riffled through a drawer, and took out a checkbook. After he wrote me a large check from his business account, I took my leave.

My candidate, my crisis, my job, my life. The check in my purse. I wasn't really thinking about any of that. I was just thinking about you, your life, this life I had given you that was yours.

AFTER DINNER, AND a full report on your first day of school (you learned a song about seasons and your library was called the "media center"), you told me why you looked a little bit sad about your surprise this morning. "It's not that I don't want to take tennis lessons," you said. "It's just that I thought you were going to tell me that I could see my dad."

17

Daylight saving ended early this year, and you played tennis in the gloaming under the court's huge white lights. Topher, your teacher, was going easy on you, or else you were even better than you were the week before; your serves cleared the net by inches, and you were working on a bit of a backhand. And fast! You could skip across the court in the time it took me to turn my head. Watching you play was like watching you become someone else. It was a surprise.

For some reason, I was finding it harder to regulate my body heat; my hands were always freezing now and so were my toes. I was wrapped in a fleece sweatshirt and a down jacket and an ugly wool afghan even though it was fifty-seven degrees out and you were, at your insistence, wearing nothing but shorts and a flimsy short-sleeve T-shirt. And your sweatband, of course. I had a seat on the bleachers right by the court. I was watching every muscle in your body all at once. I knew your father was coming, but I wasn't on high alert or anything. I barely even startled when I saw him approach.

"Hey," he said gently. He sat next to me on the bleachers; I slid over but not enough and our bodies touched a little. I wasn't wearing a wig, only a thick wool cap tight over my head. My eyebrows were sparse but I hadn't drawn them in. I did put on some lip balm, though, the shimmery kind. Mostly because I liked the way it tasted.

I could feel your father's strong familiar body next to me, his pressure. The smell of him, or just the smell of the leaves. I'd met him in the fall. That night we met, when we spent hours together at a fund-raiser in Maryland—that's how he'd smelled. That night we left the stupid hotel ballroom, walked along the weird man-made lake next to the hotel. Like we were in Paris together. Like we were somewhere really good. He loved me once, your father. I believe he did.

"Wow," he said as you returned one of Topher's driving serves.

"I know," I said. You took a dramatic little dive, rolled over once, popped right back up with your racket in your hands, tossing it back and forth. You were bending your knees, your tongue sticking out just a little.

"Is it just me or—"

"No," I said. "He really is good."

We watched you again for a few minutes. I didn't think you knew he was here; if you did, you wouldn't have been able to concentrate.

"So what's going on?" your father finally asked.

"Parent-teacher conferences are the week before Thanksgiving," I said.

He looked at me, confused.

"Jake's doing pretty well in math, but his handwriting is still terrible. Lots of boys his age have problems with small motor skills, so it's not really a big deal, but the teacher thought I might want to do some occupational therapy with him. Just, like, having him pick up small objects and stuff. Jacks. Marbles. Clearly his gross motor skills are fine."

"Kids still play with jacks?"

"Sometimes."

"Okay," your father said. We were quiet again for a while. Crows landed on a nearby tree. On the court, you were racing and grunting.

"Also I'm thinking about putting him in the accelerated Spanish program. He knows a little bit from Julisa, just some basic conversation, but he can't read or spell or anything. But there's an option if he wants to—it's like an extra hour after school. Between that and the tennis it might be too much, but on the other hand the research shows it's very helpful for children to be bilingual."

"Okay," your dad said again.

"I've talked about it with him and he says he doesn't think he wants to, but I'm not sure . . . I mean, I don't really know how many of these decisions should be left up to him."

"What does his teacher think?"

"That's what I want to ask her at the conference."

You paused for water but didn't look over at us on the bleachers. If you saw him sitting there, would you have recognized him right away?

Now Topher turned on the ball machine, stood behind you, working out some kinks in your stance that I never would have seen. Standing next to Topher you seemed so delicate, almost fragile; on your own you seemed so big to me. Six-year-olds are such funny people, so aware and capable that it's easy to forget that really they're still small and new on this earth. You adjusted your stance and whacked the next ball hard.

"I think you should come to the meeting if you want to."

Your father looked at me. "Of course I want to," he said. We watched you for another minute. "Why? I mean, why do you want me there?"

"I think we're at a point where Jake needs more people in his life," I said. "Not fewer."

He was still looking at me, and he looked—honestly, he looked sad. He didn't look rapacious. He didn't look litigious. I had to be honest with myself, and with you. "Has something changed?"

"I'm unemployed," I said. "My candidate dropped out."

"I read that in the *Times*," he said. "What about your health?"

"I don't know," I said. "My doctors are pretty insistent about staying positive, but I'm not feeling very good these days. And anyway—that's not really why. He loves you, Dave. He loves you. I have to do this for him."

Dave closed his eyes, put his fingertips on his lids.

"I want you to know it kills me."

"I know," he said, eyes still closed.

"Do you?" I asked. I was watching you while I spoke; I could not turn my head. "Do you know what it feels like to let you play with him, to let you see him? You didn't want me, but you still get him?" I tried to say this conversationally, but I was failing.

"Karen," he said.

"I loved you so much. I loved you. You broke my heart. You

told me you didn't want this child we had made. You told me that and then you let me walk out your door. And you had said you loved me. And then we made a child together and you told me to leave."

I was no longer being conversational. In fact, I was once again crying. I was desperate for you not to turn around and see me.

"Why would you have told me to leave? *You said you loved me.*" I had lost control; I was no longer myself. But I trusted myself or whoever it was I'd become in this moment. Or at least I was trying to. I was trying to make sense. "Why did you do that to me?"

"Karen."

"And now here I am." I held on to my own cold hands. "Did you love me, Dave? Was that the truth?"

Dave looked stricken. "Karen," he said. He was staring into space. I didn't expect him to say anything else, but then he did. "I didn't love you enough," he said. "I thought I did—or it was an easy thing to say, I love you. It was fun. You were fun, and I was happy. But I wasn't ready for more. I wasn't ready for what you wanted, a house and a baby and all that. I should have been more clear."

My hands were really so cold.

"I wasn't ready. I'm so sorry." I could not look at him but he might have been crying too.

But who says you get to be ready? Who says you get to take someone's heart and eat it and then decide you don't like the taste, so you spit it out and leave her there heartless, empty? An empty space inside? You don't get to do that and call yourself a grown-up. You don't get to do that and walk out forgiven. And I wanted to tell him that—calmly, orderly, I wanted to tell him—but what would have been the point, really? How could he have made it up to me now? There we were, almost seven years later. Dave was married and I wouldn't be here much longer so what would be the point of screaming at him or saying something terrible? What would be the point of telling him he was a monster? Trying to wreak my own sad vengeance even now?

He took my hand in his. If he was startled by the ice, he didn't say anything. "I will never not be sorry," he said.

I pulled my hand back, blew on it. I could keep my own damn self warm.

"It doesn't matter," I said. I didn't want to hear him apologize anymore. "My son loves you. And I love my son."

In front of us, you smacked a serve. Hit the net. "I love him too much to keep him from you. So that's why you win. I love him more than I ever loved you. More than I love myself. So he gets you. That's what he wants. I want him to have what he wants. There's no time left for more fighting." Here I was quoting my sister.

Your father squeezed his eyes shut, sniffed a little. This was the most grateful I had ever seen him. This was what he should have looked like when I told him I was pregnant with you.

"Jacob will finish his school year here. I want that for him. I want him to take tennis lessons and go to games and playdates with Kyle and everything—I want things to be as normal for him as possible. And since he wants to see you, he can see you."

Your father opened his eyes. The wind rustled his thinning hair. He had lines around his mouth I didn't remember, and around his eyes.

"But if you're going to be part of his life, you can't just be

Santa Claus, you understand? You can't dangle new pets in front of him, let him watch scary movies. There are rules about the movies he can watch. You have to learn the rules."

"What are the rules?" your father asked quietly.

"Only G-rated unless it's a cartoon or superhero. Then PG is okay. You can't let him watch violent movies. That was insane."

"I know," your father said.

"He's only six," I said. "You have to learn what that means."

"Okay," your father said.

"I'm trying to prepare him to live without me," I said. "You have to help with that."

"But you're not—"

"Please," I said. I started to shiver and wrapped my afghan a little tighter around myself. I wondered if I had just capitulated, given up the battle before your dad had to even fire a shot. But then I remembered this wasn't a battle. It wasn't even a campaign. It was you.

"Karen," Dave said, "you're such a good mother. I just . . . I want you to know how I admire everything you've done. I really— I want to be half the parent to him that you are. Not in a . . . not that I want him half the time, not that I'm trying to—"

"I know," I whispered.

"If I can be half as good at this as you are, I will be better than I ever could have imagined."

I didn't know what to say to that, so I said nothing. I tried to focus on anything else, the wind, the birds, you and your racket and the tennis net before you. My whole life seemed to be puddling around me. My girlhood on Long Island. My sister, Allison. My dreams for myself. My dreams for you.

What is this life, anyway? Why should I expect it to have been any better than it was?

How could it have been any better?

I started to shiver harder. He put his arm around me. When your practice ended and you saw that he was here, your smile bloomed like a firework. You dropped your expensive tennis racket and came racing over. "Dad!" You barreled into him. Your dad managed to hug you while keeping his strong warm arm around me.

"Hey, Jacob," your father said. "I missed you."

"I missed you too," you said, and huddled underneath his other arm.

I LET YOUR father walk us upstairs, even though the apartment was a mess, even though I had nothing to offer him besides frozen chicken nuggets and tap water.

"You guys are set up?" your father asked. "You want me to order pizza for dinner?"

"Mom, can he?"

I let your father order us a pizza. I kept waiting for that feeling to return, that feeling of capitulation, but instead I just felt like I was okay. I would survive for you. I retreated to the bedroom, took off the wool cap, tied a scarf around my head. I thought about makeup and then forgot about it. My bed was made and the medications were all lined up across my chest of drawers and the wig was on the wig stand by the window and on the night table sat a big jug of water, and there were towels piled up on one side of my bed for night sweats and a bucket next to my bed and also a walker in case I ever felt weak, but so far I'd never felt weak enough to use it (when I felt that weak, I just stayed in bed), but overall I didn't think my room looked too terrible, I mean, it didn't look like a morgue or anything. The pictures on the wall were all cheerful; they were pictures of you.

I looked over at the box where I'd been keeping this manuscript and a few other things I had for you. "Dave?" I called. He was looking at your math homework with you, I think trying to assess your handwriting. "Dave?"

He poked his head into the room.

"I want to show you some stuff," I said. The pain flared. I pretended it wasn't there.

Then your father came in, and I showed him this box, and the papers and the photographs I wanted you to have one day. I showed him my father's old hat. I showed him the album I had from when you were a baby and the album I had from when I was a baby. I showed him the platinum ring.

"When it seems like it will fit him, and he's responsible enough not to lose it, please give it to him. I think maybe at his bar mitzvah." I was kneeling by the box, your father cross-legged on the floor next to me. "You do know what a bar mitzvah is, right?"

"Karen, come on."

"It was my grandfather's. He hid with it in the forest in Hungary. From the Nazis. It belonged to his father before him. It was his wedding ring." I squeezed my fingers around it, then put it in his hand. "I think it might be a good luck charm."

"You think so?"

I considered all the luck in my life. "Yes," I said. "But now my fingers are too swollen for it. I used to wear it every day."

"I remember."

Your father took the ring and slid it on his finger, the way a person sometimes does when given a ring, but then he remembered himself and immediately started taking it off. "I'm sorry, I wasn't trying to—"

"No, you can," I said. "You can wear it until it's time for Jacob to have it." I closed my hand around his hand. "And also there's a manuscript in here, but it's for him only. It's not for you. If he has questions about it—well, it's for him when he's older. When he's eighteen. Allie knows about it, but just in case . . ." I trailed off, looked out my window for a minute. My own beautiful street. I was still holding Dave's hand.

"Just in case of what?"

A pedestrian, a bicyclist. Two taxis with their lights turned on. "I just want you to know it's there too. It's the most important thing I have for him," I said. "Besides the money. But that's kind of complicated. Lots of different accounts."

Dave looked concerned: What was I telling him, exactly? "Allie knows about that?"

"Of course," I said, even though I realized I'd been meaning to send her the paperwork, the power of attorney, the advanced directives, the bank account stuff. I'd meant to do that for months now.

"I mean, you still have lots of time, right?" Dave asked.

I said nothing. The rogue cells.

"Can I help you stand?" he asked me.

I gave him my arm, and he helped me to stand and then he helped me to the kitchen. You were sitting at the kitchen table. You were holding the pencil in that weird way you have.

"Mom, are you okay?"

"Of course," I said.

"Are you hungry?"

"Yes," I said.

"Really?" you said.

Oh, Jakey.

"I am," I said. "I'm totally starving."

"That's good," you said, and stood to give me a little hug while Dave poured us water from the tap in the refrigerator, and I pulled you close by your thin sharp shoulder.

And then the pizza came, and the three of us sat around the kitchen table. You got tomato sauce all over your face. Dave said something that made you laugh. I realized we hadn't done your twenty minutes of reading yet and we'd have to do it before bed. You told a joke about zombies that neither Dave nor I totally understood.

And then I started floating out of myself, the way I sometimes did, or the way I seemed to do more and more. As I floated, I was pleased to see us all sitting around the table: you and your mother and your father, as I'd once imagined it years ago. Eating pizza. Talking about nothing.

"Mom?"

"I'm right here, Jakey." I always would be, you know.

You took a too-big bite, whisking off half of the cheese. I wiped your face with a napkin. You squirmed and moved away. I was your mother, Jacob. I am so grateful I got to be your mother. I am so grateful you were my son.

I hope that wherever and whenever this book finds you, it finds you as happy as you were at that moment—as the two of us were, the three of us, even. Eating pizza around the kitchen table, no big deal, a Thursday night. Remember that we loved each other. And that once upon a time it was the two of us, and we were our own magical family.

So now, days later, I'm trying to think of what else I have to say to you. There's so much, Jacob, but I think I've said most of it in many different ways throughout this book. I suppose I could edit it now—I suppose there are things that I could say more carefully, that I could say better than I did. I suppose I could make it all seem prettier than it was, or that I was a better person. But I won't. That's not what this project was for.

The most important thing, Jacob, is that I loved you more than you can ever possibly imagine. The most important thing is that I always will.

And I'm so tired now—I want to finish this book while I still have the strength to make sense. I want this document to feel real to you, not like some sentimental mishmash or some whitewash. I want you to pick up this book and know the truth. The truth is that even more than I want to be healthy, I want you to be okay. Even more than I want to live forever, I want you to live forever.

But I guess the last thing I want to say in this little book of mine, Jacob, is thank you. Thank you, baby boy. For as long as I've known you, you have given me the strength I need to keep living. I look at you and I feel strong. Every day you help me feel strong.

And thank you for being eternal, so that when the time comes— whenever it comes—I will find the strength to close my eyes.

Acknowledgments

I could not have written this novel without my sister-in-law Mychi Grodstein's encouragement. She and her family are active in the fight against ovarian cancer and have all my admiration and support.

Dr. James Brust, Dr. Thomas Uldrick, and Dr. Elliot Grodstein provided crucial medical information, as did Susan Grubar's wonderful *Memoir of a Debulked Woman*.

Micah Lasher and Joshua Zeitz helped me understand the ins and outs of campaign life, and my friend Allison Jaffin taught me all about New York City politics. Jennifer Kerrs Singer provided professional insight into the way children experience grief.

The terrific writers Elisa Albert, Kelly Braffet, and Lisa Zeidner guided me as I revised this manuscript. William Boggess made enormously helpful suggestions about its structure.

The Kennedys introduced me to Mercer Island years ago and have given me the gift of a warm welcome whenever I return. Adele and Jerry Grodstein have done the same in Bergen County.

Julie Barer is the best partner a writer could have: wise, loving, and generous. My editor, Kathy Pories, is empathetic and insightful beyond imagining. I am profoundly grateful to have these two women in my life, for their smarts, their enthusiasm, and their friendships.

Nathaniel Freeman has granted me the blessing of raising a beautiful little boy. I would not have known how to write this book without him.

Ben Freeman holds my hand, reads my drafts, and pours me a glass of wine whenever I need one, and for these reasons and many more I love him dearly.

Finally, I want to acknowledge the memories of mothers I've known whose lives stand as monuments to love, especially that of my dear friend Marilyn Feingold.

OUR SHORT HISTORY

An Interview with the Author

*

Questions for Discussion

An Interview
with Lauren Grodstein and
PhillyVoice.com by Elizabeth Licorish

Provided courtesy of PhillyVoice.com

PV: What was your inspiration to write the novel?

LG: A few things got me thinking about and then writing this book. The first was that my sister-in-law's mother, a woman I was incredibly fond of, was dying of ovarian cancer when I met her. But she was still spunky, still funny, still whip-smart. Cancer slowed her down sometimes but it never took away who she was. And oh, how she worried about her daughter—what it would mean for her to get married, have children, and grow older without her. I couldn't meet this woman and know her story without wanting to write it.

The other, more mundane but even more powerful thing for me was that I wanted my son to know how much I love him. But fiction is my medium, and so this is the way I did it. One day I hope he reads the book and knows that I could never have written about Karen's love for Jake if I didn't love him so desperately.

PV: *How was the writing of* OSH *influenced by the political atmosphere in today's America?*

LG: I wrote this book way before Trump; I started it in 2012, around the time of Obama's reelection. I thought that was an interesting time, politically, but then again I've always been interested in politics in a sort of amateur way. Trump's election, of course, changed that. Now I'm interested in politics in a life-or-death, "what is happening and how do we make it stop" way. I'm not certain I would have written a story about a campaign consultant if I started the book again today. It's just too horrifying.

PV: *How did you research your protagonist's career as a political consultant?*

LG: I'm blessed with many interesting friends. One of them—my college roommate and still a dear friend—worked for [former New York mayor Michael] Bloomberg in City Hall and was an absolute encyclopedia of campaign info. She introduced me to the right people, who then introduced me to the right terms, the right game plans, the right attitudes a political consultant like Karen would have. There was so much I didn't know! How much money she'd make, for instance, or the kinds of resources that would be poured into the campaigns she'd run. I loved writing about her job and I loved talking to people who do her job in real life.

PV: *Your previous novels are written from the perspective of male protagonists; how did the experience of writing a female protagonist compare to your past work?*

LG: I never set out to write a character whose gender is one thing or another. I set out to write a specific character, and if that character happens to be male, that's the one I write, and if she's a woman, I write a woman. Writing Karen wasn't easier or harder than writing other protagonists I've created, because I've felt them in my bones just as strongly as I felt her. And even though she's a woman, her experiences are so different from mine, from her parenting (she's a single mom in Manhattan, and I'm a married one in the burbs) to the state of her body. I had to imagine her just as deeply as I've imagined my male characters. I couldn't rely on my own experiences.

PV: *Even while she's dying, Karen feels pressure to constantly apply makeup and wear a wig, which seems unique to the female experience of terminal illness. What are your thoughts regarding the pressure that sick people (especially women) feel to appear well?*

LG: It's very important to Karen that she doesn't end up marginalized (even though she does, again and again), and so she relies on what she calls her "healthy drag," the wig and the makeup and the decent clothes, so that people will still include her in the land of the vital. I think this is an exaggerated form of what many women my age and older do all the time—Botox, and competitive exercising, and SPANX, and highlights, and all the rest of that (and believe me, I'm not immune). We need to keep looking as young as possible because we know that in our culture older women are often marginalized. I work out much harder than I did when I was younger, take more care with my makeup, and frankly look better than I did in my twenties, in some ways, because suddenly it matters in a way it didn't before. It's like, if I want to be paid attention to (and I do!) I should have the wisdom of a sixty-year-old and the body of a twenty-year-old.

PV: OSH addresses facing death without faith in God. As more Americans embrace this humanist worldview, how do you think that affects our attitude toward dying?

LG: Well, the only time in my life where I wished I believed in God was when my grandmother was killed by a car crossing the street. I loved her so much and just couldn't believe she was taken from me like that, in a snap, in a second. I really wanted to imagine her somewhere in the heavens, looking down on me. Even more than that, I wanted to think that one day I'd see her again. In my heart that felt ridiculous, but that sentimental urge to believe in the supernatural was hard to get over. I was just so overwhelmed by grief.

But as time passed, and the shock lessened, I also felt great comfort in the idea that nature has its own rules, and that life— if you're lucky, like my grandmother was—life runs its course over many years, and then ends, to be replaced by new life. My grandmother is gone, but she has six great-grandchildren, and more on the way, and her life is renewed in theirs.

I guess what I mean is that Karen's life will end, but her life will continue in her son, Jake. You don't need a supernatural God to see that there is no greater blessing.

Questions for Discussion

1. What do you think Jake will make of this book if he does, indeed, open it when he turns eighteen?

2. Do you think Dave really called Karen after she told him she was pregnant?

3. Reading is very important to Karen, and she leaves a list of book suggestions for Jake when he's older. If you were going to make such a list, what would you include?

4. If you were Karen, would you let your son's father back into your life, even though he rejected you when you told him you were pregnant?

5. How do you think Megan, Dave's wife, feels about Jake? How would you react if it turned out your partner had a child he'd never known about?

6. It's been said that you can either love your child or hate your ex, but you can't do both. Do you think that's true? If not, why not?

7. Was it the right decision to explain to Jake that his mother was going to die?

8. Karen grew up in a working-class family. What effects do you think her childhood had on the way she thinks about money in her adult life?

9. Why do you think Karen seeks out Beverly Hernandez in her office? Is she acting more as a campaign adviser or as a cancer patient?

10. Karen's grandparents were Holocaust survivors who barely escaped Hungary in World War II. How do you think her understanding of their experience makes her think about her own fight with cancer?

11. Karen's advice for the adult Jake she'll never meet: read a lot, be a good neighbor, don't spend too much on useless stuff, be nice to the women you date. Would this be the advice you'd give to the generation that comes after you? What else would you say?

12. If you were Karen, would you have gone back home to New York City to try to work, or stayed in Mercer Island with Allison and allow yourself to be taken care of?

13. Karen has a hard time connecting to her father, who has dementia. Do you think she should have told her father that she was dying? Do you think he understood?

14. Why do you think Karen hints to the reporter what Ace did? Was she disgusted with Ace's behavior, or was she looking for a final crisis to manage?

15. Do you think Jake would have wanted to meet his father if Karen hadn't gotten sick?

16. Karen relies on something called "healthy drag" when she's out in the world: a wig, makeup, and nice clothes. Why is healthy drag so important to Karen? What would have happened if she'd let more people know how sick she was?

17. Are Karen's choices about work and motherhood feminist choices?

18. Do you agree with Karen that being a mother is "the condition of helping the people you love most in the world leave you"?

19. After Karen dies, do you think Jake will go to Mercer Island to be with his aunt, or do you think he will live with Dave?

KEN YANOVIAK

Lauren Grodstein is the author of four works of fiction: the *New York Times* bestseller *A Friend of the Family*, *The Explanation for Everything*, *Reproduction Is the Flaw of Love*, and the story collection *The Best of Animals*. She directs the creative writing MFA program at Rutgers-Camden and lives with her husband, son, and daughter in New Jersey.